# A Secret To Die For

# A Secret To Die For

Scott Winslow Legal Mysteries Book 3

*David P. Warren*

# Chapter One

The executive conference room of Aligor Pharmaceuticals was filling with the eighteen people invited to attend the exclusive meeting. Security stood at the door to ensure that no one else appeared. Anticipation filled the air as the seats around the expansive marble conference table were filled by corporate power players; the people key to running a Fortune 500 Company and keeping its image polished and its income in the stratosphere.

President and Chief Executive Officer Roland Cook, a tall and commanding presence, was the last to enter the room and the first to speak. His thick white hair was perfectly coifed, and his poise and control were on clear display. Today, as always, he looked like he had just stepped from the cover of GQ.

He looked around at the familiar faces and spoke with confidence. "The response to Delexane has been phenomenal and our team is to be congratulated for getting through the trials so quickly. At the rate we are going, we will be ready for new product rollout in about four months. Word is out on the street and investment capital is rolling in faster than ever. The fact that we have a cancer drug that gets results like no other is out there and hedge funds, stock funds and private investors all want a piece of the action. Just the anticipation has caused our stock to go from fifty-two dollars to eighty-eight dollars per share in the past sixty days."

He beamed as he looked around the room at members of the Board of Directors and the principal players in the Delexane trials. With a smirk, he added, "This could be the best revenue generator since Viagra."

There was a round of applause at the recognition of the importance of the product and the reminder that many people in this room would soon be multi-millionaires. Cook smiled and added, "As you know, there is massive interest in the product and the trials. You may be approached by reporters, bloggers or others hungry for information. You will smile enthusiastically and respond by stating that you are not at liberty to talk about the matter and direct the inquiry to corporate communications. They are set up to respond to all questions and the message will be consistent. We can't have anyone going off message or getting into trouble for any alleged insider trading—got it?" After heads nodded understanding, he said, "There is an updated information package that you can pick up at the door on your way out. All departments are gearing up to be ready for a fast roll out as soon as we can get FDA approval. The accelerated approval we have been seeking is likely at this point because the FDA recognizes that a breakthrough drug is critical in treating cancer, so we should plan to be on the market by the end of summer. At that point, our sales and distribution people will have a good deal of work to do in order keep up with the demand." There was another round of applause and then Cook said, "Give it your all and let's hit the ground running."

As the executives began to depart the room, glad-handing with Cook on the way out, the Director of Product Testing and Marketing, Martin Cardenas, approached Cook. Marty Cardenas had black hair that fell over his forehead, dark eyes that conveyed intelligence and a confidence that said he was comfortable in his own skin. He asked, "We're in your office in twenty minutes, right?"

Cook nodded but didn't speak, and then refocused his attention on the other executives departing the room. Marty already knew that this was a meeting Cook would just as soon avoid.

\* \* \*

**January 11**
**6:20 p.m.**
Marty Cardenas walked into the CEO's executive offices accompanied by his boss, Director of Product Development Arthur Underwood, a brilliant leader and a lanky, affable man who reminded many of Jimmy Stewart. Within a few minutes, they were escorted into an interior conference room.

Roland Cook walked into the room and took a seat at the head of the table. He looked around the room without speaking and then looked directly at Underwood. "Art, you have the floor. Tell me what was so urgent."

Art Underwood was instantly nervous. "Well, sir, we wanted you to know the latest results from the trials. It's like I mentioned a couple of weeks ago, phase three is not generating the same positive results as the first and second phases did. I'll let Marty give you the specifics."

As Marty Cardenas began, he could see that the CEO already looked annoyed. "As you know, Mr. Cook, in phase one and phase two trials we had sixty-five percent of the participants achieve great results with shrinkage of tumors and remission for some and extended life projections for others."

"Right, I know that," Cook replied.

"Yes, sir. This time the results are not what we expected. Phase one was one hundred and fifty patients and phase two was one thousand. Now that we have been measuring the results for fifteen thousand patients in phase three, the results are a long way from the results of the first two phases." Cook looked at him intently but said nothing, so he added, "We will have final results in a few weeks, but we wanted to give you a heads up that the results are showing positive impact in about twelve percent of cases and there are some side effects that didn't show in the smaller phases."

Cook frowned. "You still have to get to final numbers on this trial, right?"

"Yes, sir, about thirty days."

"So, let's see what happens. This is probably just an anomaly. This drug can make a big difference in many lives. It can revolutionize treatment and make cancer something that people can beat."

Marty tried not to grimace. "Given the size of this sample, the results are statistically much more significant than the first two phases and the side effects that didn't appear in the first two trials are also troubling."

Ever the diplomat, Arthur Underwood jumped in to reduce the tension. "We thought you should be alerted to what's coming, Mr. Cook, so that you are not blindsided by results that were not what you expected."

Cook nodded. "I think it's probably an aberration. Let's wait and gauge the result when we are done. In the meantime, this is need to know only."

"Yes, sir," Underwood responded.

"All right, thank you all for coming," Cook said, standing to make clear the meeting was over.

As Marty walked down the hall with Art Underwood, he said, "I don't think he got it."

"What?"

"I don't think he understood that we were telling him this trial is not going to give us anything close to a result that demonstrates a viable product."

"Let's get a cup of coffee," Art said, and they moved out of the building and to the coffee hut next door. After they ordered and stood outside looking at the afternoon sky and sipping coffee, Art continued the conversation. "He understands."

"What do you mean?"

"Mr. Cook has a degree in chemistry and as well as a master's degree in business. He has also been through this process associated with drug testing and chasing FDA approval about a hundred times so far and he has a good track record in making it through the process. He knew exactly what we were telling him." Marty stared at him questioningly, so Art added, "First, he really believes in the product. He has already decided that Delexane is going to help people and that this company will be heralded as the one that changed the way we deal with cancer. He believes that this company can change the whole culture surrounding cancer. No longer is it a death sentence for so many; now your chances of remission and survival go way up." He took a breath and added, "Secondly, this product could mean about a billion dollars in new stock value and hundreds of millions each year in revenue. That hasn't slipped his mind either."

"But if it doesn't do what everyone expects, then it isn't going to be worth anywhere near that amount. It could be worth nothing."

Art hesitated and then replied, "It would be a mistake to jump to that conclusion in front of Cook."

Marty wore a look of disbelief. "Surely, he knows that the drugs we test don't all work. You said he has the education and experience to know that."

"He does, Marty. But this is the big one and it has to work. He has the company all in on revolutionizing cancer treatment and he made promises along the way. We also have two competitors close on our heels. It is not a very well-kept secret that that Sutton Pharma has seventy percent in phase two trials and are now underway on their phase three trials of Excerdes. They are thinking that our phase three results are hovering at sixty-five percent and they know that's hard to match. If they knew about our twelve percent results accompanied by increased side effects, they'd already be celebrating. And Jardine Health Products is still in phase two, but they are closing the gap. If either gets better results in phase three..." he shook his head and let the words trail off, his message clear.

There was concern in Marty's expression. "You're saying that he knows the results are as good as we are representing and intends to do it anyway?"

"I'm saying that money is flowing in and he doesn't want to shut off the spigot any sooner than he has to. He waits for final results so that the stock price continues its upward trend and investment dollars keeps flowing in at a record pace in the interim."

"So, what happens when the study results are final, and we have to tell him that the results aren't there?"

"I'm not sure. Let just hope he doesn't plan to shoot the messenger."

\* \* \*

**February 2**
**6:00 p.m.**
It was like having another private audience with the Pope. Roland Cook didn't engage in meeting with employees. He met with industry captains and Senators who could affect legislation. He sometimes met with hedge fund administrators who could write a check for ten million dollars, but not employees delivering bad news.

Martin Cardenas had connected with National Sales Manager Justin Palmer seven years ago, when they were both new to Aligor. When Martin's team completed testing and blessed a product, Justin Palmer and his salespeople could rely on the fact that they had a good product to market. But he knew that when Martin red-lighted a product, there was a reason, and his review of the data made it clear that Marty was right about Delexane. Palmer had brown hair and a face five years younger than his thirty-eight years. He was the friendly sort that everyone took to immediately, and he had an uncanny ability to get people talking to him like they had known him all of their lives. He was fully attentive when others spoke, and he made them feel heard and understood; the ideal persona to head a national sales and marketing force.

The two men sat quietly in the lavishly decorated waiting area of Cook's suite, checking email messages on their phones. Arthur Underwood joined them in the lobby, with an expression that suggested his world was on fire.

There was a thin film of sweat on his forehead and he looked older than he had when Marty saw him two hours ago.

A woman in her mid-thirties approached the group and said, "If you'll follow me, Mr. Cook is ready to see you now." They walked down the hall past the two offices and a massive conference room and into Cook's private sanctuary. The woman indicated a conversation area on one side of the large room. "Please have a seat and Mr. Cook will be with you soon."

Marty and Justin took a seat on the elegant couch behind a marble coffee table and Arthur took a seat on one of the armchairs that had been placed at either the end of the coffee table. No one spoke until Roland Cook entered the room. "Hello, gentlemen," he said as he sat in the other armchair. Without wasting a second he asked, "What do we need to discuss?"

Arthur cautiously responded. "There are concerns about our recent publication of test trial results."

"Meaning what?" Cook asked impatiently.

"The data doesn't support what we published," Marty offered. Anger flashed across Cook's face as Marty added, "But if you read our latest public description of the results, you come away with the impression that the data from this larger study is consistent with our first study results and that's not accurate. We actually state that we have conducted three separate trials, which implies that the published results come from all three studies. We found positive results for sixty-five percent in the initial two phases of the study, but in phase three only twelve percent showed improvement of any kind. That significant deviation is not shown in the results we published. So, it is misleading to the public."

Cook shrugged. "This is just an anomaly. You need to go back over the data and figure out where the mistakes in your analysis can be found. We know that this is a good drug, so we just need to determine how you got to an erroneous result."

Arthur Underwood nodded and replied diplomatically, "We can reassess the data, but it seems that there are problems. If the data shows improvement to twelve percent, then it seems to me that we can't publish reports showing significant improvements to sixty-five percent of participants." Gauging the thinly veiled anger on Cook's face, Marty realized Art was pushing information that Cook didn't want to hear. He glanced over at Justin, who wore a stunned expression.

Cook checked his watch and stood. "We had positive results for sixty-five percent of the previous phases, so this product is the real deal. Let's get the final numbers corrected to assure we are properly representing the product." The three visitors nodded acknowledgment and searched for words to convince him that the results were not what he was prepared to publish. Cook didn't wait for anything further. "I have to get on to my next meeting gentlemen. Thanks for coming by." He offered his hand and they all shook before leaving the office trying to digest what had just happened.

As they left the executive offices for their own three stories below, Arthur said, "Did you get the message?"

Marty nodded. "Yeah, loud and clear."

Justin added, "I'm still in shock. He doesn't appear to be open to making any corrections to the data we are publishing."

"Hopefully, he will get there," Art offered. "When all the data has been reaffirmed, he will have to acknowledge the results. He just doesn't want to let any air out of the balloon any sooner than necessary because this is a massive money maker. The stock keeps rising with the anticipation."

"Right," Marty replied, "but if the results don't support the projections, the balloon will lose a lot of air in a big hurry. I mean, when the accuracy of what we are saying is confirmed, isn't the bottom going to fall out of the stock price anyway?"

"I think so," Art offered. "But he won't let it happen any sooner than necessary. I have to run guys, so let's talk again tomorrow."

After they said goodbye and Art disappeared from view, Justin turned to Marty and asked, "So we are we artificially inflating the stock price? Between now and the time we report the real results, there will be temptation for some to dump their stock before the market catches on; we are creating a situation that invites insider trading if people inside the company know the bottom will fall out and their stock value will be badly damaged."

"That's one more problem," Marty said. "The biggest concern is having patients buy into this therapy in large numbers if the results aren't there. People with cancer desperately need hope. How can we pretend to provide that hope based on inflated positive numbers?"

Justin stopped in his tracks. Marty looked at him and asked, "What?"

"Do you think there is a chance that the company has already provided false data to the Center for Drug Evaluation and Research to get them to make favorable reports to the FDA?"

Marty was quiet as the two shared expressions of worry, because it crossed a line when you provided data known to be inaccurate to the FDA's watchdog. "The FDA has us on a fast track program because of the importance of this drug, so we'll know for sure in just a few weeks, when the data comes back to us after their review," Marty offered.

Justin drew a breath and said, "Should we wait that long? I mean by then all of this is a long way down the road and..." He let his words trail off.

Marty was quiet for a moment and then said, "I can't help but feel like we are watching something bad unfold in real time. I don't know about you, but I don't want some Congressional inquiry two years from now asking me whether I saw it coming and never spoke out."

"I don't want that either," Justin said. He reflected a moment and then said, "We better think hard, because if we take a stand, we will be risking our careers. The choice between honesty and corporate loyalty will have some serious fallout for us."

"You think that Cook might fire us rather than correcting the data?"

Justin looked at him with wide eyes. "Not if we can convince him that we need to address the problem for the good of the company. But if he thinks we are undermining him, it comes out differently."

\* \* \*

**March 22**
**4:00 p.m.**
Marty Cardenas walked into Arthur Underwood's office and sat down in one of the two visitor chairs without saying a word. "Did Mr. Cook agree to meet with us again to discuss the trial results?"

Arthur looked up from his reading and said, "No. I asked him to schedule a meeting for you, me and Justin. He said that wouldn't be necessary and that I should come up right then and he and I would discuss whatever was on our collective minds."

"And?"

Art's expression was downcast. "I went up to see him and made the pitch, but nothing changed. He told me that he believes in the product and I need to believe in it as well. I replied that I think the product isn't what he believes it is yet. I reminded him that the data from our biggest and most significant trial does not support the statements in the public that sixty-five percent of participants saw extremely positive results."

Marty nodded. "What did he say to that?"

"He said that this is a good product and we will be able to prove it. He said we can't be distracted by an aberration that won't matter in the big picture. I resisted, telling him that the data provided cautions we needed to explore." Art shook his head. "He gave me a look that said he had heard enough. Then he told me that this was a matter of loyalty, and that I needed to be on the right side of history."

"It's now a breach of loyalty to raise concerns about the data?"

"It would seem so," Art replied, shaking his head. "All of this is pretty uncomfortable."

"This is more than uncomfortable, Art. The company is misrepresenting the results of the study and when the drug becomes available, those misrepresentations can kill people. The accuracy of our data has been confirmed and we now know that Mr. Cook has no plan to fix the misrepresentations in the public pronouncements about the success of the trials." He studied Art's worried expression for a moment and then said, "Look, I know that the money is flowing in and the stock is going through the roof, but it's just not right."

"What do you want me to say, Marty?"

Marty frowned. "I want you to say that it's wrong and that we can't sit around and let this happen."

Art leaned back in his chair and looked at Marty. "What are you proposing?"

"Let's go talk to a lawyer and see what we should do. We can keep it confidential and get some advice."

"You know how well that goes over with the company if word gets out?"

"Word doesn't get out. It's a conversation protected by the attorney-client privilege even if it never goes anywhere."

Art looked worried. "I don't know."

Marty was trying to suppress frustration as he said, "Justin and I are going to consult with an employment lawyer. At least we can learn our rights if we come forward with complaints to the FDA, or the press, or somebody." He paused a moment and added, "We'd really like you to go with us and be part of this. I know you share our reservations about what's happening."

Art leaned back in his chair and replied, "I'll go with you, but I'm not sure that I will take any action beyond that first conversation."

"Fair enough. I don't know that we will either. Let's just figure out what the possibilities are and what protections we have."

"You want to set it up?"

"A week from today at 6:00 p.m. It's all set."

"Who's the lawyer?"

"Scott Winslow."

He nodded. "I've heard the name somewhere."

"He got some good verdicts in employee rights cases."

"All right. I'll go along, but just to listen. I am not committing to doing anything else," Art replied, grudgingly. "Now get out of here and let me get back to work."

"I appreciate having you involved, Art. I get really upset about what's going on here, so I need a voice of reasonable restraint."

"Okay, but like I said, how involved I'll be is yet to be decided. Don't assume that I am in for anything more than the meeting with the lawyer."

* * *

**March 29**
**6:05 p.m.**
Art Underwood, Marty Cardenas and Justin Palmer sat in Scott Winslow's tenth floor conference room at 6:05 p.m., with cups of coffee on the table in front of them. The floor to ceiling window that formed one wall of the room looked down onto a crowded Lake Avenue in Pasadena — occupants of cars ready to be home fought against red lights, and pedestrians moving in every direction.

Scott Winslow and Donna Robbins walked into the room and extended a hand to the waiting visitors. The three executives stood to greet them.

"Gents, I'm Scott Winslow and this is my paralegal assistant, Donna." Scott is forty-four years old, six feet two inches tall and flashes deep blue eyes filled with determination. Donna is thirty-seven years old, five foot five, and has short blonde hair and a likable smile. Her large brown eyes exude warmth and sincerity, and clients typically like her from the first moment. Scott and Donna operate with the proficiency of a team that has worked together for a dozen years and know each other well.

They shook hands. "Marty, I think you spoke to Donna when you called in to make this appointment."

"Yes, that's right," Marty replied.

"I like Donna to sit in so that she has an awareness of the facts from the beginning. If this becomes a case, you will be regularly working with both of us." He sat back in his seat and said, "The first thing I want you to know is that whatever you tell me is protected by the attorney-client privilege and it will be kept strictly confidential whether the matter goes any further or not."

That announcement made Art relax. "That's good to hear because we all feel like we have our necks overly-extended."

Scott smiled and said, "I understand. Tell me about your respective roles at Aligor."

"I am the National Product Manager," Art replied. "Everything to do with each of the products Aligor markets is in my wheelhouse, from development to distribution. Marty is the Manager of Product Testing and Marketing. Anytime we conduct tests or trials, Marty's people conduct it, make sure it's done right, and assess the resulting data. Justin is the National Sales Manager. Once a product is released, he over sees the entire sales force in its sale and distribution."

"Who do you report to?" Scott asked Art.

"I report directly to the CEO, Roland Cook. These guys report to me."

"Got it," Scott replied with a nod. "From the expressions around the table, I think something distressing has happened. Can you us off by providing an overview of what's happening?"

Art looked at Marty and nodded. Marty looked at Scott and said, "We have been testing a new cancer drug. The initial trial results were extremely good. Sixty-five percent of people were getting good results. But most recently we have done a larger round of trials, our phase three trials involving fifteen thousand participants, and the results aren't the same."

"What do the latest results show?" Scott asked.

"Instead of sixty-five percent of participants coming out better, that number is only twelve percent and we don't know why. There are also a couple of side effects that could be significant that we didn't see before. We are concerned that this information is not being divulged." He drew a breath and added, "The CEO says he still believes this product will revolutionize cancer treatment. Our concern is that none of the expanded test findings are being shared by the

Company. They still use the results generated by the phase one and phase two studies and those numbers are now misleading."

"You approached the CEO about the need to change what is out in the public realm because of your findings?"

Justin nodded. "He reinforced his belief in the product and dismissed the latest data as an aberration."

Art offered, "The three of us met with him twice. The second visit was just like the first. We just weren't getting through to him, so we assembled the data in great detail and tried to set up another meeting. He refused to meet with all three of us but met with me alone. In that meeting I told him that we had been over all of the data again and what we were stating was accurate. His response was that we needed to give it time and let the positive effects of the drug be discovered by the public. When we ended the meeting, he characterized the need to let the product be released so that it can help cancer victims as a test of my loyalty."

Scott reflected a moment and asked, "So, he never acknowledged that these numbers reflect any problem with the product, is that right?"

"That's right," Marty replied. "Which is frustrating to those of us who can see these latest results are material and reflect on the performance of the product."

"I assume that if this drug could revolutionize cancer treatment, it is expected to generate big bucks?"

"Expected to and already has," Art replied. "The stock price is way up and inflow of investor capital is astounding."

"So, denying any problem is what you want to do if your primary objective is to keep the money flowing, right?" Scott concluded.

There were nods around the table. "Yes, that's true," Marty replied.

"But there's more to it than the money," Art added thoughtfully. "Cook thinks that he has found a drug that will change cancer treatment and the impact of cancer forever. He sees himself ushering in a new era where people recover from late stage cancer. He really wants that to be his legacy."

Scott nodded. "Even when he's shown that it's not working."

"Right," Justin acknowledged, entering the conversation. "We have taken him through the data. It's nowhere close to what it should be, but he doesn't want to acknowledge it. He understands the data, he simply rejects it because it doesn't match the image in his head."

"What do we do?" Marty asked. "I mean, we are now officially between a rock and a hard place. We are disloyal to Cook and the company or we make the adverse data known."

"I take it that the FDA does not have the data that Cook doesn't want to hear?"

"Seems right," Justin replied, "because he won't even acknowledge the data that undermines the drug exists. The watch dog agency that analyzes the information for the FDA is the Center for Drug Evaluation and Research. The new data should have been conveyed to them for review, but that is not happening."

Scott reflected a moment and then said, "I suggest that you prepare a memo to Cook pointing out that, as disclosed to him in prior meetings, the data shows positive results for only twelve percent of the participants and new side effects have been discovered. Ask him to confirm that he will promptly take action to address the problem, including conveying the information to the Center for Drug Evaluation and Research. Tell him that unless such essential corrective action is taken, you feel you will have no choice but to advise the Center because public safety issues are involved."

"He will likely fire us before we go to the Center," Marty added.

"He may, but then your path is clear. And going to the Center isn't just sour grapes by a fired employee because you told him you planned to do so before you were fired. If he takes no action, then you write a communication to the Center for Drug Evaluation and Research and the FDA providing the new data. Because the failure to disclose adverse testing data presents serious public safety issues, if you are the subject of retaliation for coming forward with the warnings, you will have a whistleblower claim and termination in violation of public policy claim."

Nervous faces considered this information for a time and then Marty asked, "And if we do this, will you represent us in this whistleblower claim?"

Scott considered a moment and then asked, "The company will likely take the position that you were fired for another reason, such as performance issues. Is there anything out there that would substantiate that position?"

All three men shook their heads. "Nothing I'm aware of," Art replied.

"Do you have documentation of your achievements? Things like commendations, compliments, raise and bonuses? Things that we can rely on to establish positive performance?"

"Yeah," Justin said. "Lots of it." The others nodded agreement.

"Our Firm will take the case for you whether you are fired because of your complaints before or after going the Center and the FDA." Scott regarded the attentive faces around the table and added, "The reason for preparing the communication to Cook is that there is no record that you went to him with your findings. This creates a piece of physical evidence establishing what you complained about. It helps us prove an essential element of the claim and minimizes his ability to mischaracterize the content of your communications."

"If we do this and wind up fired and in a whistleblower action, how long would a lawsuit like this take to get to conclusion?" Justin asked.

"From filing the lawsuit to trial, about a year and a half. During that time, we take depositions and obtain critical documents. We gather all of the evidence we can in preparation for trial." Scott added, "If you elect to move forward with this case, we will work on a contingency fee basis, so your only out of pocket expenses would be costs in connection with the litigation." There was quiet around the table as the three considered this painful decision. "You should take your time and consider all of this before you make a final decision," Scott offered. "If you have any additional questions, call and Donna and I will be available to provide answers."

There were nods around the room. "Thank you, Scott," Marty said. "The information that you have given us is helpful."

They all shook hands and then the three left the conference room wondering if they could do what was suggested and fearing what might come next. As they walked to the car, Marty said, "What do you think?"

Justin replied, "I like Scott. He's a smart guy, but this is going to cost us big time. I just don't know. We survive for a year and a half during the litigation. We also have to worry about how a feud with Aligor affects our ability to get work somewhere else."

Art shook his head. "I just can't do this," he said. "I'm almost sixty-years-old and just five years from when I plan to retire. I'm sorry, but I can't go tell Cook that I am about to go to a public agency to blow the whistle, and I can't think about having to look for a new job at age sixty."

"I understand," Marty said. "I'm going to talk to my wife, but I think I want to make this stand. How about you Justin?"

Justin nodded. "I'm in. I'm single, I have money put away, and I can't let Cook mislead people who are looking at this product like it's going to be their salvation in just the next few months."

Marty nodded. "I feel the same, but I have to make sure Abby is up for what all of this will mean to us personally."

# Chapter Two

Scott Winslow emerged from his day long deposition in a sexual harassment case. He had been back in his office for about thirty seconds when Donna appeared at the door. "How did it go?"

Scott grinned. "Very well. He lied to me about at least five major issues."

"Oh, good," Donna replied.

"Yep, and we have the evidence to establish that each one of them was a lie. Two with emails that he wrote before he had a motive to lie."

"That will make for great cross-examination at trial." She added, "Lee Henry just got here to see you. He's in conference room number two."

Lee and Scott had been working together for years. He was the guy Scott turned to when he needed a witness found or some evidence that was out there somewhere. Lee was a master of disguise and could hide in a crowd. He had often proven himself able to penetrate walls and emerge with evidence that seem unobtainable. "Got it, thanks," he replied. He dropped his file on the credenza and made his way to the conference room where Lee waited. Closing the door behind him he extended a hand to Lee. "How are you doing, buddy?"

"Good. Really good," he replied, grinning like the cat that just found the canary farm.

"What? What have you got?"

"I found your missing witness and served the trial subpoena."

"How did you do you it?"

"Turns out he has a number of reasons to lay low. He borrowed money from the wrong people and didn't pay it back, so I wasn't the only one looking for him."

"Great," Scott replied with a grimace. "Who doesn't want a witness like that? Sounds like a great guy."

"He's a dipshit, but he has a ten your old daughter he cares about. I followed her until he met her at his ex-wife's place this morning. Then I followed him to the rural trailer where he has been hiding. He wouldn't answer the door, so I just pretended to be one of the wrong people he's worried about."

"How did you do that?"

"You really want to know?"

"I probably shouldn't, but I do."

"While I was following his daughter for a few hours in order to find him, I took her picture. Then I wrote, 'Pretty little girl you have' on the back of a picture and slid it under the door. For some reason he perceived that as a threat, so he was really pissed. He opened the door and pointed a gun at me." Lee shrugged. "So, I took advantage of that opportunity to take the gun from his hand and replace it with the subpoena. Then I told him to have a nice day."

"Jesus, Lee."

"I also took the picture back in case he was inclined to complain about the manner of service." He was thoughtful a moment and then added, "You usually don't have dirt bag witnesses like this guy."

"Sometimes you don't get to choose your witnesses. He is the only guy present for certain events." Scott took a moment and then asked, "Do you think this guy will show up at trial?"

"He will," Lee replied with a grin.

"How can you be so sure?"

"I reminded him that if he didn't show up the court would hold him in contempt. While he thought about that I told him that his bigger concern was that I would find him again if he didn't show."

"I guess that should do it," Scott said with a pained expression.

Lee smiled and said, "Guys like him aren't particularly courageous. With the right kind of encouragement, they will do what they are supposed to, you know?"

Scott shook his head. "Remind me not to ask how you get things done." He paused and then asked, "How's Melissa?"

"She is still amazing." He chuckled and added, "She says that I'm the bad boy her mom always warned her about."

"Well, she's probably right about that." Scott shook his head. "This has to be a record relationship for you right?"

"Almost two years together and I feel like we're just getting started."

"You are hooked, my friend."

"I admit it. She drives me crazy. I asked her to marry me."

"What?" Lee Henry married?

"I know. I didn't think that would happen either. This is the first time I've ever been convinced that I could spend the rest of my life with someone and be happy."

"That is great, buddy."

"I assume she said yes?"

"Yep. Otherwise I wouldn't be grinning like an idiot."

"You are definitely hooked."

"Yeah, I know it. How are Lisa and the kids?"

"Lisa is great as always. Katie is still large and in charge. Eight years old and she thinks she knows all the answers. The other day we were talking about trials. I told her that I talk to juries because she saw one on television. She wanted to know if I had friends on juries that helped me win my cases. When I told her that I didn't know any of them before the trial, she had some serious questions about why I was purposely talking to strangers. She also suggested that if the jury was packed with friends and acquaintances, I would be most likely to win."

Lee laughed. "Sounds like her. Should be some interesting teenage years ahead," he offered with a grin.

"Not looking forward to that," Scott replied.

"How about Joey?"

"Fully recovered from his injuries and a star athlete. Next year is first year of middle school and he's got his eye on playing quarterback."

"You know, it almost makes a person want to have kids."

"You and Melissa should do that. A whole bunch of little trench-coat wearing covert operatives getting the goods on all the other kids."

"You make them sound like trouble."

"No, it would always be for good purposes. Take down the school bully, something like that."

"Now you're talking. Sounds like my kind of kid," Lee said, smiling. He paused and asked, "Before I get on the road, Donna said you needed my help with something else?"

"That's right. I was consulted by three national managers from Aligor Pharmaceuticals. They were talking hypothetically about what rights they would have if they were fired for complaining that the company was misrepresenting the test results of a new drug. Apparently, the first two trials showed positive results in the range of sixty-five percent of the participants. A damned good result. Then they did the third trial with a bigger test group and the positive results were around twelve percent. Aligor is still hyping the sixty-five percent as trials results and these two guys want to introduce a little reality to what's being published."

"Holy shit," Lee replied. "That could be a pretty big deal."

"It really could. The guys who came to me are hoping to convince the CEO to put out accurate test results. If he does, they will be fine. If not, they are thinking about becoming whistleblowers to protect the public from a cancer drug that isn't all it's supposed to be. They wanted to know their rights if they get fired for coming forward."

"How can I help?" Lee asked.

"The three guys I met with were impressive and came across as straight shooters. Donna did an initial look on each of them online; nothing negative there. I want you to do a preliminary check on them and let me know if you find anything about them that should make me want to decline their representation. Criminal records, fraudulent conduct, big judgments against them; that kind of thing."

"You got it, Scott. I'll let you know what I find within the next couple of days."

"Perfect. Want a beer?"

"I thought you'd never ask."

\* \* \*

**March 30**
**7:50 p.m.**
Marty parked his Tesla in the garage and walked into the kitchen. "I'm home," he announced to the empty room.

A familiar voice called out from upstairs. "I just beat you home. I'm changing and will be right down. Why don't you pour us a glass of wine?"

"Damned good idea," Marty replied. "I could use it."

As he poured the wine, Abby walked into the room and gave him a kiss. Her shoulder-length black hair framed high cheek bones and big blue eyes. "That's why I love coming home," he said with a grin. "You do that very well."

"You're not too bad yourself." He handed her a glass of pinot noir. "Thanks. So, how was the meeting with the lawyer?"

"It was good. He knows what he's talking about. He thinks we have a case if we are fired for raising complaints that the company is hiding negative information about the testing. He told us to communicate with Roland Cook in writing, referencing our previous conversations and letting him know that if he won't provide negative test results to the FDA, we will have no choice but to take our concerns to them."

"Holy shit. It sounds awfully scary when you say it that way."

"It is. Art already told me and Justin that he is out. With five years until retirement he doesn't want a war with the company."

"I can understand that. How about you?"

"Do I want a war with the company?"

"Yeah."

"No, but things may be headed in that direction." He looked at her with worry in his eyes. "That's what we need to talk about. I am really bothered about the company sitting on information that matters to people who are facing the worst moments of their lives."

She gave him a smile. "It sounds like you're ready to take a stand."

"Maybe, but it affects both of us because it puts my career at risk. I mean, if I'm fired landing a new job could be hard. Other employers may not want any part of my dispute with Aligor." He shook his head and added, "Cook already made it known to Art that keeping quiet about this is a matter of loyalty to the company."

Abby shrugged. "I'm proud of you for wanting to do the right thing. If you get fired, we will still be okay." She grinned and added, "I have a good job and I can be your sugar mama."

"Are you sure about this?" Marty asked. "It could mean exchanging a good career for an uncertain lawsuit."

"I know. But if the alternative is that you keep quiet and let the company give false hope to people who have to make life and death decisions, then I say let's roll the bones."

"No wonder I'm crazy about you." He put his arms around her and kissed her softly, and then with passion. With her arms around his neck, she whispered, "I've only had these casual clothes on for five minutes and I am predicting they are about to come off again."

"Good prediction," he said, kissing her again, pulling her close against him, and entirely forgetting about the worries of the day.

* * *

**March 31**
**7:00 a.m.**
Roland Cook's estate in the Lake Sherwood area of Westlake Village featured lake views from most of the rooms within the nine thousand square foot Tuscan-style structure. Walls of windows opened to allow the expansive outdoor patios and fountains that were all part of the flow from the house down to the lakefront.

The doorbell rang and Cook opened the front door promptly. "Come in, Sean. Let's have coffee outside."

The forty-six-year-old visitor with curly black hair was built like a linebacker; thick arms bulged from his short-sleeved shirt and wide shoulders filled the door. Sean Garner was a cop in a previous life who had left the force and gained success in corporate security by the time he was in his mid-thirties. A dozen years later he found himself at the top of the security pyramid for one of the fastest growing pharma companies in the world. He had an extensive security department and reported to the Vice President for Operations, except when there was a special project that Cook decided required Sean's personal attention.

"Give Mr. Garner a cup of coffee will you, Lydia?"

"Yes, sir," a woman said. She stopped cleaning the counters and poured coffee for Garner.

"Thank you, ma'am," Garner said, taking the mug.

"Let's go out back," Cook said and walked towards the patio.

As they sat down on at one of the outdoor tables that overlooked the Olympic-sized pool, Garner looked out at the beautiful blue waters of the lake that touched the other end of the yard fifty feet away. There was a gentle lapping of water onto the land. The rear yard contained through gardens, trees, gazebos and distant seating areas and stretched for an acre until it reached the shore of the lake. "This is so gorgeous," Garner offered.

"It is that," Cook replied. He looked at Garner and said, "Your message said that you learned something, is that right?"

"Yes, sir. The three of them went to see an employment lawyer. A guy named Scott Winslow."

"Art Underwood participated?"

"Yes, sir."

"I'm disappointed to hear that. He shook his head. "We can't have that happening, Sean. We are within weeks of this important new drug getting FDA approval to help people stricken with cancer. Now we must deal with three disloyal executives trying to stop us from helping those people in desperate need." He reflected a moment and then said, "This drug imperative to people in need, Sean." He paused and then added, "Initially, it will also mean about a million dollars in stock value added to your personal portfolio. And that is just the beginning."

"Yes, sir," Garner replied, his expression thoughtful. "Do you plan to fire them?"

"Not just yet, although their disloyalty certainly warrants it."

"What would you like me to do, sir?"

"I want you to convince them that this is not the way to proceed. They need to stay loyal to the company and its goals."

"Yes, sir." Garner looked towards the lake and adjacent hillsides populated with gorgeous homes like the one he was visiting. "It sure is beautiful here, sir."

"It is, Sean. And one day, you will be a neighbor if you choose."

"I would like that."

"It's not far-fetched, Sean. Your stock value is going through the roof and there could be other significant incentives if you do well with what we are discussing today." He gave Garner an insider's grin and then added, "Thank you for coming by this morning, Sean."

"Yes, sir." Garner rose and walked into the house to head for the front door.

"One more thing," Cook called out.

Garner turned back and looked at him. "Yes, sir."

"It is critical that nothing slows this project, Sean. You understand?"

"Yes, sir."

Cook furrowed his brow and said, "If the convincing requires some expenditures, they are authorized. I leave it to your discretion. I want you to use outside resources for this and not security department employees. I don't want this coming back to the Company."

Garner nodded, and added on more, "Yes, sir, I understand, and I will handle it." As he walked to the front door of the magnificent property, Garner looked around. He really could live in a place like this if his stock value continued to soar. He was confident that he could take care of this problem, as he had taken care of so many others in the past. He was paid well to make sure that big problems disappeared one way or another.

He was already contemplating ways to convince the three members of the management team who had strayed that they needed to return to Company priorities before the situation became dire. Hopefully, it could be done with reason, along with the injection of a little fear about what choosing the wrong path would mean for the Company and for each of them.

\* \* \*

## March 31
### 7:30 a.m.

Justin walked into Francine's Café, a hole in the wall restaurant with a good name among the local workforce in downtown Los Angeles. He looked around until he saw Marty Cardenas and Art Underwood sitting at a table across the bustling room. He walked over and pulled out one of the two remaining chairs. "Good morning, guys. I trust everyone has been sleeping well?" he said with a sideways grin.

"Nope," Art replied. Not well at all."

"Likewise," Marty said, shaking his head. "This really sucks."

A woman in a red apron ran up to the table carrying a pot of coffee. "You want coffee?" she asked Justin, seeing that the cups in front of Marty and Art were still full.

"I do, thanks."

She poured and then asked, "What do you want for breakfast, gents?"

"Wheat toast for me," Art said.

"A bagel with everything you can find in the kitchen," Justin asked.

"What about you, hon?" she asked Marty.

"I'll have your breakfast burrito." She gave a nod and disappeared from the table.

"So, what are we doing?" Marty asked, keeping it vague.

"Like I said yesterday, I'm out," Art replied. "In five years, I want to retire from this job."

Justin nodded. "I'm in. How about you, Marty?"

"Yeah. Abby is going along with it, so I'm in as well." He took a deep breath and said, "How about you and I meet tonight to compose the letter to Cook that Scott Winslow talked about. We'll keep Art away from it all."

"That's fine."

"My place at 8:00?" Marty offered.

"I'll be there."

"Okay. I'll call Scott's office and tell him that you and I are in."

The server in the red apron appeared with a tray and placed food in front of them. They thanked her and found themselves staring at the food, stomachs churning and not welcoming what awaited. They looked at each other, no one touching the food, and then Marty said, "I hope we can eat at some point while this case is pending. It could be a long year and a half." Art and Justin nodded, but remained silent.

"Are we sure about this, Justin?" Marty asked as the weight of what lay ahead hit him.

Justin stared at his food without speaking and then said, "I think so." The realization seemed to strike both of them simultaneously; they were on the way to being perceived as disloyal by many and a social pariah to the others who just couldn't risk being associated with them. This was not going to be a good experience.

Art looked at the expressions on their faces and offered, "Looking at you guys I feel like I just joined a funeral in progress. Cheer up, it's not too late to pull back from all of this. You haven't committed to go down this road yet." No one responded. There was a heavy silence at the table as Art studied their somber expressions, and then added, "Or maybe you have."

# Chapter Three

Marty took the elevator up two floors, turned left as he exited the hallway and walked towards the receptionist. "He's waiting for you," she said, only partially looking up from her monitor.

"Thanks," Marty replied and opened the door behind her. He walked down the corridor to the corner office occupied by Sean Garner, the corporate security guru. He gave a knock next to the open door and Garner looked up from his desk. "Come in, Marty. Thanks for coming by."

"Hi, Sean. What's going on?" Marty asked, wanting to cut to the chase and figure out why he had been summoned here. Seldom did Marty see Garner outside senior management meetings.

"Take a seat, Marty. Do you want some coffee?"

"No, I'm good, thanks." Marty was quiet. This was Garner's party, so he could fill the silence when he was ready.

"Mr. Cook is a little concerned, Marty. He asked me to reach out to you."

"Reach out? Does he believe that I am in some kind of trouble?"

Garner smiled. "In a manner of speaking, I suppose."

"A little vague, Sean. What's on his mind that required this meeting?"

"I think you know. There is some concern that you may be attempting to undermine the release of Delexane."

Marty stared at him in disbelief. "Undermine?" he asked. "Is undermining the same thing as voicing concerns that the tests no longer support the information the company is releasing?"

Garner gave him a stern look. "Obviously, Mr. Cook doesn't see it that way. He believes that the results you refer to are just an anomaly, and we are on the threshold of changing cancer treatment and the way the world looks at cancer. You must admit, that's a pretty big moment."

"That moment will be wonderful, Sean. We just aren't there yet with this product." He was quiet for a moment, feeling frustrated at the message not being communicated. "Is there something else that you want to tell me?" Marty asked.

"Only the obvious."

"Which is?"

"You've been a part of corporate culture for a long time, Marty. You know that it is extremely important to be a team player at critical times."

"I've always considered myself exactly that and I still do," Marty replied. "That's what I am when I'm working hard to test a product, when I'm singing a product's praises, and when I'm raising concerns about a product not being everything that we hoped it would be."

It was Garner's turn to remain quiet. After a time, he said, "Mr. Cook just wanted to make sure you understood the importance of this product to the company and to the consumer," Garner offered. He leaned forward in his chair. "This is revolutionary, Marty. So far, no other company is where we are in releasing such a product."

"Sean, I've been dealing with this product since before testing. I know what it represents and what it can be for the company. I also understand how important it is to the public that we get it right."

Garner offered a grin that was not particularly friendly and then said, "Thanks for coming by, Marty. I'm glad that we had this opportunity to talk."

"Sure," Marty replied. "Anytime." When he reached the door, he turned back and said, "You know, Sean, I hope Mr. Cook understands that having concerns about the quality of the product we are about to turn loose on society doesn't equate to disloyalty."

Garner furrowed his brow. "It can be a concern when your actions appear to undermine the direction that the team is taking. I will relay our conversation and your position to Mr. Cook," Garner replied, turning his attention back to his computer. Marty stood for a moment, wanting to find a way to further express his genuine concern. Garner never looked back at him, so he turned and walked out of the office.

When he arrived back at his office, Marty was shaking. He was nervous and he was angry at the way Cook was painting him. Marty grabbed his phone and punched in Justin's number.

"Justin Palmer."

"Justin, this is Marty. You won't believe what just happened."

"Yes, I will. My first guess is that you got a request to drop what you were doing and visit with Sean Garner."

"You too?"

"Yeah, about an hour ago."

"And?" Marty asked, "How did it affect your perspective?"

"I'm really not much for intimidation tactics. I've been pissed off ever since that meeting. I told him that I disagree with his assessment and I wanted to tell him and Cook to go fuck themselves."

"We probably shouldn't do that, but I can relate." Marty paused and then asked, "So, do you want to move forward with the letter to Cook?"

"More than ever."

"Okay, I finalized the letter. I've already signed it. Do you want to stop by my office and add your signature?"

"Yeah. Let's deliver it first thing in the morning."

"Consider it done." Marty said. When he hung up, he stared out the window, considering what this game of chicken with his career might cause. Maybe Cook could be persuaded to see the significance of the new findings. Perhaps he would agree to further studies before the product was released. That would be a compromise that would work for everyone.

* * *

**April 2**
**5:55 p.m.**
The cars remaining on the third floor of the parking structure were a scattered few as Marty walked towards his, where Justin waited, leaning on the driver's door with a concerned expression. "Did you send the letter?" he asked.

"As a matter of fact, I delivered it to Cook's personal assistant just before 9:00 a.m."

"No response?"

"Not a word from anyone all day. I kept staring at the phone, expecting to be summoned."

"How do we know that he read it yet?" Justin asked.

"I guess we don't, but it seems like he would give it his immediate attention, not knowing how soon we planned to go to the FDA. My guess is that he read it and he is considering his options."

Justin was quiet for a moment, and then replied. "I guess we are committed now, wherever this leads."

Marty nodded slowly, sharing the uncomfortable realization that sides had been chosen. "We have crossed a line and I am not sure there is any way back. I have an uncomfortable foreboding about what lies ahead, my friend."

\* \* \*

## April 2
### 9:45 p.m.

The lights of the executive suite far above city streets were still burning. Roland Cook poured two glasses of bourbon at the bar near his desk and walked over to the conversation area on the far side of the office with sleeves rolled up and tie loosened around his neck. He handed his visitor one of the glasses.

"Thank you," Sean Garner replied, taking a sip of the bourbon. He studied Cook for a moment without speaking. He had seen those eyes angry before. This meeting was not going to be about good news. "What's happening, boss?" he asked as Cook sat down in one of the armchairs.

"Read that," Cook replied, pointing to the letter he had received from Marty Cardenas and Justin Palmer earlier in the day.

Garner took a few minutes to read the letter demanding that Cook make corrections to the published data concerning the trials of Delexane, referring to the lower positive results of the phase three study and the newly discovered side effects. "What are you going to do?" Garner asked with concern.

He narrowed his eyes as he said, "No one blackmails me, Sean. These guys have forgotten who they are. They do not get to decide what happens with our new discoveries," he said angrily. He paused and then added, "We have a revolutionary drug on the immediate horizon. Something that will change the way people look at cancer forever. I will not let disloyal employees cast doubt on the product or substitute their judgment for mine."

"I understand, sir." Garner said, nodding. He waited to see if Cook would add more. When he said nothing further Garner asked, "What would you like me to do?"

"They will each get a written response from me in the morning, telling them that their input is appreciated and will be given full consideration." He savored a sip of the bourbon and then added, "Both are in the same meeting at 8:30 a.m. When they return to their offices, my letter will be waiting for them. It will make it hard for them to claim that we are not considering their position."

"Yes, sir. I understand."

"They will no longer have data and email access in the morning. As soon as they return from their meeting, they will be asked to meet with me at 11:00 a.m. and 11:15 a.m., when they will be terminated. I want you to personally walk them out of the building to make sure that they don't take or access anything that belongs to the Company."

Sean Garner nodded, swirling the ice in his glass. He was a little shocked at how fast the decision had been made to fire them, but he wasn't about to make his reaction known. He took a drink and then said, "I'll also check around after they leave and make sure nothing has been disturbed."

"Good. That will be fine, Sean." After a moment, Cook added, "I appreciate you coming by tonight."

Garner realized that he had just heard the signal that the meeting was over. He took one more sip and said, "Good bourbon," as he stood to leave.

Cook nodded. "I'm glad you have an appreciation for the good stuff; I see more of it in your future, Sean. Have a good evening."

\* \* \*

## April 5
### 12:45 p.m.

Justin carried a box to the elevator. Co-workers tried not to be seen watching him being escorted out of the building with desk and wall pictures, two coffee mugs, a light jacket and a couple of souvenir paperweights — everything that had converted a generic office into his home away from home. Years of belonging to a company and a purpose, undone in an instant. As they reached the elevator, Sean Garner looked at him and said, "I'm sorry I had to walk you out, Justin. No hard feelings." Justin gave him a nod as they boarded the elevator without any further discussion. This was really it, he told himself as the elevator moved towards the ground floor. He felt anger growing inside him. There would be an announcement that the National Sales Manager is 'no longer with us' and his staff would wonder what had happened for a few days. Then he would be replaced and forgotten, just like that.

As Justin stepped from the elevator in the lobby, the words that Cook had spoken echoed in his head. "Justin, it's not working out and we have decided to go in a different leadership direction." Just like that. It was the end of a career in a matter of seconds. He turned to Sean Garner and asked, "Are we okay here or do you plan on seeing me all the way home?"

Garner shrugged. "I'm sorry, man. Just doing my job."

Justin nodded. "You know what, Sean? I was too," he replied and then turned and walked towards the parking structure elevators.

Garner spoke to his back. "Nothing personal man."

Justin stopped in his tracks and looked back at Garner, outrage in his eyes. He shook his head and said, "Are you kidding? This is about as personal as it gets."

Garner gave a nod and then turned and got back into one of the elevators. Before moving into the garage elevator, Justin dialed Marty's cell and waited.

"Hi, Justin. How was it?"

"Where are you?" Justin asked.

"I was the first wave escorted out. I'm at Francine's Café, waiting for you. I was pretty sure you'd be following along shortly."

"I guess Francine's is our new office. I'll meet you there in fifteen minutes."

\* \* \*

Justin walked into Francine's Café and took a seat across from Marty. He shook his head. "Holy shit. Did we make a mistake?" he asked.

"I don't know," Marty replied, shaking his head. "I'm feeling a lot less secure about all this than I did yesterday."

"Yeah, Justin replied. I knew that this might happen at some point, but I didn't expect it in twenty-four hours."

"I guess we both thought that there would be some warning it was coming. We send him a memo yesterday and we're escorted out today. I feel like I just got hit by a truck."

"I agree. And do you know what else?" Justin asked.

"What else?"

"Sean Garner is an asshole. It's not just that he's doing Cook's dirty work, it's that you can see he is taken some kind of perverse pleasure in it."

Marty nodded. "He really did seem to be in his glory as he carried out this execution. His moment in the spotlight."

"Is Art still employed?" Justin asked.

Marty nodded solemnly. "Yeah, he's still there. I think what happened to us conveys a pretty strong message that he needs to silently launch the product without objection."

"Do you think we can get him to help us?" Marty posed.

Justin shook his head. "This morning I would have said that there is no doubt. After the message that our abrupt ouster communicates, he probably wouldn't dare. I think we have to be careful about what we ask him to do."

Marty reflected and then replied, "I think you're right. He's been good to us for a long time and I don't want to hang his ass out to dry."

\* \* \*

## April 5
### 5:20 p.m.
Donna walked Marty and Justin to the conference room. "Here are the retainers for your review. If you have any questions, discuss them with Scott before you sign."

"Shall do," Marty responded. "Thanks."

Scott entered the conference room about two minutes later, and both men handed him their signed retainers. "No questions?" Scott asked.

"Nope, I'm good with the agreement," Justin responded.

"Yeah, me too," Marty said.

"So, Cook pulled the trigger today?" Scott asked.

"Yeah, and gave us this letter in response to ours," Marty said, handing Scott a copy.

Scott reviewed the carefully worded response to the complaints that Marty and Justin had delivered to Cook.

*Thank you for your letter. Please know that the Company will seriously consider the points you raised in connection with our further assessment of the Delexane studies that are under way. We are excited about the promise of this new drug. At the same time, we want to assure that all information is considered.*

Scott smiled. "This guy is no fool. He's working hard to create some doubt about the reasons for your terminations. He's also trying to sound like he cares about the new drug's safety issues you raised, to negate any inference that your complaints were the reason you were terminated." Scott was quiet for a moment, and then asked, "Do either of you have any documentation concerning the drug and its performance in the trials?"

"Not yet," Justin said. "We were walked out suddenly and without notice. I'm kicking myself for not having taken a copy of the phase three results home. Now I'm hoping we can get Art to help us."

"But he's not here today because he is risk adverse, right?" Scott asked. "I mean he wants to survive the next five years at Aligor so that he can retire."

"Yeah, that's true. So it will be hard to expose him to the risk of helping us."

"We'll have to think about the best way to handle that issue," Scott said. "Once we file the lawsuit, I will send Aligor a demand for production of documents that they have to respond to under oath. It would be nice if we knew we had the real thing just in case what they give us isn't it, but we have time to work on whether there is a way to get it." Scott was quiet and then said, "In a couple of days, we'll have the lawsuit done and ready for your review. Once you review the document and tell us that we have the facts right, we can get it filed. Can you guys come in the next few days to look it over?"

"Sure," Marty replied. "My schedule is suddenly much lighter," he offered with a sardonic smile.

"Me too." Justin offered, "I suddenly have time on my hands."

Scott smiled. "Okay, gents. We'll call you to set it up as soon as the lawsuit has been drafted."

"See you then," Marty offered. He and Justin left the building silently, feeling the weight of their decision.

\* \* \*

**April 7**
**8:20 a.m.**
Donna sat in the conference room with Marty and Justin. When they finished their review of the proposed lawsuit, Justin said, "I made just a couple of minor date corrections." He handed the document to Donna.

"Likewise," Marty replied. He paused and then added, "You guys did a good job of describing the retaliation and the whole scenario leading up to it." He handed her his copy of the lawsuit and handwritten complaints.

Donna reviewed the changes they had made and said, "Like I mentioned, Scott's in court this morning, but I'm confident he will have no issue with your corrections. I will make them for his review and in all likelihood the Complaint will be filed in court tomorrow. We'll get it served within the next few days and we're off and running," she added.

"Thank you, Donna. We appreciate you guys already."

"We'll keep you posted," Donna said. "Please provide us with any other documents you locate concerning your performance, raises, bonuses, promotions, accomplishments and everything positive you can find. The more evidence supporting our claims the better."

"Okay," Marty replied. "I'll dig through old documents. I need a project anyway."

They shook hands and the two men left the law offices and walked out to the parking lot. "Should be an interesting ride," Justin offered as some consolation to the loss they shared.

Marty shook his head. "I guess, but I'd rather be back at work having too much to do. We have too much time to think about all this."

"Right. Even when I'm supposed to be sleeping, I'm playing all of this over in my head. Mostly, I'm just pissed off that the company would do this to me because I want them to tell everyone the truth about the results."

"They say that losing a career is like losing a loved one and I can see how that is true. I think I'm grieving the loss. I'm helpless, angry and mostly sad."

"Want to get some breakfast?" Justin asked. "I'm hungry as well as pissed off."

"I know I have time for that. I don't even need to check my calendar."

They laughed as they climbed into their cars and headed for Barney's Coffee Shop. Maybe bacon, eggs, and a lot of coffee would fix the problem and make them feel better.

# Chapter Four

Sandi and Art Underwood walked down the street from their downtown apartment to Francine's Café for their Sunday morning brunch, a ritual that had been part of their lives ever since they sold their big suburban home and moved to an apartment in the city five years ago. Art took his wife's hand and gave her a troubled smile. He looked at her and still saw the beautiful girl he had married so many years ago. Sandi was one of those people who always looked younger than her age, something that's a problem when you're twenty but a blessing when you're in your sixties and still look fifty. Her hair was black and flipped under at her shoulders. Her green eyes were almost liquid and seemed to drink in everything around her. She had a natural beauty and an unpretentious manner about her.

The streets were less congested than they were during the week, but the sidewalks were busy with pedestrians taking a walk, looking in store windows, or finding a spot at one of many restaurants offering elaborate Sunday brunch. Sandi and Art bypassed the street seating and walked into Francine's where the hostess waited. Their usual table was saved for them at the same time every Sunday. As they were seated and given menus, Sandi studied her husband's expression. After thirty-two years of marriage, she knew her husband as well as she knew herself, and she hadn't seen Art this distracted for a long time. He was uncharacteristically quiet and withdrawn. His usual Sunday morning smile had been replaced by a look of concern.

"Are you all right?" she asked, putting her hand on his.

He nodded. "I'm okay."

"But not really," she replied. "I know you too well, partner."

He gave her a pained smile. "I feel a little trapped. I haven't been fired, but in order to be deemed loyal and protect my career, I have to keep a bad secret and I don't feel good about it." He sat back in his chair and added, "I'm staying quiet just to save my own skin; it's like I lack the courage to do what's right the way Marty and Justin did."

"Marty and Justin are young. They have long careers ahead and can take a chance on a lawsuit at this junction in their lives. You and I need these last few years with Aligor. You and I both love our jobs, right? You still love the challenge and excitement of your job. It's the same way I feel about nursing."

"Yeah, that's all true. It just doesn't make me feel any better. I don't feel like a profile in courage when I watch my co-workers gamble everything to do what they think is right and I just watch it all from the sidelines."

"So, you're feeling like a coward for not standing up?"

He nodded and gave her a downturned expression. "Exactly."

"You're still you on the inside. So, maybe there is some way you will be able to help when it matters. Who knows where this goes from here, but we are a long way from the conclusion of all this, right?"

He considered her offering and nodded. Maybe he could give them a statement or summon the strength to support them in some other significant way. "You have always been able to find a way to make me feel better, no matter how bad things look. No wonder I adore you." He gave her a wide smile and then said, "Let's order a great brunch and then catch a good movie. I'll worry about all of this tomorrow."

"Try not to worry so much, sweetheart. I think a time will come when you can help the cause without losing everything. We just have to be patient and wait for the right moment."

"Thanks for understanding, Sandi. I want to support Marty and Justin because in my heart I know that what they are doing is right." He considered a moment and then said, "This is not just a problem for Marty and Justin, it's a problem for sick people who need help. Thousands of people are desperate for any last-minute cancer treatment they can find. They've already been told that doctors can only make things less painful until their time comes. Now Aligor is telling them that there's an answer that there will be improvements in two out of three people. It's just not true."

She nodded thoughtfully. "And that's another good reason to assist them in this fight. As for me, I'm going to do my best to convince my hospital not to buy Delexane, but the influence I can have is equivalent to one bucket of water in a lake. I want this fight to play out and I want you to support Marty and Justin, too. I just think that maybe we can do that best with you on the inside."

He nodded. "The third round of the trials told us that only one in eight can expect to see positive results from the drug, and even then, some people will have side effects that weren't previously in the mix." He shook his head. "These stricken folks will want to try anything that might help, whatever the odds. We just have to be sure that they are not getting bad information as a basis to make a life or death decision." It was her turn to smile widely. "What?" He asked.

"I was listening to how much you care. Now you know the reason I'm supportive of you. You're a good man, Charlie Brown."

\* \* \*

**May 18**
**6:00 p.m.**
Nikki, the receptionist, buzzed Scott.

"What's up, Nikki?"

"I'm heading out for the day and Doug Gibson is on line 1." Doug was a senior partner with Gentry Marsden, a law firm three hundred lawyers strong, who had been retained to defend Aligor in the lawsuit brought by Marty and Justin.

"Thanks, Nikki. Have a good evening." He punched a button and said, "Scott Winslow."

"Scott, Doug Gibson."

"Hi, Doug. What's up?"

"As you know, our firm represents Aligor in the action you brought on behalf of Cardenas and Palmer."

"I am aware of that, yes."

"I wanted to introduce myself as I will be lead counsel for the defense." Which meant there would be two other lawyers doing the day to day grunt work on the case and Gibson would be calling the shots.

"Okay, good to meet you, Doug. I've had cases against several of your partners in the past."

"Yeah, I know that. I also wanted to call you to tell you personally that we have serious problems with your demand for production of documents."

"What problems do you have?"

"These are confidential and proprietary materials."

"First of all," Scott replied, "the personnel documents of my clients and their employment histories are not protected. As to the drug testing documents we are seeking, any confidentiality claims are easily handled. We sign a confidentiality agreement stating that the responsive documents will only be used for prosecution of this case and not otherwise disclosed."

There was a silence and then Gibson said, "That is not enough."

"Okay, I'll give you a first draft choice for next season as well."

"Funny. Scott, the information requested is Aligor proprietary material, and it implicates third party privacy rights."

"I wish you guys cared as much about privacy when you take my clients' deposition and try to invade theirs at every turn."

"Look," Gibson replied with an angry edge to his voice, "I was just giving you a heads-up."

"A heads-up that you are planning to disregard your discovery obligations. This is an easy fix. In the first round you provide statistical from the Delexane trials without identifying specific patients. If we need more, we'll fight for it."

"I'm afraid that won't do it, Scott."

"Because?"

"Because it's both proprietary and confidential, like I said."

"And why doesn't my solution work?" Scott asked.

"You would definitely want individual information, and that is protected by the right to privacy of all those patients."

"Wait, let me make sure I have this right. You're not going to give me the statistical data that doesn't include names because you think I'll want more?"

"Right."

"So, if I want more and you don't agree that I'm entitled to it, you object to further production at that time."

"No, I don't think so. Anyway, you'll be receiving our objections in the next day or two."

"That's not going to do it for me, Doug. We will be making a motion to compel production of documents and the court will decide."

"Fine. Go for it." With that, Gibson was gone. It was the tough guy posturing that seemed to happen at the beginning of a case when both sides were staking out their territory. He made notes about the content of the call so that the argument he had been given for why he was to be stiffed could be recited to the court. It was time to pull some corporate teeth to get the documents he needed.

* * *

## May 20
## 8:05 a.m.

Marty Cardenas and Justin Palmer carried their cups of coffee into the conference room. Scott Winslow walked into the room and greeted them as they took a seat. "Hi gentlemen, how are you?"

"Good now," Justin said, pointing to his cup. "You guys make really good coffee."

"I hear that often," Scott said. "Maybe we should add that to our website. "Employment counseling, employment litigation and great coffee."

"I think so," Marty said. "The Firm that has it all."

Scott said, "What is it that you guys wanted to discuss? From Justin's call, it sounds like you have some good news."

"That's right," Justin said. "We know that you are getting ready to argue motions about whether we get the Delexane trials data, and we've been concerned that the court might buy Aligor's arguments and not give us the data. So, we found a better way."

"Lay it on me," Scott replied. "I'm always open to better ways."

"After wrestling with whether to put him in the pariah position that we occupy, I decided to talk to Art Underwood. He wants to help if he can and he will make a copy of the critical data for us, provided we don't disclose where it came from," Justin offered. "Even though he won't be part of any lawsuit, I think he may step up to help us get the documents because he believes in the cause."

"We owe him a beer or two," Marty suggested with a smile.

"You probably do, but it's a little more complicated than that," Scott interjected.

"How so?" Marty asked.

"This is proprietary information. The lawyer representing the Company will accuse you of theft and may even file a cross-complaint against you for stealing Company secrets. They will also take your depositions in the case and ask you where you got this confidential material."

"Well," Marty offered, "we sure as hell won't tell them that we got it from Art."

"There's the rub, guys. You are under oath and can't lie in your depositions, and I can't be a party to lying in your depositions."

"So, what are you saying?" Justin asked.

"I'm saying that if you get documents from Art, you're going to have to say that you got them from Art."

"I can't do that," Marty replied.

Everyone was quiet for a moment, and then Scott said, "Let's take a few days and work on ideas that would allow us to collect the documents without implicating you guys or requiring that you identify Art," Scott said. "Then we'll talk about it one more time."

"I don't know how we can do that, but it will be a good piece of work if you can figure that out." Marty offered.

"It will take some thought," Scott said, nodding.

"Okay," Marty said, "Let us know what we can do to help. It turns out that we have time on our hands like never before."

Justin let out a forced laugh. "A little humor as we whistle past the graveyard, right Marty?"

\* \* \*

## June 8
### 9:05 a.m.

Judge Thomas Garrett always seemed annoyed. The perpetual bad mood of someone who would rather be somewhere else, but who had been on the bench for over twenty years and didn't really know where else to go. Every time he visited Judge Garrett's courtroom, Scott envisioned a bumper sticker on the bench that said "I'd rather be fishing."

Judge Garrett looked over the glasses perched halfway down his nose at lawyers who bothered him, which was seemingly all of them, no matter what they said. The clerk announced, "Cardenas and Palmer v. Aligor Pharmaceuticals" and Scott took his place at the counsel table reserved for the plaintiff. Doug Gibson appeared at the defense table next to him.

"Scott Winslow for plaintiffs Cardenas and Palmer, your Honor."

"Doug Gibson for Defendants."

The judge looked unhappily at both sides and then said, "I have read the motion and the opposition. We have two issues. Plaintiff wants a copy of the product trials documentation for each of the three trials and also seeks the identity of those who participated in the trials. Let's take one issue at a time. Mr. Winslow, you want to be heard?"

"Yes, your Honor. My clients were fired after complaining that Defendant was not properly disclosing trial results. Instead, Defendant was releasing incomplete and inaccurate data that didn't include the significant results of the third and biggest study. In other words, we believe that they were misleading the public in matters of public health and safety. We are entitled to see the drug trials documentation so that we can demonstrate where the information was improperly withheld from results that were made public to create positive expectations for the product."

"Mr. Gibson?"

"Your Honor, this is highly confidential information. Not only are the materials proprietary, the privacy rights of all of the participants are in issue and we, as well as this court, must respect those privacy rights. What's more, plaintiffs don't need this information. They were both terminated for reasons having nothing to do with these trials and they know it."

"Mr. Winslow?"

"Both clients have positive evaluations and great work histories. Counsel can argue that there was some other unlikely reason for the termination of these successful executives, but the issue is whether they were terminated for unlawful reasons. Unless the Defendant is prepared to admit that it terminated Mr. Cardenas and Mr. Palmer because of their complaints about false test result information being disseminated, we are going to need to show what the results were and that they were hidden. We are entitled to the documents to establish those facts. Defendants cannot he heard to deny there is anything wrong with the data they released and hide the critical documents from view."

Judge Garrett nodded.

"Your Honor," Gibson urged, "this is extremely confidential material that implicates medical condition and privacy rights of each of the participants. There is no way this information should be out there in the public eye."

Judge Garrett sat back in his chair. "Mr. Winslow offered a confidentiality agreement that would allow disclosure of this information only to witnesses and for preparation of the case for trial. I think that protects your client's confidentiality concerns and I'm going to order the trial data produced within the next two weeks. Now, as to issue number two, the identity of study participants, I have a problem with that, Mr. Winslow."

"Your Honor, each of the participants is a percipient witness in the case. Defendants urge that certain results were achieved, and we need to be able to test the accuracy of what they are saying when those statements can be compared with the facts about the participants."

"May I?" Gibson asked.

"Yes, Mr. Gibson," Judge Garrett responded attentively.

"Every one of these participants have privacy rights implicated in these requests and none of them have consented to give plaintiffs person, medical information about themselves and their lives. This cannot happen without their consent."

Judge Garrett nodded slowly. "I believe that I agree with that," he said slowly.

"Your Honor, there is a way to handle those concerns. I propose that we have an order that a notice of this case be delivered to each of the participants along with the form I designed and attached to our motion. It gives the patient our contact information and allows them to call us or provide for a signature. If they sign the form consenting to our inquiry, then we get to call them."

"That isn't necessary for this case and the trial participants should not have to deal with those issues," Gibson urged.

The judge studied both sides for a moment with an expression that said they were both a pain in the ass. After a time, he said, "Let me consider that further. I will take the matter under submission and send you my ruling on it within the next couple of days. Anything else?"

"No, your Honor. Thank you," Scott replied.

"Nothing further, your Honor," Gibson added.

"Goodbye gentlemen. Next case."

* * *

**June 12**
**3:00 p.m.**

"Scott, Marty Cardenas is on line 1," Nikki said into the intercom.

"Thanks, Nikki." Scott punched a button. "Hi, Marty. I bet you're returning my call from earlier today."

"I am."

"I was calling to tell you that the judge sent his ruling. Aligor is ordered to produce the test results, not identifying individual participants. At this point, he denied our request to send a letter to the participants telling them of the case and allowing us to contact them if they sign and return the notice."

"Well, I'm glad we get the results of the trials but I'm not sure why we can't talk to participants."

"The judge apparently bought the argument about their rights to privacy."

"Any word on when we get the test data?"

"They had two weeks from June 8, so they have until the 22$^{nd}$ to get it to us. I'll let you and Justin know as soon as we have it."

"Thanks, Scott."

"How are you doing with all of this?"

"It's all surreal at this point. I've been putting out word of my availability to those in the industry that I have known a long time, but so far no one is calling to hire me or even just to talk."

"Are you doing okay emotionally?"

"Been better. My self-worth has been suffering lately. I had no idea how much of my self-image was derived from my career, or at least having one."

"You're right about that. When something so important gets taken away, it turns everything upside down. You should consider talking to a counselor to help you through. They can be helpful in these situations."

"I've been thinking about that. I have a friend who just gave me the name of a counselor and I think I'll make an appointment. Hopefully I can land a new job soon. I know that it would help if I had work to focus on again."

"Do you and Justin talk frequently?"

"Almost daily. Somehow, it's good not to feel like you're doing this alone, you know."

"I get it. Hang in there, Marty. I'll be back with you as soon as I have any update."

"Thanks, Scott. It's good to have you on our team."

* * *

**June 23**
**8:00 a.m.**
Scott and Donna walked into the conference room with coffee in hand. Marty Cardenas and Justin Palmer were still staring at copies of the same twenty-nine-page document they had been given a half hour before. For a few moments, neither looked up as Scott and Donna took a seat and prepared to take notes.

A full three minutes later, Marty closed the document and looked at Justin. He shook his head as Justin looked at him with wide eyes.

"Let us in on it." Scott said, anxious for interpretation of the looks of shock.

Marty shook his head and waved the report in his hand. "These results have been altered, Scott. I can't remember all the details, but I know that these numbers just aren't right."

"Are you sure?" Scott asked.

"I'm sure."

"Jason, how about you?"

"I agree. I'm not as intimately familiar with all of the numbers as Marty, who lived and breathed this stuff. But there are differences that I can see as well. These are not the real numbers."

Scott nodded. "Marty, can you and Justin go through the document page by page and note all places where you are confident the report has been modified. Also include what you believe the correct information should be."

"We can do that," Marty said.

Scott shook his head. "We have to find a way to get hold of the real documents for purposes of comparison."

\* \* \*

**June 24**
**6:45 p.m.**
"Hi, Lee. This is Scott Winslow. Call me when you get this so we can brainstorm for a few minutes about some evidence for the Aligor drug case. I'll be in the office for another twenty minutes or so. After that, get me on my cell."

After leaving the message, Scott returned his attention to preparing for a deposition. It was five minutes later that the phone rang. Scott recognized the number. "Lee, how are you?"

"I'm good. I got your message. How can I help?"

"Thanks for your email confirming that the three Aligor employees I talked to have clean backgrounds. Marty Cardenas and Justin Palmer were fired, and Art Underwood is still there. Justin told me that Underwood is prepared to help us by providing a copy of the critical test results, so I want to find a way to get that material while avoiding having my guys get the material directly from Art Underwood. If it comes into their possession, the defense lawyers will be all over them in deposition about where they got proprietary information. If they don't perjure themselves by denying the documents came from Underwood, he will be unceremoniously fired, and may also get sued. So, I want to do away with the connection between my clients and access to the documents."

"Got it," Lee said. "Let me jump into the middle of it with Art Underwood. If I come up with the documents and give them to you, your guys accurately say they weren't involved in the acquisition."

"That's what I was hoping you would say. We are on the same page here."

"No problem," Lee replied. "Give me his number and I'll call Underwood tonight and see what we can set up so that Underwood doesn't have to acknowledge that he was involved either."

"Thanks, Lee. Let me know if you and Underwood can work something out. He's nervous about putting his ass on the line because he's five years from retirement, but he wants to help if he isn't too far out on a limb."

"Got it. We can protect him too. I'll just have him copy and leave the documents somewhere that I can find a way to access them, so he doesn't have to hand me anything, or even meet with me."

Scott knew better than to ask how that would happen. Lee Henry could hide in a crowd or stand alone and go unnoticed. He would know everything that took place in his location of choice and no one else would know that he had been there. "Sounds good, Lee. Keep me posted."

\* \* \*

**June 24**
**8:30 p.m.**
Lee dialed the number Scott had given him. It was answered on the second ring.

"Art Underwood."

"Hi Art, my name is Lee Henry. I'm an investigator who works with Scott Winslow. Do you have a couple of minutes to talk?"

"Yes, sure."

"I understand that you are prepared to copy some documents to share."

"That's right," Art replied. He paused and then said, "Justin and Marty shouldn't have been fired. They were trying to do what was right. I hope they understand why I can't get involved in the litigation at this stage of my career." He sounded like a man who felt guilty, like a man who cared.

"They understand, Art. They really do. And they want to keep you as far from this as possible. So, I have a slightly different proposal to make."

"I'm listening."

"What if you copied the documents and didn't give them to anyone."

"Sounds good so far," Art replied. "What do I do with them?"

"How many pages are we talking about?" Lee asked.

"About thirty pages."

"You simply leave them in a brown envelope on your desk by noon tomorrow and go to lunch between noon and one."

"And then?"

"And then nothing. Anyone asks you about it, you never gave documents to anyone."

"Okay, that works for me. I'm just not sure how that gets them to you."

"If someone asks, you can say that you never gave them to anyone. If they ask how the documents got to Marty or Justin, you can accurately say that it's a mystery to you, right?"

"Well, yeah. The whole thing is actually pretty mysterious. This is a secure building and I have no idea how you can get to anything in my office."

"Then you can see how that is just perfect. I'll worry about the rest of it."

"Okay. I'll hope that you know how to make yourself invisible."

Lee smiled because that's exactly what he knew how to do.

# Chapter Five

Lee Henry parked a white van in one of the visitor parking places and walked into the Aligor Pharmaceuticals building. Lee wore hair that was much greyer than his own and a little uncombed. He had a newly placed birthmark on his right cheek and a grey, walrus mustache that made him look a little like John Bolton's blue-collar brother. His overalls displayed an "Emperor Elevators" logo on the breast pocket and Lee completed the outfit with an expression of impatience. Carrying a tool case, he walked over to the security desk and said, "I'm here to conduct the quarterly elevator inspection."

The young security guard looked puzzled. He examined a document in front of him for a few moments and then said, "I don't see anything about that on the schedule."

Lee shrugged as if to say not my problem. The guy looked at the list again. Lee said, "Look, man, I have five stops this afternoon and my partner is out sick. I can get this inspection done in about twenty minutes and then we can send the new certifications out."

"I understand. I just don't know…"

Lee shrugged. "Don't worry about it, I'll just go on to my next one and tell my people you didn't have my visit on your list. Like I said, I have five stops this afternoon, so if you don't want your certification, I'm on my way."

"Twenty minutes?" the young man asked with a worried expression.

"Right. I'm going to ride the elevators and check the controls. That's it, man."

"Okay, go ahead, but sign in first."

"Sure thing," Lee said, picking up the pen and signing and undecipherable name. "See you in about twenty minutes and we'll be done with this for another three months and we'll be that much closer to the weekend," Lee said, giving the guard a smile and then walking towards the elevator bank.

Lee rode to the twenty-seventh floor hit the emergency stop on the elevator. He used tape to make an "X" across the open elevator door and disappeared into the restroom down the hall. Once inside, he took off the overalls, exposing a white shirt and blue tie and suit pants. He pulled a pair of polished slip-ons from his tool kit and left the tool kit and the overalls in a stall, locked from the inside. He climbed under the door and made his way out of the restroom and down the hall. He entered the open door of Art Underwood's office and walked over to his desk, picking up a large brown envelope identified with the words "For review."

As he walked along the hall towards the elevator, a woman came out of an office and looked at him. "Can I help you, sir?"

"I was going to stop and see a friend while in the building, but he's not here."

"Who is it? Maybe I can give him a message."

Still wearing the grey wig, Lee gave her his best fatherly grin and said, "You are very kind. Thanks so much but I'll just give him a call." He walked on and then turned back and said, "Thanks again for being so nice." She couldn't help but return the smile before she stepped back into the office.

Lee quickly returned to the restroom and crawled under the door of the locked stall. He slid the envelope into a compartment on the bottom of the toolbox and removed another envelope from the same location. He shimmied back into the overalls and made his way back to the elevator where he removed the tape and hit the emergency stop button one more time. He took the elevator to the lobby and walked over to the guard desk, where his nervous young friend looked relieved to see him returning even more quickly than estimated.

Lee said, "Thanks, good buddy. You can let building management know that the elevators are going to be re-certified. Official certifications will come in the mail in about a month. They tell me it will be two or three weeks, but it's really taking them about thirty days."

The young man smiled contentedly and said, "Sounds great. Will you sign out for me before you go?"

"Of course," Lee said. "I almost forgot." He checked his watch and put the accurate time in the box that said "out," across from the signature that no one would be able to read. He looked at the young security guard and said, "Have a good day man."

"You too. Good luck with all your other stops."

Lee shook his head. "It's a pain in the ass. I'm just glad it's Friday." He gave a wave and then turned and walked out of the building without looking back.

\* \* \*

**June 25**
**3:01 p.m.**

Donna stepped into Scott's office and handed him an envelope. "Here are the drug trial documents from Aligor. The elevator repair man just dropped them off."

"What?"

"Truly, it took me a couple of minutes to figure out it was Lee. The guy is amazing with disguises."

Scott laughed. "I don't think I've ever had documents delivered by an elevator repair man before. This is a first." Scott opened the envelope and began to decipher the contents. "Let's set up an appointment for Marty and Justin to come in and interpret some of these findings and compare them with what Aligor produced."

"I'll give them a call and set it up," Donna replied.

Scott shook his head. "Lee figured out a way to pick up the documents so that Art Underwood can accurately say he never gave them to anyone."

"Right," Donna said. "Our clients can testify that they didn't remove any Aligor confidential documents." She grinned. "Where else would one get proprietary documents? They were delivered by the elevator repair man."

\* \* \*

**June 25**
**9:20 p.m.**

Sean Garner punched a private number and waited. It was answered on the third ring. "Yes?"

"Sorry to disturb you at home, sir, but it's important."

"What is it, Sean?" Cook asked, sounding impatient.

"You know that our copy machines used at the executive levels take an electronic picture of documents copied on the machine?"

"Yes," Cook replied.

"I checked the emails and copy machines previously used by Marty Cardenas and Justin Palmer. No inappropriate copies taken. But today I checked Art Underwood's machine and found that the phase three test results had been copied."

There was quiet for a moment before Cook said, "Okay, but Art is entitled to access that information as part of his job."

"Yes, sir, but what I know so far is that the documents were copied on Art's machine at 11:15 a.m., and then Art went to lunch at noon and had an out of the office appointment this afternoon. My concern is whether he shared this material with the other two. I not sure why he would copy it today, but I walked around his office tonight and didn't find it. So, we don't know if he handed over this material or not."

Cook was quiet for a time and then said, "You'll have to look Art in the eyes and ask him about it directly, Sean. It's Friday night and I don't want to wait the whole weekend to get to the bottom of this."

"I'll meet with him in the morning. His office says he plans to be in for a couple of hours to finish up a few things."

"Call me as soon as you do. If he delivered those documents to the lawyer, it is a problem."

"Yes, sir."

\* \* \*

## June 26
### 7:35 a.m.

Art Underwood walked into his office, set his briefcase down on the floor and jumped a foot when he saw a figure standing across the room staring at him.

He took a moment to gather himself and then said, "Did you and I have an appointment this morning, Sean?"

"No, no appointment," Garner replied.

They were silent a moment, and then Art said, "What can I do for you?"

"You can answer a question or two," Garner replied. "What happened to the Delexane trial data you copied yesterday?"

"What?"

"You made a copy of the trial data yesterday morning. Where is it?"

"I'm not comfortable with this conversation, Sean. I'm also not comfortable with being spoken to like I'm sort of a suspect." He shook his head. "You can leave now, Sean."

"I'm afraid that you need to answer this question, Art."

"No. No, I don't. I've been dedicated to this company for a long time and I don't have to justify myself to you."

"The question comes directly from Mr. Cook," Garner replied with a shrug, "so I'm sure you want to answer."

"I see," Art said thoughtfully. "In that case, Mr. Cook and I will discuss any question that he has when he and I talk."

"It would be a lot easier to simply answer my questions. You are forgetting that I am the security chief around here."

Art looked Garner directly in the eyes. "I'm not forgetting anything and whether it would be easier or not, I don't answer to you, Sean." He paused a moment and added, "If you'll excuse me, I have work to do." Garner stared at Art with daggers in his eyes. He didn't move and he didn't speak. "Anything else?" Art asked in a calm voice. Without a word, Garner turned and moved quickly out the door.

Art was doing his best to stay in control, but his heart was racing. They knew he had made a copy of the Delexane trial data. Holy shit. He needed to have a copy of the document in his possession by the time of his next meeting with Cook and he couldn't make the copy here, where whatever was copied was apparently being recorded. He needed to find a public copy machine in order to take a picture of an extremely confidential document, so that he could have a copy to replace the one that had mysteriously made its way to Scott Winslow. It was all getting crazy.

\* \* \*

**June 26**
**8:45 a.m.**
"Marty, this is an emergency. Call me back right away on my cell." Art Underwood paced the office turning it over in his mind. He was going to hear from Cook, and he was going to have to respond.

Art picked up his phone and jacket and walked out of the office. "Sheila," he said to the assistant sitting outside his office, "I have an errand. I expect to be back in about an hour." She nodded as he made his way as quickly as possible to the elevator and out to the parking lot. His pulse was racing, and he felt flushed. He climbed into his Audi and drove out of the Aligor parking lot. As he made his way towards the local mall, a place he was going because no one would suspect he would go there, his phone rang.

He looked at the number and said, "Marty, I need help."

"What is it?" Marty asked with concern. "What's the matter?"

"They know that I made a copy of the Delexane trial results. The bastards can actually tell a copy was made on my copy machine. Sean Garner showed up and asked to see it."

"What?"

"Yeah. He came on behalf of Mr. Cook. He said that he wanted me to show him that I still had the document."

"How did you handle it?" Marty asked.

"I told him that I didn't answer to him. I had to buy some time. I can't print another copy to show Cook I have the copy, or they will know it. I need you guys to get me back the document I gave to you."

"Okay, I understand," Marty said. "I will get it from Scott Winslow and deliver it to you."

"Perfect," Art replied. "I hope you can do it fast."

"I talked to Scott this morning and I know that he's in his office, so I should be able to meet you within half an hour. "I'll call you as I leave Scott's office. Where do you want to meet?"

"I'll meet you at Francine's Café."

\* \* \*

**June 26**
**10:25 a.m.**
As Art pulled into Francine's parking lot, his phone rang. He recognized the number as coming from the executive offices of Roland Cook. He ignored the call and slipped the phone into his pocket and looked around the restaurant until he saw Marty Cardenas at a table in the far corner. As Art approached the table, Marty pulled an envelope from his briefcase. He handed the envelope to Art, who looked extremely worried. "This is the original you gave us, so if they have a way of determining whether it came from an Aligor copy machine, it will pass the test."

Art nodded. "Thanks, Marty. Cook is getting paranoid about this. To him this is loyalty or betrayal." Art took a deep breath and then said, "I can't stay for coffee. I want to get back to the campus and put this back in my office. Garner showed up in my office demanding answers. I told him I didn't report to him and had nothing to say. A few minutes ago, I got a call from Cook's office, so I know what's coming next. Anyway, these guys want assurance that I still have the document that was printed."

"I understand, Art, but there's something you should know." Marty's turn to take a breath.

"What is it?"

"Aligor produced a copy of the report to Scott Winslow in connection with the case."

"Okay," Art replied. "No problem."

"But there is a problem; a big one. The report we got is not the one you provided. It had been sanitized to eliminate questions raised by the third level trials. They changed the numbers to justify their statements that sixty percent of participants benefitted from the study."

"Oh my God," Art replied, frozen in place. He pushed both hands through his hair and worked to compose himself. "They are going to know the source of the real report as soon as they know you have it."

"That won't come out right away. Scott tells me it could be several months before we have to make any reference to the real document." Art nodded, fear and worry in his eyes. "Scott is working on a way to create doubt as to where we got it when they learn we have the real data."

"All right," Art said, not sounding particularly hopeful, but unable to find any other words. He gave Marty a tepid smile and turned to walk out of the restaurant. Marty watched his friend and former boss leave the restaurant, feeling responsible for Art's anxiety. They had to find some way to make sure Art wasn't blamed when it was uncovered that Scott had the real data in addition to the sanitized version that Aligor produced. Art's career hung in the balance, so it had to be pretty damned convincing.

Marty stood and left five dollars on the table for his cup of coffee and then walked to the front door. It was then that he felt his own blood pressure spike as he caught a glimpse of Sean Garner watching from the other side of the restaurant.

* * *

Art made his way back to the office with the critical document in his brief case and feeling like a heavy load had been lifted from his shoulders. With the trial data back in his hands, he could prove that the only copy he had made was still in his possession. He could return to work and stop worrying about whether top management thought he was a traitor. Even so, the experience left him feeling uneasy.

When he entered his office, Art took the document from his briefcase and began to review the data one more time, considering whether there was any way to dismiss any of these results as a "one-off," but he already knew the answer. As he reviewed the trial data the knot in his stomach returned. Did Cook really believe what he said about Delexane being a great drug or was he simply focused on the big payoff that the drug promised and willing to do what it takes to get there? He sat back in his chair and he knew that there was no other way to view this product. It was not ready for FDA approval or marketing and inducing the public to believe that this product could be some miracle treatment for their cancer was simply cruel. The phase three trials demonstrated that their chances of improvement were about the same as if they took one of several other cancer drugs on the market, but now there were new side effects that had not been well-studied.

Art checked his watch. He had to get a few things finished and wanted to get out of the office so that he could avoid any further discussion while he had a chance to digest all that he had learned. As he walked from his office obsessing about how he could continue to stay neutral in the face of what he knew, his phone rang. He looked down at the number and saw that it was Marty Cardenas. He had no time to talk now, so he would have to call Marty back tonight. He let the call go to voicemail.

* * *

**June 26**
**11:30 a.m.**
"So, what do you think you witnessed?" Roland Cook asked Sean Garner up in the executive sanctuary. Cook stood, leaning against his desk, arms folded as Garner sat in one of the visitor chairs feeling a little too close to his boss.

Garner thought a moment, and then said, "I think I saw Marty Cardenas delivering documents to Art, rather than the other way around. Maybe information or questions from Marty's lawyer, I don't know."

Cook nodded. "You told him that you knew he made a copy of the trial data, right?"

"Yes, sir," Garner offered, nodding.

"And then you see Marty Cardenas giving a document to Art, correct?"

Sean thought for a moment and then his eyes widened, and he replied, "Shit. I bet I was watching Marty give back the document that Art had already delivered, so that he had the one that came from our machine in his possession."

"I think that's right, Sean, but you have to find out for sure whether their lawyers have been given the trial results. If that's true, it creates untenable complications."

"I will find out."

"Talk to Art again and convince him it's in his best interests to tell us whether he has given anything to the lawyers."

"Yes, sir."

"And do it off campus."

"I will definitely find out," Garner said. This was his opportunity to convince Cook that he had what it takes to be part of the inner circle and he was going to make it count.

# Chapter Six

Art and Sandi Underwood made their way to dinner at "Temptation Tacos," a favorite hole-in-the-wall restaurant for spicy food. Sandi could see the worry on her husband's face and worked hard to get him to forget his concerns and enjoy the moment. As they finished the meal, she said, "That was really great. No cooking and no dishes involved."

"It was great," he replied, and then he got quiet.

"Talk to me, Art. I know that you are struggling."

"Sorry, I don't want to seem distant. I feel like I am sitting out an important fight. Like a coward."

"You are helping them though, right? I mean you got them the key document."

He nodded. "True, but I feel like I'm hiding rather than declaring my participation in the fight."

Sandi shrugged. "So what? Discretion is the better part of valor." She touched his hand and then added, "And you can probably help more while you are still on the inside, right?"

"I suppose that's true."

"So, stop beating yourself up already."

Art nodded and took her hand. "Thank you," he offered with a warm smile.

"For what?" she asked.

"For always being there when I need you. Just for being you."

They drove home and he gave her a kiss before climbing out of the car. "I can't believe my group agreed to a book club meeting on a Saturday night. I must have been spacing out when we agreed to this."

"I know how that goes," he offered. "I'll see you at home in a couple of hours."

"I'll see you then, sweetheart." As he watched her drive away, he smiled. He had the familiar feeling that she was the best thing in his world. She always seemed to be his emotional rescue. When things were difficult, stressful or disappointing, she was always there to make him feel better. He was one hell of a lucky guy.

Art pulled out his key and entered the apartment building. He rode the elevator to the fifth floor and then walked to the end of the hall. He unlocked the door and went inside, then grabbed a beer and walked onto the balcony to look at the night. The moon was almost full and shone in ghostly fashion beyond the fog beginning to take hold. There were wisps of white clouds drifting across the sky. He loosened his tie and sat down in one of the two recliners facing the television and turned on the baseball game. The Dodgers were playing someone; maybe Arizona.

He watched the Dodger pitcher strike out a batter. A minor success given that the Dodgers were trailing by four at the end of the sixth inning. As the next batter walked to the plate, the doorbell rang. Art wondered who that could be, especially seeing as no one had buzzed to be let in at the locked front door of the building. Whoever it was must have been followed a tenant in or gained access through another tenant's intercom.

"Who is it?" Art asked as he walked to the door. There was no response. "Who is it?" Another knock. Art opened the door slightly, without disengaging the chain that secured the door. "What are you doing here?" he asked the familiar figure.

"I need to talk to you, Art," Sean Garner said evenly.

"Talk to me at the office," Art replied. "This is my home."

"I'm here because Mr. Cook wants me to talk to you tonight."

"Monday, Sean."

Garner furrowed his brow. "Open the fucking door," he said, loudly.

"No, Sean. Get out of here."

Garner stepped back one pace and gave the door a hard kick, breaking the chain and slamming the door into Art, who fell to the floor. "We need to talk,"

Garner said again as he stepped inside the apartment and pushed the door closed behind him.

"You son of a bitch," Art screamed. "Get out of my house." He walked over to the phone in the living room and picked it up.

Garner ran towards him and jerked the phone from his hands. "You're not calling anyone," he said. "We are going to talk."

Art was so angry that he was shaking. "Get out," he yelled one more time. Garner didn't move.

"You're going to tell me if you gave proprietary company documents to Cardenas and Palmer."

"I'm going to tell you nothing, you son of a bitch. You go tell Cook he can talk to me at work or fire me, but I am not telling you anything."

Anger flared in Garner's eyes as he walked over and grabbed Art by the arm. "I've had enough of your arrogant bullshit. You need to start talking now."

"Let go of me."

"Start talking. Did you give Delexane trials documents to Cardenas and Palmer?"

"No, I didn't give them documents."

"So why is it that I saw Cardenas giving them back to you at Francine's?"

"I don't know what you're talking about," Art replied. "Get out!"

Garner punched Art in the gut. As Art stood bent over trying to recover his breath, Garner said, "Start talking."

Art took a swing at the bigger, muscular Garner, which he easily deflected. Garner grabbed Art by the neck and moved him across the room backwards to the closed balcony door. He opened the door with his left hand as his right maintained a tight grip on Art's neck. Art found himself struggling for air again, as Garner pushed him to the edge of the balcony, which was surround by a five-foot stucco wall in a half-circle. He lifted Art off his feet and onto the balcony wall, pushing him back so that his head swung out away from the building. "You ready to talk now, asshole?"

Art couldn't say a word. He tore at the hands that held his throat, desperate to find his way back to secure footing. Garner pushed him back further, until he was almost horizontal, leaning out over the balcony rail and into the nothingness five floors up. Art couldn't speak or breathe. He tried to loosen the grip on his throat so that he could get enough air. He ripped desperately at the hands that gripped is neck so tightly, with Garner yelling, "Are you ready to talk yet?" Art wanted to nod, but he was held immobile. Then something went terribly wrong. A balance point was reached, and Garner lost his hold on Art. Gravity pulled Art from the balcony and into the night air. Sean Garner tried to grab him again but could barely touch his shoulder as he disappeared downward into the night. As Garner looked down, it was if he was watching the fall in slow motion. The ambient light kept him in view until he saw Art hit the ground five floors below. A second later he heard the horrific sound, like an enormous lightbulb shattering as Art's body broke on the concrete. His limbs were positioned unnaturally, and he lay motionless below.

Garner stood helplessly staring for a few moments in disbelief as he gazed down at the broken body slightly illuminated by apartment lighting and ambient city light. What should he do? Should he call for help? He found himself staring at Art's body below for several minutes and then he made his decision. He ran from the apartment, closing the door behind him and down the stairwell to the front of the building. Breathing hard, he ran down the block to where he had parked his Audi and climbed inside. He was shaking as he held the tightly to the wheel. He felt like he was going to throw up. Holy shit, what had he done?

Garner started the car and drove home, the images of Art leaving his grip and falling through space playing over and over in his mind. He wanted to close his eyes to clear the images, but he knew that they weren't going to go away. He started considering conditions back at the apartment. Was it a crime scene? Was there evidence of his presence somewhere that he hadn't considered? Garner didn't think so. No one saw him walk into the building or leave it. Someone opened the front door without leaving their own apartment. He had said he was there to see Cindy Mason in apartment 3, whoever she was. He was still shaking as he arrived home twenty minutes later, but he was pretty sure that there was no evidence he had ever been to Art Underwood's apartment. His thoughts returned to the critical moments — losing his grip as Underwood went off the balcony, that awful popping sound as he hit the pavement, and looking down to see the body strewn unnaturally five stories below.

Garner told himself he was in the clear, but he was shaking and afraid he might throw up. He drove in no particular direction, trying to calm himself as he played it all back in his mind. Was there anything that could prove he was at Underwood's apartment tonight? He should have worn gloves. Fingerprints could be in a couple of random places and if they were ever found, he would have to admit that he had visited Underwood at some point, but fingerprints couldn't be dated. Fibers from clothing? He thought it unlikely that there was anything unique enough to track to him. He really was in the clear.

Sean saw a sign that said, "Blue Ridge Saloon." He pulled into the pot-holed parking lot and climbed out of the Audi. He walked to the side of the red-brick building and threw up. He held on to the wall and closed his eyes, feeling dizzy and desperately tried to get the images of Art Underwood's final moments out of his mind. The moments he seemed suspended in space, the terrifying fall and that awful sound. He took several deep breaths and then made his way into the bar. There were a couple of guys playing pool and three others at the bar. The bartender was a grey-haired woman in her fifties. "What will it be?" she asked as he took a seat.

"Scotch," he replied, then added, "Make it a double."

She poured his drink and placed it on the bar in front of him. "You okay, mister?" she asked with concern. He just nodded, unable to find any words. "You don't look good. You sure you're okay?"

He was anything but okay, but he made himself nod again. "I'm fine," he finally managed. He emptied the glass and asked for a refill. Maybe a couple more of these and the images would stop, he told himself. What was he going to do? An answer came to him when he finished his fourth drink. He threw thirty dollars on the counter and made for the door.

As he ran out the door, the bartender shrugged, "Nice talking to you, man," she said to the empty seat and a couple of the other patrons chuckled.

With too much alcohol in his system and without regard for cops, Garner drove quickly. He raced down the freeway for a dozen miles and then took the off-ramp at a hazardous speed. After five minutes of driving along side streets, he raced up the long private driveway and parked under the front portico. He climbed out of the car and pounded on the door. He waited almost no time at all before pounding again.

An unhappy Roland Cook opened the door and stared at him. "What are you doing here, Sean?"

"Sorry to bother you, sir, but things went terribly wrong."

"Can it wait until tomorrow at the office?"

"No, sir."

Cook gave him a disapproving look and then said, "Come inside." Garner followed him into the house and Cook gestured to a couch in the big living room. Cook sat in a big armchair and looked at him. He looked in Garner's eyes and said, "Are you drunk?"

"No. I mean I was drinking but I'm too scared to be drunk."

"Come with me," Cook said. He led the way to the kitchen and then brewed a single cup of black coffee, which he handed to Garner. Garner took the cup with both hands and took a drink. He nodded a thank you and drank again. Cook waited a moment and then asked, "So, what is the emergency?"

"Art Underwood is dead."

"You fucking killed him?" Cook asked with wide eyes.

"No...I mean he fell from the balcony in his apartment," Garner muttered.

Cook stared at him incredulously and asked, "What were you doing while he fell?"

"I held him out over the balcony and asked questions about whether he gave the trial results to Cardenas and Palmer."

"And you let go?" Cook asked.

"I don't know how it happened. Somehow my grip came loose and he was suddenly falling."

"Oh shit, Sean. What the fuck have you done?" Cook was distressed and angry.

"I don't know what happened, it all just got out of control. I didn't mean to let it happen."

Cook was quiet for a moment and then asked, "How do you know that he's dead?"

"His apartment is on the fifth floor." He paused, drawing a breath, trying not to think of the detail, and then added, "I saw what happened to him."

Cook was quiet again. After a time, he asked the critical question. "Have you reported any of it to the police or to anyone?"

"No, sir. I came right to you."

"Did anyone see you there? Any witnesses to anything you did?"

"No."

"Anyone see you anywhere around the building?"

"I don't think so, no. Not even the person who unlocked to the front door to let me inside. I pretended to be someone's relative in another unit."

"Were there cameras in the building?" Cook asked.

Garner reflected a moment and then said, "No, I didn't see any." He reflected a moment and then added, "I don't think that there were any cameras."

"So how does anyone connect you to what happened?"

Garner nodded slowly. "I guess they don't."

"So, what are you going to do? You don't plan to turn yourself in to the police, do you?"

Garner reflected a moment and then said, "I can't. I mean, I would go to jail."

"Right," Cook replied, evenly. "So, you go home and live your life. It never happened and you weren't there."

Garner nodded. "I understand."

Cook was silent a moment and then said, "Did Art tell you?"

"What?"

"Did Art tell you whether he gave the trial data to Cardenas and Palmer?"

"No, he never did."

Cook shook his head, dismissive of Garner. "Okay, Sean, get out of here. You were never there." As he walked Garner to the front door, Cook added, "And you were never here."

*      *      *

## June 27
### 4:00 a.m.

Sandi Underwood sat on the couch in her apartment, her eyes red and swollen and her face a picture of despair. Her life partner had been taken from her and he would never be back. It was all surreal. Two plain-clothes detectives sat across from her in armchairs while a forensics team worked the apartment for clues and uniformed officers guarded the doors. She was surrounded by strangers, yet she was all alone.

The lead detective had long, shoulder-length black hair and wide hazel eyes that were both sympathetic and analytical. She wore a blue suit that made her look more like a lawyer than a cop. Olivia Blake was thirty-nine years old. She had been a detective for the past five years and a street cop for ten before that. She waited until Sandi Underwood looked at her and then said, "I'm so sorry, Mrs. Underwood, but we need to ask you more questions so that we can find whoever did this, okay?" Sandi couldn't find words but managed to nod. "You said that you went to book club and got home a little after 10:00 p.m., right?"

"Yes, that's right," she managed.

"Was anyone coming over to see your husband while you were gone?"

"No, Art was going to relax and watch the game."

Olivia's partner, Ed Farris, was a detective of three years, but older than her by a decade. He wore a grey suit with loosened blue tie. His hair was short and greying. He listened carefully as Olivia continued.

"When you got home, the first responders were already here, right?"

"Yes."

"How did you learn that something had happened to your husband?" she asked.

It occurred to Sandi that 'something had happened' was a pretty empty euphemism for sudden death or maybe murder. She looked at Olivia and then put her hands over her swollen eyes for a few moments. When she looked up, she said, "I thought maybe Art ran to the store or something. Then a uniformed officer knocked on the door and told me that Art had been found down below..." She let her words trail off and covered her eyes. "Oh, my God," she gasped. "This just can't be happening."

"Is there anyone who had a grudge against your husband? Anyone angry at him or looking for revenge for something?"

"No, detective. Art was a good guy that everyone loved. I can't imagine anyone wanting to hurt him." She thought for a moment about Aligor, but he was one of the good guys who stayed with the company, not one of those who were suing them. Besides, corporations don't kill employees who upset them. "I can't think of anyone."

"Okay, Mrs. Underwood. The forensics team has finished their evaluation and we are going to leave you and let you rest as best you can. I'll be in touch as we have more questions or if we learn anything. Thank you."

As they stepped outside, Olivia asked the uniformed cop at the door. "Did you get to the apartment manager?"

"Yeah, he's over there. The guy in the blue shirt."

"Thanks," she said and moved towards the building manager, who appeared to be in his seventies, and painfully thin. "You are Mack Langford, the manager of the building?"

"Yeah," he said, nodding.

"So how do I find out who visited apartment 5C?"

"I don't know. We have a locked door, but we don't have security people and we don't make anyone sign-in or anything like that. The front door is always locked, so you either have a key or someone in one of the apartments has to let you into the building."

"Have you had break-ins or vandalism before? Any kind of crime around the building?" Olivia asked.

"No, ma'am. What we have here is a high-end building in an expensive neighborhood. In my ten years here the closest thing I've seen to any crime or vandalism is a hopscotch game chalked on the sidewalk."

Olivia nodded. All of this confirmed her suspicions that this was not a random crime. Besides, random crimes are usually more like drive-by shootings. If you want to kill a stranger, you pick the easy target, not one behind walls you have to break into. It's the low hanging fruit you go after, unless you have a target or you're sending a specific message to a certain group. "You found the body?"

"No, I was second to the scene. Mrs. Tiffany in 1B was first to see what happened because the sound was right outside her patio. I think she's going to have nightmares about it for some time. I mean, he was pretty badly broken. She was really shaken up when I got to the scene. About two minutes later the paramedics and the police showed up."

"I'll take a couple of uniforms and we'll knock on doors," Ed Farris said. "Maybe we can figure out if someone other than the victim let an intruder inside the building. Maybe they saw the person or can describe the voice."

Olivia nodded. "Yeah, go ahead. Let's wake people up and find what we need before any of the residents leave for work." As her partner walked away, she turned back to the apartment manager.

"Thank you, Mr. Langford. I'll call you if we have other questions."

"Okay, detective," Langford said. She watched him turn and walk away slowly. Her thoughts returned to Sandi Underwood. She had some hard days ahead. It's hard enough to lose the person you consider your life's mate, but to have it happen like this wrapped the loss in horror.

# Chapter Seven

Marty Cardenas and Justin Palmer sat in the Simmons and Winslow conference room nervously waiting to see Scott Winslow. Donna walked into the room wearing a troubled expression and sat down, holding tightly to a mug of coffee. "I'm so sorry, guys. This is all pretty shocking," she offered, looking at the two worried faces.

"It's unbelievable," Marty said, shaking his head. "And I know that Art did not take his own life. I'm sure of it. Something else happened here."

Scott walked into the room and took a seat. He looked at his clients and said, "I'm so sorry, guys. I know Art was a big part of your lives." They nodded agreement without finding words to speak. Scott studied them a moment and added, "So, it could have been an accident, right?"

Justin looked at him with a furrowed brow. "There is no way that Art was home alone and had a fall over a five-foot wall and down five stories. No way. Someone was there and arranged the fall. It can't help thinking Aligor had something to do with it."

"Maybe," Scott replied, "but why would Aligor go after Art? He's the only one of the three of you who's not coming after them."

"I might have thought the same way except for one thing," Marty replied. "There was pressure on Art to produce the copy of the Delexane trials data that Garner knew he had copied. So I met with him at Francine's yesterday and gave him the envelope. As Art walked out of the restaurant, I looked across the room and Sean Garner was sitting there watching us."

"That's disturbing," Scott replied. "Did you tell Art what you saw?"

"I tried. Right after I saw Garner, I called Art several times to let him know we were being watched, but he didn't return the call. Next thing I know, Sandi Underwood calls me crying and tells me that Art's dead." Marty drew in a breath and added, "Justin and I went by to see her this morning before we came to see you."

"How is she holding up?" Scott asked.

"Not well. Not well at all."

They were quiet for a few moments, contemplating the horrific news. After a time, Scott said, "The police will be investigating how this happened, although they probably won't go public with their findings for a while." There were nods from Marty and Justin. "I'll have Lee look around and see what he can find out about all of this. Sometimes he finds a way to connect with information most people can't."

Marty and Justin considered this and then Marty said, "I'd appreciate anything he finds out because I tell you, Scott, I am scared shitless at this point. This is a powerful company and if they just took out a guy for feeding us information, what would they do to us?"

"I agree that it's scary," Scott replied, "but we don't want to make too big a leap. So far it is all based on assumptions. We don't have any evidence that Aligor was involved. At this point, it could be anyone. It could even be a suicide, even though none of us think Art would do that."

Marty shook his head. "Art was a mentor to me and a guy with a moral compass who cared about what we were doing inside the company. He may have been a little nervous about all this, but he was also even and upbeat. There is no way you can convince me that Art took his own life. He loved his wife and kids, he loved his life, and he was in for the full term of this life. Someone was there and threw him off that balcony."

Justin nodded. "You're right, we won't jump to unsupported conclusions, but we also shouldn't take any chances just in case there are no coincidences. We have to find out if the company was involved." He leaned forward in his chair and said, "I've been thinking about this ever since we got word. It's not as far-fetched as it sounds. Delexane is already worth millions and it will be worth billions to Aligor. The stock price has set records with the anticipation of this new drug and added about a hundred million dollars to shareholder value, and the drug hasn't even been released yet. It's being touted as the answer to cancer and it's going to sell at a record-setting pace worldwide as soon as the FDA approval happens, which is only a few weeks away. You with me?"

"I am," Scott replied nodding.

Justin continued, "So think about what happens if word gets out that the company is misrepresenting results and the product isn't reliable. The sales are gone and there is a stock sell-off." He looked at the three faces in the room and added, "So, what would they do to prevent the whole thing from coming unraveled and a loss of billions?"

There was a protracted silence as that statement settled on the room. The possibilities were daunting.

\* \* \*

**June 28**
**12:30 p.m.**
Lee Henry dialed a number and waited. "Sargent Chuck Miller," a familiar voice responded on the second ring.

"Chuck, Lee Henry."

"No shit. About time man. I know you're a ghost when you're working, but not where your friends are concerned, right?"

"Sorry, man. I know it has been a while. How about a beer tomorrow night after work at The Barn."

"Yeah, I'm in. Meet you there at 7:00."

"I'll get the first round," Lee said.

"Yep, because you also want me to do something for you, right?"

"Yeah, I have a little favor in mind."

"What do you need?"

"I have a client with an interest in what happened to Art Underwood. I went out to the scene. I know there are no cameras in the building, but I noted there are a couple of commercial cameras that might have picked up a visitor to his apartment. One is in the back across the street and the other is in the market a couple of doors down. You guys track any video yet?"

"Nothing on the bank video but the mini-mart video picked up something. It's distant, a little fuzzy and hard to identify anyone, but we have two people who showed up at the door, one man and one woman. So far, we haven't identified either of them but we're working on it. I'll show you the video if you agree to share what you find out."

"You got it. When can I see it?"

"How about late this afternoon. The detectives on the case are Olivia Blake and Ed Farris. I am going to be in a meeting with them at 4:30. Can you meet us at the station at around 5:30?"

"I'll be there."

\* \* \*

**June 28**
**4:15 p.m.**
Sandi Underwood walked slowly through the park. Wiping away her tears, she watched smiling children run up the stairs of the slide and race downward. Mothers watched their little ones, and couples walked hand in hand. It was a gorgeous day in a wonderful place, but for her, nothing would ever be the same. It was as if time had stopped completely on the saddest day of her life.

Art had been beside her for thirty-two years. She barely remembered a time when they were not a team, and now he was suddenly gone. He would never speak to her again. It felt like her heart might explode. How could she live in a world without him by her side? There was no place that didn't hold their memories. Restaurants, movies, shop windows, hiking trails and their home. She could never again be with him, but the reminders were constant, each a new wound.

Sandi walked home and unlocked her front door. She sat down in the living room with a view of the balcony where Art's life had suddenly, inexplicably ended. How could she live here, looking at that balcony every day? How could she be all alone with his memory every night? But there were no answers. There were only questions; questions and the deepest of sorrows.

The funeral service was going to be closed coffin, they had told her. There were too many broken bones in his face to allow him to be shown. Sandi gasped as she heard those words. She had seen damage like that working in emergency and trauma units over the years. These were images that never went away.

It wasn't that she so desperately needed an open casket service, it was just knowing that Art had been so badly injured that it was irreparable, and knowing that someone had entered their home and done this to him. She walked around the apartment not knowing what she was looking for, hoping that some comfort could be found somewhere in the empty rooms.

\* \* \*

**June 28**
**5:25 p.m.**
Lee was ushered from the police department waiting room to the detectives' office where Chuck Miller sat on one of eight desks in the large, rectangular room and a man and a woman stood next to him. He smiled and extended a hand. "Hi, Chuck. How the hell are you?"

"I'm good," Chuck Miller responded, grinning. "This is Detective Oliva Blake and Detective Ed Farris. They are investigating Art Underwood's death."

Lee shook hands with each of them. Olivia Blake gave him a wry grin and said, "Good to meet you, Lee. Chuck tells me that you are a good guy. Is that right?"

Lee grinned. "Who am I to say? I guess it depends who you are as to whether you think so. Cops tend to like me more than perps."

"He also says you are both competent and cocky."

"Really?" Lee asked. "I wondered what he'd say when I'm not around. I was hoping for intelligent, charming and extremely humble."

Olivia smiled. The small talk over, and she asked, "How can we help you, Lee?" She was an attractive woman with intelligent eyes and a friendly smile. Ed Farris wore a skeptical look, like a guy who had heard his share of bullshit on the street. He was also less rumpled and better looking in a suit than most cops, who generally wore it like it was an unnatural skin that didn't quite fit.

"I have a client who shares an interest in figuring out who helped Art Underwood off his balcony."

"We aren't sure that anyone helped yet," Blake replied.

Lee furrowed his brow. "Seems likely. There was an unwelcome visitor, right?" Lee asked. "Chuck told me that the chain lock on the front door had been broken, so the logical conclusion is that someone forced their way into the apartment."

"Right," Blake said, "and maybe a broken chain just tells us that someone got a little aggressive with entry, not that anyone was a killer."

"I understand, but someone breaking into apartment right before Art Underwood just came home from work and makes a decision to fly off the balcony seems unlikely to me. And what I'm picking up about Art makes it unlikely that he was ready to do it alone." No one spoke, so Lee said, "Chuck tells me that you were able to get some video of arrivals at the unit from the mini-mart camera."

"That's right," Olivia Blake said. "The video is distant and grainy, so we haven't been able to identify anyone yet, but we have one woman and one man showing up at the door within the critical window. Step into the conference room and we'll run it for you."

They walked a few steps down a narrow hallway and then moved into an inside conference room with a large oval table. They took a seat and Ed Farris moved to the end of the table and hit a button, running the video on a wall-screen in fast-forward mode. It was so grainy and fuzzy that it almost appeared like the video was taken through conditions of a major electrical storm. Farris slowed the video when the outline of a woman approached the front door of the apartment units. The time display showed 7:02 p.m. Best he could tell, she was middle-aged, Caucasian and very fuzzy. Someone released the front door lock and let into the building quickly after her arrival. The second visitor, an equally fuzzy Caucasian male, appeared at the door at 8:31 p.m. Despite the grainy and distant portrait, Lee thought he recognized the image because he knew what he was looking for. Lee had seen pictures of Sean Garner and despite the lack of clarity of the video, his build was a physical match. He didn't let on that he had an idea about the identity of the man. He simply shook his head and asked, "You got anything on the identity of either of these two yet?"

"Not yet, Lee," Olivia offered. "The poor quality and the angles make facial recognition software ineffective, so we're trying to chase ID's down with leg work. We are showing pictures taken from the video to the residents to figure out who they came to see and why. If we can eliminate them as visitors to the Underwood unit then it becomes more likely that this was a suicide."

Lee nodded. "Can you give me copies of the stills you took from the video?"

"We can do that," Blake said.

"And as we agreed," Chuck Miller interposed, "if you learn anything at all, you are going to keep Olivia and Ed in the loop."

"That's right," Lee said, doing his best to ooze cooperation. "We're all working towards the same end here."

Olivia handed Lee two still photos of each visitor. "These are what we're working with to find the connection to Underwood," she said.

"Thank you, Olivia. Great to meet you. And likewise, Ed."

"Good to meet you as well, Lee," Farris offered. Blake smiled and said, "I think Chuck's description of you might work better than yours."

They laughed and shook hands. "I'll see you after work tomorrow," he offered to Chuck Miller. As he left the office of the detectives, Lee contemplated the grainy closed-circuit images. He was already planning a meeting with Sean Garner.

* * *

**June 29**
**3:00 p.m.**
The greyness of the afternoon sky befitted the deep sadness of the occasion as they gathered before the closed, flag-draped casket to say farewell to a devoted husband, father, and friend. There was a picture of Art that Sandi had chosen, perched on an easel and portrayed a smiling Art the way they would all want to remember him. He wore a golf shirt, a light jacket and a wide smile. The photo captured the sparkle in his eyes and the love for life he embodied.

Sandi and the two adult sons she and Art had raised together were seated and a hundred others who came to honor Art stood, while three uniformed soldiers of the Army stood at ease, in anticipation of their role in honoring their fallen brother. The grandfatherly pastor read passages from the Bible focused on the promise of eternal life. He spoke of how Arthur Underwood's time serving God in this world had passed. He spoke compassionately of the qualities that all who knew Art admired and would always remember. Memories of a good man overcame all of those who knew and loved Art and tears overwhelmed every sorrow-filled eye.

Marty and Abby Cardenas stood next to Justin Palmer as they listened to the pastor's words describe the man that they knew so well. It didn't seem possible that Art was gone forever. To Marty and Justin, he had been a mentor, an inspiration and a devoted friend who cared about doing what was right. To Sandi, he was everything, and everything had been taken from her.

As he listened to the words paying tribute to Art, Marty had overwhelming feelings of guilt about his own responsibility for the death of his friend. If only he hadn't drawn Art into his battle with Aligor. He had never considered that it might be dangerous for Art to provide evidence from inside the company. It was all so hopelessly careless, and it had cost more than he could have imagined. He glanced at the sorrow on Sandi's face; he would give anything to take that away. She was all alone with her eyes tearful and her heart breaking; doing her best just to make it through this day.

Marty returned his full attention to the words being spoken. The pastor finished speaking of Art's accomplishments in this life, as a devoted husband, a caring father, and a friend to many. "Art was the kind of guy that we all want to be. I've heard what family and friends say comes to mind when they think of Art and it's all about his devotion, his values, and the fact that he was always there for those he cared about." He let the tribute settle on the group and said, "We are now going to have a few words from Daniel, Art's oldest son."

Daniel stepped up next to the pastor. He was a handsome young man who bore a striking resemblance to his father. "Thank you for those good thoughts and prayers for our father," he told the pastor.

Daniel looked out at all of the family and friends who had come to pay tribute. He pushed tears from his eyes as he tried to find words. He took a quiet moment to pull back the emotion and then he began. "I'm Daniel Underwood. Many of you know me, but all of you knew my father. First, I want to thank you for coming to honor my father. I really appreciate it and I know my mom and my brother, Alex, do as well." He wiped a tear and said, "My dad taught me about the things that are important in life. Watching how he lived is how I learned how to respect others, how to honor my word, and how to love."

There was a deep quiet as everyone in the crowd felt the weight of the immense sorrow that Daniel carried. Daniel looked around the gathering for a moment and then added, "I had a rare blessing in this world. I lived my whole life with an unconditional love from both my parents. It is a gift like no other and I realize that now, more than ever. When that kind of love surrounds you, there is always something to come home to and your life is always important." He took a deep breath and then said, "My father was a smart, caring man. When he faced tough choices, I watched as he invariably did the right thing regardless of the personal cost." Daniel pushed back a tear and looked to the sky. He drew a deep breath and said, "I am so honored that you are my father. I will always hold on to what you taught me." He put his hand to his heart and said, "I love you, Dad."

Sandi watched her brave son and forced a smile as he approached her. What was left of her heart went out to him and Alex for the loss of their dad. Maybe sharing the deepest of losses with her boys could help her make it through. Daniel walked over and hugged his mother and then his brother, who was too torn up to speak. Those few in the crowd who weren't crying before he spoke were crying now.

The man Daniel had described so personally was the Art Underwood that Marty and Justin had come to know. Marty and Justin cried as they reflected on a world that had been deprived of the caring and compassion of Art Underwood. How could this have happened? It just didn't seem possible.

The pastor reminded the group that Art was many things to many people and that everyone in attendance had personal stories of how Art made a difference in their lives. He ended by saying, "Art did much to mirror the way Jesus taught us to live. To reach out to those around us with kindness and compassion, and with a strength born of love. To honor him, we must all try to live those values every day."

The three uniformed soldiers walked over and took the flag from the top of the coffin. Two of the soldiers carefully folded the flag while the Army Captain looked on, directing their movements. The Captain saluted the two men, taking the folded flag, and then she walked to where Sandi sat, got down on one knee and awarded the flag to Sandi. "Thank you, Mrs. Underwood, for your husband's service on behalf of a grateful nation." While the Army Captain held Sandi's hand and expressed the country's gratitude, a new round of tears engulfed the heartbroken group saying their final farewells to a man who had been an inspiration. Justin pushed a tear away and remembered a quote that had touched him. "When it is your time to go, what you take with you is the love you leave behind."

* * *

## June 30
### 3:20 a.m.

Sean Garner was looking down on a flailing body as it fell helplessly through the air. There was a scream, a look of terror and then that awful sound as the falling body hit pavement. Sean awakened with a start. His heart was racing, and he was sweating.

He looked at the clock on his bedside table and saw that it was 5:00 a.m. He found it hard to catch his breath as he looked around the darkened room desperate for the reassurance of familiar surroundings. He climbed out of bed and walked around the house without turning lights on, feeling uneasy. Almost without conscious decision, he made his way to his liquor cupboard and poured a glass of Scotch, downed it in two hard pulls and then refilled the glass.

Sean sat down at the kitchen table without turning on the light. Once he was awake, it was always hard to get back to sleep. He was troubled by the dream. How long would that be part of his life? He wanted to reassure himself. Wasn't it all good news? Underwood brought this on himself; Sean had simply protected the company from a traitor. He had eliminated one of their enemies. Maybe a few bad dreams were just the cost of doing what had to be done. Now that he was awake, he felt the relief that came with knowing there was no evidence to tie him to Underwood's death. It was all going to be fine.

Sean walked to the kitchen counter and turned on the coffee pot. Maybe Cardenas and Palmer would learn something about the cost of betraying the company from what happened to Art Underwood. It placed guilt at the feet of each of them. They would know that their actions were responsible for what had happened to Art and the will to push their lawsuit would be weakened. With a little more pressure applied in the right way, they might be compelled to dismiss their lawsuits and walk away. When that happened, Sean would be recognized as the guy who made it work. He would do the hard work that no one else would undertake. Cook didn't want to get his hands dirty, but he wanted it done.

Sean smiled as it occurred to him that this might be the beginning of his trip to the executive suite. If his next step was to make sure that Cardenas and Palmer end their lawsuits, the Company would make billions as Delexane rolled out and he would be the man responsible. He could soon be living in a mansion down the street from Mr. Cook. Maybe everything was falling into place.

# Chapter Eight

Lee Henry examined the area where Art Underwood's body had been found, five stories below his apartment balcony. The distance was considerable, and Lee reflected that Art must have been terrified during the last moments of his life. Lee walked to the front of the building and studied the surroundings. He walked the street in front of the building and along the block in both directions, noting the location of the mini-market and the bank that Sergeant Chuck Miller had described. Both were reasonably close to the front of the apartment building. The bank cameras had picked up nothing, but the film from the mini mart had presented the grainy footage that seemed to depict Sean Garner's image.

Lee made his way up to Art and Sandi's apartment and knocked. The woman who answered looked to be in her late fifties or early sixties, petite and attractive. She had penetrating eyes that studied him as he introduced himself.

"Ms. Underwood, I'm Lee Henry. I am the investigator who works with Scott Winslow."

A weak smile emerged as she said, "Yes, Lee. Marty and Justin told me about you. Please come in."

Lee stepped inside to find a comfortable, well-decorated apartment. A couch and two armchairs formed a conversation area over a round coffee table. Across the room was a slider for access to the balcony that now loomed large. "I hope I'm not disturbing you, Ms. Underwood," Lee said, looking her way.

"No, it's okay. How about some coffee?"

"That sounds good," Lee replied.

"And please call me Sandi."

"All right, Sandi." He reflected a moment and said, "I'm so sorry about what happened to Art."

Her green eyes flashed, and her expression changed became serious, almost angry. "Let there be no doubt, my husband did not take his own life. Someone did this to him, Lee."

Lee nodded. "If that is true, I want to help you find out who did it."

Those eyes narrowed as she said, "There is no *if.* Art had second thoughts about not joining the lawsuit. He thought that Marty and Justin were showing the courage of their convictions and he wanted to help them." She shook her head. "Then the Company cross-examined him about whether he had shared a copy of the Delexane trial results with Marty and Justin. He showed them that he had the copy he printed and the same night he suddenly goes off our balcony and falls five floors." Lee nodded but didn't speak. She handed him a cup of coffee and continued. "My husband wanted to support what his co-workers were doing. He was not depressed, and he did not kill himself. I know Art as well as I know myself and I can tell you that there is no way he would take his own life." In her words Lee could hear that she was adamant, and she was angry.

Lee nodded. "I understand. I know that Marty and Justin agree that he wouldn't kill himself. I've also been told that the chain on the door was broken, so it appears that someone forced their way into the apartment." She nodded silently, so he continued, "Did you find any other indication that someone else was in the apartment the night Art died?"

She shook her head. "Just the broken chain."

"Someone was here, so maybe someone else saw who it was," Lee offered.

"The police say that they have not identified any witnesses."

Lee shook his head. "I'll see what I can do to assist. Thank you for the coffee."

Sandi gave him a soft smile. "I'm sorry for the intensity of my reactions. It's just that..." she let the words trail away.

"No apology necessary, Sandi," Lee replied. "I'm so sorry about what happened." She was a strong, determined woman and Lee liked her already. He walked to the door and then turned back to her and added, "I'm also sorry I didn't have the opportunity to get to know Art. I know I would have liked him."

* * *

**July 1**
**11:30 a.m.**

"Scott, Doug Gibson is on line three," Nikki advised through the intercom.

"Thanks," Scott replied, punching a button. "Hi, Doug."

"Scott," Gibson replied coolly and then went momentarily quiet. "I have some disconcerting information," Gibson offered after a moment.

"Oh, what would that be?" Scott asked.

"It appears that your clients may have been creating false data regarding the test trials."

"I knew someone was," Scott replied evenly, "but I think you have it a little bit backwards. Aligor is publishing false data. Last time I checked, that was your client, right?"

"You are not hearing me, Scott. I'm telling you that your clients are using false data to hurt Aligor. That means the biggest defamation lawsuit that they can imagine. You with me now?"

"Sure. Alice through the looking glass." Scott paused a moment and then said, "I'm hearing you. It even sounds like you're saying this with a straight face."

Gibson's turn to pause. After a time, he said, "I think you're being rather flip about something important."

"Does your client really think that bringing a frivolous claim against two long-term employees they fired is going to help them? Don't they have enough of a PR and legal nightmare already?"

"That's your answer? I tell you that your clients are fabricating trial results and that's what I get?"

"My answer is that your client is better off not making their situation worse by using false allegations to enable a cover-up."

"I thought that having this information would help you assess the problems with your case," Gibson replied.

"Thanks for the call, Doug. You may want to have a sit-down with your client to keep them getting in even deeper."

When Gibson hung up, Scott thought about the call. Maybe Gibson really believed the story his client was pitching, but it didn't much matter. It was a heads-up all right, and one that he would act on. It meant that Aligor was not only going to push their false data from the trials, they were also going to tell the world that Marty Cardenas and Justin Palmer were the ones falsifying data.

Scott punched some numbers on his phone.

"Hi, Scott," came the reply.

"Marty, I just got a call from the Aligor lawyer. He told me that Aligor is saying you and Justin fabricated your numbers. I think it was an attempt to create a problem for us that would make us want to settle the case, but it means that they are going to go on pushing their false test trial results and saying that your numbers were manufactured to assist in a lawsuit."

"Shit," Marty replied. "What do we do?"

"We've got the data, so we get witnesses who back up the reality that you know. Those who can identify the data you have as the real deal. We need statements from a couple of well-placed employees who know that the numbers you and Justin complained about are the accurate test results."

"I understand," Marty responded. "The first name that comes to mind is Art. He would have been great." There was a moment of quiet and then Marty added, "some people won't get involved because there's too much on the line and they want to stay employed. There are a few I know well enough that they might help, and even if they won't they will keep to themselves that they were approached. Let me see what I can do."

"Great," Scott replied. "I'm going to put in a similar call to Justin. Maybe you guys can brainstorm and let's see who you can line up to assist. We can get whoever will help to sign declarations and keep them in our back pocket until Aligor starts to argue to the Court that we are fabricating data."

There was a moment of quiet and then Mary said, "It's disappointing that they have gone so far as to falsify test results in order to defend the lawsuit. After all these years, I thought that they had more integrity."

"I'm sorry, Marty. Sometimes when it comes to defending a claim a company will do almost anything, particularly when there is a lot at stake."

"I'm on it, Scott. I'll let you know whether I am able to get colleagues to step forward and testify about the accurate test trial results. There are a number of people who could, but some will not want to take sides against the Company."

"You're right about that. It's always easier not to get involved, so you have to sell the need based on relationships or what's the right thing to do. If they aren't buying, all you can do is move on and try the next person. Securing witness support is a matter of approach and persistence, but it's an imprecise art."

"I like to think that if someone came to me to be a witness to truth that I knew, I would step forward. Knowing that, I think there are others who will feel the same way."

"As you think about personalities, there will be those that you know are least likely to help and most likely to go back to the Company and share what you are seeking. Take those people off your list and go after the people you believe will see it as a matter of honesty or integrity."

After a few moments of thought, Marty asked, "It's something of a guessing game, isn't it?"

"It is that, but we are talking educated guesses. Trust your gut to tell you who you can count on to help. In my experience, we can usually assess the likely response from someone we know or have dealt with. Courage in one situation translates to the next, as does the desire not to make waves."

"I'll give it my best shot," Marty said.

"After you take your shot, if a potential witness is on the fence, ask them if they will talk to me and I'll try and give them a reason to step forward."

"Good. The legal stuff makes people nervous, so you can be my closer. I'll keep you posted on how it goes."

\* \* \*

## July 2
### 7:30 a.m.

Lee Henry enjoyed early morning visits to adversaries. There was something about climbing into their heads before they were properly awake and while they wanted tranquility with that first cup of coffee. He pulled up to this morning's target residence. It was middle America. A small, well-maintained house in a neighborhood comprised of more of the same. He knocked on the door and waited. No response. He knocked again. After a few moments, a stone-faced Sean Garner opened the door and stared at Lee silently. His hair was uncombed, his shirt half buttoned, and he was shoeless. "What do you want?" he finally asked.

"I thought that you and I should chat for a few minutes," Lee offered evenly.

"About what? And who are you?" Garner asked impatiently.

"About you, and I'm a concerned citizen."

"What the fuck do you want?" Garner said with distaste.

"No need to be unpleasant," Lee replied evenly. "Were you at Art Underwood's apartment the night he died?"

For an instant, a look of alarm flashed across Garner's face and then he said, "I'm not going to tell you anything. Who are you?"

He stepped back away from the door and prepared to close it, but Lee stepped into the doorway and held up his left hand to prevent any attempt to close it. "Answer my question," Lee instructed and stared into Garner's eyes.

"Show me a badge," Garner demanded.

"I never said I was a cop."

"Then get the fuck out of here."

"I do know lots of cops," Lee said, thoughtfully. "I can get one here in no time at all, if necessary."

There was quiet while Garner glared at Lee wearing an angry look. "You can get the fuck off my property before I throw you off," Garner yelled, anger taking hold.

Lee decided that psychology might be the most effective route. He smiled and said, "You can try that, but it's really not productive. You worked with Art, right? I assumed that you respected him and would want to help like his other co-workers. Am I right about that?"

Garner studied him for a few moments and then said, "Is that it?"

Lee nodded and said, "Yeah, it's a pretty simple question."

"Yeah, I respected his abilities."

"So, as this was someone you respected or cared about, then you probably want to know what happened. And either you were at Art Underwood's home the night he died, or you weren't. If you were, I'd like to know what you learned. If not, you probably can't help me with the events of that night."

Garner stood motionless, apparently trying to make sense of all this. When he finally spoke, Garner's tone was different. "I worked with Art Underwood and I thought he was a talented executive. I was shocked to hear the news of his death."

"Does that mean you were not at his apartment the night he died?" Lee persisted.

Garner shot him an angry look and then replied, "Yeah, it means that."

"I appreciate your cooperation." Lee was confident that Garner was the guy in the grainy pictures and Garner had lied to him. Either he was nervous about being near the scene of a crime or that he had something to hide. Given that Garner had an extensive background in security, being a witness would not likely bother him. The smart money said he knew what happened that night. Lee held his gaze for a time and then smiled. "Thanks for your time," he said cordially. Garner stood frozen and speechless as Lee turned away.

Lee walked from the porch and down the driveway. As he walked past Garner's Audi, Lee turned and looked back towards the house. Garner was still in
the same place, watching him carefully. Lee gave Garner a smile and a wave
with his left hand as he slipped a GPS in a magnetic case under the left rear
wheel well with his right. "Have a good day," Lee yelled with a smile.

"Who the fuck are you?" Garner yelled back.

"Just a friend," Lee replied with a smile.

* * *

**July 2**
**11:38 a.m.**

Calling someone who has been a friend for a long time is usually a welcome
respite in a busy day; a few moments of pleasure. Today Marty found himself
nervous at that prospect, because this was not the usual call. This time he had
to be vulnerable. He had to ask that friend for a big favor, one that he needed
desperately, but that could damage his friend's career. It made for tension that
didn't feel good as he pushed a single button on his phone and waited.

"Pete McMillan," the familiar voice announced after the second ring.

"Hi, Pete. It's Marty."

"Marty, how are you? Everything okay?"

"Well, as okay as it can be under the circumstances," Marty offered.

"We should get together sometime soon," Pete said, awkwardly.

"Yes, we should." There was an uncomfortable silence and Marty guessed
Pete knew there was a reason for the call. "Pete, you and I worked side by side
for almost five years. You know the same things that I do," Marty Cardenas
said into his phone speaking to one of his former lieutenants and instinctively
glancing around him to be sure no one was listening. Marty walked along a
residential street and made his way towards a large community park where
little children played under watchful eyes of parents, some attentive and some
seemingly preoccupied. The park sidewalks meandered under cover of massive
oaks and evergreens. The sun made its way through the canopies overhead to
warm the park's inhabitants and cast shadows on the pavement below.

There was a moment of silence and then Pete's stressed voice retorted, "You
don't know how it is around here now. I would love to be able to talk to you
about all of it, but I can't. It's like we're spies dealing with international secrets.

Everyone is watching everyone. Everyone is looking for..." He paused mid-sentence and then added, "the next Marty Cardenas."

"Meaning what?" Marty asked, already knowing what was coming.

"Marty... you and Justin are considered traitors by management and they are doing their best to make sure that you can't get to anyone else."

"Like you?"

"Yes, like me. That's why I walked out to the parking deck when I saw your number on my phone. I can't talk to you from the office. There are eyes watching everyone who worked with you and Justin."

"You mean everyone who knows what we know about the trials?"

"I guess so, yes."

Ahead Marty saw the walkways of the park become dirt and meander around a small lake, or maybe a large pond, where ducks quacked, and heron stood in regal, motionless positions. He could feel his blood pressure rise and he was working to maintain an even tone. "And what we both know, Pete, is that they are lying about the Delexane results. They have released a false report for phase three of the trials. You know that what that report says isn't accurate because you've seen the real one. Shit, you helped develop the real one."

"I understand Marty, but I don't think you do. For me to stand up and say that would be career suicide."

"Are you telling me that you can stand by and let the Company make false statements to people who will have one chance to decide which course of treatment to take before their cancer gets too far along? I'm not trying to judge you, my friend, I just think that we need to call them out on this." Marty could tell that his voice sounded angrier than he intended.

There was an awkward silence before Pete spoke. "I think about it every day, but there has to be a way for me to do what's right without taking a bullet for doing it."

"Here's the ultimate question, Pete. Will you let them publish false study results and look the other way while the money flows?" There was a quiet that said too much, and Marty felt his heart sink. "At least please tell me you'll think more about what I'm saying, Pete. There are too many people affected by what we do here."

"I will, Marty. I can definitely tell you that I'll think about it because I think about it all the time."

"Can we talk again?"

"We can talk again in a few days. I'm not promising anything, but I'll think, and we'll talk. Let me call you next time. I can't be in the wrong place when I field a call like this."

"I understand," Marty offered. He hesitated and then added, "Sorry if I sounded angry or frustrated, it's just that emotions are pretty high right about now."

"I understand," Pete replied. "Talk to you soon."

Marty hung up and turned to retrace his steps. He walked around the pond and back into the forested area, thinking hard about the prospects. Pete was the second person he thought might come through. The first had already apologetically declined. It was becoming clear that no one was in a big hurry to join Marty and Justin in taking on the corporate monolith. Economic survival dictated that they follow a course of moderation and steer clear of those considered enemies by Aligor. Apparently, he and Justin were now both at the top of that list.

As Marty walked through the park, a figure emerged from the adjacent trees. Marty stopped in his tracks as Sean Garner stood in front of him in jeans and a plaid shirt. Garner stared at Marty like he was the one out of place. "What do you think you're going to accomplish with all this?" he asked. Without waiting for an answer, he added, "You are in way over your head, Marty. You don't want to continue down this road because I assure you, nothing good will come of it."

Marty was trying hard not to appear nervous. "You're following me around just to drop off some other obscure threat, Sean?"

Garner smiled. "I can make it less obscure if needed, but I think you get the picture. At least I hope you do. You and Abby have a great life and a lot to look forward to, right? You don't want to lose all that."

"Why don't we have the rest of this conversation at the police department? You can explain to the cops why you are threatening me."

Garner smiled. "This is all easy enough to explain. People who used to work together ran into each other in the park. With concern for your well-being, I suggested that you end the fraud you are engaged in, but you wouldn't have it. I think they would understand that." Garner shrugged. "I suspect we won't need to go that far because it won't help you. What you do or don't do in response to the warning is entirely up to you, but when the opportunity arises, I strongly suggest that you take what is offered and get your case settled and behind you.

Your future will look so much brighter if you do." Garner grinned and then added, "Enjoy the park," as he turned and walked back into the trees.

Marty stood watching Garner's back until he disappeared from view. Should he go to the police? If he did, what could he say that would make sense? There was no specific threat that Garner couldn't talk around, just as he had a few minutes ago. Garner would say they had a conversation about him committing fraud. As Marty walked slowly back towards the park entry, he could feel his blood pressure on the rise. Is there anything they wouldn't do to handle him? If they murdered Art for helping him, why wouldn't they find a way for him to have an accident? Worse yet, what if they came after Abby? For the first time, Marty was fully aware of what he was up against and he was really scared.

# Chapter Nine

June 30
2:30 p.m.

Emma Franklin wore the kind of smile the way one wears a disguise. It was a façade she used to prevent others from seeing that her world had fallen apart and she was barely hanging on, but no one close to her was fooled. She was not quite thirty-four and living each day had become a challenge. Trying to avoid having her despair appear obvious to anyone she met was becoming difficult. Tears lingered just below the surface and she had never felt so vulnerable, but she worked hard to wear a smile whenever Christopher was looking her way.

They watched the children playing together at the dining room table from the couch in the living room. The kids were all smiling and laughing, and it should have been a happy time, but the looming threat that hung over them like a dark cloud colored every day now. Michael took her hand but for a time they remained silent in their feelings of helplessness. "What are we going to do?" she asked. A question she now posed almost daily, seeking some kind of reassurance. It was painfully rhetorical, because there was no good answer.

Michael took a deep breath. "I just don't know, sweetheart. Each day is a little worse than the one before and nothing seems to be working." He hesitated a moment and then added, "My heart breaks when I see the pain in his eyes. It is just so unfair."

Emma nodded, trying her best to make it through one more helpless moment; a drop of water in an ocean. She looked over at the five kids at the dining room table and forced a smile. "He's having fun," she offered.

Michael nodded. "I want him to have fun every minute of every day. I keep hoping for progress with his treatment, but I have to fight this desperate feeling that we are running out of time."

Emma nodded, "I'm so scared of that, Michael. I feel like it could all come crashing down on us."

It had been the kind of a day that kids and parents love. A smiling Christopher had four friends with him to celebrate his fifth birthday, which included a trip to the zoo and a party with hot dogs, cake and ice cream. Emma looked over at the smiling children and could see that they were all having fun. That should make things okay, she told herself, but it was all she could do to hold back the tears.

Christopher had become the most important part of their lives. Michael had been making a name for himself at the University and Emma was near her master's degree when Christopher Michael Franklin was born. From the first look into his perfect face, all doubts about their ability to be good parents vanished. Emma and Michael were captivated and knew that they would do anything for this little man. He was their instant priority. He was gorgeous. He was a miracle.

Christopher was a handsome child with big blue eyes, rosy cheeks and a mop of black hair, and he had brightened the world the moment of his arrival. He learned to read at age three and was tackling multi-syllabic words by age four. His blue eyes sparkled with wonder as he drank in the world around him and posed questions about all he saw. You could see those questions form in his eyes as he looked at something new or unclear. Why are shadows different sizes? Why do they go away? What makes rain? Why do I have to eat vegetables, and when staring at and actually reading a menu in a restaurant, what is albacore? He had a natural need to know what words meant, how things worked and why things were as they were.

And Christopher was brave, more than any child should ever have to be. He had pain that he described as 'the hurt inside." His rosy cheeks had become sunken and his wondrous eyes were surrounded by darkening circles. He also had to battle nausea from the drugs infused into his system for the past five weeks to attack the cancer. It was all Emma could do to watch her little son sit with a needle in his arm that delivered poisons she knew would kill cancer cells and healthy cells. The treatment process seemed so cruel and it was almost impossible for a parent to watch.

Michael got an offer for an associate professor position at Georgetown University in Washington, D.C. Three months later, Emma completed her master's degree and took a position on the staff of democratic Senator Edward Jamison, where she would help develop bills, persuade support from others on the Hill, and brief the senator on pending legislation. Emma's dreams were realized with the opportunity to make a difference in public policy — she pushed for domestic programs that mattered and she had the ability to persuade, induce and cajole others to join the fight. Emma and Michael were chasing their career dreams for about sixty hours each week. It was a magnificent time in their lives when the only dilemma was the guilt that consumed working parents who loved every moment with their children and wanted to miss none of them. Emma had been in her new job for about three months when everything came crashing down.

It had been a downhill fight since they learned what was happening four months earlier. At first, Christopher developed a wheeze. A cold? The flu? Maybe an allergy? They went to their family doctor and then to an allergist, but nothing of consequence was discovered. The wheezing should have gone away, but it didn't. Christopher then began complaining that his chest hurt. They went back to the family doctor and the diagnostic process began. Blood testing, x-rays, an MRI and ultimately, something Michael and Emma had never heard of and couldn't pronounce, a metaiodobenzylguanidine (MIBG) scan.

It was then that Emma and Michael were told that they needed to meet with an oncologist. They met with Dr. Mitchel Rayburn who studied the test results and did a couple more tests. Then they sat down in chairs across Dr. Rayburn's desk and looked into his pained face as he told them the news that would destroy their lives. Christopher had something known as a neuroblastoma. It was cancer, stage III cancer to be precise, which meant it was not just localized but had spread to nearby tissues and lymph nodes. It had not yet moved to more distant organs of his body but that was the immediate threat. Emma felt like she had been hit by a truck. In the days that followed, the fear was paralyzing.

\* \* \*

**June 30**
**5:40 p.m.**
Justin Palmer checked the time on his phone. He was supposed to meet her at 6:00 p.m., so it was time to go. He reluctantly picked up his keys and walked to the door of his condo. He shook his head, considering just how much first

dates suck. They were endlessly awkward and seldom amounted to more than money spent and hours counted down until it was over.

It seemed to Justin that there were very few soulmates out there, but everyone you knew had someone in mind who was just right for you. What could he look forward to tonight? There was the toothy smile greeting, the search for small talk worthy of sharing and which is not too revealing, the desperate attempts to find the right balance between being interested in your date and divulging something significant about yourself, assuming you knew what that might be. You searched for the right words to express something meaningful to someone who didn't know you at all and, in all likelihood, didn't share your values. You both brought all your past relationship baggage to the date, looking at each other through the lens of past mistakes, and seeking to avoid becoming involved with a person who possessed whatever characteristics you believe drove your last relationship into oblivion.

Justin chuckled to himself about his jaded attitude and figured he better get it under control, or he'd be looking for the exit before he even met this woman. All he knew about her was that she was that she was an accountant and, those most scary of words, she had a great personality. According to his brother Nate, who Justin saw once a month, this was the perfect woman for him.

It was 6:02 as Justin walked through the door of the Golden Dragon, a fish restaurant that borrowed a Chinese restaurant's name for some unknown reason. He looked around the restaurant. There were three of four couples and as many families. About ten people sat at an elaborate semi-circular bar. The hostess approached Justin a he surveyed the restaurant and asked, "Are you looking for someone?"

"Yes, but I don't know who." He grinned as the door opened and a woman walked in looking around as she entered.

"Maybe her," the insightful hostess offered with a grin.

Justin turned around to see a woman in her mid-thirties with long red hair, high cheek bones, a small, slightly upturned nose and liquid green eyes. "Jessica Morris?" Justin asked.

She nodded. "Yeah. You must be Justin."

"I am," he replied, studying her a little too long. Nate forgot to mention that she was beautiful.

"You been waiting long?" she asked.

"No. I just got here."

"Glad you two found each other," the young hostess said with a smile. "You have a reservation?"

"Yes," Justin replied. For Palmer at 6:00."

She glanced at a book on the podium and nodded. "Yep, we have you. Follow me."

The hostess took them to a cozy table with a view of the street, where people strolled along the sidewalk in both directions. The overhead lights were low and the soft light between them came from a candle enclosed in glass.

"How are you?" Justin asked lamely, wishing he had picked a better question to start the conversation.

She looked at him with a smile and said, "I'm all right, how about you?"

"I'm good... now."

"Oh?" she asked. "Now?"

"Right. My brother forgot to tell me that you were gorgeous."

She leaned back in her chair. "Thanks, although I have to say it doesn't mean all that much to be admired for one's looks. If you look okay, you do. It's hardly an accomplishment."

"Sorry," Justin offered. "I meant it well."

"I know. I'm sorry, Justin. It's just that every time I meet a guy I get graded on my looks and I find it annoying. I'm more than my outward appearance."

"I get it. I mean I'm cute, too, so I understand."

"Are you now?" she asked, shaking her head.

"Just kidding. So, tell me something about yourself. My brother said you're an accountant?"

"Not exactly. I'm an auditor."

A young woman with a great smile appeared beside the table and said, "Good evening, folks. Can I get you something to drink?"

"I'll have a glass of the house red," Jessica replied. "Thank you."

"That sounds good. I'll do the same," Justin said.

"I'll be right back with the wine and to take your order."

"Who do you work for?"

"Elegy Partnerships. They invest in different companies. I like to refer to them as a minority owner in almost everything. When they are considering an acquisition, my team does an analysis of their assets, liabilities, and net worth."

"To make sure no one's been cooking the books?" Justin asked with a grin.

"For sure," she replied, nodding. "And to make sure the anticipated value is really there before the financial commitment is made. What do you do?"

Justin hesitated a moment. It was the first time he'd had to tell someone new about the job he didn't have anymore. "Until recently I was National Sales Manager for a drug company," he offered. Just answering the question was like a gut punch; an open wound. She nodded but didn't ask any questions and he appreciated her restraint. "So, do you know my brother, Nick?" he asked.

"Not really. My sister works at the same company as your brother. I'm not sure how they got around to talking about trying to put you and me together."

He smiled and said, "I can't imagine how that came about, but I'm glad it did."

She regarded him thoughtfully and then smiled. "So far, I am too," she said. "And my sister never gets it right. She has set me up about four times. Let's just say past experience made me reluctant to agree to come and meet you."

The smiling server put a glass of wine in front of each of them and said, "Enjoy. Do you know what you'd like for dinner?"

"I'll try the smoked salmon," Jessica said.

"Great. How about you, sir?"

"I'll go with the halibut."

"I'll get the order in and be back to check on you." She took the menus and stepped away from the table.

"She's nice," Jessica said.

He nodded and their eyes engaged from a few moments. "What do you like to do for fun when you're not working?" Justin asked.

"I like reading, going for walks," she hesitated and then added, "and taking road trips to places I've never seen. How about you?"

"I love reading, biking and hiking. I really like your road trip idea, too. I've always found it fascinating to be a stranger in some town you don't know, anonymously trying a local cafe and seeing the sights."

"Do you know where you would like to explore?" she asked.

"I have a couple of ideas," he said, grinning widely.

"What?"

"Salem, Oregon in the summer and Sedona in the winter."

"Yes, good choices," she said. "Another thing I like is film festivals and I think that both of those cities have them."

Their plates were delivered and placed in front of them.

"Looks great," Jessica said.

"Can I get you two anything else?" the server asked.

Justin looked at Jessica and then said, "I think we're good. Thank you."

"My pleasure," the server replied as she moved away.

There was no shortage of dinner conversation and the date was anything but awkward. When they finished the meal, feeling relaxed, Justin insisted on paying the check. Jessica resisted at first, but then gave him a smile and thanked him. She added, "But it's my turn next time."

"Perfect," Justin replied, "because I really want there to be a next time."

Jessica touched his hand and said, "Me too. This was really nice."

They walked out of the restaurant together and Justin found himself not wanting to say goodbye. "Can I have your number?"

She nodded. "If I can have yours."

They exchanged phones and entered their contact information. When their phones had been returned, she said, "I'm parked down the block." She pointed down the street.

"Can I walk you to your car?"

She nodded. "I would like that."

He took her hand as they walked down the well-lit evening street. She didn't resist. "I had a great time," he said, squeezing her hand.

"Yeah, me too."

"How about Friday? Maybe a movie?"

"Okay," she replied. "Call me and we'll make a plan." She stopped in front of a blue Hyundai and said, "This is me."

Almost before he knew he was going to do it, Justin leaned towards her. She met him halfway and the kiss was wonderful. "Goodnight," he said, turning back to wave to her one more time as he walked back towards his car. His heart was racing and he couldn't stop grinning. This first date was the kind that could overcome his skepticism. There was something special about this woman.

Justin climbed into his car in the restaurant lot, paid the attendant on the way out and started towards home. As he drove, Justin noticed a car behind him that seemed to stay behind him. He wasn't given to any kind of paranoia, but then again, life had changed recently. He made a right turn and then a quick left. The dark colored Audi stayed with him. He made another left and then another. The Audi followed.

He asked himself if he was being crazy. Why would anyone be following him? He wasn't someone in a critical role. In fact, these days he was in no role at all. He pulled to the side of the road and waited as the Audi went past him without hesitation and disappeared into the city lights ahead. So much for his paranoid fantasies.

He took a deep breath and his thoughts returned to the wonderful evening with Jessica. She was something special and he was already looking forward to seeing her again. Maybe his brother and her sister finally got one right. Justin was still smiling as he pulled into his driveway, hitting the visor button and watching his garage door begin to open. He drove into the garage and climbed out of the car. He walked to the internal door that lead into the kitchen and found it locked, which was weird because he never locked this door. He pulled keys from his pocket and unlocked the door. He walked into the kitchen and flipped on the lights. He let out a yell as he looked up to see a man leaning against his kitchen counter. The man was Sean Garner.

"What the fuck are you doing in my house?" Justin yelled, angrily.

Garner's stern countenance turned slowly to a smile. "I thought it was important that you understood just how vulnerable you are," Garner said. Looking at the fear in Justin's eyes, he added, "I think you're getting the picture."

"My alarm was turned on."

Garner shrugged. "Yeah, that's part of the heads up. They are really not too difficult to disengage. Understand?"

Justin was trying hard not to let this former work associate turned home invader see the level of his concern. "What do you want?" he asked as assertively as he could.

"I want to help you, Justin. I want to help you make the right decisions."

Justin furrowed his brow. "Meaning?"

"When you get the chance to settle your case in the near future, don't wait."

"Or what?" Justin asked, needing to know what kind of a threat this was.

"Or you might be depriving seriously ill people of their right to the best treatment possible. Is that what you want to achieve?"

"Are you kidding? I gave my all to this project. I wanted the Company to tell the truth about the test results, that's all. You might remember that I was fired because I wanted the truth to come out."

"I understand your need to stick to that position so that you can justify what you've done, but the Company has made it clear that we know you are pushing false results. I'm sure your lawyer shared that information with you, right?"

Justin held his gaze. "If what I'm saying is not correct about the Company's misrepresentation of the test trial results, then the Company would not want to pressure me to settle, so this meeting wouldn't he happening." He shook his head. "Now get the fuck out or I'll call the police."

Garner showed no perceptible reaction to Justin's anger. He was quiet for a moment and then said, "That was a pretty lady you were dating tonight." Justin was distressed by the comment. Was it one more threat or just the creepiness of knowing Garner had been watching him all evening? Garner shrugged. "This was just a friendly warning, Justin. I'd pay attention if I were you." Not waiting for an answer he said, "I'll show myself out and you can reactivate your alarm."

When Garner walked out the front door, Justin walked to the living room window and lifted the curtain. He watched Garner walk down the driveway and then move along the street. He put both locks on the door and reactivated the alarm. It was more than unsettling. His heart was pounding as he leaned against the secured front door and replayed the conversation in his head. They were coming after him. He grabbed his phone and dialed Marty. Maybe he would have an idea about how to handle this crazy shit.

\* \* \*

**July 1**
**9:00 a.m.**
The outdoor seating at Maxie's Restaurant catered to the hungry in a hurry. Sean Garner sat at a patio table enjoying the morning sunshine and a breakfast of scrambled eggs and bacon. About half of the ten round tables around him were occupied and two servers constantly ran in and out of the restaurant delivering coffee and breakfasts and picking up the remnants. Overhead was a massive awning shielding the customers from direct sunlight. All around those enjoying breakfast, shoppers occupied the morning sidewalks as they moved between stores. Cars populated the two-lane road, but the morning rush was almost over and the pace had slowed.

Sean reflected on his accomplishments and considered his next moves. His visits to Marty Cardenas and Justin Palmer had been successful and just reliving those visits gave him a thrill. The control he had exerted was empowering. Sean knew he had the ability to make this happen and he wasn't about to let up. He sensed that they were both scared and with just a little more motivation could be made anxious to put the case behind them. His next move would have to be direct and leave no doubt that there was no longer a choice; they would settle their cases and his rise to the top of the corporate world would be complete. Cook had endorsed Garner's plan to provide settlement motivation to Cardenas and Palmer, but he didn't want to know the details. Those were up to Sean. He could determine how to execute the instruction and Cook would supply whatever he needed to get the job done but Cook planned to keep his distance and maintain plausible deniability — Cook would know nothing about what Sean was doing, but he would celebrate the result.

Lee Henry stood inside the restaurant, near the hallway that lead to the restrooms. From there he had a clear view of Sean Garner on the patio. He checked the time; about thirty seconds to go. Lee watched as a teenage server wearing an apron and a warm smile walked to Sean's table and refilled his cup. Sean said, "Thank..." but before he could finish the thought, there was a tremendous crash at the table next to his. A young woman in business attire had knocked over a table and fell to the floor in the process, a meal strewn all around her. She had blood on her forehead and wasn't moving as Sean ran over to where she was laying on her back. After a moment, she opened her eyes and looked up at Sean and the crowd that had gathered around her. "I am so embarrassed," she offered timidly.

"Don't worry," one of the servers said, "the EMT's are on the way."

"I'm fine," the young woman said climbing to her feet. "Much better off than this skirt," she said looking down.

"You sure you're okay?" Sean asked.

She smiled. "I'm all right. Thanks for asking."

The woman stood and immediately walked out of the restaurant, so Sean turned and made his way back to his table and sat down. It took a moment before he realized that his phone was no longer on the table. He searched under the table and all around before beginning to panic. There were things on his phone that no one could see. He reminded himself that if someone had stolen his phone, the security protections he had built into the phone would keep the thief away from confidential information, but he would have to pull all of the information from his backup hard drive. It also didn't look good when security chiefs were the victims of a crime.

Sean called two servers over and said, "My phone is missing. I went to help the woman who fell and when I returned it was gone from my table."

"We'll help you look," said one of the servers, a young man with long hair and tattoo covered arms. The other server was the young woman who had served Sean his breakfast. They both searched under the tables and throughout the patio area, but neither found the missing phone. "I'll check with the hostess," the young woman said, "in case someone turned it in."

Sean nodded, now angry. It was probably some kid or maybe an addict who stole and sold phones to support a habit. "Thanks," he said, still inspecting the area all around him. Seeing one that looked like his, he asked a man seated four tables away, "Is that your phone?"

"It is," the man said, showing him the photo of an unfamiliar woman and child that served as its wallpaper.

Sean nodded and continued searching. After about ten minutes it became clear that he was not going to find the phone. The young woman who had been Sean's server returned shaking her head. "It hasn't been turned in yet." She looked a little perplexed and then asked, "How do we reach you if it shows up? Is there some other number we can call?"

"Yeah," Sean said, handing the woman a business card.

"We'll call you if we find it."

"Thanks," he responded, and walked away contemplating what confidential information, passwords and other access a thief might be able to get to if he was a techy rather than a junky.

His first stop after leaving the restaurant was to get a new phone. There were too many calls he couldn't afford to miss. As soon as he had the latest iPhone model in his possession, he forwarded calls from his old number to his new one to assure that he would miss nothing, and his focus returned to ending the Cardenas and Palmer lawsuit. He was going to make sure it happened sooner rather than later.

\* \* \*

**July 1**
**4:40 p.m.**
Scott emerged from a deposition and Donna met him in the hallway. "Catch me up," he asked as they walked.

"Okay, the proposed date for the Mills mediation is set for three weeks from today, the brief on Cordova has been updated, the other side wants to continue the motions on the Banks case while we discuss settlement and you have about a dozen calls including one from Gibson. Also, Justin Palmer is one the phone right now and says it's important."

Scott nodded. "Tell them that the date is agreeable on Mills. That will give us ten days to get the last declaration we need and finalize the brief. I'll look at the Cordova brief tonight. And tell them no on continuance of the Banks motions. We already talked settlement and it isn't working. I'll call Gibson and the others, and I'll take Justin Palmer's call now."

"Got it," Donna replied, walking down the hallway towards her office. "Tell me what Justin says when you have a chance. He sounds pretty excited."

Scott walked into his office and picked up the phone. "Hi Justin, it's Scott. What's happening?"

"I have a witness."

"Tell me," Scott replied excitedly.

"Edward Barnes says that he will support us."

"What's his position?"

"He is the Director of Compliance. The guy who counsels managers to assure that the Company acts in compliance with state and federal laws. Apparently, something has hit a nerve and he is ready to talk to you."

"What is he prepared to say?" Scott asked.

"He will say that he has been pressured to give out information that is not wholly accurate about the Delexane trials. You want to talk to him?"

"So, he is at Director level? That is right under the vice presidents, right?"

"Yeah, that's right."

Scott reflected for a moment and then said, "He's too high up the food chain for me to talk to directly."

"Really?" Justin asked.

"Yeah. Ethics guidelines prohibit one lawyer from talking to another lawyer's client directly. It's easy to identify the other lawyer's client where individuals are concerned, but in the corporate environment it's a little trickier. I am allowed to talk to non-management and middle managers, but the higher up the chain we go, the more likely it is that I am talking to the other attorney's client, which is prohibited. Director Level is uncomfortably in that danger area."

"So what do we do?" Justin asked.

"I can't talk to him about it, but you can. Tell me what Ed Barnes is prepared to say and we'll put it in affidavit form. You take it to him and have him assure it's accurate and then sign it. If he has any concerns about what's in the document, have him notate them and we will make changes the same day. He can then sign the revised document and we have it in our pocket for future use."

"Got it."

"So, what do you believe he will agree to say under oath?"

"He will say that he knows that the test results the company is putting out pertain to the first and second trials but are not accurate with respect to the bigger, third trial."

"So how does he know that what he is being asked to put out to the public about the Delexane trials isn't right?"

"Well, he heard it from me, Marty and Art, and he has seen the actual results."

"What he heard from you, Marty and Art isn't all that helpful because it's hearsay, but if he saw the results and he can identify the copy we have as accurate, then we have something."

"Got it," Justin replied. "I'll confirm that with him while you guys prepare the document."

"Perfect," Scott said. "Call me back to make sure we have it accurately and we'll have the document ready for signing tomorrow morning."

"There's something else," Marty added.

"What's that?"

"Sean Garner, the Aligor Security Director, followed me the other night and threatened me."

"Threatened you how?"

"He showed up in my house. He said that I was pushing false information to injure the company."

"He was in your house?" Scott said, incredulous.

"Yeah, he told me that he wanted to show me how little security home alarms provide."

Scott considered a moment and then said, "Let me consider how we deal with this guy."

"Thanks," Justin replied. "I'll keep you posted if anything else happens. I'll also get hold of Ed and get clarity on what he will say in his statement."

"Great news," Scott replied. "Talk to you soon." When he hung up, he sat back in his chair and thought about the contents of the statement he would draft for Edward Barnes. If one of the managers on the inside committed to a statement that his clients were telling the truth about the drug trial results, it also meant that the new version that Aligor was putting out was false. After a few moments he turned his attention to the intimidation aimed at his clients by Sean Garner. He might have to consider filing for a restraining order to keep Garner away from Marty and Justin, but he would wait for Lee to report in on Garner before moving further down that road.

# Chapter Ten

**July 2**
**11:00 a.m.**

Emma watched Christopher as he sat on the floor, legs folded under him, reading "The Big Book of Tell Me Why." It was made for a child with his hungry curiosity about everything; he loved to pull out obscure facts about animals and start a sentence with "Did you know that..." Did you know that hummingbirds flap their wings ten to fifteen times every second?" or "Did you know that they fly at 49 miles per hour?"

"I had no idea," Emma replied with honest interest.

"Yeah," he said, returning his attention to studying the book that held such fascination and looking for the next remarkable fact to report.

He was a force of happiness living in a world that interjected pain into his life every day. Emma contemplated the next doctor's appointment with dread. She was consumed by the possibility that her loving son might never make it to his next birthday. Every waking thought was about doing anything and everything to assure his survival, and restful sleep was no longer possible.

First had come questions about possible surgery. The doctors had done a number of tests and then told her and Michael that removing the neuroblastoma surgically was not a possible course of action because the cancer had spread to adjacent tissues and lymph nodes. It had to be treated with chemotherapy. They told Christopher that he was going to have a needle in his arm to put medicine into his system, so that he could get all better. He nodded agreeably and said, "Okay, Mommy. Then can we get ice cream?" Emma nodded because she couldn't say a word without crying.

Emma's childhood had been so easy that she had taken happiness and the existence of a future for granted. She had been blessed in many ways and everything had always fallen into place for her. In high school she was student body president, debate team leader and ultimately, valedictorian. Her parents had always believed that the sky was the limit for Emma and were confident that the world would soon know it as well. There was little doubt that she could be whatever she wanted to be. Her strength of character, as much as her brilliance, made her a natural leader. The boys found her attractive, although some were intimidated by the intelligence that sparkled in her eyes.

At age eighteen, Emma took her flawless academic history, her impressive extracurricular resume and her 4.4 grade point average and entered Stanford University. Four years later, she took her 3.9 grade point average from Stanford into the graduate program to pursue her Master's in Public Administration.

Emma had met Michael Franklin in the first year of her graduate program. He was an instructor working to become an associate professor, two years older than Emma and equally brilliant. In class, he posed questions using the Socratic Method common to law schools, asking a question that led to a likely answer, and then modifying the question to make the response less likely and modifying the facts again to illustrate that answers are often illusive and the questions exist in a world of greys rather than black and white. He skillfully illustrated that when you secured one public policy priority, you could easily sacrifice another as competing interests were always in play. Emma loved these discussions that sometimes became intense and drew classroom advocates to competing positions about how tax money is best spent to benefit the greatest number.

Then came the day after an early afternoon class, when she saw Michael sitting in under a red-flowering gum tree eating a sandwich, surrounded by students walking across the tree-lined campus in every direction. The extraordinary flowers of the red gum were like huddled sea urchins of dynamic red, gathered tightly and brightly on every massive branch. The effect was a tree alight with bright red flame.

"I wondered what you did when you left the classroom," she asked with a smile.

"I eat, soak up the sun and watch students scurry around. I am pretty impressive when it comes to multi-tasking."

She sat down next to him and said, "Obviously true," she replied, and then added, "Can I join you?"

"Sure. Pull up some grass and open your lunch bag."

She sat next to him and asked, "Do you always eat alone?"

He grinned and replied, "Maybe not after today. Do you want to have lunch with me tomorrow?"

"Yes, that would be nice."

The next day, and most days thereafter, they met under the same stunning tree and ate lunch together, consumed in conversation about funding schools, defense spending, health care, climate change and taxation — every public policy issue that Congress was addressing or needed to address. They shared a perspective on many issues and engaged in rigorous debate where their views differed. After they had tackled the country's biggest problems, the conversation took a turn to books, movies and cooking. It wasn't very long before their discussions went beyond lunches and they began taking other meals together. They took walks around the campus hiking and that led to hiking in local hills. At some unspecified moment that neither of them could identify, the relationship grew. They held hands, went to movies, engaged in endless reading in the same room and then began to share a bed. All of it brought them ever closer.

It was just short of a year from that first lunch under the red gum tree when Michael got down on one knee in the middle of a popular Italian restaurant and watched her eyes grow wide. He said, "Emma, I love you and I want to share life with you forever. Please be my wife."

Surrounding customers broke into cheers and applause as Emma began to cry. She threw her arms around him and squealed with joy. When she could talk, she yelled, "A thousand yeses. I love you."

Two months later, they had been married in a gorgeous setting beside the ocean in Half Moon Bay, surrounded by close friends and family. Emma had never been so happy. They lived together for a year chasing busy schedules and ambitions that were now within reach.

One night while they were sitting in the living room reading after dinner, Emma walked over to Michael and put her arms around his neck. She kissed him softly and said, "We may need a slightly bigger place."

He looked around and nodded. "We may need to get all of these books in electronic format, right?"

"Well, that would help, but we're also going to need a second bedroom."

"Really?" he said as his eyes flew open. "We're having a baby?"

She nodded and smiled. "Is that okay?"

"It's wonderful. Oh my God Emma, thank you."

"My pleasure," she replied, kissing him softly.

"Is it a boy or a girl?" he asked, excitedly.

"Yes," she replied with a smile. He laughed and she added, "We will find out in the next couple of weeks."

He kissed her and said, "I hope this little person is just like you."

"Parts of me and parts of you and his or her own original contribution. A brand-new life like no other," she had said in wonderment. Now those days of celebration and happiness seemed like another life in a distant universe. They had been replaced by constant fear as they watched their precious son's condition deteriorate.

\* \* \*

**July 2**
**2:45 p.m.**
Sean Garner felt restless and anxious to move to the next step. It was a good first effort with Cardenas and Palmer. They were both scared; he could feel it. Now he needed an effective move to push them into a state of panic. At a certain point, the fear and uncertainty would overwhelm them, and they would want the lawsuit to be over. He considered another surprise one on one meeting with each of them. Maybe one of them or, better yet, someone they cared about, should have an accident. As Sean considered the next move, the new phone he had purchased rang.

"Mr. Garner?" an unknown male voice asked.

"Yes," Sean replied in guarded tones.

"This is Bobby King at Maxie's restaurant. We have recovered your phone and you can pick it up anytime you'd like."

"Really? Where did you find it?"

"A guy stopped by with the phone. He said his daughter found it in the patio area and asked that he return it."

"Wow. Do you know who the guy is?"

"Nope. He wore overalls that said the name of some elevator company. He just said that he thought someone would be looking for it, so he wanted to get it back to the owner as soon as possible."

"Great," Sean replied, "feeling an immense sense of relief. "I'll be there to pick it up in an hour." He owed a big thank you to some unknown elevator company employee and his daughter.

"It will be waiting for you at the hostess desk."

"Perfect," Sean said, grinning widely.

\* \* \*

## July 2
### 6:00 p.m.

Sean Garner opened his front door to find an attractive woman with shoulder length black hair and piercing hazel eyes standing on the porch. She wore a dark suit and a white blouse, and she was accompanied by an older man with greying hair and a serious expression. The woman flashed a badge and said, "Sean Garner?"

"Yes," Sean said, surprised.

"I am Detective Olivia Blake and this is Detective Ed Farris." The middle-aged man beside her wore a look that said he was suspicious of something. "Can we come inside?"

"What's this about?" Garner asked.

She watched his eyes as she replied, "Do you want to let us inside to tell you or do you want to have the conversation here?"

"Okay," he replied, sounding unsure.

They stepped into the entry hallway and Olivia Blake said, "You worked with Arthur Underwood, do I have that right?"

"Yes. Well, I didn't work with him every day, but we were both employees of Aligor Pharmaceuticals."

"Right. You're aware that he died on June 26th, right?"

"Yes. I was shocked to hear that."

"Were you at his house anytime on the night he died?"

"Uh, no."

"Were you anywhere near his house that night?"

"No. I was home."

"Was anyone here with you that night?"

"No, just me. There was a ballgame I wanted to catch that night. Why are you asking?"

"Just doing some legwork. We had a suggestion that you might have been in the area of Art and Sandi Underwood's apartment that night."

"Not me," Sean replied confidently. "I was right here."

"Okay, thanks. It's our job to talk to anyone who might know something. You never know when you will turn up a witness to something important."

"I understand," Sean replied, having fully regained his composure.

"Oh, one more thing," she asked, reflecting for a moment. "Have you been following Mr. Cardenas or Mr. Palmer?"

A brief hesitation as Sean was caught off guard. "What? No, of course not. I have seen them around town, but I steer clear because my employer is in litigation with them."

She nodded and replied, "Well, thanks for your time, Mr. Garner. Have a good evening."

"Yeah, you too," Sean said, closing the door as they walked down the pathway. He was annoyed with himself for having been caught off-guard. He had to be poised at all times. That too, was part of the job.

As they walked towards the car, Olivia asked, "What do you think?"

"I don't know. "He denied it, just like Lee said he would, but so what? What do you think that Lee is up to?" He reflected a moment and then said, "If the shadowy image on the CCTV feed really is Garner, then he was in that building to see Art Underwood, right? And if he got in to see Underwood, then is it coincidence that Underwood went off the balcony that night? I can make an argument for how it could be Garner, but we don't have any real evidence yet."

"Right," Olivia replied, nodding. "We did this interview because Lee Henry talked our boss into it. I'm thinking that maybe Lee knows something that he isn't sharing. If that's true, it pisses me off. I don't want to be used to run down clues for a private investigator."

\* \* \*

**July 2**
**9:22 p.m.**
The isolated enormity of the vast executive suite was magnified in the absence of human life. The offices and conference rooms that surrounded the wide hallways and extravagant furnishings had an eerie feel. It had the feel of space to left unattended in the wake of an apocalyptic event, as if the last human had vanished without explanation.

Sean Garner made his way through the maze of luxury alone, the mouse following a daunting path in search of distant cheese or in fear of imminent electric shock. The sense of not belonging had always been immense, but these days Sean fancied himself as destined for bigger things. He knocked on the door of the expansive office and Randal Cook replied, "Come in, Sean." Cook sat on the couch in the conversation area near the door, reviewing documents and nursing a drink.

"Good evening, Mr. Cook."

"Sit," Cook directed, gesturing to the couch perpendicular to the chair he occupied. "You want a bourbon?"

"Yes, sir. That sounds good."

Cook stood and walked to a bar in the corner, dropped ice cubes in a glass and poured what Sean recognized from the shape of the bottle and the rider on the cap as Blanton's — at a couple of hundred dollars a bottle, something he had never tried. Cook handed him the glass and said, "Try that," with a wide grin.

He took a sip and nodded. "Amazing," he offered, taking one more sip.

Cook sat down in his chair and said, "So, you have something important that you think I need to know?"

"Yes, sir. I thought it best we spoke in person rather than on the phone."

"I see," Cook replied, sounding perturbed. "I assume this means that the problem is taken care of?"

"I think so, yes."

"Meaning?"

"Meaning that I think they are ready to receive a settlement offer that allows them to walk away with some money and save face. They sign the settlement agreement with confidentiality provisions and this problem is behind us." Sean smiled, enjoying the moment as Cook considered his message.

Cook nodded and then replied, "Well, if it's as you say, then you have indeed handled the assignment well. I will have our lawyers reach out to the lawyer for Cardenas and Winslow and put the deal together. Assuming this all comes together, you will not be disappointed in the outcome for you personally, Sean." He gave Sean a satisfied smile and added, "Thanks for coming by." He stood to signal the end of the meeting. As Sean stepped towards the door, Cook clapped him on the back and said, "Thanks for the update. I'll have our legal folks run with this and we'll know if what you've done so far motivates a quick settlement."

"Yes, sir," Sean replied.

As Sean made his way out of the opulent suite, elation took hold. Cook had acknowledged that he would be rewarded. What had he said? "You will not be disappointed in the outcome." He was about to join the elite. Time for a celebration. Some good bourbon of his own was in order.

* * *

**July 2**
**11:42 p.m.**
Sean Garner sat at the bar of the Carbon Club, a high-end bar that featured elegant glassware and cherry wood everything. The servers delivered hors d'oeuvres on china plates, wearing bow ties, black jackets and deferential smiles. Couples occupied broad armchairs at four of the twenty tables scattered around the high-ceilinged club room. There was a man in a blue suit with loosened tie sitting at the other end of the curved bar sending and receiving messages on his phone. "I'll have one more," Sean said to the jacketed bartender, who was filling his glass within seconds. As Sean started on his fourth Woodford Reserve Bourbon, he knew that his bar tab would climb to about two hundred or so, but it didn't matter — this was a big night he would long remember. He had hoped there would be a woman he could flirt with and maybe get laid, but no such luck. All the women were accompanied, so it was just him and the Woodford.

Two of the couples stood and left the club during the next ten minutes. The crowd had thinned, and Sean decided that it was time for him to take off and get some sleep. The morning would come quickly, and he had a lot to accomplish back in the office. Sean waved a farewell to the bartender who responded with a nod and a smile. "Take care, sir," he offered as Sean made his way to the door.

As Sean walked out the front door he felt the bite of the cold night air and an empty street. The moon's light was blocked by clouds and the night was dark. It was unusually chilly for July in southern California. Sean made his way to the parking area behind the building, where only three cars awaited their owners. His was against the building wall and as he approached, he saw a figure seated on the hood of his car. He hesitated a moment, as he wondered who it could be. He walked more slowly towards the car, the cold night air and the shock of the stranger clearing his mind of bourbon fuzziness.

"That's my car," he said to the figure in a stern voice as he approached.

"Right. Which made it the ideal place to wait for you. I knew you had to come out of there sooner or later."

"You're that private investigator asshole that I talked to once before." He shook his head. "I don't have anything to say to you." He stopped about three feet from where Lee sat and said, "And get the fuck off my car."

Lee smiled but didn't move. "You seem to be in a bad mood for someone who has been out having a good time this evening."

Sean folded his arms and stared at Lee silently. Lee held his eyes and said nothing. Sean was getting angry at this intrusion. "What do you want?"

"I'm concerned, Sean. I thought we understood one another, but you lied to me." Lee added, shaking his head.

"Get the fuck off my car," Sean growled.

"Just resting while we talk. You know Sean, when you lie about your involvement in a homicide, you just get yourself into deep shit."

"You're not a cop and I don't need to talk to you. You are harassing me." Sean exploded, "now get the fuck off my car."

"Harassing you?" Lee asked evenly. "Like you did to Marty Contreras by the lake? Or more like you did to Justin Palmer by showing up uninvited in his home? You mean that kind of harassment?" Sean eyes went wide with shock and then blazed with anger. Lee added, "I don't think that you are pathological, so you must believe that your company is worth killing for in the name of loyalty. Either way, you're going to have to account Sean."

Sean glared at Lee in silence for a time and then said, "You think I can't come find you, too? I know who you are." Sean growled.

Lee shrugged. "My identity is not a secret and you have a security background, so I would hope you could find me. Then again, you don't need to find me because I'm sitting in front of you." Lee studied the fire in Garner's eyes without emotional reaction. After a time, Lee said, "Your loyalty is misplaced, Sean. Think about what you're doing. In the name of some misguided allegiance, you are helping a company make money at the expense of people who are ill or dying. The most vulnerable among us are being sold a bill of goods so that they make one last ill-advised purchase before they die. Is that what you want to achieve?"

"The results are not what you think they are. It's not like Cardenas and Palmer say it is."

"It's exactly like they say it is. You know it and I know it. Think about what you are endorsing here. Most people trained in law enforcement or high up in the security industry wouldn't buy into the bullshit you seem to have swallowed."

Garner furrowed his brow. "Get off my car."

Lee studied Garner a moment. "There's no mystery here. It's pretty clear what you are doing, Sean. Just remember that you are going to answer for what you did to Art Underwood. Now you're attempting to intimidate Marty Cardenas and Justin Palmer. And for what? To cover a company trying to steal money from desperate people fighting for their last days?"

Garner growled, "I don't like be accused of things I didn't do. Not by anyone. Maybe I should call the police."

Lee nodded. "You should call them so that you can explain your recent actions."

"I don't know where you get your information, but you need a new source. You need to get off my car and get the fuck out of here," Garner snarled. "Next time I see you, you won't walk away."

Lee didn't move. He shook his head. "One more threat to add to your recent list of accomplishments. For a novice criminal, your record just keeps on growing. Let's see, you tracked and threatened Marty Cardenas in a public park and you broke into Justin Palmer's house to intimidate and threaten him. So, this would be your third assault based on threats, along with one breaking and entering and, of course, one murder." Lee raised his hands and added, "Oh, and lying to the police. I almost forget that one. But ask yourself why you are going down the path." Lee shrugged and added, "Don't forget, you are going to have to account for all of this."

"You son of a bitch," Sean yelled. Sean's eyes were ablaze as he drew back a fist.

Lee stared at him. "You don't want to do that, Sean," Lee offered with a menacing grin. No one spoke for a time and then Lee added. "I'm hoping you can come to terms with this. Your criminal acts aren't even for a good reason."

Lee stood up and looked directly and unflinchingly into Sean's eyes. "And right before you go to sleep at night, think about what you did to Art Underwood. Then think about Sandi Underwood. She'll be trying to get to sleep, too." For a protracted period of silence Lee held Garner's gaze. Then Lee walked a few feet away from Sean. He turned back and said, "We'll talk again, Sean."

"Count on it," Sean Garner yelled angrily.

\* \* \*

## July 3
### 9:15 a.m.

Donna stood in Scott's doorway while she and Scott updated on critical projects. "We have another week on the Cameron brief, so I thought I'd take the outline you did and jump into it next."

"Good. Also, kick out a letter on Winston about the late discovery responses and I need rough interrogatories and a request to produce documents to go out to the other side on Barker."

"Shall do," Donna replied, scribbling notes on a yellow pad.

There was a buzz and a voice filled the air. "Scott, there is a guy named Edward Barnes on line three. He says he worked with Justin Palmer at Aligor." The disembodied intercom voice belonged to the receptionist Nikki Ryan.

Donna's eyes widened. "He's the manager who worked with Justin Palmer. He probably wants to talk about the declaration, but are you allowed to talk to the guy?" she asked.

Scott shrugged. "High level executives are generally represented by the corporation's attorneys so probably not. But let's get some detail and we'll see where it takes us."

He punched a button on the phone and said, "Scott Winslow here."

"Mr. Winslow, its Edward Barnes. I worked with Justin Palmer and I want to talk to you about the declaration your office prepared for my signature."

Scott hesitated. "Mr. Barnes, you are a current employee at Director Level?"

"That's right."

"Then you and I can't talk because you are represented by counsel who represents Aligor. I can't talk to the other guy's client without him being on the call."

"I'm not represented. To the contrary, I refused representation. I was told Aligor's lawyer would represent me if I was called as a witness and I said no thanks. I told them I didn't want or need a lawyer." He paused a moment and then added, "The reason I'm calling you is to give you a head's-up. I'm just not sure that I can sign a declaration."

"Was the content of the declaration accurate? I mean, did we get anything wrong?"

"No, you didn't get anything wrong. It's just that I have to survive in this environment, and it has been made pretty clear that to help Marty or Justin would be a fatal mistake."

"I'm sorry to hear you say that, Edward. Justin was grateful for your participation and your willingness to stand up. I'm sure he will be disappointed."

There was a long, awkward pause and then Barnes spoke thoughtfully. "Your clients are brave, Scott. They have taken on a Goliath because they believe in what they are doing. The flip side of that coin is that heroes are lonely and sometimes they starve. This is a major red line, and to cross it is to risk everything. You're asking me to put my career on the line for this."

Scott said, "I understand being nervous, but there is a lot at stake here. There is no sugar coating this. You know what the Company is doing. They are marketing a product to people who are clinging to their last hope. If no one speaks up, we all know that they are going to continue peddling false information. If you have a spouse or child with cancer and you are down to the last desperate attempts to find any drug that might extend their life, you need the whole picture. Millions of people could make that critical decision based on false information." Scott paused to let that settle and then added, "Isn't it the ultimate example of putting money ahead of humanity; deceiving people whose lives depend on accurate information? They are planning to make billions at the expense of people who are dying by feeding them false information about why they should make Delexane their last hope, Edward."

"I understand," Barnes replied, "and I think I just heard part of your jury argument, but you need to understand that my whole career will be over. Not just at Aligor, but in an industry that suddenly closes when you are at odds with one of its big players. How are Marty and Justin doing finding new jobs?" They both knew the answer to that rhetorical question. Barnes was quiet for a moment and added, "Like I said, I think that Marty and Justin are incredibly brave, but I have to support my family."

"You have to make this decision but think about it. First, they lie about test trial results, omitting all of the bad information that came from the phase three trials. When Marty and Justin stood up and tried to get them to make it right, they got fired. And now Aligor is going even further, accusing them of falsifying information when they come forward with the real test results. They are now denying the real test results, not just omitting to disclose them in reporting but claiming that the real numbers are fabrications." Scott paused a moment and then added, "Edward, you know that Marty and Justin are telling the truth and that the documents they have are the real test trial data. The Company is lying about all of this and they want you to lie for them."

"The product could do some good," Barnes offered. "I mean the early data was really positive."

"That's right. Maybe the product could be useful to some people, but only if the people have real information in making their decision. Otherwise, it's a false choice. As it is, the Company is claiming much better results than the tests reveal and ignoring critical side effects that appeared in phase three. If you have a family member with cancer and you have to choose a course of treatment, don't you need to know the truth? Is there anything more important to anyone in that position? And that could be any of us next year or even next month."

"I understand all that, but my whole career..." he let the words trail off.

It was Scott's turn to go quiet. After a few moments, he spoke. "My clients tell me that you are a man of integrity, Edward, and they really need you to step up and tell the whole truth. If you decide you can't help with declaration, I will have no choice but to go in a different direction. I will subpoena you and take your deposition so that you can answer these questions under oath. You sound like a man of integrity to me too, and I don't think you will perjure yourself to cover up the Company's fraud."

Barnes spoke in tones became quiet resignation, "So it comes out the same for me, either way."

"The declaration is the option that allows you to stay under the radar for a while. We tuck it in a file for later usage. If I take your deposition, your testimony is available to both sides right away."

"This smacks of some kind of lawyer blackmail," Barnes said, unhappily.

"Not really, Edward. It just gives you a heads-up on how the alternatives play out so you can make an informed decision. Something the Company isn't doing for the public."

There was a prolonged silence. "If I sign the declaration, when does the company learn that I did?"

"I can't tell you exactly, but it won't be right away. We will hold it until we need it for a motion, a mediation or trial. It's likely to be a month to several months down the road."

There was an extended silence, and Scott was concerned that Barnes might have hung up. Then Barnes said, "I've been going back and forth on whether

I sign this declaration ever since Justin brought it to me. I want to help Justin and Marty because I think what the Company is doing here isn't right. I just don't want to be collateral damage. People are already looking at me closely just because I worked with Justin and they know that he and I are friends. There is perpetual scrutiny to see who is aligned with the enemy."

"I really get that," Scott responded earnestly. "It's hard to take a big personal risk to do what's right."

"Would you sign it in my position?"

"I have a built-in bias because I obviously have a horse in this race, but yes, I would. I think what Aligor is doing constitutes a fraud on the public that could cost many people their lives."

There was another silence and then Barnes replied, "Okay, Scott. I will sign the declaration and give it to Justin. I hope I don't come to regret this decision."

"For what it's worth, I think you are doing what's right in a hard situation."

"I think so, too. That's why I'm doing it." He paused and then added, "But I may be the next one coming to consult with you."

"You know that I can't assure you that these guys won't fire you. Like you say, the company is watching you. But keep in mind that if they fired you and then you signed the declaration, they would argue that you aren't believable and that you only did it because they had to fire a bad employee, you know, the whole disgruntled employee thing. If you sign the declaration and then you're later fired, you have a stronger claim for wrongful termination. Your position is much better if your complaints about the company's fraud are documented before they fire you and make up some bullshit reason like you were a poor performer or we decided to go in a different management direction, whatever the hell that means."

"I understand. I feel like I'm caught between a rock and a hard place, but it's going to make me do the right thing. I may just have to get my family used to having me around the house more." He let out an uncomfortable chuckle and then added, "Anyway, Justin will have the signed declaration by the end of the day. I'm also going to keep your number handy in case my career starts to slide into the abyss." Scott thought he detected a combination of satisfaction and resignation in his voice as Barnes spoke.

"I hope nothing bad comes of it, but I'll be available if you need to talk. Take care of yourself."

"I will. You will hear from me if I'm suddenly on the street."

As he hung up, the intercom buzzed again. Nikki said, "Scott, you have Doug Gibson on line 2."

"Okay, thanks." He punched a button and said, "What's up, Doug?"

"No small talk today?"

"Yeah, sure. How's the family?"

"They are doing okay."

"Great. So, what do you need? In my experience you only call to resist discovery or accuse my clients of making up the test results that we both know are real."

"A little testy. Not in a good mood today, huh?" Gibson asked playfully.

"I guess you hit me at the right time. I have a low tolerance for bullshit today. So, what's up?"

"Well, even when I don't think much of a case, part of my job is to assess settlement possibilities, so that's what I'm doing. Do your clients want to try to settle their case? Hopefully, they are in a better mood than you are."

"All right," Scott replied. "I have to hand it to you, that was a pretty good line. As far as settlement, we're open to talking but we can't hold the conversation alone. So far, I've heard lots of bullshit accusations, but no offers. And when opposing counsel starts out the conversation by stating that they don't think much of a case, you can understand why I'm not optimistic with respect to our chances of settlement."

"Well it's clear that we have different views about the quality of the case," Gibson replied. "My client doesn't see that you have a winning hand to play, but litigation is expensive, and they want to spend their time working on their business rather than ours."

"I know how they are spending their time on business, and that's part of the problem. But like I said, I'm listening," Scott offered evenly. "I'm always willing to hear an offer, but with one caveat. If your client thinks we're talking costs of defense they are sadly mistaken."

"Do you want to mediate this case?"

"Maybe. I'd like to know your opening offer before going to mediation because I want to make sure that we're not wasting our time."

"You haven't given me a demand."

"True, but then again, you've never asked for one. Give me a few days to talk to my clients and I'll get back to you."

"Fair enough. Talk to you then."

* * *

## July 3
### 1:20 p.m.
Sean Garner couldn't get the meeting with the guy he had now identified as Lee Henry out of his mind. He hadn't slept well, replaying the encounter countless times over in his mind. Sean was in the office at 7:00 a.m., slightly hung over and in a foul mood from his late-night meeting.

His first action of the day had been to make inquiries about the people around Cardenas' and Palmer's attorney, Scott Winslow. From there he connected the dots to Winslow's frequent investigator, Lee Henry, by talking to a colleague in the corporate security field who had worked with Lee and held him in high regard.

Sean thought about ways to go after Lee Henry but decided to set that aside. The best way to get to him was to turn up the heat on the clients Scott Winslow and Lee Henry represented. Another visit to Marty Cardenas and Justin Palmer would convince all of them that no one was going to fuck with him. If he leaned on them one more time, he could force a low settlement of the case and reap the rewards. He thought again about Cook's house and what it would be like to live in that exquisite Lake Sherwood neighborhood. It was all within his reach, so it was time to push the envelope a little further.

* * *

## July 3
### 6:02 p.m.
Justin pulled up to the curb and then looked himself over before getting out of the car. A comb of the hair, a straightening of the collar and one deep breath — he was as ready as he was going to get. He climbed out of the car and walked up the driveway and into the apartment building, finding his way to the elevator and fearing that maybe their first date had been a fluke. He was looking forward to seeing Jessica again but it seemed too good to be true. Maybe his obsessive thoughts about her since their first date had overstated the match made in heaven aspects of it all. He knew that, notwithstanding his jaded attitude, he was capable of putting a woman on a pedestal, but he wanted so much for this to be real.

He emerged from the teakwood elevator and made his way to apartment 222. He pushed the doorbell and waited. After a moment, she opened the door wearing a wide smile and said, "Hi, Justin. Come on in." She stood aside and gestured toward the couch. "Give me just a minute to put my shoes on and we can go."

She disappeared down a hallway, leaving him to look around the living room. Two armchairs, the couch he sat on and a marble coffee table. There were built-in bookshelves on each side of the credenza that held the flat screen television. Adjacent to the living room there was a breakfast nook that looked out onto the back garden. Next to the nook was a small kitchen boasting a blue-flecked granite. As he surveyed the area, Jessica reemerged wearing dark slacks and a silky blue top. Her eyes sparkled as she regarded him.

"You look lovely," he said softly.

"Why thank you. That's not a word I hear much these days. I like it." She gave him a smile and added, "Have you been thinking about our first date?"

He shook his head. "Only constantly."

She laughed. "Yeah, me too. That and wondering if the second date would be as much fun."

He nodded. "Well, let's find out. How about Hooper's for dinner?"

"Sounds good," she replied.

They walked from the apartment and Justin took her hand as they walked down the driveway towards the car. She gave him a smile and his hand a squeeze. As they pulled away from the curb, a black Audi followed.

* * *

Hooper's had a reputation as a romantic place for good reason. Soft lighting and alcoves with private tables, blooming flowers and a massive stone fireplace in the center of the restaurant. The offerings included white tablecloths, good wine and wonderful food. It was a setting for countless birthdays, anniversaries and marriage proposals. As they walked in, the young hostess in a black and silver evening dress asked, "You folks have a reservation?"

"Yes, Justin Palmer at 6:40 p.m."

She scanned a book and nodded, "I see it. Your table is ready. Are we celebrating anything special this evening?"

They looked at each other and Justin said, "Yes we are. We are celebrating the beginning of a beautiful relationship."

The hostess smiled and said, "Oh, that's so nice. My boyfriend and I had one of those dates six months ago."

"Great," Jessica replied. "I'm glad you have someone special."

"We just broke up, actually."

"Sorry to hear that," Jessica offered, commiserating as they followed the woman to their table in the back of the restaurant.

When they sat down, Justin smiled and said, "I think you were set up."

"No kidding. She had a relationship just like this one and then they broke up. Nice."

"Our very own Hooper's cautionary tale," Justin offered, "when all we wanted was dinner."

They were laughing as a young male server approached the table. "I like working with happy couples," he said. "Can I get you something to drink?"

"What's your house red?" Jessica asked.

"Opolo Mountain Zinfandel. It is really good."

"Guaranteed?" Justin asked playfully.

"Guaranteed," the young man said without missing a beat. "If you don't love it, I'll drink it for you."

"Perfect," Jessica responded with a chuckle.

"Make it two," Justin said. "The guarantee sold me."

The young man laughed and quickly disappeared from the table. "What?" Jessica asked. "You're looking at me with a crooked smile."

"I'm already enjoying the moment with you."

She nodded. "You say the sweetest things, Justin." She considered a moment and asked, "Have you ever been married?"

"Nope. I was close once."

"What happened?"

"About two weeks before the wedding she decided that she didn't want to be married. She had an epiphany of some weird kind and wanted to spend a couple of years traveling through Europe and staying in hostels."

"Wow," Jessica responded. "That must have been a nasty surprise."

"Yeah, as was the fact that she wanted to do it with a good friend of mine."

"Holy shit," Jessica replied. "That's awful."

"It was, but it was a long time ago. For obvious reasons, I'm glad I never married her."

"And no one has tempted you since then?"

"Nope. I hadn't found the one I wanted to spend my forever with."

The smiling waiter returned to the table with two glasses of wine. He set them down and said, "I think you're going to like it, but don't forget the guarantee."

"We won't forget," Justin said.

"Do you want to order now?" the server asked.

"Specials?"

"Yes. Wild caught salmon with amazing risotto and filet mignon with house baked potatoes."

"Same guarantee?" Justin asked with a smile.

"Absolutely. I love all of it," the smiling server offered.

"You got me again. I'll have the salmon," Justin said.

"Make it two. That sounds perfect," Jessica added.

As the smiling server left the table, Justin returned the question. "How about you? Ever been married?"

"I was married for two years," she said, the smile leaving her face. "He was a nice guy who believed it was always five o'clock somewhere. He wouldn't stop drinking and his need for alcohol took over our lives. After things got rough, I came to understand the principles of al anon. I wasn't going to sit on the sidelines and watch him drink himself to death while I hoped he'd stop. So, I left."

"How did he take it?"

"Not well. He begged me to stay. Made more of the same promises I'd heard frequently. Of course, by then I knew they were empty promises. So, I said goodbye."

"Are you still in touch?"

She shook her head. "I heard from mutual friends that his liver gave out, and he died five years after we split up. It made me really sad because at one time I thought him and me belonged together."

"I'm sorry," Justin offered.

She hesitated before speaking. "Somehow that final outcome seemed inescapable, but I wish he had been able to recover and start over."

"Anyone in your life now?"

"Yeah. There's a guy I think I really like," she said, smiling at him.

"What a nice coincidence," he said.

Dinner was delivered to the table and they ate in silence for a time. "I'm even comfortable being quiet with you," Justin said.

"Yeah, me too. It's not awkward."

The conversation came easily as well, and as they finished the meal, the waiter dropped off the check. He considered their plates and said, "Looks like I won't be reaping the benefits of the guarantee tonight. Have a good night, folks." They laughed as he disappeared from the table.

Jessica put a card on the check as Justin was reaching for his wallet. "My turn," she said. "Remember?"

"Well, thank you," he said with a grin.

"My pleasure," she replied. "It really is."

"What would you like to do after dinner?" he asked.

"How about we go for a walk around my neighborhood?" she suggested. "And maybe curl up on my couch and catch a movie."

"I like it," Justin said.

As they walked from the restaurant to Justin's car, he took her hand.

"Thank you for dinner," he said, smiling. "My turn next time."

"Okay. Deal."

He opened the passenger door and she slid inside. "Justin, there's a note on your windshield," Jessica pointed out.

He walked around the car and plucked the note from under the windshield wiper. It was computer generated. "I am ALWAYS watching. Do the right thing."

As he got into the car, Jessica noted the concern in his expression. "What was it?" she asked. He hesitated and then handed her the note. She wrinkled her nose. "This is pretty cryptic. Is it from Santa?"

He laughed hysterically. "Not hardly," he said. "This guy is the furthest thing from Santa. I'll tell you about it while we take our walk and then I'll hope you're not too worried to hang out with me."

"Sounds serious," she replied, her eyes wide. She then grinned wryly. "So, do you have a secret side I don't know about? Are you a fugitive in search of a one-armed man or something like that?"

"Nope, I'm a product manager in search of a woman with a great sense of humor. So, I think I'm in luck."

# Chapter Eleven

**July 4**
**3:30 p.m.**

A slight breeze blew from the west, moving the trees softly and giving the warm afternoon a delightful tropical feel. Marty and Abby Cardenas held hands as they walked the dirt path through the park. Flowers and wild grasses bloomed all around them as birds sang their songs in praise of nature. It was one of those moments Marty wanted to record and play back when the stresses over-whelmed him.

"It feels like we are a million miles away from anything stressful out here," Marty said, squeezing Abby's hand.

"It's amazing," she replied. "Reminds me of our trip to Mendocino a few years ago. The submission of the will to the majesty of nature."

"Wow," he replied, "that's pretty deep."

"I'm just a philosophical kind of woman."

"I think so. I also remember that we got naked and made love in wild grass not far from the beach."

She grinned. "I remember that, too. It was really great." She stopped in her tracks, ending his forward momentum as she clung tightly to his hand.

"What's the matter?" Marty asked, turning towards her and staring at her shocked expression.

"That man ahead of us on the bench. He was on the first bench when we entered the park. We've been walking quickly and in a straight line."

"Yeah, that's right."

"So how did he get here and settled on that bench ahead of us?"

Marty turned his attention to the man on the bench and felt his heart stall. It was Sean Garner, sitting there and staring at them. Marty walked quickly over to him, but he didn't move. "What are you doing here?"

Garner smiled. "Relaxing and reading the paper." He pointed to the newspaper on the bench beside him. "It's a beautiful day, isn't it?"

"Bullshit!" Marty yelled. "Why don't you leave us alone?"

Garner shrugged. "Just enjoying the holiday. You came over to speak to me, remember?"

"What do you want, Sean? You were seated at the first bench when we entered, and you had to move fast to get here before we did. So, no bullshit, Sean, what do you want?"

"I'm just enjoying this gorgeous day. Days like this make me appreciate the things that are really important, you know. Things like loyalty and trust." He grinned and laced his fingers in front of him. He looked thoughtful for a moment and then added, "And family. You have to take good care of family and keep them safe, right?"

Marty glared at Sean and said, "I don't understand how you could have done what you did to Art."

"You think I did something to Art, huh? Accidents happen, Marty." He shrugged and added, "We all need to be aware of that."

Marty shook his head and yelled, "Fuck you, you son of a bitch." He turned and walked back to where Abby waited. He was shaking with some combination of fear and anger. This fucking guy was deranged.

"You all right?" Abby asked. Marty nodded. "That's him, isn't it? The security guy who was watching you and Art?"

"That's him."

"Why is he following us?"

"Let's walk while we talk," Marty said, taking her arm. They moved past Sean without looking at him. "I think there is something wrong with the guy. He features himself some sort of corporate secret agent and he's out to stop me and Justin from pursuing our lawsuit."

She looked at him with worried eyes. "Do you think he's really dangerous?"

Marty drew a breath and said, "Maybe. Art is dead and he may have had something to do with that."

"You mean that this guy might come after us?"

"I don't know. He's working a course of intimidation. I told you about my previous meeting with him in the park and the son of a bitch actually broke into Justin's house. None of it is normal behavior."

"What are we going to do?" Abby asked.

"I'm not sure." He glanced behind him to make sure they weren't being followed, but the pathway was clear back to a group of hikers fifty feet behind. "I haven't been chased by a well-trained psychopath before."

"Should we call the police?"

"What do we tell them? That we saw him twice in the park and he said we have to be careful because accidents happen? And that I said fuck you Sean? That doesn't make me sound very intimidated as I think about it." He shook his head. "I know he's already been interviewed by the police after Art's death. That didn't seem to go anywhere."

"Maybe we need to tell them what he said today. You interpreted what he said as a threat, right?"

"I did. Don't the police need to know that?"

He nodded and said, "Maybe, but I'm a little concerned that it will color their opinion of us more than him. I mean, he was pretty indirect. His words don't sound all that threatening. You had to be there to get the impact."

Abby wore a worried expression. "It's really creepy Marty. When we go watch the fireworks tonight, will this guy be there? I feel like we are going to being looking over our shoulders all the time to see if he is watching from the shadows."

"You're right. I feel that way, too." He pulled back on what he was going to add and went quiet.

"There is something else you aren't saying."

He nodded. "I believe that this son of bitch killed Art. If that's true, he'll do most anything."

"Which is why we really have to go to the police, Marty," Abby asserted. "We can't play games with this guy."

His eyes opened wide as he looked at her. "I think I know what to do."

"Does it involve calling the police?" she asked.

They reached the parking lot and climbed into the car. He turned to her and said, "He's doing all of this to keep us quiet and get us to end the lawsuit so that the Company doesn't have to deal with what it did with the drug trials."

"I got that part," Abby replied.

"I think we have been too passive. We need to push back. Justin and I need to start telling the world what Aligor is doing and not just wait to let it come out in a courtroom."

She considered a moment and then asked, "You think Scott Winslow would agree?"

"Probably not."

She regarded him curiously. "How do you start getting your story out?"

"Nothing you can't get out there with the help of the news media and the internet."

She shook her head disapprovingly. "Maybe we should just get targets tattooed across our backs, as long as we are in the business of doing what it takes to make sure someone comes after us." He then lifted her hand to his lips and kissed it. "Jesus, Marty. You can kiss me all you want, but I'm not going to think this is a good idea." She shook her head in dismay. "Am I supposed to smile and be glad that we don't live in a five-story apartment building and leave it at that? You are planning to pick up a stick and poke the bear. You are messing with someone who knows no limits. I understand your desire to stand up for what's right, Marty, but if this guy is crazy, I don't want us to be the collateral damage."

Marty grinned. "Oh, I don't think we'll be collateral, we'll be the primary target."

"And I'm supposed to think that's funny, right?" she interjected unhappily.

"Sorry, just a little whistling past the graveyard I guess."

"Don't antagonize this crazy bastard, Marty. Let's just lay low." She hesitated and as they arrived home, she added, "Maybe it's time to let the lawsuit go. I know that what you are doing is right, but who wants to die for a claim?"

Marty hit the garage door button on the visor and pulled into the garage. He turned off the engine and then looked at her. "That's exactly what this guy wants. He's attempting to intimidate us into dismissing the case." He shook his head and then said, "I need to take a stand, Abby. I've already committed to the litigation and the Aligor executives are slamming me throughout the Company and all around the industry. Sean Garner is going even further to get to us, and I don't think he's doing it without Cook's consent."

Her eyes filled with worry. "I keep thinking about Art Underwood, Marty. I don't want to be the next Aligor widow who had a husband fighting the good fight."

"I understand, but this fight isn't just about us. There are families out there struggling through the final days of cancer in a family member and they are going to rely on the doctored findings Aligor puts out." She nodded her understanding but didn't look convinced. "I think that it's time to join the public fight so that everyone knows why we are doing this." He stopped the car in the garage but didn't get out. He turned and took both of her hands. "I need your support, sweetheart."

"This is really dangerous, and we are not covert operatives of some kind."

His expression conveyed his commitment as he said, "Please, Abby. This is a fight I have to have."

She silently drew a breath and then said, "Okay, but if the crazy guy following us around, shoots us, or pushes us off a cliff, I'm going to say I told you so."

He smiled widely, feeling grateful to have her in his life. How lucky can one guy be?

* * *

**July 5**
**1:15 p.m.**
"Thank you for meeting me," Sandi Underwood said. The three women sat at an umbrella covered table between the bar and grill known as The Tropics and the busy pedestrian sidewalk. "I know I made it sound urgent, but I want to start by saying that I'm buying lunch and the margaritas."

"That sounds great," Abby replied. "I'm ready for that."

"I'm in as well," Jessica replied. She looked at Sandi as if waiting for more and then added, "It sounded like you had some urgent business when we talked on the phone."

The conversation was silenced when a woman with a wide smile and a Tropics apron stopped by the table. "What will it be today, ladies?"

"Margaritas all around," Sandi answered. "And I'll have a chicken salad."

The server looked at Abby. "A BLT, please."

"And you?" the server said to Jessica with a smile.

"The chicken salad sounds great."

"Okay, ladies. I'm on it," the woman said, racing away from their table.

"Where were we?" Sandi asked. "Oh yeah, the urgent business of today." She gathered her thoughts a moment and then said, "I have been feeling lost. I am reminded of Art everywhere I look, and I miss him so much." Her eyes were moist, but she held back the tears. "I want to know who killed him and I want whoever it is to be held accountable." She took a breath and then said, "I spoke with the two detectives working on the case and they don't have much, but I need to know who murdered my husband. I thought maybe we could share ideas."

Abby wore a look of concern. "We're not cops, Sandi. How can we do anything they can't with all the tools they have?"

"I know. Maybe it's silly, but I just can't do *nothing.*" She studied their worried expressions and then said, "I'm not asking you to get involved in a shootout, just to brainstorm with me. We share ideas and we see what comes of it. If nothing, we're no worse off, but at least we're trying to come up with an answer. I need that."

Abby nodded. "Okay, I just don't think I have much information."

Sandi said, "Let's think about what we already know. There is a grainy video of a man at the door of our building before Art was murdered. I also know that Art was being watched by Sean Garner in the days before he died and that the grainy video image is consistent with Garner's build." She paused and then said, "I understand that Garner has been invading your lives to cause Marty and Justin to walk away from the lawsuit. I want to know what you both know so that I can assemble all of the facts and meet with the police. We can be the boost the investigation needs."

Jessica and Abby both wore doubtful expressions. "I'm not sure about us finding a killer the cops can't," Jessica offered.

"I'm not either," Sandi replied, "but I need to do something." She reflected and then asked, "What was your encounter with Garner like?"

"Damned creepy," Abby answered, shaking her head. "We saw him at the beginning of a hike. Then we walked at a good pace and he was magically there ahead of us, sitting on a bench and waiting. Marty went over to him and they had words. When he came back, Marty told me that he had threatened us."

The server stepped up to the table with a tray. "Here we are," she said, placing margaritas, two salads, and one sandwich on the table. Anything else I can get for you?"

"No, looks great," Abby offered.

"Enjoy," she said.

Jessica renewed the conversation as the woman walked away. "He broke into Justin's house and threatened him, talking about how alarm security is just an illusion and how we are more vulnerable than we think. And he left a note on Justin's car saying that he's always watching. The guy is truly a piece of work."

"What about Lee?" Jessica asked. "I think he's climbing into figuring out what happened."

"Yeah, he is. If anyone can figure this out, he might be the guy," Abby replied.

"What else can we do?" Jessica asked.

"I knocked on the door of all of my neighbors and no one seemed to know anything," Sandi said.

"You really are doing an investigation." Jessica said.

"Yeah, I'm just without a plan to get further."

"You and the police," Abby offered.

"Well, I'm ahead of them," Sandi said. "They are still not sure he didn't kill himself. Makes me mad, but they don't know him like I do."

Jessica said, "Well, we can share any other information or interactions with this weird guy."

"Yeah, we can do that much," Abby added.

"You have any other ideas?" Sandi asked. They shook their heads and returned their attention to lunch.

Abby understood why Sandi was desperate to do something to cope with the immense loss, but she believed their chances of figuring out who killed Art before the cops do were about as good as their chances of winning the next lottery. Still, she would help a friend any way she could.

"I feel better just talking to you both," Sandi said with a smile.

Jessica nodded. "It's good to see you both. Whether we turn out to be good sleuths or not, I like the friendships we have here."

"Me too." Abby said with a grin. "The margaritas help as well."

* * *

**July 5**
**3:12 p.m.**
Michael and Emma sat in Dr. Rayburn's office, each minute a torturous eternity as they waited for his arrival. They held hands and shared looks of worry, watching the clock on the wall as it moved twelve minutes past their meeting time.

Dr. Rayburn walked into the office, his expression solemn, and said, "Sorry I'm a little late. I had a consult that ran longer than expected."

"We understand," Michael replied, wanting to get to talking about Christopher. "What news do you have for us?" he asked, unable to wait another moment.

"I reviewed the results and consulted with two other oncologists on the hospital's team." They nodded without speaking. "The treatment is not working as we had hoped," he said, softly. He wore a strained expression as he groped for the words that would hurt the least. "There is minimal shrinkage of the tumor; not enough to lead us to believe that the treatment we are currently using can be successful. We are going to need to change the drugs." Emma and Michael stared at him silently, fear in their eyes. "It doesn't mean that chemotherapy will not work," Dr. Rayburn offered. "It means we need to adjust the drugs that we are using. We have other weapons in our medical arsenal," he offered, seeing their pained expressions.

"It may still work?" Michael asked, feeling the desperation rise.

"Yes. You have to understand that some cancers respond to one particular drug regimen and others require a different regimen. It's not clear what course of treatment will work on a specific patient, so we often have to take our best shot at the right one and if it doesn't work, try again with another."

Michael nodded slowly. Emma asked, "And sometimes none of them work?" When she saw his expression, Emma wished she could retrieve the question. Dr. Rayburn nodded. "But in many cases, we make a change and we get better results. So, we don't want to give up hope."

Their spirits came crashing down once again. Emma was pushing back tears as she listened to what she heard as a pronouncement that the threat to her son's life was greater than ever. They needed to try something else because everything that they had tried isn't working. As she listened, Emma felt the blood rushing through her veins. She was finding it hard to breathe and the doctor's voice seemed to be coming from miles away in some remote echo chamber.

When they left the meeting with Dr. Rayburn, Emma went directly to the restroom down the hall and threw up. She cried as she cleaned up in front of the bathroom mirror and then she stepped out into the hallway and almost fell down on a bench. She began sobbing as Michael walked towards her and put his arms around her. People walked by and gave them sympathetic looks, after all, they were people who knew what kind of news was delivered in these offices.

\* \* \*

**July 6**
**8:05 a.m.**
Scott Winslow refilled his coffee cup and then picked up the phone. He waited through five rings and then the answer came. "Gentry Marsden, how may I direct your call?"

"Doug Gibson please."

"One moment and I'll see if he's available. Who's calling?"

Scott smiled. Undoubtedly his availability would vary based on whether he wanted to talk to the caller. "Scott Winslow."

"Yes, Mr. Winslow. Hang on."

The response was rapid. "Hi, Scott. How are you? In the office nice and early," he added.

"I'm well, Doug, how about you? I noticed you were in early enough to take my call." As he spoke, Scott noted that his small talk quotient felt a little higher today.

"I'm doing great. I like to get here before everyone arrives. It's quiet and I can get something done."

"I understand," Scott replied.

"So, where are we with respect to a settlement demand?" Gibson inquired.

"Well, Doug, we do have a settlement demand for you. Our demand is two-fold. Part one is $750,000 for each of Mr. Cardenas and Mr. Palmer. That represents about three year's earnings and benefits and $100,000 in emotional distress damages for each."

There was a moment of quiet and then Gibson said, "Yeah, we feared that the parties saw case value differently, didn't we." Scott didn't respond, so Gibson added, "All that and there's a part two?" Gibson asked.

"Part two is your client tells the truth to the public. They release the real numbers. We don't care if they say they recalculated, that these are the latest figures, or that they just remembered how to do the math. How they explain it can be the subject of negotiation, so long as they don't try to fault my clients." He paused a moment to let that settle in and then added, "We're not asking that they admit to fraud or wrongdoing, we are only asking that they put the real numbers out there, so patients have the complete test results in making critical decisions. A creative explanation for the delay is okay with us and if we come to an understanding concerning that explanation, my clients will agree not to dispute the reason given."

"The obvious problem with your proposal is that my client already has put out the correct information and your clients are attempting to distort it for their own benefit."

"I understand that has been their line for the press, but it's total bullshit, Doug. Anyway, please convey our settlement demand. Let us know your settlement offer and we will jointly decide if it's worthwhile to go to mediation. Just know that any offer that contains a confidentiality provision to muzzle my clients and doesn't correct the public misperceptions your folks created will be rejected."

"I'll pass it on, but I wouldn't hold your breath."

"I stopped holding my breath after the first week in this business. Anyway, let me know if your client would like to consider a settlement that includes sharing reality with the public."

"I think your reality is different than mine."

"How about that. And we're not even politicians."

Gibson chuckled and said, "I'll get back with you concerning our response as soon as I can."

"One more thing," Scott interjected. "We are going to amend the Complaint to include causes of action for retaliation and assault. Your client's security chief, Sean Garner, threatening my clients in an attempt to intimidate them into ending or settling the lawsuit. You might want to tell him that such conduct won't play well to a jury."

"I don't know what you're talking about," Gibson replied, suddenly serious. "I haven't heard anything about this."

"I'll have the Amended Complaint for your review in the next few days and it will include all the particulars. Get ready to be even more surprised."

* * *

## July 6
### 11:30 a.m.

Lee Henry drank coffee in the seating area outside Ida's Coffee Barn, with a view of the busy street. Olivia Blake and Ed Farris walked up to his table with cups of coffee in hand and sat down. "Hi, Lee," Olivia said, smiling.

"Hi, Olivia. Ed." Lee nodded at Farris who returned the nod. "I wanted to update you on what I've learned." They both looked at him without expression. "That is part of our deal, right?"

"Yes, it is."

"Aligor's Security Director, Sean Garner, has been up to no good. First, he lied to you guys."

"About what?"

"He told you the same thing he told me, that he was not at Art Underwood's place the night Underwood went off the fifth-floor balcony."

"And we now know he was there?" Farris asked with interest.

"We do."

"How?" Blake asked.

"Cell phone data places him right where he said he wasn't." He tapped a file in front of him.

Blake narrowed her eyes and asked, "And how did we get that?"

Lee smiled. "I have a few connections."

"Yeah, but we don't have a warrant for that information. The Supreme Court decided a couple of years ago that we can't get that information without a warrant."

"I'm familiar with the Carpenter case," Lee said, grinning. "Which is why it's good that you guys have friends who are outside law enforcement, like me, because private citizens aren't required to get warrants. You guys get tips from citizens are the time."

Blake shook her head and said, "Except that private citizens don't usually call us with cell phone location data. Most informants don't know what that is, and those who do have no way of getting it. If we put statements in subpoena affidavits that we got cell phone location data from an anonymous caller, the judge would find it absurd and probably decide that we lied in our affidavits, call us in and rake us over the coals before referring us for an Internal Affairs investigation or prosecution for perjury."

Farris added, "Citizens with information tell us about a piece of physical evidence or name a witness. They never happen to have cell location data."

"Details," Lee said. "There are a few of us who find a way." He took a sip of coffee. "So, now you take the information you have about Garner, including the fact that there was a guy who looked like him on the closed circuit video you reviewed and I'll leave it to you to figure out how to use that information to get the warrant you don't have yet. If you can do that, you know that warrant will lead you to learn that Garner lied to you."

Blake shook her head. "Interesting, but it's not enough. We aren't the FBI so there is no statute that makes it a crime to lie to us. People do it all the time."

"I agree," Lee replied. "But when it gets to trial it can be pretty damn powerful when the jury learns that the defendant lied about key issues, right?"

"True, but so far we still don't have enough to get anywhere near a trial. The fact that he lied about being at the building isn't a crime by itself."

"Figure out a way to turn the information I've given you into a phone company warrant, and then you'll get the cell location data through conventional means. You should also know that Sean Garner has been harassing Marty Cardenas and Justin Palmer, attempting to intimidate them into dismissing their case. That course of intimidation includes breaking into Palmer's house."

"What did he do there?"

"Waited for Palmer to come home and then told him that security systems don't really protect people like everyone thinks they do."

"Okay," Farris said. "We have a possible assault. Got anything else? I mean, how else does he intimidate them?"

"Showing up at all hours to see them in public places and point out that things will not go well for them."

Blake considered and then said. "We'll keep on the Underwood investigation and see what else turns up, but unless you want some kind of misdemeanor charge that likely won't go anywhere, we can't take him down based on what there is so far."

Lee smiled. "I get it. I'm just keeping you guys in the loop like I said I would. What you do with the information is up to you."

"We will submit affidavits to try for a warrant to get the cell data you've already got," Blake offered. "Let us know if you find anything else."

"Have you got anything to share?" Lee asked.

"No, we don't have anything that you don't."

"Call me when you find something. This is still a two-way street, right?"

"Yeah, that's right," Farris replied. "That is the deal."

Blake smiled and said, "This is a pretty strange arrangement. We are not used to sharing information with private investigators. Normally we tell them not to mess with the investigation. With you, well there is the arrangement Chuck Miller made and then there is the fact that you've given us more than we've given you." She paused and said, "It's also pretty obvious that you know how to handle yourself. Besides," she added, "if we told you to back off, you wouldn't do it anyway."

"I think that sums it up pretty well," Lee replied. He tossed his coffee cup into a nearby trashcan. "See you later. I've got another appointment."

"Okay, thanks, Lee," Farris offered.

When Lee left, Blake looked at Farris and said, "I was wrong about that guy. He is on his game."

Farris nodded. "I agree. He is also pretty unrestrained. It's hard to predict what a guy like that will do next."

Blake nodded. "That's for sure. Although I don't think I know anyone else like him."

"Me either. Imagine being able to move in the shadows with no rules?"

"It's a cop's dream come true, partner."

# Chapter Twelve

Justin and Marty sat in Brambles' Bar on stools that were no longer entirely vertical. The combined effect of large men and fifty years of operation had taken their toll. The bar was dinged and scratched and its operator, Floyd, was eighty and still tending bar. The place was the poster child for deferred maintenance, but its personality was undeniable.

"I've got to get out of here," Justin said.

"We've only been here for twenty minutes and I was looking forward to a second beer."

"I know, but after ten minutes on these seats I realize that my butt is just not shaped that way." They both chuckled. "Besides, I've got a date with Jessica at 7:00."

Marty nodded. "You seem pretty serious about her."

Justin grinned. "Yeah, I guess I am. I love being with her, man. She just might be the keeper."

"That's great news, buddy." Marty was quiet for a moment, and then said, "Do you think our case is going to settle?"

"Nope. I mean Scott didn't think so either when we met with him to discuss the settlement demand. Part of me would sure like to see that happen," Justin added.

"I know what you mean. The litigation is stressful and it's screwing with our ability to get new work."

"Not to mention the batshit crazy stuff from Sean Garner."

"Yeah, not to mention that. That guy is…" Marty's words were interrupted by Justin's cellphone.

Justin looked down at the phone and said, "It's Jessica. I'm going to take it, okay?"

"Sure."

"Hi, Jess. I hope you're not calling to cancel our date this evening." There was a silence and then Justin said "What?" and his eyes grew wide. "Holy shit, I'll be right there."

"What is it?" Marty asked, concerned.

"I think Garner is sitting outside her apartment building watching her."

"I'll follow you over there," Marty said. Justin nodded and threw a ten on the bar as they raced outside to the parking lot.

They moved down the freeway as fast as traffic would allow. Justin stayed on the phone with Jessica, who pulled back the drapes to periodically glance at Sean Garner standing on her sidewalk and staring directly up at her apartment. At Justin's insistence, she hung up and dialed 911 and told the dispatcher of the man outside staring at her. He hadn't done anything yet, but he had appeared before and she felt it was threatening.

Justin and Marty exited the freeway and made their way down busy streets. When they pulled onto Jessica's street, the lights of two police cars illuminated the night. They parked behind the police cars and walked up the driveway. Three uniformed officers and Jessica stood in the entryway, and she periodically glanced towards the street.

The police officers looked their way as they approached. "It's okay," Jessica said, watching their reaction. "That's my boyfriend."

"Is everything okay?" Justin asked.

"Yeah, he left before the officers got here," Jessica offered, and then threw her arms around Justin. "He just stood there… staring. He was truly creepy."

"I'm so sorry, sweetheart. This guy this all about intimidation and trying to pressure us on behalf of the Company."

"I'm not used to having some guy just stand and stare at me. Right before these officers got here, I went outside to talk to him. As I approached him, he moved away. It was all a little unnerving."

"If you have a suspicious character outside, ma'am, don't go out there. You never know what you're going to get," the tallest of the officers instructed.

"At the time I just thought I could figure out what was happening. It wasn't overtly threatening, I mean the guy never spoke. It was just all so weird," Jessica said.

"There will be a report on file, ma'am. If anything should happen, call us right away."

"Yes, I will," Jessica said, putting an arm around Justin.

"Have a good day folks," one of the officers said and they walked toward their cars. "We're not far away if something should happen."

As they watched the police walk away Justin asked, "Are you okay?"

"Yes, really. It wasn't all that bad. I just wasn't sure what I was getting into."

"I think he is dangerous, Jessica. The same guy who left the note on my car."

"Santa?" Jessica asked.

"Yeah, Santa," Justin replied, and Marty stared at them trying to figure out where the conversation had taken a turn that he couldn't follow. "By the way," Justin added, "weird circumstances for an introduction, but this is my good friend Marty Cardenas."

"Hi, Marty. I've heard good things about you, and I've been looking forward to meeting you."

"Yes, likewise," Marty offered. "I believe that you have done good things for the happiness quotient of my friend here."

"That would be mutual," she replied, looking at Justin and smiling. "Please, come in for a few minutes."

"I don't want to delay your date," Marty said, before committing.

"It's fine, Marty. Really, come in for a little while."

As they walked into Jessica's apartment, she asked, "How about a beer, guys?"

"That sounds great, if you guys don't mind me staying for a little longer."

"We don't mind," Jessica offered.

As she moved into the kitchen, Marty said, "She's really great, man."

"Yeah, she is amazing."

He paused a moment and then Marty said, "I sure don't like Garner showing up here."

"Yeah. It's Garner's latest not too subtle message conveying that he knows where I'm vulnerable."

"There has to be some way out of this," Marty replied, shaking his head. "It just keeps getting crazier. I say we take it all public right away."

Jessica came back into the living room carrying three beers and handed one to each of them. "Thanks," Marty said.

"Yeah, thank you, Jessica."

"You guys are looking pretty serious," she replied, smiling. "Don't worry, I've never been afraid of Santa, not even the Stephen King version we seem to be witnessing."

\* \* \*

After the three disappeared into the apartment building, Sean Garner extricated himself from a hedge across the street that had provided cover as he watched. He smiled to himself and began making his way back to his car, satisfied that the move had been just enough to let Justin Palmer know that his new love could be a target; that they were all vulnerable whenever Sean decided to make his move. He was confident he was wearing down their defenses. Soon they would realize that the only way to be safe was to settle their lawsuit and move on. Little by little, like moves in a chess game, he would expose their weaknesses and move in for the kill; unless they resigned first.

Sean was feeling good as he climbed into his car. It had been another good day. He knew that he had to keep denying any involvement with Art Underwood's death but part of him wanted them to know he had been involved, so that they knew what they were up against and what they risked if they didn't comply with his demands. Still, he drove home feeling satisfied. He wasn't far from the day that Mr. Cook would be meeting with him in private to share good bourbon and discuss his new salary and bonus structure. It was all close at hand.

Sean pulled into his driveway, pushed the visor button and waited as the garage door opened. He closed the door behind him and walked through the interior garage door into the kitchen, immediately feeling that something was wrong. The familiar sound of the chirping alarm as he entered the room was conspicuously absent. He moved cautiously through the dark house without turning on any lights. There was no sound and room by room, he found that the house was empty.

He moved back to the kitchen and flipped two light switches. He poured himself a bourbon and threw it back, feeling it warm his throat. It was then that he saw the typewritten note at the kitchen table. He found himself looking around. Stupid. He had just searched the house and he knew no one was here. He walked over to the note. Picking it up, he read, "You were right. Alarms are entirely an illusion and easily penetrated. They provide a false sense of security to those who aren't secure at all. Anyway, Sean, don't forget that you are going to be held accountable for what you've done. Karma comes knocking." Behind the note was a picture of Art and Sandi Underwood looking into each other eyes and sharing the smiles of lovers.

Sean felt his blood pressure rise. He knew who had done this — the face and the name. He wanted to scream. He picked up his glass and threw it across the room, watching it shatter against the wall. That son of a bitch had been in his house, taunting him and throwing down a gauntlet. Lee Henry was going to find out that he was in over his head.

* * *

**July 7**
**1:12 p.m.**
Scott drove through town on his way to Westwood, where he was meeting with a lawyer and his client who wanted him to assume the role of lead counsel on a sexual harassment case shortly before trial. His cell rang and he picked it up. "Scott Winslow."

"Hi, Scott. Doug Gibson."

"You tracked me down, just when I thought you'd never find me." There was silence. "I'm kidding."

"Your office said you'd probably want to talk to me as soon as possible so they gave me your cell number."

"I figured that, and I'll get even with them later."

Gibson chuckled, unsure whether that was really a joke. "Anyway, I have a response to your settlement demand."

"Lay it on me," Scott said.

"They will pay each of your guys $150,000 for full release and confidentiality agreement."

"What about part two?" Scott asked.

"There is no part two."

"Which means your guys want to go on lying to the public about the efficacy of their product."

"Let's not have that discussion again," Gibson replied. "It doesn't get us any- where."

"That's true. I'm having trouble making you see the light. The proposed settlement amounts are too low, but there is an even bigger problem. You can tell your client that there will be no confidentiality agreement and no settlement unless making the public aware of the real test trial results is part of the deal."

"They already have," Gibson said, testily. "Your clients are trying to fabricate a new reality."

"Here we go again," Scott said. "You have our position. I don't see any sense in mediating the case if your people aren't prepared to address the inaccurate test results they continue to publish."

There was a pause and then Gibson asked, "Are you saying there is no way you'll ever have your clients sign a confidentiality agreement in connection with this case?"

"Nope, I'm not saying that. They will sign a confidentiality agreement provided part of the agreement is that the public is given accurate and complete test results. Like I said before, we don't even need you to tell anybody your client did anything wrong. Just publish the accurate numbers and identify the results as the final numbers so that potential buyers know what they are buying. Tell the world recalculations were in order, that certain results were disqualified or that divine intervention led to correction of these final conclusions."

"Like I said, we don't agree that there are inaccuracies so that's not going to happen."

"Maybe some of this will be clarified when I take your client's deposition next week. I'm sure Mr. Cook will be able to shed light on some of the issues."

"I already know what his testimony will be. Perhaps once you've heard how well he comes across your settlement posture will change."

"Perhaps. In any case, we may then be ready to decide if we mediate the case or just go see a jury and see what they think."

"You mean you're not willing to waive jury?" Gibson joked.

"Nope. I'll waive judge, but I'm keeping the jury. In the interim, you know our position. Please pass it on to your client."

"I will pass it on. Take it easy."

"Yeah, you too."

* * *

**July 7**
**4:20 p.m.**
Marty Cardenas always had an eye on the news. In his years with Aligor he was periodically interviewed concerning products being developed and those scheduled for release. He liked journalists and what they did. They are information predators. If you know something newsworthy, they are on the way. If there is something newsworthy about you, look out because they need that too. They are smart and by definition inquisitive, and endlessly persistent.

They are also invaluable because they are the only access to information inside government entities and big corporations. And as soon as the story is uncovered, it is available for public consumption. Suddenly, what was hidden is everywhere — blogs, tweets and cable news interviews over "Breaking News" banners.

If you're the lucky reporter who gets the story, the cable hosts put you on to say what you wrote and what you meant. In that way, no one has to read anything at all. You can be steeped in news filtered through the confirmation bias of your selected source in a prompt and tidy delivery, and all with minimal effort.

Marty Cardenas turned on the news to get the identity of the reporter who was today's winning predator. She was New York Times reporter Lindsay Ackerman, answering questions for Jake Tapper about Aligor Pharmaceutcals' announcement that their amazing new cancer drug, Delexane, was within a couple of weeks of approval by the FDA.

"What will that mean in terms of public access?" Jake inquired.

"We are told that a week after that the FDA approval happens, the drug will be available almost everywhere."

"What about cost?"

"Prices have not been announced, but it may be expensive."

"And tell us why this drug is so different?"

"Well, Jake, Aligor's statement includes information that there were positive test trial results with a stunning sixty-five percent of participants. Sixty-five percent of those taking the drug found tumors shrinking."

"Wow, that's impressive. What else can you tell us about this new drug?" Jake asked Lindsay Ackerman.

"We know that competitors are testing products, but they are behind Aligor in the process. At this point, Delexane's sixty-five percent success rate seems to put it in a league of its own. As a result, there is likely to be a run on the stuff as soon as it hits the market. And apparently, it shrinks tumors in connection with several different types of cancer. It hasn't been released yet and they say the demand is sky high. It looks like Aligor has a winner here."

Marty's emotions were swirling as he watched the report. This was horrible news. The Company was digging in; committing to releasing the drug to the public without fixing the misleading statistics and the release was going to be soon. His anger rose as he considered that they were going to mislead the dying and their families to rake in big bucks before anyone had the opportunity to learn the truth.

And now they had CNN and the other cable news channels to help market the product with a free advertising campaign. Marty found himself some combination of angry and sad. Even though he knew this day was coming, Marty found it hard to believe as he watched it unfold. He had been holding out hope that something would stop them, that they would realize that they needed to fix the statistical lies before they went to market. Now it was clear that there would be no last-minute fix. People would be misled by these statistics and maybe they would they bet their dying breath on this drug. It was despicable in the same way as elder abuse; taking advantage of the most vulnerable who were not in a position to protect themselves.

Marty called Justin but got voicemail. "Hi, Justin. CNN just announced that Aligor is expecting FDA approval of Delexane in the next couple of weeks. They are not hesitating. They are going right at the public with their bullshit. The news release even boasted their sixty-five percent success rate in trials. I want us to do an interview about the bullshit in their statistics. We need to stop these guys from cashing in on the backs of the sick and the dying. If you agree, we'll call Scott and talk to him about getting the truth out there publicly. Call me."

# Chapter Thirteen

**July 8**

**7:10 a.m.**

The intercom was already buzzing.

"Donna, you're in early this morning."

"Yeah, I thought so until I saw you were already here. I wanted to catch up on my review of the subpoenaed records on three different cases so I can get you the initial review memo. By the way, Lee is on line 3."

"Thanks, Donna. You're amazing." Scott punched the line 3 button. "Lee, how are you?"

"I'm good, buddy. I wanted to give you a heads-up because the latest may come back to you in some way. Like through some pissed-off defense lawyer."

"What did you do to whom? Weird question but it gets where I wanted to go."

"I gave Sean Garner a little taste of his own bullshit. I paid a visit to his home, turned off his alarm and left him a note. I figured he should get a feel for how that registered with Justin."

"Uh huh. And what did this note you left him say?"

"Security alarms provide an illusion of security."

"Anything else?"

"Yeah, I pointed out that he would need to account for what he has done, and I left him a picture of Art and Sandi Underwood to contemplate."

"You sure know how to get under someone's skin, Lee."

"Thank you."

"I'm not sure that was a compliment. I just know that whenever you poke a bear, I get some shit from various directions."

"I know, but it's a good trade-off. This asshole plays by intimidation and harassment. Our people don't know how to deal with him, so the intimidation works. Worse yet, this crazy bastard's self-image seems to get bigger every time he engages one of the clients. He needs to know that someone will come take him down." He paused and said, "I'm convinced that he threw Art Underwood off his balcony and if he's going to come after anyone else, I want it to be me rather than Marty or Justin."

"I don't disagree with you but do your best to stop short of getting yourself thrown off the balcony. Good investigators are hard to find, and I've become rather attached to you over the years. Besides, I want to go to your wedding in seventy-four days."

"You know how many days it is?"

"I'm on my game, too, you know. Besides that, my calendar tells me all that."

"Nice."

"Yep. So, don't make a widow of Melissa before the wedding day."

"I don't think that's technically possible."

"Perhaps not. Maybe widow is not the right word, but whatever you call a dead fiancée, Melissa will be upset if you become one of them. Besides, I'm not sure the wedding gift Lisa and I got you is returnable." They laughed and then Scott added, "Thanks for the update. If I hear about it from someone else, I'll try not to smile. I also get the impression you're enjoying torturing this guy."

"I have to admit that I am. He's a bully and I hate that. I also think he has delusions of grandeur, thinking that he's going to get this case dismissed and be the Aligor hero."

"While you're needling this guy, keep in mind that's it better if we get him to back off than if you force a high noon type shootout."

"I hope it works out that way, but I'm not sure. So far this guy isn't giving an inch."

"All right, Gary Cooper, just make sure he draws first."

"You got it."

Scott grinned as he hung up just in time to hear the next intercom buzz. "Hi, Donna."

"Scott, Justin and Marty are here for the appointment you set last night. I saw the Aligor announcement on the news, so I'm not surprised they wanted to see us today."

"Yeah, they are going to push for our blessing to go public with their side of the story."

"Are they going to get it?" Donna said.

"Feeding the press is never what I want to do. Too many ways to have something come back and bite you." He shrugged. "Can you bring them into the conference room and feed them some calming decaf? Then stay for the meeting."

"You got it."

As he walked into the conference room a few minutes later and saw the expressions on his clients' faces, Scott could tell that they were both pretty worked up. Donna gave him a raised eyebrow look that told him the same. "Hi, Marty. Hi, Justin. I guess we have some issues to discuss this morning," Scott offered to begin the meeting.

"You could say that," Marty offered. "We can't stay muzzled anymore, Scott. I know that you believe in trying cases in the courts and not in the press, but there are limits. Aligor is priming the pump to sell record amounts of Delexane. The data that they are publishing is the same misleading bullshit and they are days from distribution. They've even got the news channels reading their promos, so it's a major free advertising campaign."

Scott nodded. "I understand the problem. So how are you guys proposing to handle it?"

"That's easy," Justin responded, sitting forward in his chair. "I've had calls from two reporters in the last twenty-four hours. They want to hear our side of the story and we want to tell it. Otherwise, everyone is saturated with Aligor's version of reality."

"I understand," Scott said thoughtfully. "I saw some of this stuff, too. I didn't hear anyone mention the facts alleged in the complaint, just that there is a whistleblower lawsuit by two former employees who dispute some of what the Company says."

"That's right," Marty agreed. "That's all our side of the story is getting."

"You guys have to know that anything you say in the press is permanent. If you make a single mistake it will be played back over and over until they find your next one."

"But we can't let them get away with this stuff. It's blatantly false and it's getting lots of airtime."

"I get it. It's not that I want to muzzle you guys, it's just that if you make a statement that is incorrect, or even overstate anything, there is a permanent record that can be brought to the jury's attention with the suggestion that you lie when it suits you. That's why talking to the press is so dangerous." He looked at his silent clients and then added, "So, how about if we fashion a statement for release that is built around the allegations of the lawsuit. You know, put it in your own words but stick to the pre-planned points to stay clear of trouble. So, you stick to key facts. You were in executive positions, you were involved in the phase three trials and saw the results first-hand, and you know that the percentage of participants who saw a reduction in tumor size was much lower than the Company is stating. They know it and they fired us for complaining about the issue." Marty and Justin were both furiously scribbling notes as Scott spoke.

"You will then get a question like, 'You're saying that Aligor is lying?' Your response is that 'I'm saying that they are giving you inaccurate information. You can decide for yourself whether they are doing so on purpose, but they had the real results.' You then state that the reported should review the lawsuit for the facts and decline further questions. How does that work for you guys?"

Marty nodded. "I like it. I take your point about how it can be dangerous, so I like this approach."

"Justin, how about you?"

Justin wore a thoughtful expression. He reflected a moment and then said, "Yeah, I'll do my best to stick with that narrative," he said with a grin.

Scott gave him a look and he said, "Okay. Count me in and I'm returning reporter phone calls this morning. Breaking news ahead CNN."

"Do it this afternoon. Give me a couple of hours to email ideas to share and statements to avoid, then have at it."

"That works," Justin replied nodding.

"Marty?"

"Yeah, okay."

"All right, guys, we have a plan. If they call me I will add that you were fired for complaining that the Company was not being accurate with the phase three trial results and I will be happy to provide a copy of the lawsuit to anyone who wants to read these incredibly serious allegations."

"This is a relief," Marty said. "I think we are ready to go and I'm feeling optimistic for the first time in a while."

"I'm with you," Justin added. "Let's go make a splash."

After the clients shook hands with Scott and Donna and walked from the conference room, Donna gave Scott a smile.

"What?" he asked.

"Nothing. I just didn't think you were going to endorse this plan."

"What the hell," Scott replied, "the other side isn't hesitating to spill total bullshit across the country. These guys should have the chance to be heard, so long as we have control of the message."

"I like the idea," Donna said. "I think that they should be heard, and I think it might make a difference to the jury pool that will be affected by Aligor's statements."

As Justin walked back to his car, feeling good, his phone rang, and he didn't recognize the number.

He hit the answer button and said, "Justin Palmer."

"Mr. Palmer, this is Jane Curtis with Mandeville Drug Company. We are looking for a new product manager and one of our people, Don Nelson, got word that you might be interested. Is that right?"

"Yes, perhaps so."

"Can you come and meet with our management team tomorrow?"

"Tell me what time and I'll be there," he responded, feeling hopeful for the first time in a long time.

* * *

## July 9
### 7:00 a.m.

Sean rang the bell adjacent to massive double doors, giving rise to the sounds of a grandfather clock chiming the hour. The door was opened promptly, and he could see through the open wall of windows into the park-like yard. "Follow me, sir," a woman wearing an apron and a serious expression offered and then turned and walked through the house. He followed her through the open wall of windows to the extensive porch and its marble flooring, statuettes and overview all the way to Lake Sherwood. Roland Cook sat at a table drinking coffee with a thoughtful expression. He didn't stand as Sean arrived. "Sit, please, Sean."

Sean selected a seat that allowed a marvelous lake view and said, "Good morning, sir."

This time no coffee was offered. Cook started by leaning back in his chair and giving Sean a disapproving look. "Sean, we can't have this," Cook directed unhappily.

"Sir?"

"I assume that you've heard the latest news surrounding Delexane? Cardenas and Palmer were each interviewed by the press and said that the numbers we are relating are false." He shook his head. "One of the interviewers concluded by stating that what these well-placed executives had to say raise some serious questions as the product is about to be released. We can't have that, Sean. And as I understood it, you were going to do what it takes to make this case go away. Isn't that what you told me?"

"Yes, sir, and I feel like I've been making progress. It's just that…"

Cook interrupted, "Progress? You call this progress? These guys are all over cable raining on our parade. The stock actually slid this morning based on the doubt they are creating." He shook his head. "I thought that you could handle this, Sean. I mean, we're prepared to settle the case, and you were supposed to be motivating them to be reasonable. They are telling our lawyers that there will be no settlement unless it includes our obligation to retract our stated results and adopt their numbers. So how much have you motivated them, Sean?"

"I know that they are getting nervous, so it's moving in the right direction."

"Not that I can tell from the video clips of their interviews." Cook ran both hands through his hair. He was clearly agitated. "Do I need to get someone else involved in handling this project, Sean? We are about to release the product and we don't need this negative energy around it." He shook his head. "I made it clear that this could be big for your career and that your reward would be substantial; substantial enough to live in this neighborhood and have your own lake view. But, if you're not up for the task, then we will find other ways to motivate settlement."

"I am up for the task, sir. I can move it along faster."

Cook was quiet for a time and then he said, "I'm disappointed, Sean. I can give you a few more days. If we don't have measurable progress within that time, I'm going to have to pull you from this project and give it to someone else."

Sean nodded. "I can do it. You'll see the progress you want for sure."

"All right, Sean. Just know that this is your last shot."

"Yes, sir," Sean replied.

"That's all for now."

"Yes, sir, "Sean said again. He stood and walked back through the house stinging from the rebuke. He couldn't lose all that this project and what it would bring him. He told himself that he had to make something happen quickly. He had three or four days, so something better start happening now. As he walked to his car, he looked around at the magnificent homes that surrounded him, all on two or three acre lots. He was going to pull off this coup, or he was going to be buried in corporate mediocrity with no chance at making this his neighborhood. He looked around again at the colonials with massive columns and the beautiful cape cod style homes with four and five dormer windows. There was no doubt in his mind that this was going to be his neighborhood. He would make it happen, starting today.

* * *

**July 9**
**3:15 p.m.**
Justin walked into 5515 Flower Street, where he was going to have his first interview since being fired by Aligor. He signed in at the guard station and took the elevator to the twenty-ninth floor. As the elevator door opened, Justin could see the words 'Mandeville Drug Company' in four-foot letters on the wall. To his right was a secure door to a hallway and on his left was a receptionist and waiting area. After checking in with the receptionist, Justin sat down on one of the couches to wait. Less than a minute later, the receptionist said, "If you will follow me, Mr. Nelson will see you now."

Justin nodded and followed her down a corridor that led to countless window offices on his left and interior offices on his right. She deposited him half-way down the corridor, sticking her head into a large office and saying, "Here is Mr. Palmer."

Nelson stood and shook hands with Justin. He looked about forty and wore a big smile and a mop of hair that was almost combed. "Hi, Justin. Take a seat," he offered. As he sat Justin glanced at the surrounding office, he could see that Nelson was making the transition to electronic files slower than most. Reports, files and other documents were piled on his desk, credenza and the other visitor chair.

"Hi, Don. I appreciate you thinking of me and it's good to see you again."

"Yeah, you too. I remembered your good work when we worked together on the Product Development Standards Committee, so I thought of you immediately when the Product Marketing Director position opened up." He handed Justin a two-page document containing an overview description of the position. "This will be familiar to you," Nelson said.

Justin scanned the position description and nodded. "It is," Justin replied. "It's what I do."

"Yeah, it's perfect," Nelson offered. "When I told my boss that I thought we should talk to you about the position, he was more than a little interested. Do you know Jerrod Nichols, our Senior Vice President of Marketing and Sales?"

"I've met him once or twice," Justin said.

"Well, he thinks highly of you. He says if you want the job then we should extend an offer."

"Wonderful," Justin replied with a smile. "I am very interested."

Nelson nodded. "The only thing you have to do is get rid of your case with Aligor."

"What?" Justin asked.

Nelson shrugged. "Justin, it's political. We do some contract work for Aligor products. It's only about five percent of our business, but it's five percent the board doesn't want to lose."

"Well, that's disappointing," Justin said. "I really think I would be a good fit here."

"We think so too, man. Like I say, I have the green light to negotiate salary and benefits with you and I don't think you would be disappointed."

"But the lawsuit has to disappear, or you find someone else."

Nelson nodded slowly. "That's what I've been told."

Justin nodded. "Tell me what you have in mind for the salary."

"We're prepared to offer $185,000 plus annual stock options of five hundred shares per year and a 401K, and we'll contribute what you do up to five percent of salary per year."

Justin nodded. "We are definitely in the right ballpark here. I just have to think about what I do with the case. I'd feel better if getting rid of the case wasn't a job requirement."

"Yeah, I know," Nelson offered, with an understanding nod. "That's somebody else's requirement. I just know that I want you here."

Justin smiled. "Thanks, Don. I really appreciate that." He stood and shook hands with Nelson. "How long do I have to figure out what to do with the case?"

"You're the one we want, so I can keep the job open for two or three weeks if I know you're coming. But I need a commitment in the next few days or I'll have to talk to other candidates. Here's my card. I wrote my cell number on it so you can call me over the weekend."

"Got it," Justin said. "Let me give it some thought, and I'll get back to you."

"Great," Nelson replied. "I hope to be working with you, Justin."

As he walked from Nelson's office, Justin the anxiety of competing demands. He wanted this job, but he couldn't just give up on the lawsuit. Maybe a settlement could be reached, he thought. And there was something else needling him, something in the back of his mind that said it wasn't right that his hiring should be conditional on his eliminating his lawsuit against Aligor.

When Justin left the office, Don Nelson dialed a number and waited.

"How did it go?" a voice asked.

"Very well. I mean he's well-qualified and I want him on our team."

"Good, what about the lawsuit?"

"He's thinking about that, Sean. He wants to find a way to make this work."

"Mr. Cook considers this a personal favor, Don. He won't forget it and Aligor won't forget it."

"Happy to help out. Like I say, I'd like to have him here, so I hope it all works out."

"Let me know when he gets back to you to confirm he's going to get rid of his lawsuit and come to work for Mandeville."

"You got it."

\* \* \*

By the time Justin reached his car he felt burdened by the weight of the decision. He desperately wanted to get back to work and to be able to focus on doing what he was made to do, but there was something wrong with conditioning his employment on ending his lawsuit against Aligor. He pulled out his phone and called Marty.

"Hi Justin. How was the interview?"

"Okay, I guess. I'm really not sure."

"Did they offer you a job?"

"They did."

"Is it a good one?"

"Seems like it."

"Well, that's great. Congratulations, buddy."

"I'm not sure it's that great."

"Why?"

"They are conditioning the job offer on my ending my lawsuit against Aligor."

"You're kidding? Why should they care about your claims against someone else?"

"Apparently, five percent of their business is through their contracts with Aligor."

Marty was quiet for a time and then asked. "That puts you in a tough situation. What are you going to do?"

"I don't know. I told them I had to think about it before I made my decision. I want the job, but I don't feel good about the condition."

"I get it. I wouldn't like that either." Marty paused and then added, "You have to do what you think is best, so you won't get any pressure from me."

"I appreciate that. I think I'll be torturing myself about this decision over the weekend."

"Call me and let me know what you decide."

"You'll be the first." Justin was quiet for a moment and then added, "Even if I do this, if we both don't settle, I'll still be a witness for you."

"I appreciate that," Marty said. "I hope they don't squeeze you to prevent you from doing that."

"There's no way, man. They can squeeze all day. I will be there to testify. Anyway, I'll call you as soon as I figure this out."

"I'll be waiting." Marty paused and then added, "You have to do what's right, Justin. No hard feelings if you decide you need to walk away from the lawsuit."

"Thanks for saying that. No matter what, I want us to stay friends."

"We will, whatever you decide."

\* \* \*

## July 9
### 5:45 p.m.

Scott was going to get out of the office by 5:15 so that he could meet Lisa, Katy and Joey for dinner at 5:30. He made a few last-minute additions to his to-do list for several different cases and then grabbed his jacket. The phone rang and he looked at the number. He recognized Doug Gibson's direct line and hesitated. Then he picked up. "What's happening, Doug?"

"Hi, Scott. Some good news. I have $225,000 for each of your guys to settle the case."

"What about part two? The public correction of what has been put out there."

"Nope. Just the money and a release. Anyway, tell them and let's see if we can get this case settled."

"I'll tell them, but I won't recommend it."

"You have my cell. Call me if you want to talk further about resolving the case."

"I'll find you if there's anything to talk about," Scott replied and hung up.

Scott raced to the elevator, glancing at his watch. He was now twenty minutes late for dinner and he hadn't made it to the car yet. As the elevator doors opened on the ground floor, Katy stood there with her hand on her hip, the perfect picture of indignance. "You're late, Dad. But we knew you would be, so we came here."

Scott grinned at his eight-year-old with all the answers and looked around to see Lisa grinning and Joey throwing a tennis ball into the air. "Hi, late man," Lisa offered. She gave him a kiss and said, "Your own private welcoming party." She looked around and said, "Joey, don't throw that so high. I don't want you to hit one of the light fixtures." It was just like home.

"Hi, Joe. Come over here and give me a hug, dude."

"Wait. Two more throws."

With that, they walked over to the garage elevators and waited for a ride to their right. Scott smiled widely. It was already a great family dinner.

* * *

## July 10
### 11:05 a.m.
Justin usually loved Saturday mornings — unscheduled time that could be spent on any project he desired, or on nothing at all. But today wasn't one of those fun and relaxing mornings. He had been torturing himself about the job with Mandeville. He wanted to get back to work and he wanted that job. In addition, his bank account could use a little help. At the same time, it was eating at him that his lawsuit against Aligor had to go away before they would hire him. It was one more example of how the industry was controlled by a few conglomerates. If you were at odds with one of the monsters, all doors closed tightly, and you were shut out. They deprived you of the oxygen you needed when they fired you, and then they made sure the paramedics never came to your aid.

After having suffered a fitful night of obsession, Justin made his decision. He was not going to have someone else decide he needed to end his lawsuit with Aligor as a condition to hiring him. Bringing this lawsuit was standing up for what was right, and he would not lay down just to get another job. He called Marty and shared his decision and then he called Don Nelson and advised he could not join them if it meant he had to give up the lawsuit. Don said he understood but sounded disappointed. It was done and Justin felt the relief that comes with making a tough decision and then realizing that that decision felt right. He called Jessica and told her what he had decided, and she was supportive, as he knew she would be. They made a plan that Justin would pick her up at 6:30 p.m. for dinner and his sense of relief was complete. It was going to be a good day after all.

# Chapter Fourteen

They were to meet with the doctors again in a couple of days and Emma had a sense of foreboding about the meeting. In her gut, she knew that Christopher was not doing better. Her father was her best and brightest remaining ray of hope. He had said that he would help, yet nothing had happened yet. She had seen a news report that the FDA was set to bless Aligor's new drug, Delexane, in a matter of days, and as CEO of Aligor, her dad could get it for her quickly. Roland Cook controlled the product with the best odds of saving his grandson.

She dialed the phone and waited. On the second ring it was answered, "Hello, dear."

"Hi, Mom."

"Will I see you this weekend?"

"Yes, I think so." She paused and said, "Is Dad there?"

"No, he's at work. He never gets home this early."

Emma hesitated and then said, "Mom, I called to talk about Dad's new drug. He said he was going to help us, but nothing has happened."

Helen Cook drew her identity from her role as Roland Cook's wife. She had never been employed in her own right but was a hostess for her husband's business contacts whenever there was need. There were frequent cocktail parties at the Cooks' elaborate home, featuring catered dinners and important players in the pharmaceutical industry and political circles. She had always been the 'stand by your man' kind of woman.

"He will help you, Emma. He told me that he will."

"But when? Christopher is not getting any better and we really need him to do something now." She knew her frustration was showing, but it couldn't be helped. "I'm really worried, Mom. I called Dad a couple of days ago and then again this morning, but he hasn't called me back yet."

"You know how busy he is, sweetheart." Her mother was someone who felt duty-bound to protect her father from any incoming negative comments or even thoughts.

Emma was incensed at the suggestion that her father was too busy to save his grandson's life. She took a deep breath before gathering herself and saying, "I know Mom, but this is about the most important thing in our lives."

"I'll talk to him tonight, sweetheart. I know he will help Christopher in every way he can."

"Have him call me as soon as you can."

"I will. Give Christopher a hug for grandma, okay?"

"Okay."

\* \* \*

## July 10
### 5:40 p.m.

Justin swapped jeans for slacks, put on a long-sleeved shirt and his black leather jacket. He checked himself in the mirror and gave a nod of approval. He felt the excitement of spending the evening with Jessica. He looked forward to holding her hand and to walking down the street towards the restaurant, browsing store windows as they walked. Being with Jessica was becoming a priority — she was direct, intelligent and she made him smile. He wanted all of that right now.

Justin made sure all of the doors were locked and flipped the alarm switch, reflecting on the fact that doing so had not kept Sean Garner out in the past, and then made his way to the garage. He backed the car out and scanned the neighborhood, assuring himself that there was no one ready to break into the house as he pulled away. All was in order. He started down the street and in his rear-view mirror noticed a dark sedan pulling away from the curb behind him. He drove to the corner and made a right turn. The sedan followed. He made the next left and it stayed with him. He stopped at a traffic light and made a U-turn when the light changed to green. The sedan followed. He made two more lefts and the sedan was suddenly gone. He felt an immense sense of relief and then wondered if he was ever followed at all, or whether it was simply heightened paranoia in the wake of his encounters with Sean Garner.

Justin entered the freeway and made his way to Jessica's, his thoughts returning to his decision not to end his lawsuit for the price of a new job. It was the right decision. Not because of what he might get out of the lawsuit, but out of the need to make Aligor accountable and to deny their seemingly unlimited reach. Justin told himself that there would be other opportunities that didn't require him to protect Aligor. He pulled off the freeway, glancing in the rearview once again. No sign of the dark sedan. He shook his head. It's amazing what the mind can do. A short time later he pulled into the parking area of Jessica's apartment building and found an open parking place marked 'visitor.' He would talk to Jessica about his decision to decline the job offer and she would be honest with him about what she thought.

Justin climbed out of the car and had taken about ten steps towards the apartment building when he noticed it. The dark sedan had stopped right behind his car and two men got out of the car and ran towards him. They were each carrying something. He raised his hands in a defensive posture and asked, "What do you want?" as the first man swung a tire-iron that connected with his midsection. He doubled over and the other man connected with his shoulder. One more across his back and Justin hit the ground, where he was struck and kicked repeatedly. His midsection, his back, his shoulders, and then a blow to the head. A distant voice said, "What did you do?" just as Justin lost consciousness. The two men turned and ran, leaving him bleeding on the pavement.

A young man saw Justin and ran over to him. His face was bloodied, and he wasn't moving. The young man called 911 and gave a description of what he saw and his location, as others started to gather. Jessica came out of the building to wait for Justin and saw the commotion. As she walked over to the growing crowd, she saw him on the ground, bloodied and broken. She ran calling his name, but he was unresponsive. She sat on the ground with Justin's head on her lap. He wasn't breathing. Someone handed her a jacket to place under his head as she began to administer CPR, pushing hard on his chest in rhythm and calling to him. "Justin. Justin please wake up." She pumped at his chest, working desperately to restore function to his lungs.

A minute later, an ambulance and a fire truck pulled up and the paramedics came running towards her carrying medical bags. "Let me take over, ma'am," a very young man with short hair and determined eyes told her. She moved and he began to work on Justin's chest. Jessica watched in disbelief as the two paramedics took turns keeping the CPR going. There was a sudden gasp and a sputter and Justin was coughing and then breathing. The crowd broke into applause as his breath returned. Without wasting a moment, the EMT's monitored Justin's vitals, assessed his injuries and hooked him up to an IV. His neck was stabilized with a board and he was loaded into the back of the ambulance.

"Are you his wife?" the paramedic asked.

"Girlfriend," she said.

"Do you want to ride with him to the hospital?"

"Yes," she said, nodding, a fearful expression on her face.

"All right. If he wakes up, yours is the first face he should see." One of the paramedics turned to Jessica and offered her a hand. He helped her into the ambulance, and she took a seat beside Justin and took his hand.

The paramedic working on Justin spoke to some disembodied voice in an emergency medical facility as they raced towards the hospital.

"Is he going to be okay?" Jessica posed through tears.

"I hope so, ma'am, but he has significant injuries that need to be assessed in a hospital."

As much as he loved to hold her hand, it seemed that he could feel nothing; no movement and his breathing had become shallow. She said a prayer as the ambulance made its way through town. She had no idea and didn't care which hospital they were going to, she just wanted to get there in time.

The ambulance screamed through the streets, slowing for red lights and racing around corners. It came to a stop and the EMT who drove was almost instantly at the back of the ambulance, pulling the gurney out and bringing its legs down so that Justin's elevation barely changed. The EMT's stationed themselves back and front of the gurney and raced through the emergency room doors. As they entered, an ER doctor joined them and asked them to update. He asked questions and they responded as they raced into one of the emergency bays. The doctor examined Justin and then said, "I want a CT and an MRI of his head. We need to know what kind of damage this wound did."

"I'll set it up," a nurse said and raced away towards the bank of desks that surrounded the examining rooms.

The doctor turned to Jessica and asked what had happened. She described how she had found him, collapsed on the pavement, no longer breathing.

"He has suffered some serious blunt force trauma injuries. My guess is that he was attacked with one or more metal objects, like a crowbar." He paused and wiped his brow. Then he said, "We are going to do some testing." He pointed to a door and said, "That's our waiting room. As soon as we have some information for you, we'll come and find you. It may be a couple of hours before we have anything to report."

"He's going to be okay, right?"

"I can't tell you too much about the degree of injury yet, but one thing is sure, he is better than the way you found him. He is breathing entirely on his own."

\* \* \*

## July 10
### 8:45 p.m.

As the nine o'clock hour approached, Justin's waiting room had filled up. His support group now included Marty and Abby Cardenas, Scott and Lisa Winslow, and Lee Henry and Melissa Carter. Jessica relayed the story of the gathering crowd and how she found Justin beaten and no longer breathing. She praised the EMT's who got him breathing again and everyone hugged her and gave her encouragement. The clock seemed to have slowed almost to a stop as the waited to learn what the tests would reveal. All seven sat in the interior waiting room, periodically glancing at giant wall clock, pacing and sharing agonized looks as they awaited word about Justin's injuries, or at least some assurance that he would pull through.

They repeatedly looked to the door where the doctor was going to emerge to give then an update whenever there was the slightest sound from that direction, which prompted another round of shared, worried glances and clock-watching. A half-hour later, the doorway opened and a doctor wearing blue scrubs and a mask pulled down around her chin approached, Jessica found herself shaking.

"Are you all here for Justin Palmer?" she asked and drew nods from around the room. "I'm Dr. Morris, I've been administering the testing."

"Is he going to be okay?" Jessica asked.

The doctor's face was anything but reassuring as she carefully chose her words. "He has three broken ribs and a punctured lung, all of which he should recover from over time. The bigger problem is head injury. We've done both a CT and an MRI. We do not see signs of brain injury, but he suffered a hematoma during the attack, and we are going to have to perform surgery to drain the hematoma." The doctor looked around at concerned faces nodding their understanding, and then looked at Jessica and asked, "Are you his wife?"

"No, I'm his girlfriend."

"Is there a relative present? We want to get a consent for the surgery."

There were concerned expressions around the room as the information was digested. Jessica replied, "His mom passed away last year, and I have no idea where his father is at this point. He has no brothers and sisters."

The doctor nodded. "I understand." Surgery needed to be performed and she wanted someone's consent, so she asked Jessica, "Will you sign the consent forms?"

"If you say it's needed, I will, yes." She was quiet for a moment and then said, "I'm familiar with the term hematoma, but I'm not precisely sure I know specifically what it is, I mean medically. I've always thought of it like a bruise inside the skin. Is that right?" Jessica asked with concern.

"You are on the right track. A hematoma occurs when a larger blood vessel is damaged. When the blood vessel wall is broken, blood leaks into the surrounding tissue. Sometimes, like in this case, the accumulation of blood where it shouldn't be can create a danger of pressure and swelling on the brain. So, we want to go in and drain the hematoma to eliminate the blood build up and prevent increased pressure on Justin's brain."

Jessica looked around nervously and saw the nods of acknowledgment.

"Is it a high percentage surgery?" Scott asked. "I mean, how dangerous is the procedure?"

"All such surgery poses some risk," Dr. Morris replied, and then added, "but the location of this hematoma makes it less perilous than many. While I can't make guarantees, I feel pretty good about our chances of success here."

"I'll sign whatever you need," Jessica said. "I want him back, so take good care of him," she added with worried eyes.

Dr. Morris gave her understanding smile, empathizing with Jessica's fear. "We will do our best. It may be three or four more hours before I can report again. If you want to go, we can take your phone number and call you."

Jessica shook her head. "I'll be right here," she urged. "I'm not going anywhere."

There were nods of agreement all around the room. The doctor gave a nod and walked out the way she had come.

"Scott and Lisa, you can go home for the kids and I could call you," Jessica offered.

"Nope. We have a sitter who will spend the night and we are going to stay right here with you," Lisa replied. Scott nodded in agreement.

"We're here to stay as well," Marty said. "I don't think there's a chance we could sleep a wink tonight anyway."

\* \* \*

**July 10**
**10:30 p.m.**
Sean Garner turned off the television and made his way down the hall. Time to get a little sleep. Tomorrow was going to be a big day — the day Palmer and Cardenas decided that they needed to settle their case and move on with their lives. The confrontation that had been scheduled for earlier this evening was going to make clear that they had no choice. Sean shed his clothing and moved into the bathroom. His cell phone rang. He stared at the unfamiliar number for a time and then hit a button, "Yes."

"Mr. Garner?"

"Yes."

"Something went wrong this evening," a man with a deep voice said, sounding distressed.

"What do you mean? And why are you calling me?" Sean did not want to hear this, and he didn't want to hear from whoever this was.

"He was hit in the head. I don't think he was breathing."

"What? Why would you do that?"

"It wasn't me. It was the other guy. But I couldn't reach my contact and I thought you should know. I'm not sure if he's still alive."

"Jesus Christ." Sean felt a rising sense of panic. "This call never happened and don't ever call me again." Sean hung up and put a hand over his face. This was going to be news. These fucking idiots killed Palmer. They were supposed to be the best at what they did. He needed to get word to Mr. Cook, so Cook wasn't blindsided by the morning news. Should he call or should he go over there? He dialed a number and waited. There was no response. The voicemail message was simply a generic "No one is available at this time."

"Call me," Sean said. "It's important that I talk to you before the morning news breaks." Sean hung up, reflecting on the call. It was okay because he had not spoken Cook's name or his own. He thought again about the message he had just received. Maybe it wasn't all that bad. Justin Palmer had been attacked and killed in some random event that had nothing to do with Sean or Aligor. Half of the lawsuit would be gone, and Cardenas would get the message about the need to be done with the other half. It could all be very good news.

* * *

## July 11
### 2:35 a.m.

Coffee cups littered the tables of the waiting room where Justin's supporters had been the only occupants for a number of hours. They had periodic conversation, moved around the room from time to time and occasionally dropped off for moments of sleep. In the still of the early morning hours, a shadow appeared in the entry door and then Doctor Morris came into view, tugging at her mask.

"Hi everyone." She looked over at Jessica, whose face was alight with anticipation. "It went well," she said with a smile. "The hematoma was successfully drained, and a damaged artery repaired. We'll have to wait a little longer to assure that there are no motor or other deficits from the head trauma or from time spent without oxygen. If all is okay there, the rest will heal in time." She paused and drank in the looks of relief around the room. "Now go home and get some sleep. Maybe he'll be awake this afternoon."

There were nods around the room. "Thank you, Dr. Morris," Jessica offered. Appreciation and relief echoed around the room.

"Truly, my pleasure," she replied. "He obviously has a good support group to assist him from here." After she turned and walked from the room, the group shared hugs and expressions of relief. They picked up their limited belongings and walked to the door, now talking Justin's successful surgery, the need for sleep and the day ahead when they would be able to speak with him. As they reached the parking lot, Jessica said, "I just remembered that I don't have a car. I came in the ambulance with Justin. Can someone give me a ride home?" Everyone volunteered.

# Chapter Fifteen

**July 11**
**3:10 a.m.**
Lee and Melissa drove to his place, where they spent most nights together these days. The relationship had started almost two years ago with his investigation of the harassment and rape of Melissa's boss, Sarah Willis, at the request of Scott Winslow. Melissa had been determined to help Sarah get justice, and there had been a mutual attraction between she and Lee that was immediate. Melissa was smart, witty, insightful, and incredibly hot and he was even more attracted to her now than had been then.

As they drove home, Melissa said, "You are quiet. You're in your work mode thinking about what happened to Justin and what you're going to do about it."

He smiled. It was amazing how she could read him. "I am," he replied. "I don't think he would have been there for the attack last night, but I know that Sean Garner is behind this. I know it in my gut and my technology will prove it."

"I knew it," she offered. "But do me one favor."

"What's that?" he asked.

"Be really careful with this guy. He scares me. His behaviors suggest that he is both driven and irrational. He's like some kind of a cult character who can justify anything in the name of his cause."

"I think you're right about that," Lee replied, nodding.

"I know that Art Underwood and Justin Palmer aren't able to handle themselves like you, but this pyscho is dangerous because there doesn't seem to be any out of bounds for him." She took his hand and said, "And I want to keep you."

"I'll be careful," he offered. "I want to keep you, too. I think your gut feelings about Garner are exactly right. Not exactly a typical corporate executive. More than a little nuts and all-in on getting to his objective." He reflected a moment and added, "This guy is also at the top of the security food chain, which means two things; he has some skills that make him more of a threat that most and he has the ear of Cook, the Aligor CEO Scott is about to depose. Cook may know some of what Garner is up doing, but whether he fesses up to that is another story."

They pulled into the driveway and opened the garage. When they parked the car and walked into the house, Melissa kissed him passionately and said, "I'm going to bed. Wanna come?"

"I do," he replied, grinning widely.

They walked into the bedroom and shed their clothes, then resumed the kiss they started in the hall. It was a good kiss. He entered her and they moaned, moving rhythmically and holding each other tight. They disappeared into the all-consuming lovemaking; all other thoughts and time itself disappear into the intimacy. They were as one, and they were alone in the universe.

They held each other in after-love contentment, drifting in and out of sleep until Lee checked the clock and saw that over an hour and a half had gone by in their blissful escape. He kissed Melissa and said, "Sleep well, sweetheart," and then he slid out of bed and made his way over to the coffee pot. He brewed a cup and then sat down at his computer. With the spyware he had inserted into Garner's phone, he could pull down the calls coming and going. He found an incoming call from a number that he had not seen before. It came in at 10:30 p.m., a few hours after the attack on Justin. It was followed by a call from Garner to another number and a return call from that same number shortly before 6:00 a.m. He looked at the clock. It was just after six now, so this last call was just a few minutes ago. He smiled to himself. As soon as he ran these numbers and obtained ID's of the callers and call recipients, he would be ready to move.

* * *

**July 11**
**5:50 a.m.**
Sean was awakened by the phone. Through a fog, he groaned, "Hello."

"Sean, what is it?"

The voice of Roland Cook brought him awake. "Yes, sir. Something went wrong last night. It has been reported to me that he may be dead."

"What? How could that be?"

"There was a blow to the head and..."

"No details. God Dammit. You handle this." There was a click and Cook was gone.

How could he handle this? If Palmer was dead, then unless he was Lazarus, he wasn't likely to come back. He turned on the television and checked local news. There were stories of protest, a carjacking and a domestic disturbance. He was getting ready to give up when the mid-thirties woman with long blond hair said, "A man was beaten by two assailants outside of a local apartment building last night. He was taken to the hospital, but his condition is unknown. His name has not yet been released, but we will provide more information about who he is and his condition as soon as it is available."

If he was dead, the reporter didn't know it. Sean decided to call the hospital to try to get an update. If he could simply get an acknowledgement that he was there, then Palmer was still alive despite the late-night call from the gravely voice.

* * *

## July 11
### 8:08 a.m.

After a couple of hours of fitful sleep, Jessica made her way back to the hospital, where she learned that her relationship with Justin had to change if she wanted easy access to his hospital room. The tip was delivered by a compassionate nurse, who told her that if she described herself as his girlfriend, her access would be more limited than if she characterized herself as his fiancée.

Whatever it took, she was determined to be at his bedside when he woke up, so she was now his fiancée. She walked into room 242 and pulled a chair up by Justin's side. He slept peacefully, undoubtedly still under the anesthetic, while machines measured his vitals and periodically beeped and buzzed. She thought about how close she had come to losing this man who had burst into her life so full of energy and love. He had changed the color of her world from shades of gray to the brightest of colors. Shit, maybe she was in love with him already. Could that be? She wasn't a believer in love at first sight. You had to know someone's character rather than just how hot they were and whether they flashed a handsome smile. Just the same, in no time at all he had become an important part of her life and she wanted him beside her.

She took Justin's hand in hers and said, "You gave me a scare last night." She reflected a moment and then added, "I don't know where you and I are going from here, but I know that I don't want to think about living without you. I'm going to need you to fully recover so that we can go walking together again. Perhaps someplace we don't find Sean Garner."

Justin slept as machines reflected his every heartbeat, his blood pressure and oxygen saturation. From a purely mechanical point of view, he seemed to be doing well. Jessica felt fear rising as the thought that he might have some level of brain damage as yet undetected struck her. How long had he been without oxygen? In the fear and chaos that surrounded the attack, she didn't have an accurate measure of the time elapsed until the EMTs had restored his breathing. Maybe it had been too long. Maybe she wouldn't get back the Justin she had come to know. It was a helpless feeling as she moved from relief about the surgery result to fear as she contemplated his oxygen deprivation.

She squeezed his hand and whispered, "You come back to me, Justin. I think that I am in love with you."

\* \* \*

**July 11**
**10:30 a.m.**
Marty and Abby Cardenas wore somber expressions as they were escorted into Scott Winslow's office. Scott stood and greeted them, "Hi, Abby. Hi, Marty, come on in and grab a seat."

"Hello, Scott," they both replied, clearly sounding down. "Thanks for meeting with us on a Sunday morning," Marty said. They took seats in Scott's visitor chairs and Marty shook his head. "I checked with the hospital," he offered. "Justin isn't awake yet and they wouldn't give me any other news over the phone."

Scott nodded. "I called too. They said that last night's procedure went well, which we all knew, but there were no other updates."

Marty was quiet for a moment and then said, "I think you can guess why I wanted to see you on an emergency basis."

"I think so, yes."

Marty shook his head. "It's all just stunning. First Art is murdered and now someone beats Justin to within an inch of his life. I'm looking behind me so much that I have neck spasms. I feel like I'm walking around with a target on my back."

"I understand," Scott replied. "It is unsettling."

"That's the understatement of the year. We are both scared shitless. We're worried about Justin and wondering when my turn comes." Marty was quiet a moment and then said, "I'm sorry, Scott, but we are thinking that maybe we attempt to talk Aligor up to the best settlement number possible, see if we can get them to give me a letter of reference as part of the deal and get the case settled before it gets all of us killed."

Scott nodded. He reflected a moment and said, "I thought that might be the reason you wanted to meet this morning and I understand it." He reflected and then said, "You know that you walking away is the goal of what Garner and his thugs are doing right? This is the bully who demands your lunch money and threatens you if you don't turn it over. And that by handing over the case they are getting precisely what their tactics intended."

Abby's eyes grew wide and she sounded angry as she said, "I don't give a fuck, Scott. I don't won't my husband dead or disabled by Aligor's henchmen. We have a good life together and we want to keep it."

"Besides," Marty added, "the school bully keeps coming until you stand up to him and then backs away. These guys are actually hurting and killing people. I remember the school bully, but I don't think we had a school psychopath."

"I get it," Scott acknowledged. "Can I ask you to hold off for a little while? I was talking to Lee this morning and he has some clues about what happened. He's following the trail right now and will update us on what he finds in the next few days."

"What trail?" Marty asked. "As far as I know the police don't have any idea who attacked Justin."

"Lee has ways of getting to places others don't see. It's not my first experience with those abilities," Scott said.

"So, does he think he knows who attacked Justin?"

"He thinks he will follow the trail and find out if we give him a couple of days. Besides, we don't want the defense to think we're conducting a fire sale in trying to settle the case. If they see desperation, the offers go down."

Marty looked at Abby. "I'll go with whatever you want," she said to her husband.

Marty turned to Scott and said, "Okay, a couple of days and if we don't have any information that makes a big difference in the way things look, we start trying to settle the case. Until then, I'll lay low and sit facing doors and windows."

"I have a slightly different proposal," Scott replied.

"Okay, we're listening," Marty said.

"Give me until the end of this week. Cook's deposition is Thursday and I want to go after him. By Friday, we'll know Cook's testimony and where we have him locked into lies. I'll also have a full report from Lee by then. In the interim, you guys take two or three days away from home. Go stay at a nice hotel where you know no one and no one knows you. We'll meet back here Friday morning at 10:00 and you can make your final decision about whether we try and settle the case based on what Lee and I come up with."

"What do you think?" Marty asked Abby.

"Your call, but I'm not opposed to the idea. We could go see Justin this afternoon and leave from the hospital."

"That sounds okay," Marty replied. He thought for a few moments and then said, "I just can't believe this is happening, Scott. I don't like the feeling that there's a contract out on my life."

"I don't like that either," Abby said. "If you keep talking, I may want to change whatever vote I have in all this."

"Your vote weighs the same as mine," Marty said, grabbing her hand. "If you're not comfortable, we won't do it."

Abby gave her husband a smile. After a moment she said, "Let's give Scott the time he needs. We'll figure out a way to lay low and defend ourselves if need be until then."

Marty nodded. He looked back at Scott and said, "Okay. Good luck with the things you and Lee plan on chasing and we'll see you Friday morning."

"If something happens call me and Lee, okay? We will both drop everything if you need us."

"Okay. Good luck to all of us," Marty replied with a smile. They shook Scott's hand and headed for the door. Before they left, Marty turned and added, "If you hear that a refrigerator fell on me, just know that it wasn't an accident." He laughed as he walked out. More gallows humor.

\* \* \*

**July 11**
**10:55 a.m.**

Lee identified the target condo on Carmen Drive in Camarillo. The man commanding his attention was Robert Roth, known to his peers on the street as Bucky Roth. He had two prior convictions, one for assault and battery after beating up a local business manager and the other for violating a restraining order to harass an ex-girlfriend. He sounded like a peach of a guy. The booking photos depicted a man who should be unmistakable; his features included a large head with little hair, small, angry eyes, a full scraggly beard and an overweight body. This was one of the guys Sean Garner had chosen to go after Justin Palmer. Not exactly the typical circles in which Garner moved. He couldn't use his connections in the security industry for this kind of a job, so he had to find a street thug. Lee considered that those facts worked in his favor. Lee also guessed that this idiot wasn't supposed to stop Justin from breathing and leave him for dead, so the late-night call was to tell Sean something had gone wrong. You also get what you pay for and this guy must have been a bargain.

Lee walked casually to the front door and knocked. No answer. He pulled a tool from his pocket and inserted it into the lock. There was a click and he was inside. He closed the door behind him and took a slow walk around the condo. The guy was a collector. There were pizza boxes in a pile on the kitchen table, a couple of them open and displaying remnants of used food that could probably be carbon-dated. There were scattered beer cans in lieu of knick-knacks. It appeared that wherever one placed a beer can became its permanent home. There were no pictures on the wall and no pictures of familial humans anywhere.

Lee made his way into the bedroom, where a mattress sat on the floor with loose blankets and a pillow piled in the middle. There was a single dresser, which Lee searched. Then he looked underneath and behind the dresser for anything that might be secreted with a little tape. Nothing.

There were no computers or laptop devices and no chargers or other paraphernalia to suggest they existed. The guy was low tech, which meant that any notes would be handwritten. Lee searched the kitchen drawers, turning up rusty utensils and a few mouse droppings. In a drawer at the end of the counter, he found a rusted old Saturday night special. He put it in his pocket and moved on. Then he saw the calendar, a magnet holding it on the side of the refrigerator out of view. He pulled it down and looked at the dates, finding nothing. Then he turned it over to find notes that included the name Justin Palmer, July 10, the phone number that was used for the late-night call to Sean Garner and another number Lee hadn't seen before. The words 'hurt him' were written underneath.

Lee took the calendar with him as he left the condo. He had no idea when his target would return, so he decided to get a few things done and return later in the day. If Bucky Roth wasn't here when he returned, he would visit Bucky's known hangout, although he would much prefer the effect and the privacy of surprising Bucky at home. Lee considered dialing the number that he couldn't identify but decided to wait until after his in-person visit with Bucky Roth.

\* \* \*

**July 11**
**3:15 p.m.**
Since arriving at the hospital, Jessica left Justin's bedside twice to get bad machine coffee and go to the bathroom and once to get a salad from the hospital cafeteria. Justin had slept peaceably, neither waking nor suffering any medical crises. She had been hearing the beeps and buzzes of the machines attached to Justin for so long, they were no longer noticeable. Like crickets on a summer night, you can stop hearing them by listening long enough.

Jessica sat at his bedside reading an article about the pandemic, protests and the general pandemonium that had characterized 2020. It was a wonder that the world made it through all of that craziness. She began to fall asleep, her head falling forward, causing her to jerk awake. She looked up at the monitor that reflected Justin's blood pressure, with new readings every fifteen minutes. One hundred ten over seventy-five; not bad at all. As she stood to stretch, she looked down and saw Justin's eyes open. "Justin, hi sweetheart."

He looked disoriented. A man coming out of a dense fog. He raised his eyes and saw her. His eyes widened and a smile appeared. "Jessica," he announced with recognition and a smile.

"Are you okay?" she asked, taking his hand.

"I think so," he said.

She leaned over the bed and cautiously gave him a kiss. "I'm so glad you are okay."

"I'm in a hospital?" he asked, glancing around him.

"Yeah. You were attacked."

He nodded. "There were two guys with pipes. I remember being hit, but nothing else."

"How are you feeling?" she asked.

"My right side and my chest hurts."

"You have three broken ribs. You also had a hematoma. They drained it last night. That's why the bandages on your head."

He nodded. After a moment he said, "And am I?"

"Are you what?"

"Going to be okay? You said you were glad I was going to be okay."

"Your brain is working. You know who I am and where you are. Do you know what year it is?"

"Yep. I know who the president is, who the governor is and that I am really thirsty. Am I allowed to have water?"

"Ice chips," she offered, pulling a paper cup from the tray next to the bed.

"Close enough." He worked on ice chips for a few moments and then said. "Did the police catch the guys who came after me?"

"Not yet. I know that they are working on it and so is Lee Henry."

He nodded. "It's Sean Garner."

"I think so, too. He wants you and Marty to walk away from the lawsuit. Marty said that he would be here," she looked at her watch and added, "in about ten minutes from now. He and Abby are scared. I know they talked to Scott Winslow about settling the case before you and him both share Art's fate."

Justin nodded but didn't speak. A nurse walked in and said, "Hey, welcome back Mr. Palmer. We figured you'd be opening your eyes pretty soon now." She stared at him and said, "I need to examine you, okay?"

"Sure thing. I'm not real busy."

"Ooh, well, your sense of humor isn't broken. Nice."

She shone a light in his eyes, prodded him and examined the numbers the machines were posting and then said, "So how are we feeling?"

"Well, I can't speak for all of us, but I'm doing pretty good except for the broken stuff. It hurts sometimes when I breathe deeply."

"Excellent," the smiling nurse said.

"Excellent that I'm hurt?" Justin asked.

"Nope. Excellent that you are lucid. Your mind seems to be intact."

"At least as much as it was before," he replied, smiling.

She grinned widely. "Wow." She looked over at Jessica. "He really is back. Good prognosis for his sense of humor as well." She walked to the door and then looked back. "You kids behave now, and I'll check in from time to time."

Jessica leaned over and put her cheek to Justin's. "I'd love to hug you, but I know it would hurt. I missed you so much, Justin."

There was a tear in her eye. "You're crying." he said.

"Yes, you're a master of the obvious," she replied through tears.

"But why? I'm really going to be okay."

She nodded, momentarily unable to speak, and then she said, "I thought I might lose you."

# Chapter Sixteen

Lee parked across the street from Bucky Roth's condo. Kids played ball outside in the middle of the street, constantly interrupting their games for passing cars as people made their way home from work. Lee smiled at their persistence as they repeatedly stepped aside and then moved back into the street with their baseball gear. A ball came in his direction, so he picked it up and tossed it to a lanky young man who was functioning as a catcher. "Thanks, mister," the kid said. Lee gave him a wave of acknowledgment and moved onto the condo property. There was a pickup in the space reserved for Bucky's condo.

Lee made his way to the front door and knocked. No response, so he knocked again. This time a big man opened the door and assessed him. "What do you need?" he asked.

Lee smiled and said, "I was wondering if you could tell me..." He never finished his sentence. Instead, he punched Bucky Roth in his midsection and watched the man bend over and then fall to his knees, trying to catch his breath. Lee quickly checked him for weapons and found none. "Mind if I come in?" he asked and stepped around the gasping Bucky without waiting for a response. He gave Bucky a moment to recover enough to function and then said, "You and I need to talk, Bucky."

"Who the fuck are you, man?"

"I am the embodiment of your conscience, and I'm here to make you feel better about yourself and what you've been doing." He smiled.

Bucky slowly hoisted himself off the floor. He held on to an armchair with his right hand. As he steadied himself, he stared at Lee, considering his options.

Then he slowly moved towards a kitchen drawer. Lee shook his head. "It's not there anymore."

Bucky froze. "What?" he asked in disbelief.

"Your old Saturday night special isn't there anymore. You can check for yourself."

Bucky opened the drawer and stared at nothing. His gun was gone. He wore a puzzled look as he turned back to Lee and asked, "How did you do that?"

"Magic," Lee replied. "Now, let's talk. If you move a couple of those old pizza boxes and whatever varmints they now contain, you'll be able to take a seat on the couch."

Bucky wore the look of a cornered animal and he glanced at Lee and then considered the distance to the doors while he assessed the odds. Lee shook his head. "You don't want to make any mistakes right now, Bucky. That would just piss me off, and that will make this visit harder on you."

"What do you want?"

"You and I are going to have a talk and your chances of coming out of this are directly related to the honesty of your answers. You may even be able to stay out of jail."

"Show me some ID. I want your badge number, man. You violated my civil rights in ten different ways."

"I don't remember telling you that I was a cop."

Bucky smiled and said, "Then you're a home invader and I can just beat the shit out of you."

Lee shrugged. "You can try. Come to think of it, if you had a gun, you could shoot me, right?"

Bucky looked away and then flew at Lee like a linebacker making a neck-high tackle. Lee ducked from his waist and when Bucky was on top of him stood and used Bucky's momentum to throw him into the air and into the wall, headfirst. There was a tremendous crash at the moment of impact and chunks of wallboard and paint flew into the air and came to earth on and around Bucky Roth. For a moment Bucky didn't move and Lee thought he might be out cold. After a time, he let out a pained groan.

"How about we talk now?" Lee asked. He waited while Bucky pulled himself to his feet for the second time and made his way over to the couch, his fighting spirit no longer evident.

"You have a chance to save yourself."

"From what?"

"From taking all the heat for the beating delivered to Justin Palmer."

"Who?"

Lee glared at Bucky and said, "You are going to get one more shot at this. If you give me another bullshit answer, you and I will wait for the cops and they will take you in now. We know that you called Sean Garner on the night of the attack. We have that call recorded, so be really careful what you tell me now."

Bucky gave him a look of concern. "How are you here before any cops?"

"I'm working with them, so I'm in a position to help you. Or not. So, make it good. Why don't you start with you beating Palmer to the point that he stopped breathing?"

"That wasn't my fault. After he was hit in the head he was out and didn't look like he was alive."

"And that wasn't supposed to happen. You were just supposed to scare him, Bucky."

"It wasn't me, man. I didn't do it."

"I know that. It was the other guy. What's his name?"

"Come on, I can't tell you that."

"I've already got his number." Lee pulled out his phone and read he the number he had recorded from Bucky's notes on the calendar, which caused Bucky to look to his refrigerator. "It's not there anymore. So, you can tell me who this guy is, or we can get him through this number and then there's no extra credit for you in your current predicament." Bucky was quiet for a moment. "The clock is ticking." Lee said.

"I only know him as Clyde J."

"Have you worked with him before?"

"Nope."

"He's the one who hit Palmer in the head?"

"How do I find Clyde J.?"

"Call him."

"Come on, he's not going to take my call. I mean, I could have the cops run the number and get him that way, but that won't help you any."

Bucky shook his big head. "The only ways I know to reach him is with that number or to see him at The Horn."

"The beer bar on Van Nuys Blvd.?"

"Yeah."

"What does Clyde look like?"

"Big guy. Like two hundred seventy pounds and six foot three. Untrimmed beard and grey hair, long at the back. Wears it in a ponytail."

"How did you get this assignment?"

"George Fletcher put Clyde and me together. He said he had easy work. Took half hour and paid two grand a piece. All we had to do was rough a guy up to give him a scare."

"So, how did you get Garner's number?"

"George was going to be out of town when we were doing the job. I told him I needed the number in case of emergency." He paused and added, "I also wanted to know who to go see if we weren't paid."

Lee gave him a thoughtful nod. "Okay, Bucky. Tomorrow, you are going to meet me here at 6:00 p.m. I will have a statement that you will sign under oath."

"I don't know, man."

"Well, I could call the cops and have them take your statement over the next few hours. You're still on probation, right?"

"Huh," he grunted.

"If the cops take your statement, you are going to be violated and wind up back inside. If you sign mine, I will sit on it for a while. If the information comes out at some point, I'll tell them that you were fully cooperative and recommend against finding any probation violation."

"How do I know that they will listen to you?"

"I could call them now and demonstrate that if you like."

Her was quiet for a time and then he held up both hands and replied, "Okay, man."

"You make me look for you tomorrow and all bets are off. Be here at 6:00 p.m."

"I'll be here."

Lee walked to the door and turned back. "Don't make me look for you, Bucky." He walked out of the condo, which was now a little worse for wear. As he walked to his car, he considered updating the Detectives Olivia Blake and Ed Farris so that they didn't feel he was sitting on important information. Maybe later. First, he would go find Clyde J. at The Horn.

Bucky waited about five minutes to make sure that Lee wasn't coming back, then he dialed the number. It rang four times. "You've reached the voicemail of Sean Garner. Leave a message and I will get back to you at first opportunity."

"You know who this is. A man was here to see me, and I thought you needed to know. He's now off to find my associate at The Horn Bar on Van Nuys Blvd. Better call me back as soon as you can." He hung up.

Fifteen minutes later, Bucky's phone rang. "Yeah," he said.

"I thought I told you not to call me. What part of that didn't you understand.?"

"Okay, man. I thought you would want to know that a guy was here shaking me for information about that Palmer fellow."

"What did the dude look like?"

"He looked like a cop to me. Hard eyes and maybe forty. Short hair and a wrap around. I tried to put him down, but he was pretty fast."

"So, what did you tell him?"

"That I was hired to scare Palmer. That's all. He's going to see the other guy on that job. Clyde J."

"Why did you give him the guy's name?"

"I didn't want to go to jail and I didn't want to fight this guy anymore."

"How long ago did the guy leave you?"

"Left around twenty minutes ago."

"You got a phone number for Clyde?"

"No."

"What does he look like?"

Bucky repeated the description he had given to Lee and then added, "You can't miss him. He's as big as a fucking house."

"What time does your buddy go to The Horn?"

"No clue. Nights I guess," Bucky replied.

"All right. Don't fucking call me again," Garner said angrily.

Lee sat in his car outside The Horn listening to the conversation between Garner and Bucky. Tapping Garner's phone was still paying off. He now had a call tying Garner to the attack on Justin Palmer. He also knew he was not the only one who would be looking for Clyde. Garner would have to find Clyde, too. He would want to make sure that Clyde didn't also talk to Lee, so he would likely show up right here. And right here wasn't much. A shack-like bar with a dirt parking lot and a set of bull horns hanging above an open door. There were three cars in the parking lot. One might be Clyde, or they all might be guys ready for a beer at 2:00 in the afternoon. Unless Clyde was one of those three people, Lee would have to check back later.

Lee walked into the bar through a creaky door and looked around. There were two old guys at a table in one corner and a guy who looked like a construction worker at the bar. A tall thin man with a cowboy shirt stood, or leaned, behind the bar. "Can I help you, mister?"

"Yeah. You know a guy named Clyde?"

"Who's asking?"

"I am."

"And who would you be?"

"I'm Clyde's long-lost twin brother," Lee said. He pulled two twenties from his wallet and added, "Do you remember now? Big guy, grey ponytail."

"Yep. I know Clyde. Usually shows up here around 5:00 or 5:30 most nights." He reached out and took the money from Lee's hand.

"Great, have him give me a call." He wrote a phone number on a napkin and handed it to the bartender. "Just tell him I'd like to catch up."

"Sure," the bartender replied, not sounding convinced, but stuffing the forty dollars into his jeans.

"Thanks," Lee said, turning and walking for the door. He knew Clyde wasn't going to voluntarily call a stranger. The number he had given the bartender wasn't real. It was just so that Clyde could disregard the message and attend to his beer. He wouldn't be looking behind him when Lee returned.

Everything seemed to be coming together until Lee stepped outside of The Horn to see a big man with a ponytail standing in the parking lot and pointing a gun in his direction. "Don't move suddenly, man, I have a nervous trigger finger."

Lee lifted his arms. "Okay, I'm not moving fast or at all. What can I do for you?"

Clyde looked at the street that passed in front of the building and seemed to be assessing. "Walk around the back of the building." Lee hesitated a moment, not wanting an isolated location with a guy holding a gun on him. "Move," Clyde yelled, waving the gun.

They walked around the side of the building and then to the rear, which was nothing more than an alley where deliveries could be made to the back of two or three businesses. "Stop right here," Clyde said. Lee looked at him silently, arms in the air. "You can get yourself shot if you spend your time looking for me."

"So I gather," Lee replied evenly.

"What do you want?" the big man asked, the gun pointed at Lee's chest.

"I just wanted to ask you a couple of questions, Clyde."

"About what?"

"About the work that you and Bucky did for Sean Garner."

"I don't know anyone named Garner."

"The job you got from Fletcher. Beating up a guy named Palmer."

"I'm not telling you shit. And you aren't really in a position to ask me any questions."

"Good point, Clyde. Lower the gun and I'll be on my way," Lee offered evenly.

"I think maybe you need to answer a couple of my questions."

"Okay, what do you need to know?"

"Why are you asking questions?"

"It's my job. I investigate things."

"For whom?" Clyde said, emphasizing the 'm'.

"For a client."

Clyde waved the gun. "Who is?"

"Can't say."

"You can say if you'd rather not be shot in the knee cap."

"No, you don't understand. I'm ethically not allowed to reveal my client who wants to remain confidential. I just came to talk to you. I wanted to know if there was anything you could share about what happened to Justin Palmer."

The big man shook his head. "Just a casual question, right?" He shook his head. "That's bullshit, man. I happen to know that you were squeezing Bucky. You even threw him around a little. But you can't throw me, man."

"Nope, it looks like I can't."

"You need to stay the fuck away from me and from Bucky. You got it?"

"I've got it. How about you put the gun down while we talk?"

"I don't think so," Clyde snarled. "You think you're some kind of hot shit. I have nothing to say to you."

"Okay, that's up to you. No problem."

Clyde shook his head and the ponytail wagged. "I'm not fucking around. You come anywhere near me or Bucky again and I use the gun. Got it?"

"I've got it."

"Get the fuck out of here."

Lee turned and began walking away. When he was a few feet away, he looked back at Clyde, who was still pointing the gun in his direction and took a couple of pictures with a palm-sized camera. He smiled and couldn't resist saying, "Nice talking to you, Clyde." Clyde stared back at him angrily but didn't speak.

\* \* \*

**July 11**
**2:10 p.m.**
Justin had drifted in and out of consciousness, and the nursing staff had drifted in and out of the room to keep an eye on him and the mechanical monsters that surrounded him.

He opened his eyes to see Jessica looking at him with a caring smile. Through the fog he found a smile of his own, even though his head was pounding, and his ribs were aching.

"Hi again," she offered, taking his hand.

"Hi, Jessica." He closed his eyes a moment to help him better focus. When he opened them, he said, "Thank you for being here."

"There's nowhere else I could possibly be."

"I think I screwed up our date."

"You did. It was thoughtless of you to get attacked before we went out to dinner."

He laughed and immediately grimaced, promptly the recollection that laughter and cracked ribs didn't coexist well. "Can I have more ice?"

"I don't know. Let me check the calorie count."

He laughed again and said, "Ouch. Don't make me laugh."

As they spoke, Marty and Abby walked into the room, followed closely by Sandi Underwood. "Hi, Justin," Marty said. "It's about time you woke up."

"No one make me laugh, please."

"Hi, Abby and Sandi," Justin said with a weak smile.

They stood next to him and Abby said, "Are you doing okay?"

"Yep. All except for the pain."

Sandi took his hand and said, "I'm so glad you're still here, Justin." She swallowed hard and added, "I'm convinced that they are after all of you."

"We're convinced of that too, Sandi," Marty replied. "We have to make a final decision about what we do about it," he said, looking from Sandi to Justin.

Justin's eyes narrowed. "Garner engineered this."

Everyone nodded agreement. "It's getting pretty clear that there's nowhere he won't go to get what he wants," Marty said. "We have to decide whether we accept settlement offers and walk away while we still can."

"What do you think?" Justin asked.

He looked at Abby and then back at Justin. "We're thinking maybe it's time to take whatever deal we can and move on with life. We are risking everything here." Justin looked at him and didn't speak, so Marty asked, "What do you think, partner?"

"I think 'fuck them.' If they want to take another shot at me, that's fine. Next time I won't be unarmed. I won't be intimidated into letting these guys defraud everyone in desperate straits just so that they can make money."

Marty smiled. "Some people are pretty hard to convince," he replied. "Part of me wants to say the same thing."

"Think about Art," Sandi said, softly. "I'd give anything to have him back."

"I am thinking about Art," Justin said, sounding indignant. "These bastards murdered by friend and now they are after us. I am not walking away. I'll fight them in court, and I'll fight whoever they send on the street if that's what it takes."

"I think these guys achieved a result that they didn't intend," Marty said, grinning. "You seem more determined than ever."

"I am, dammit."

Jessica looked at him with wide eyes. "Don't get yourself killed, Justin. I don't know that I have any vote, but this was close enough for me. I want you around."

"And I want to be around you, sweetheart," he heard himself say, noting that was the first time he had ever referred to her in that way. "You have a vote and I want to hear what you think, but I cannot walk away from this." He paused and then said, "You know, when I fell off to sleep a little while ago, I dreamed about those two guys beating me with tire irons. It was so real I could feel the pain all over again."

"That's because you still have the pain; you have several cracked ribs. But I take your point. I just don't know if those nightmares are chased away by continuing to fight these guys."

Justin smiled. "I'll let you know."

"You are one stubborn son of a gun."

"You're just figuring that out? How long have we worked together?"

Marty just grinned at Justin, causing Abby to look at her husband and say, "Do not tell me that Justin is convincing you to stay in this case."

Marty shrugged. "There is something to be said for determination."

"Yes, there is. In this case it's stupid. Do you both want to keep going until they actually kill you?" Abby asked.

Justin frowned. "That's not how I would explain the goal, no."

"Tell them not to do this, Sandi," Abby urged.

Sandi shook her head. "You guys know how I vote. I lost the man I've adored my whole adult life." She took a deep breath, trying to deal with the emotion that was right at the surface. She shook her head and added, "My heart hurts all the time and my whole world feels empty. I don't want this to happen to Abby or Jessica."

Justin attempted to move in bed and flinched as rib pain stabbed him sharply. He held Jessica's hand and looked from her to Sandi. "Art was a hero of mine. He was a man of character doing what he thought was right, and I have to do the same."

Sandi wore a sad expression. She nodded and said, "Art would have said something just like and look what happened; it cost us everything." She shook her head. "These guys are relentless. Don't you get it? There are billions of dollars involved and there is something happening that doesn't come out of the Aligor board room; they have put together some kind of a back channel to dispatch people instructed to end challenges by going right at those who dare to bring them."

The room got quiet for a time. Justin grimaced as he moved slightly and then he said, "I do get it, Sandi, I really do. It's just not okay with me." He shook his head slowly, because it hurt as well. "There are people who will die from the choice to use Delexane. They need to know that it isn't what Aligor says it is and I will do what it takes to bring that into the light. I won't be intimidated by Sean Garner or any of the thugs he sends after me."

"Look at you, Justin, you're lying in a hospital bed after emergency surgery and you're still playing tough guy," Marty said.

"Yep, and maybe they'll finish the job next time, but I still won't give up. But next time, I'll be looking behind me and fighting back."

"Right. And with broken ribs that make any movement painful, you'll be a force to be reckoned with."

Justin studied Marty a moment and then asked, "So, are you checking out?"

Marty smiled. "I don't think so." Abby stared at him, startled. He shrugged and said, "I can't leave this helpless fool all alone in this."

"Yes, you can," Abby prompted. "Before you're next in a hospital bed or the morgue." Marty just shrugged. "Jesus, you two piss me off," Abby said and walked out of the room.

Justin grinned. "You better chase her down or you might be divorced even before you get killed."

"You are fucking unbelievable," Marty replied. "How can you take all this so lightly?" Even as he said it, he couldn't help but admire his friend's strength. He knew what was right and he wasn't going to be intimidated. As crazy as it seemed, Marty decided that he should stay in this thing with Justin.

"Just a little more gallows humor. Helps you keep things in perspective."

"None of this is in any kind of perspective," Marty replied and left the room to find Abby. It was going to take some real work to convince her that he should stay in the lawsuit with Justin, or at least not to kill him for making that decision.

After Marty left the room, Jessica looked at Justin with wide eyes.

"What?" he asked.

"I just never thought I'd fall for somebody so dammed stubborn."

He grinned. "You're falling for me, huh?"

She shook her head. "Shut up. You are impossible."

# Chapter Seventeen

**July 12**
**7:05 a.m.**

Marty woke up to find that Abby was already dressed and ready for work. She kissed him and said, "I'm worried."

"About what?" he asked, still trying to wake up.

"About us getting killed, Marty. What else?" She was quiet for a moment and then added, "I know you. You're impressed with what Justin said yesterday and you're thinking about staying in the lawsuit."

He nodded slowly. "I was impressed with Justin's commitment to getting Aligor to tell the truth, even after getting the shit kicked out of him."

"Yep," she replied. "It's so courageous it crosses the thin line into stupid. How are we going to feel when he's the next one to sail off a rooftop? And what if it's you? I don't want to join the widows' club, Marty."

"I know, sweetheart. Can I brush my teeth and take a shower before we finish this conversation? It may take a while."

"I have an early appointment and I have to go. We'll finish the conversation tonight. Just give it some thought, please Marty."

"I will." He smiled, stood up, and gave her a kiss. "See you tonight." As she walked out, he was already aware that the conversation they had just postponed would not be pleasant. That feeling is what told him that he had made his decision and he was going to stay in the lawsuit with Justin. He wondered whether being thrown off a building would be worse than the friction that would come his way when he shared his final decision to stay in the case with Abby. It was not going to be pretty.

\* \* \*

**July 12**
**5:50 p.m.**

Lee got out of his car and walked towards Bucky's condo carrying a thin file. As he expected, the old pickup registered to one Clyde James Jackson aka Clyde J. was parked on the street. As he walked, Lee watched the same group of kids he had seen on his last visit playing ball in the street, caught up in the long days of summer and the thoughts of getting one more at-bat before mom called for dinner.

Lee hit a button on his phone and said, "He's here. Give me two minutes and then come on in. I'll keep the line open so you can hear the initial exchange." He hesitated a moment and then added, "Thanks for your help with this one."

"It's not for free," Detective Olivia Blake replied. "You're going to owe us for this one."

"Understood," Lee said. "See you inside."

Lee knocked at the door of the condo and waited. He didn't have to wait long. The door opened and Clyde J. stood there pointing his gun directly at Lee. "Whoa!" Lee exclaimed. "Be careful with that thing, Clyde. I have an appointment with Bucky," he offered, gesturing to Bucky, who stood in the living room and watched the exchange.

"You remember what I told you, man?" He didn't wait for an answer. "I told you that if you show up near me or Bucky again, I was going to use this. Didn't I tell you that?"

"You did tell me that, Clyde."

"So now I'm gonna have to put a bullet in you."

Lee raised his arms and said, "Just as a matter of principle, right?" Clyde looked momentarily confused and then his expression returned to anger. Lee said, "I'm unarmed. Don't shoot."

"Too late, man. You're..."

He was interrupted by the words, "Drop the gun. This is the police." Olivia Blake and Ed Farris stood three feet outside the open door with their guns drawn and pointed at Clyde. He hesitated and Farris yelled, "Last chance jerkoff, drop the gun or we drop you."

Slowly, Clyde lowered his weapon and the two detectives rushed inside. Farris spun the man and Blake put hand cuffs on him in what seemed like a single move. Olivia Blake injected, "Clyde Jackson, you are under arrest for two counts of assault with a deadly weapon and possession of a firearm in violation of your probation. You have the right to remain silent. If you waive that right anything you say can and will be used against you in a court of law. You have the right to counsel. If you cannot afford legal counsel, counsel will be appointed for you..."

As the Miranda warning reached its end, Lee moved towards Bucky, who looked decidedly nervous. When Blake looked at Bucky, he responded, "I didn't do anything. I don't have a gun."

Blake and Farris perp-walked Clyde to their unmarked sedan. Lee turned to Bucky and said, "Okay, let's get down to business. Here is the declaration we agreed you would sign, testifying that you were hired to beat up Justin Palmer. It also includes the fact that you spoke personally to Sean Garner about the hiring and contains details about his words to you. Read it and sign."

"Why should I? Clyde has already been busted and he's going to turn me in anyway."

"Were you listening when the arrest was made? Clyde is a guy on parole who is going to be violated for carrying a gun and he's going to be charged with assault with a deadly weapon for pointing a gun at me on two occasions. No one said anything about battery or attempted murder for the attack on Justin Palmer, right?" Bucky thought a moment and then nodded. "You tell the truth about the attack on Palmer by signing this declaration and I won't say anything about the attack on Palmer. I can't guarantee the police don't find out about it somehow, but I won't take it to them."

"I don't know."

"Okay, suit yourself, Bucky. You and Clyde can both face attempted murder and battery charges for the attack on Palmer. Let's see how that works out for you. As I understand it, you have a couple of priors, one that includes beating up a guy, so you're probably looking at a guaranteed ten-year stretch. Is that your best call?" Bucky wore a pained expression but remained silent. "Once I walk out of here, this deal is gone." Bucky looked flustered. Lee shook his head. "If that's the way you want to do this, I'm out of here. Those two detectives will be back for you shortly and you can tell a judge why you attacked and almost killed Justin Palmer. You can also explain to Clyde how the attack on Palmer suddenly got added to his list of charges."

That possibility seemed to move the needle and Bucky found his voice. "Okay, okay. I'll sign."

Lee handed Bucky the document. He stared at it blankly for period of time and then signed it with a shaking hand. Lee picked up the paper and said, "I think you made the right decision, Bucky." He walked out of the condo while Bucky watched in stunned silence.

As he reached the street, Lee yelled "Nice hit" to a tall boy who ran towards a manhole cover in the street after hitting a high fly into someone's front yard.

"Thanks, mister," the kid replied once he was safely on the manhole cover serving as the base. Lee smiled and climbed into his car. As he pulled away from the curb, he hit a button on his phone. It was time to update Scott Winslow on the removal of Clyde J. as an impediment and the newly acquired declaration from Bucky.

\* \* \*

**July 13**
**5:50 p.m.**
Justin and Jessica looked towards the hospital room door to see Dr. Morris step inside wearing a white coat and carrying what looked like a small iPad. As she approached the bed, she smiled and asked, "How are you feeling, Justin?"

"It hurts when I laugh, move or breathe, otherwise I'm fine." He laughed and flinched, demonstrating the problem.

She smiled and said, "Yeah, fractured ribs are like that. I wish I could tell you that next week the pain would be gone, but recovery will be slow and gradual." He nodded his head in understanding and she added, "I hear you've been walking the halls. Is that right?"

"It is. I know it's good for me to keep moving. I also don't have much else to do."

"Keep it up. Medically, you are looking pretty good. I think we are going to keep you here for a couple more days to keep an eye on your head. If everything looks good at that point you can go home to heal and continue walking."

"Great," Justin replied. "My own hallway is less crowded."

Dr. Morris shook her head and looked over at Jessica. "A sense of humor is a really good indication he's on the back way to good health."

"Yep," Jessica replied with a groan.

Doctor Morris smiled. "It doesn't mean it's easy to take that humor, only that he's on the way back."

"Hey, you know that I'm right here and I can hear you, right?" Justin said with a smile.

\* \* \*

**July 15**
**9:30 a.m.**

Roland Cook walked into the Simmons and Winslow conference room wearing a suit that probably cost five thousand dollars. He mumbled a quick greeting to the room and then sat at the conference room table with his hands folded in front him. He looked some combination of unhappy and angry.

He was out of his element. Those at the top of the Fortune 500 weren't used to having to answer questions for anyone else, but he didn't get where he was by showing weakness and there would be none today. He would take on Scott Winslow without hesitation.

Scott and Doug Gibson attached the microphones to their shirts and Gibson asked Cook to do the same with his. The videographer and the court reporter each announced that they were ready to proceed. The videographer was a man of about forty, with a beard and a clean-shaven head. The court reporter was a woman in her mid-thirties with red hair and a confident manner. Scott gave her a nod signaling his readiness and she turned her attention to Roland Cook and said, "Raise your right hand, sir." Cook did so and she recited, "Do you solemnly swear to tell the truth, the whole truth and nothing but the truth, so help you, God?"

"Yes," Cook replied and returned his hand to his side and his gaze to Scott.

"Good morning, Mr. Cook. Do you understand that you are testifying under oath today and that your testimony is subject to the penalties of perjury?"

"Yes," Cook replied.

"Did you have the opportunity to meet with your attorney at some point before we began today?"

"Yes."

"Good. At the risk of being redundant about matters he may have shared with you, I want to go over a few ground rules that govern this proceeding so that you have them in mind and so that you and I are on the same page. First of all, make sure that you understand each question before you respond. If I ask you a question you don't understand, don't answer it. Tell me that you didn't understand, and I will rephrase it. Will you do that?"

"Yes."

"With that in mind, if you answer a question, I am going to assume that you understood it and I'm going to ask a judge and a jury to make that same assumption. Understood?"

"Yes."

"Just because you understand a question, however, doesn't mean that you are going to know the answer to every question I ask. If you don't know, just say that. No one wants you to guess about information you simply don't have. Understood?"

"Yes."

"I may ask you about a date or time of some event, and if you don't recall specifically, I am entitled to your best estimate."

"Okay."

"You have in mind the distinction between a guess and a best estimate?"

"Yes, I do."

"Your attorney may object to questions from time to time to preserve his objections for the record. Unless he instructs you not to answer, you are obligated to answer the question after he puts his objection on the record. Understood?"

"I understand."

"Great. Any questions about the procedure before we go further?"

"No."

"What documents did you review in anticipation of your deposition here today?"

"The documents that Justin and Martin produced and the documents that the Company produced in this lawsuit."

"What else?"

"That's it," Cook said.

"How about the personnel files of Mr. Cardenas?"

"No."

"Did you review Mr. Palmer's personnel file?"

"No."

"What is your position with Aligor?"

"I am its CEO."

"How long have you been in that role?"

"Six years."

"Did you hold any position with Aligor before that?"

"No."

"And what are your duties?"

There was a brief look of impatience and then he took a breath and replied, "I make day to day business decisions concerning company operations and I keep the Board of Directors informed of critical matters."

Scott spent the next two hours taking Cook through his education and the positions he held before arriving at Aligor as its CEO. It was the kind of background that Cook wasn't anxious to discuss. His expression evidenced his unhappiness with having to put up with this inquiry. Once he had the rhythm of such questioning, Scott made a sudden change in direction.

"Mr. Cook, Justin Palmer didn't report directly to you, did he?"

"No."

"Marty Cardenas didn't report directly to you either, correct?"

"Correct."

"To whom did they report?"

"Arthur Underwood."

"And Mr. Underwood reported directly to you?"

"Right."

"And that was true from the time you joined the Company until Mr. Palmer and Mr. Cardenas were terminated?"

"Right."

"I object," Gibson interjected. "Assumes facts not in evidence."

Scott smiled and asked Cook, "Mr. Palmer and Mr. Cardenas were both fired, correct?"

"Yes."

"Who made the decision to fire Mr. Palmer?"

"I did."

"How about Mr. Cardenas? Who made the decision to fire him?"

"I did."

"When did you decide to fire Marty Cardenas in relation to his termination date?"

"I don't remember."

"What is your best estimate? Was it a year before, a month before, a day before?"

"Maybe a couple of weeks before."

"Why did you fire him?"

"I was not happy with his work."

"When did you cease being happy with his work?"

"It had been a while, maybe a year."

"How did you document your dissatisfaction during that last year of his employment?"

"I don't know that I ever did."

"Why?"

"I didn't see the need."

"What documents exist that show any inadequacy in Marty's performance?"

He was quiet for a time and then said, "I don't remember."

"But there are documents commending his work during that last year, aren't there?"

"Maybe, I don't know."

"Well, let me refresh your recollection. Let me show you exhibit 1." Scott laid a copy of an email in front of Cook.

"What is this?"

"It's an email," Cook replied curtly.

"In the first paragraph, read the sentence beginning with the words 'well done'."

"Well done, Marty. You have been way out front in getting Enderma to market. You are on top of your game as usual. Nice work."

"Did you write that?"

"Yes."

"And this is dated about two months before Marty's termination, correct?"

He was quiet for a time and then said, "I guess so, yes. But this is only part of the story."

"Meaning what?"

"Meaning I was unhappy with other things."

"I see, but none of those things are written down, correct?"

"I don't write everything down."

"So, in answer to my question, none of those things are written down, correct?"

"Correct."

"Let me show you something else you did write down. We will mark this document as Exhibit 2. Is this an email dated about six weeks before Marty's termination?"

Cook did a quick calculation and then said, "Yes, roughly."

"Did you write this one, too?"

"Yes."

"To commend Marty on a successful meeting that led to a new contract?"

"Yes."

"Let me show you Exhibit 3. Is this a letter that you wrote to Marty congratulating him on his extraordinary efforts?"

"That's what it says."

"You did write it?"

"Yes."

"And this one would have been between six and seven months before his termination?"

"Yes."

"You gave him this commendation letter with a check reflecting a six percent bonus?"

"Objection to the characterization of the document as a commendation letter," Gibson offered, desperate to interrupt the momentum of what was happening.

"You can answer," Scott said.

"Yes, but others also got bonuses."

"Anyone else get six percent?"

"Yes."

"Who?"

"Four of five people."

"Does that include Justin Palmer?"

"Yes."

"And a week or two after this letter of commendation is when you decided that you weren't satisfied with his performance, right?"

"Yes, that's right."

"What specifically happened between the date of this commendation letter and two weeks later that made you conclude that Mr. Cardenas was not properly performing?"

"It was not just one thing."

"Well, what things were there?"

Cook seemed some combination of angry and flustered as he said, "His attitude was a problem."

"How did that manifest itself?"

"I don't like the way he talked to me. Like he was in charge."

"During the last six months of his employment, Mr. Cardenas was also com-plaining that phase three of the test trials for Delexane were not yielding the same results as the first and second phases?"

"It wasn't clear what was happening at that point."

"There were fifteen thousand people in the phase three test, correct?"

"Yes."

"And only five hundred fifty in phase 2?"

"Yes."

"And just fifty participants in phase one?"

"Right."

"And what's the purpose of expanding the group's size with each phase?

"To see if the results differ when it is extended to larger numbers."

"You want to figure out success rate on a larger scale?"

"Yes."

"And you're also testing for side effects?"

"Right."

"And Marty told you that the results were not as good in phase 3?"

"He said he had some concerns."

"He told you what those concerns were, didn't he?"

"He told you that the sixty five percent tumor shrinkage rate from the earlier phases weren't holding up?"

"I don't recall that."

"You don't recall it, or it didn't happen?"

"I don't recall."

"Didn't he also tell you that the phase three test results also include greater numbers of side effects?"

"No."

"In fact, Mr. Cook, didn't you hear complaints or concerns from Marty Contr-eras, Justin Palmer and Director of Product Development Art Underwood that the tumor size reduction results of phase three were not as good as the first two phases?"

"They had minor concerns that didn't amount to anything."

"How many times did they come to you with these minor concerns?"

"Three, maybe."

Over what period of time?"

Cook took some time to assess and then replied, "Two or three months?"

"And did these minor concerns alert you to the fact that they were not meeting standards for FDA approval?"

"No."

"Did they tell you that there were concerns about possible side effects from the phase three study?"

"I don't recall."

"Did they tell you that the results Aligor continued to publish were not consistent with phase three findings?"

"I don't recall that either. They simply said that they had concerns, but those all got worked out as the test results were finalized."

"Let me show you Exhibit 4. Is this document the phase three test results?"

"No."

"What is it?"

"I hate to say it, but it is a fraudulent document that your clients created to twist the results to their purpose in justifying this lawsuit."

"What about these results is inaccurate?"

"Everything. The percentage of tumor reduction was not less than ten percent but was up in the sixty-percentile range as in the first two phases."

"Anything else that is inaccurate?"

"There were no concerns with additional side effects when all the results were in."

"When was this document created?"

"I have no idea. You'd have to ask your clients."

"Let me show you Exhibit 5, purporting to represent very different results from the phase three study. I'll represent that this is a document that your attorneys produced in discovery. What is this document?"

"These are the real results from phase three. As you can see, there are no side effect issues reflected and the positive results are about sixty-two percent."

"When was this document prepared?"

"In the normal course, I'm not sure exactly when."

"Who prepared it?"

"A whole group of employees."

"Who?"

"Your clients, Art Underwood, Edward Barnes, Pete McMillan and, of course, the entire Board of Directors."

"Who is Mr. Barnes?"

"He is our Compliance Director."

"Does he know what he's doing when it comes to testing results and assuring that a product is ready for approval?"

"Absolutely. He knows his stuff."

"And who is Mr. McMillan?"

"He is one of two Managers of Product Testing. Jeff Sanchez is the other."

"Is Mr. McMillan well informed about a product's testing and readiness to market?"

"Definitely," Cook said emphatically.

"And is that the case for the past three years?"

"Yes."

"Was anyone else involved in preparing this document?"

"Maybe, but I can't name others off the top of my head."

"So, all of the persons you just named would testify to the accuracy of this document, correct?"

"Yes, that's correct."

Scott decided to change direction abruptly. "Who is Sean Garner?"

"Our Director of Security."

"What's his job?"

"Overseeing all security matters for the Company. Asset protection, technology and patent protection, everything to keep our products and people secure."

"Does that include safety issues?"

"So, he's supposed to protect, rather than endanger employees, correct?"

"Yes, of course."

"Was Mr. Garner at Art Underwood's condo the night Mr. Underwood died?"

"Objection. Calls for speculation," Gibson interjected.

"I don't have any knowledge of that, and I can't imagine any reason he would be."

"Was Mr. Underwood under any pressure by you or Mr. Garner for allegedly assisting Mr. Cardenas and Mr. Palmer with their lawsuit?"

"No, of course not." Cook did a good job of looking and sounding indignant.

"Did Mr. Garner threaten Mr. Cardenas if he didn't dismiss his lawsuit?"

"Calls for speculation again, counsel," Gibson said, sounding annoyed.

"I don't have personal knowledge, but I'm sure he would not."

"Are you aware that Mr. Garner broke into Justin Palmer's house and threatened him?"

"Same objection," Gibson said.

"Not to my knowledge and I think you are defaming Mr. Garner," Cook replied angrily.

Scott knew he was getting under Cook's skin. "Did Mr. Garner have any role in bringing about the attack on Justin Palmer that put his life in danger and caused him severe injuries?"

"I find this insulting and inappropriate," Cook said loudly.

"Counsel, I agree. This is not Garner's deposition and these wild allegations make no sense."

Scott ignored Gibson and turned his attention to Cook. "You can answer, sir. Do you have the question in mind?"

"I do and the answer is no."

"Did you receive a phone call from Mr. Garner at about 2:00 a.m. the morning following the attack on Mr. Palmer?"

Gibson said, "You can't be serious about this stuff, Scott. Don't waste our time."

Scott looked at Gibson and said, "I'm very serious, Mr. Gibson. Mr. Palmer was severely beaten and for a time after the attack stopped breathing. His injuries necessitated immediate surgery. It doesn't get much more serious." He turned his attention back to Cook. "So, did that phone call happen?"

"I don't recall that."

Scott held Cook's gaze for a time and then asked, "Did you call Mr. Garner at about 5:50 a.m. that same morning?"

"I don't know."

"Does he generally call you at 2:00 a.m.?"

"No, but there have been times when we've had to speak in the middle of the night."

Scott liked that answer. "How many times did that take place in the past three months?"

"Twice."

"And it would have to be an important matter to prompt a call in the middle of the night, correct?"

"Yes, I suppose so."

"So, you'd remember one that happened just a few days ago if you'd had such a middle of the night or early morning conversation, wouldn't you?"

"I'm sure I would."

"And there was no such call at either 2:00 a.m. to you or at 5:50 a.m. by you to Mr. Garner?"

"No."

"Let's take a break here," Gibson said.

"Fine," Scott agreed. "Can we keep it to ten minutes so that we can get through the deposition today?"

"Yeah, sure," Gibson agreed. Now Gibson would go ask his client where he thinks I'm getting this middle of the night phone call line of inquiry and what it's all about.

As Scott made some additional notes, Donna walked into the conference room and asked, "How's it going?"

"Good," Scott replied, with a grin. "He's locked into a number of positions that he won't be able to defend and a little shaken up. Between the documents we obtained, the declarations from Barnes and Bucky and the other information Lee furnished, we have some real surprises to lay on these guys at trial."

"Sounds great," she replied.

"Let's set the deposition of Pete McMillan. He doesn't want to supply a declaration to support Marty and Justin, but I don't think he'll lie under oath to cover the Company's ass."

"You got it. I'll get it set and send the notice of deposition. Talk to you when you're done."

Scott awaited the return of Cook and Gibson, readying to take him through Justin Palmer's positive performance history and the lack of any paper trail to justify his termination. He went through all of the congratulatory emails and memos that decorated Justin's file one at a time, having Cook acknowledge that he had written each and created no documents critical of Justin's performance. As the deposition concluded, Cook would be locked into testimony acknowledging the trail of positive performance of both of his clients and testimony about the Delexane phase three test results that was contradicted by documents and witnesses.

The timing of the termination decision coincided with the voicing of complaints about Delexane's phase three results not measuring up. Before that, there were commendations, not criticisms. The lack of any justifiable grounds to terminate Marty and Justin, their termination in the wake of their complaints about the false reporting on Delexane, along with proof that Aligor had manufactured a false report concerning the phase three trials should play well to a jury likely to believe that the public should be protected from false information about drugs and that whistleblowers should be protected for trying to bring the truth from the shadows.

Next he would take the deposition of Sean Garner and get him to deny all of his own conduct under oath. Sean Garner added an entirely new element, threatening and trying to coerce Marty and Justin even after the termination. Testimony by Marty, Justin and Lee about Sean Garner's actions could add an additional dimension concerning how far Aligor's executives would go to protect its secrets about the deficiencies in its product, including making threats, breaking into homes and physical attacks.

Scott wasn't sure that Cook expressly authorized the conduct, but with middle of the night phone calls between Garner and Cook were pretty good circumstantial evidence that Cook knew it was going on while doing his best to maintain plausible deniability. It would all be given to twelve people to dissect and reassemble, and hopefully, it would provide accountability for his clients and shine a light on the product for those with the greatest need for good information.

# Chapter Eighteen

Lee was satisfied with the mileage he had gotten from his Emperor Elevator uniform. Seldom was he able to use the same disguise on multiple occasions, but this one kept working. No one noticed an elevator repair guy going about his business. Of course, he was now in a residential area and there were no elevators in sight, but elevator repair guys had to live somewhere, and they would likely get up early to go about their esoteric tasks.

The morning was overcast, and most people weren't yet out on the streets. Lee drove the rented van past Sean Garner's place slowly, noting that the garage was closed. There were lights on inside the house, telling him that Garner was still inside. He parked three houses away and waited, where he could see the front door of the house and the garage door without being noticed. A half-hour later, Garner's garage door opened, and he backed out onto the street and sped away. Lee followed at a safe distance as Garner drove directly to the Aligor corporate offices. The guard at the gate waved Garner through and Lee pulled up to the gate and smiled at the young man. "Another day of fun," Lee offered, rolling his eyes.

The guard smiled and checked his list. "I don't see elevator reps on the list today."

Lee shook his head. "That happens sometimes. I was only called about the elevator problem last night, so I guess they didn't have time to get it on the list. It shouldn't take too long, but if you want, I'll go and let the bosses work it out."

The guard shook his head. "You're probably on the list inside. Just stop at the guard station and check in inside the front door."

"You got it man. Have a good day."

"Yeah, you too."

Lee drove in and made his way towards the front door and then changed direction and moved towards the employee parking lot. It was evident that Garner had discovered the bug Lee had placed on his phone, because the flow of data had suddenly stopped. The GPS he had previously placed on Garner's car had also stopped functioning, so it had either been found, fallen off, or failed mechanically. Lee decided it had to be a priority to know where this reckless bastard was at all times. He found Garner's car parked in the executive parking closest the building. He located a visitor spot not far away and parked the van, then made his way back to Garner's car and searched for the GPS he had planted. It was still there, so it had to be a mechanical failure. He removed the failed GPS and replaced it with another, sliding it inside his rear wheel-well on the passenger side. He climbed back into the van and took off, now able to keep an eye on Garner's whereabouts once again. One way or another, he had to make sure that Garner didn't come after the clients when they least expected a visit. If only he had been able to do the same for Art Underwood.

\* \* \*

**July 16**

**8:10 a.m.**

Christopher's face looked bruised and beaten around his eyes. All of his youthful energy was gone, and he was perpetually tired. Christopher suffered chest pain that made him cry and broke the hearts of his parents. His battered appearance was a reminder, not that any was needed, of what Christopher faced every day of his young life. As she watched his pain, Emma would sometimes have to find a reason to leave the room for a few minutes so that he didn't see her tears.

Another meeting in Dr. Rayburn's office. They were never good. It was the place they went periodically to get the latest bad news. Emma and Michael sat in the visitor chairs awaiting his arrival.

Emma took Michael's hand and squeezed. "I'm so scared, Michael."

He nodded slowly. An acknowledgment without an answer because there was no answer; because he was desperately scared, too. "Maybe it is better news this time," he heard himself mumble without conviction.

Dr. Rayburn entered the room. He wore a white coat over his shirt and tie. The attire he always wore. He said, "Good morning Emma and Michael," as he took a seat behind his desk and then looked up at them. There was a moment of silence while he searched his mind for the right words; the way to say what he had to say without being more downcast than necessary. "The results are not what we had hoped."

His simple words were knives to the heart. Emma felt like she might come apart at that moment. She put both hands over her face for a moment and then took deep breaths. She looked over at Michael. His eyes were closed and there were tears at the corner of his eyes. Dr. Rayburn gave them a moment to make sure they could hear what came next. "I think that we have to change courses at this point. With your consent, we will start immunotherapy."

There was a prolonged silence and then Michael asked, "How does that work?"

"Essentially, it's a regimen of drugs that stimulate the immune system to attack and kill the cancer cells."

"Will it work?" Emma posed, already knowing that she had asked the impossible.

"Sometimes it works. I can't guarantee the result, but it is successful sometimes." He drew a breath and forced a sad smile. "Like I said before, we never really know what works best in an individual case. When something doesn't work, we try something else until we find what begins to destroy the cancer cells."

Emma nodded slowly and said, "Sometimes nothing works, right?"

Dr. Rayburn sat back in his chair and folded his hands together. After a moment he said, "Yes, sometimes that's true."

Emma had no idea why she had just forced Dr. Rayburn to say that Christopher might die. One more hopeless question in a sea of questions without answers. "When do we start this new course of treatment?" she asked.

"We start tomorrow morning."

"Okay," she offered, looking down at her hands. She looked up at him and said, "Thank you for all that your team is trying to do for Christopher. I don't want to sound like I am ungrateful. I just…" she let the words trail off.

"There is no need to apologize or explain," he replied with an empathetic smile. "I know that it is very hard to learn that something else has not worked."

As they walked from his office, Emma found herself thinking of all of the wonderful parts of life that Christopher may never experience. He might not even make it through grade school years. Would he have a chance to be on a debate team? Would he know the excitement of preparing for his first day of college or his wedding day? It was all so unfair. Was this disease somewhere deep in the generations of her genes or of Michael's? The genes they carry had likely done this to an innocent child before he had the chance to live. And with these obsessive thoughts came endless guilt over factors they could not control.

\* \* \*

**July 16**
**8:40 a.m.**
Marty and Abby Cardenas sat in Scott's office and Justin was on the telephone from the hospital. Scott spent fifteen minutes detailing Cook's testimony concerning their termination, the reasons he offered, the competing phase three reports and his lack of awareness concerning Sean Garner's threats and assaults. Scott also updated them on the information Lee reported. When he was done, Scott said, "So, thanks for giving us a few extra days to assemble all of the information we could before making your final decision about whether we go forward. My gut tells me that after yesterday's deposition, Aligor will have even greater motivation to resolve the case, so if you choose it settled, I can probably get them to up the ante to get it done. What do you all think?"

Justin was the first to speak. "I've already told Marty and Abby. I'm in this until we get where we need to go. For me, this is about a company that I loved going down the wrong path. I don't want to take money to make me be quiet while they rip off the public. So, if we go to trial and lose, I'm still okay. I just want the facts to come out. And I'm hoping Jessica will stand by me because I want her in my life. I know decisions that put loved ones in danger are hard to accept, but I just have to do this." He paused a moment and then added, "She just gave me a nod, so all of my reason to walk away is now gone."

Scott nodded and looked at Marty. "How about you, Marty? I want you to know that what you do with your case is your decision and I will respect whatever decision you make."

"First, thanks for that, Scott. And thanks for your good work. You and Lee have done a hell of a job for us," Marty said. He reflected a moment and then added, "I'm not ready to jump out of the case. Abby is ready for us to end it because of the danger and I understand that, but I just can't. So, we are still in this case."

Scott nodded and then looked at Abby. "I understand your concern and I recognize that this is not easy given the craziness coming from Sean Garner."

Abby shook her head. "I want you to know that I would make a deal to end this today, Scott. I don't need our family being threatened or attacked. They beat up Justin and they probably killed Art Underwood, so I know that there is nothing they won't do to protect the billions that this product is going to bring them. I don't want me or my husband to be their next victims."

"I understand, Abby. I really do," Scott offered.

"But," she said hesitating, "my husband wants this lawsuit to continue and I am going to stand by him for now. If this gets worse, however, I am going to push hard to stop it. None of this is worth dying for."

"I agree with that," Justin interjected, "and I have no intention of letting these guys end me, but I also won't be intimidated out of doing the right thing."

"Look," Scott added, "I can't tell you that this isn't dangerous. I know what these guys have been doing. They beat Justin almost to death and they threatened all of you. One of the guys who came after Justin also pulled a gun on Lee, and it was touch and go for a while, so I would understand if you wanted to end this." He drew a breath and added, "It's like litigating in court while being strong-armed by the mafia on the street at the same time. So, let me ask one more time. You all still on board?"

"I'm in," Justin replied without hesitation.

Marty looked at Abby, who said, "Yeah, we are, too. But try to make a deal to get us out of this nightmare."

"As long as the deal includes Aligor correcting the phase three results publicly," Justin added.

"I agree," Marty added.

"Okay, I'll work on it, but I have to tell you that I'm not optimistic. These guys may pay more to settle the case, but they don't want to concede that the product is flawed because it will stop the inflow of money that has been coming from everywhere."

"Then no deal," Justin replied evenly. Marty and Abby nodded agreement and then Marty remembered that Justin could not see them and verbalized, "Agreed."

\* \* \*

**July 17**
**9:35 a.m.**

Michael was late again, and students sat waiting. He had called in to have an assistant let his class know he would be a few minutes late, but by the time he got there the hour-long class was almost half over. He apologized profusely to the class and told them of yet another personal emergency. He assured them that he would cover all of the material. There were distressed expressions around the room, but no one complained. At the end of the class, Michael apologized once more and returned to his office to find a note requesting that he meet with the university chancellor.

He went to the chancellor's office at the appointed hour and was escorted directly into the beautiful sanctuary. Chancellor Theodore Nelson stood to greet Michael, extending a hand. "Good afternoon, Michael. Thank you for meeting with me. Please sit." He directed Michael to the conference table that seated ten on the far side of the room, adjacent to the marble fireplace.

"Yes, sir," Michael replied, taking a seat.

Nelson, in his early sixties, had a full head of perfectly coifed grey hair and a warm smile. "How is Christopher doing?"

Michael didn't expect that question and he almost broke down. He moved his mouth to answer but couldn't find words. After a time, he managed to say, "Not very well, sir. As you might imagine, we are struggling."

Nelson nodded, empathy in his expression. "I understand and I'm sorry," he offered. After a pause, he said, "Michael, you are a good instructor and I see you having a track toward a full professor position. I don't want you to hurt that future by being unable to perform the duties while you are going through these times." He paused to let that sink in, and then added, "I want you to consider a sabbatical for the remainder of this semester. We have someone who can step in for you to complete the remaining eight weeks. You can either return to work next semester or take one additional semester as part of the sabbatical."

Michael's reaction changed from nervousness about his career as he realized how kindly he was being treated. This meeting could have much harsher. "I know that I have been missing too much time and I'm really sorry. It's just that we need to spend as much time as we can with Christopher right now..."

Nelson shook his head. "There is no need to explain, Michael. We understand."

Michael was barely holding himself together. "I appreciate what you are saying, sir. It's just that our medical expense has been astronomical. We have help from family, but I want to do all I can to contribute to Christopher's care."

"Let me be as supportively direct as I can. You would not be doing your career any favors to keep going this way." He looked directly into Michael's liquid eyes and said, "Take the time and be with your son. We will protect your career here. Believe me, Michael, I understand."

Michael nodded. "Yes. Thank you, sir. I really appreciate your concern." Michael shook Nelson's hand and walked from the office. It wasn't until the following day, when he said farewell to another assistant professor that he learned how painfully real Nelson's empathy was — he had lost a daughter to cancer.

* * *

**July 17**
**10:10 a.m.**
A woman appeared at Roland Cook's office door. "Excuse me, sir. I just fielded a call from Mr. Stevens. He said that he will be by to see you at three o'clock."

"Okay, Marie. Thanks." The woman disappeared from the doorway and Cook sat back in his chair with his hands joined behind his head. Albert Stevens was the only guy who could get away with demanding an appointment with the CEO when it suited him. And this wasn't good news. Cook new what the president of the board of directors wanted to talk about. The Cardenas and Palmer case was making too big a splash and the wrong people were getting wet. Add that to questions in his deposition about Garner's actions and midnight phone calls and the shitstorm seemed to be closing in on him. Cook didn't like feeling exposed and someone needed to account. He hit a button and got a "Yes, sir," in response.

"Marie, I'm expecting Sean Garner. Send him in as soon as he arrives."

"He just walked in, sir."

"Okay, send him back."

It took the better part of a minute for Garner to make it from executive reception through the maze of anterooms and offices that got him to Cook. He stood at the door and knocked rather timidly, waiting for approval to step inside. When Cook looked up at the door, his expression showed his discontent. "Come in and close the door."

Sean Garner walked inside the opulent office and closed the door. He walked a considerable distance to Cook's desk and sat down. Nothing else had been said. Cook leaned back in his chair and drew a deep breath. "What the fuck is going on, Sean?"

"What do you mean, sir?"

"Well, starting with the mess that surrounds almost killing Palmer, things are pretty bad. The cops are knocking on doors. Does that come back to you?"

"No way. No one can identify me as part of that incident."

"I had my deposition taken yesterday by Cardenas' and Palmer's lawyer. He asked me questions about you calling me in the middle of the night and me calling you back at slightly before 6:00 a.m. How is that possible, Sean?"

There was concern in Garner's eyes as he considered the question. After a prolonged period of uncomfortable silence, he said, "I don't know how that's possible." He flashed on the temporary disappearance of his phone, but there was no way he was revealing that to Cook.

"Well, that's the thing, Sean. It happened and you have no idea how," Cook replied unhappily. "That does not fill me with confidence concerning whatever you're doing."

"I'm working on giving these guys incentives to settle, it has just taken a little longer than I anticipated."

"A little longer than you anticipated? Are you kidding? There's more to it than that, Sean. One of these guys was almost killed and both of them, at least according to you, were scared shitless, but nobody is folding their tent and going home. So far, you've done nothing except make these guys dig in and get us too much press attention." Cook's eyes narrowed as he said, "I don't want probing questions from the press or the cops about whether Aligor is coming after these guys. This needs to stay under the radar or it impacts the product and the investment in the product."

Garner nodded his understanding. "What do you want me to do?"

Cook stared at him like he had just proposed that aliens were landing in the parking lot. "You were to take care of this, and I wasn't to have specifics. Do you recall that?"

"Yes, sir. I recall."

"So, now that this situation is what it is, I don't want you to make it worse. I don't want a discussion of our former employees being beaten to near death on cable news. I don't need lame attempts to motivate settlement that don't work.

What I needed, Sean, was for you to complete the assignment you were given professionally and quietly. That didn't happen." He shook his head in apparent disappointment. I'm going to need you to stay away from this now. You are drawing too much attention to yourself and to the Company."

"You can't mean that. I've gone all in on this."

"I do mean it. You need to lie low before things get worse. I will have the legal people again to make a deal and I don't need you screwing it up by giving them anything else to work with."

Sean tried desperately not to yell out in anger, but he had given so much to this effort to suddenly just be told he was out. "I can make it work, boss. Just give me a little longer."

"What part of this don't you understand, Sean? You have made the situation worse and there is already enough pressure around all of this."

Was that the end of his big bonus, his recognition, his future? Just like that? He had been looking up to this man as the one who would open the door to his future at the top of the economic ladder. Cook was an ungrateful son of a bitch. The silence had been protracted. Cook was just staring at him awaiting his response. "Okay. I understand," he heard himself say, but he knew he would not stay away from it. He would get this done with or without Cook's help.

"All right. Thanks for coming in, Sean."

Sean stood and walked from the office feeling angry, disappointed and more determined than ever to find a way to shut this lawsuit down. The Company would know that he had pulled it off, even after they gave up hope.

# Chapter Nineteen

**July 17**
**11:05 a.m.**
"Doug Gibson is on line 1, Scott."

"Thanks, Nikki." Scott hit a button and said, "Hi, Doug. Thanks for returning my call so quickly."

"What's up?"

"I just heard the news that Delexane's final review by the FDA is about to conclude and will be available for prescription within a week."

"Yes, that's right."

"Then this is the point of no return, Doug."

"Meaning what?"

"Meaning this is the last chance to fix misrepresentations the Company has made before they are stuck with what they represented to get the product across the finish line."

"We've had this conversation before, Scott."

"But this is the final moment that the Company has control of its own destiny."

There was a protracted silence and then Gibson said, "I've been meaning to call you as well. Are you available to sit down and talk today?" He didn't wait for an answer before adding, "Meet me for lunch at Saddleback. We can eat outside and talk privately."

"I'm not sure it's going to be productive," Scott replied.

"I can't guarantee the outcome, but I won't waste your time."

Scott hesitated a moment and then said, "Okay, 1:00."

"Are you bringing anyone?" Scott asked.

"No. I'll see you there," Gibson said and hung up. Scott had a feeling this was going to be a conversation about settling the case on terms that did not include fixing the phase three testing misrepresentation that were still out there in the public mind. Until a couple of weeks ago, he knew that Justin and Marty would not have agreed to a settlement that didn't include correcting the public misrepresentations about the product. But things had changed. They had both been threatened repeatedly, and in Justin's case, beaten up, and they may be at the point where they would make to settle without the public protections they had been demanding. He knew that Abby was a strong proponent of stepping back from the lawsuit before anyone else got hurt, and who could blame her? Art Underwood had been killed and Justin had been beaten and left at death's door. With that history and billions of dollars at stake, she was right to conclude that the case is as dangerous as it gets. He wanted to talk to both of his clients before the meeting with Gibson, so he knew just where they stood. It was still possible that they might elect different paths, with one ready to settle and the other ready to push on. He started with Marty, waiting while the phone rang. Whatever they chose, it had to be their decision because Scott would not play down the personal danger in going forward to trial.

* * *

**July 17**
**12:45 p.m.**
Roland Cook studied his ringing cell phone, trying to anticipate the conversation that would occur when he answered. His daughter was in so much pain and his wonderful grandson wasn't going to make it. He knew he had to act now, with or without FDA approval. His grandson couldn't hold on any longer.

He hit a button on the phone and said, "Hello, sweetheart."

"Dad, if you can do anything," his daughter's voice said through tears. "The treatment's not working, and Christopher won't make it much longer the way we are going."

"I understand, Emma. I really do. I'm working on it right now and it won't be much longer, I promise you."

There was quiet for a time and then she replied, "It can't wait. We are going to lose him, and he means everything to me. Please, Dad. Please."

His head was pounding, and he had never felt so helpless. He loved his daughter and adored his grandson. He had to make something happen for

Christopher, but there were problems. Problems with the absence of FDA approval and maybe, problems with Delexane. "It will happen, baby. I give you my word that I will see to it."

"It has to be now, Dad. There is no more time." Emma said goodbye, wondering if it wasn't already too late for her father to assist. "Please God, help me with this," she said as she stood holding the phone. "There just has to be a way."

* * *

**July 17**
**1:11 p.m.**
They ordered hamburgers that were too large to eat without guaranteeing work for the dry cleaner and sat at a table surrounded by extensive lawns and tall pine trees. Scott expected to see a deer family stop by for leftovers. It was a little bit of Yosemite with your fast food. His conversations with Marty and Justin had confirmed that, much to Abby's and Jessica's chagrin, they were not wavering in their position despite recent events. The only way it settled was if Aligor corrected the misleading data that had been repeatedly pushed into public consciousness.

"My client would like to get this case settled," Doug Gibson managed between bites. "It's a distraction from their primary focus."

"I won't ask what their primary focus is, but I know it's not full disclosure."

"Jesus, Scott. Are you trying to antagonize, or do you want to talk?"

"I'm listening," Scott replied, sounding skeptical.

"I'm so glad," came the frustrated reply. "Anyway, my clients would like to resolve the case and they are prepared to pay each of your clients $500,000 if we do it now. Naturally, we want confidentiality as part of the deal."

"Naturally," Scott replied, sarcastically. "Doug, how many times have we had this conversation? My guys want yours to correct the record as part of any settlement. They don't want the general public mislead about the quality of the product they are peddling."

"There is no correction needed, so that won't happen." He thought for a moment and then Gibson said, "If you go to trial, assuming you win, your guys are going to get money damages for their dismissal. That's it."

"And?"

"And you're asking for something you can't get at trial. There's no incentive in that for my client."

"That's okay with us. The trial will shine a light on all of the issues that we are discussing. The termination of my clients occurred because they complained about product problems and the misleading publication of test results, so all of that comes out and all of it gets reported by the media. Whatever the jury's verdict, the case brings all of the issues into the light, and the public gets an awareness of the deficiencies in the product. That is what my clients are after."

Gibson shook his head. "You know, your clients could end up being prose-cuted for fraud as a result of this case."

"So, let me make sure I have this right. My clients are perpetrating a fraud on your client who is therefore willing to pay them half a million dollars each, is that right?"

"And maybe they shouldn't, but they would like to move beyond this case. That doesn't mean your guys won't have to answer criminal charges if the prosecutor decides to move forward."

"Now you really are wasting my time," Scott replied. "You know, your guys can fix the problem with a simple disclosure correcting their..." he hesitated a moment and then said, "well let's call it a mistake. They correct the record with truthful information and the product gets marketed without resistance."

"Except that there is no mistake. Your guys created all of this to support their claims, even to the point of making false test results."

"Okay, Doug, you have a client to represent and you're a good advocate. When we show that our results are the real results, then you can keep serving your client by getting them to deal with the truth. Just keep an open mind."

"We both need to keep an open mind." Gibson was quiet for a moment and then asked, "So, I take this a rejection of the offer?"

"Yes," Scott said, "an unequivocal rejection."

"You are a stubborn son of a bitch."

"Yeah, I've heard that before," Scott replied, "but it gives us some common ground."

Doug Gibson couldn't help but chuckle. "All right. You know what we are not going to do, so go talk to your people and see if there is some other way to get this case resolved. If not, both sides will use a scatter gun approach and there will be way too much collateral damage."

\* \* \*

**July 17**
**3:05 p.m.**
Albert Stevens walked into the inner sanctum five minutes later than his self-scheduled appointment and sat down on the couch. Stevens had short grey hair and glasses perched on his nose below large brown eyes. At 6' 3" and two hundred fifty pounds, he was an imposing figure. He was a thoughtful man. He spoke softly, but there was unmistakable strength behind his words.

"Good afternoon, Albert," Roland Cook said, moving around his desk and taking a position in one of the armchairs across from the couch.

Stevens nodded. "I guess you know why I'm here, Roland."

"I have a general idea, but why don't you tell me specifically what's on your mind."

Stevens nodded slowly, his expression downcast. "The Board is very concerned. The Cardenas and Palmer case is driving a great deal of media discussion. We are hearing blurbs on cable and social media every day now. They are saying that we are engaging in fraud and we are getting calls that suggest they are scoring points and gaining followers with this campaign. We need it to stop, Roland. These two guys are the only real impediment to our roll out of Delexane and this controversy could end up costing the company millions."

Cook leaned back in his chair. He nodded and said, "I've been listening to all the chatter and we're trying to get rid of the case. I have the lawyers trying to make a deal now."

"It has to happen, Roland. Negotiate your best deal but give them what it takes to make it go away."

"It's not quite that simple," Cook replied.

"Why not?"

"Because they are demanding that we change our phase three results as part of any settlement."

Stevens was quiet for a time, and then he asked, "Are there some problems with our numbers?"

"We don't think so," Cook replied, "but we know the dispute hurts us."

"I can tell you that the Board will support you if you have to modify the numbers a little bit to get this done." Stevens looked directly at Cook and said, "We need this dispute to end. Our numbers are currently in the spotlight every day, and it's nothing compared to the attention that will be coming if this case goes to trial."

"I understand," Cook offered, "but they don't want to modify the numbers a little. They want to take our effectiveness rate from phase three from sixty-five percent to twelve percent."

Stevens studied him silently. "Are they right?"

"No. Our people have not agreed with them."

"Okay, then. Work to compromise, but if we are right about the numbers, we'll take the fight to the end." He paused and added, "If you learn anything different, you get hold of me right away. The Board needs to stay on top of this."

"I will," Cook said. "If I hear something contrary, I'll call you."

Stevens said, "Okay, thanks." He stood and shook hands with Cook, but before he walked out of the office he asked, "What did Art Underwood think about the numbers?"

Cook hesitated a little too long and Stevens said, "I see. You know, I respected Art. He was a dedicated man who knew his stuff. If he had concerns about this, then I do too." Albert Stevens walked out of the office without looking back, leaving Roland Cook thinking that he needed to do make a deal and make this all go away.

\* \* \*

**July 19**
**8:00 a.m.**

Olivia Blake put down the phone just in time to get buzzed one more time. She picked up the phone and an intercom voice said, "Detective Blake, I have another call for you."

"Take a message for me, Lilly. I've been on three in a row while I have Mrs. Underwood sitting here waiting to talk to me."

"Shall do."

"Have you seen Ed?"

"Yep. He just walked by and said to tell you he's on his way."

As she put down the phone, Olivia Blake gave Sandi a smile and shook her head. "Sorry to keep you waiting, it has just been pretty crazy around here."

"It's okay," Sandi replied. "I understand."

Ed Farris walked into the small office, where three chairs barely fit between stacks of files. "Hi, Mrs. Underwood," Farris said, offering her a hand.

They shook and Sandi said, "You guys are busy I know. It's not easy to get an audience with you."

Olivia smiled. "We're sorry, but we're down a detective and up a number of serious crimes." She took a breath and said, "So, what can we do for you?"

"You can tell me that you have Sean Garner in custody."

The detectives regarded each other, and Olivia said, "No, did someone tell you he was in custody?"

She shook her head. "No one told me that he was in custody, but he killed my husband and he should be."

Farris wore a serious expression. "We can't say that you're wrong, but as of now we don't have the evidence to prove that he killed your husband, Mrs. Underwood."

"You'll excuse me if I disagree," she said, sounding annoyed. "It seems pretty damned obvious to me. He was outside the door of our building right before he broke the lock and entered, he's been harassing Marty Cardenas and Justin Palmer, broke into Palmer's house to threaten him and then had him beat up." She shook her head. "What more could you possibly need?"

"We can't specifically identify Garner as the man in the distant, grainy photos. We can establish that he was in the vicinity that night, but we can't prove Garner was ever in your apartment. There were no fingerprints or other physical evidence that ties him to the scene. Threatening Cardenas and Palmer is assault, and breaking and entering when he entered Palmer's residence, but that doesn't prove that he murdered your husband."

Sandi wore a look of frustration. "You aren't going to get him, are you? You're going to let him get away with it," she said with some combination of disgust and disapproval.

"If he did it, we'll get him. You need to be patient because we have to do it right. When we arrest him need to have enough evidence to prevent some defense attorney from getting him off with a slap on the wrist." She sat back in her chair. "I know it's taking time, Sandi, but we have to be able to prove our case. Trust me when I tell you that we are working on it every day."

"Right, with one fewer detective and many other cases."

"There are some things I can't change," Olivia offered. "We will keep you informed as we find new connections. I promise."

Sandi slowly nodded. There was an extended period of silence while she considered her response. Then she stood and said, "Thanks for your time. Please keep me informed. You can call me anytime."

"We will," Farris offered. "Definitely."

She walked towards the door and then stopped. She looked back at the two detectives and in even tones said, "My husband was a good man."

"We've heard that from everyone who knows him," Olivia said with sincerity.

Sandi nodded and then said, "Please get this asshole."

"Yes, ma'am," Farris replied. "We will do all we can."

As Sandi walked to her car, she had the disappointing realization that these detectives were good people who worked hard, but if they didn't have the evidence to convict Sean Garner now, how would they get it? Didn't the likelihood of finding the evidence they needed diminish with every day that passed? Was Art's murder going to become one more case that goes cold? He was owed so much more than that.

# Chapter Twenty

Emma and Michael told Christopher that these were new drugs that the doctors were going to give him. He looked beaten and bruised from some combination of the disease and the treatment. He had lost weight and his face was shadowy and gaunt.

"It's going to make me better?" he asked, hopefully. One more knife to the heart.

"We sure hope so, son," Michael said, putting his arm around Christopher. "Sorry it is taking so long to get you well."

The immunotherapy brought a new round of suffering for a child who had been through far too much. Christopher woke up in the middle of the night with complaints of stomach pain. Emma sat next to him on his race car shaped bed and hugged him as he cried out in pain. It was all so cruel and heartbreaking.

Medically, Dr. Rayburn had alerted them to the possibility. The pain was an anticipated symptom of the treatment and there was a regiment of pain medication available, but that medication had to be adjusted, something that could take a couple of weeks. Watching their son in pain, bruised and battered by this horrific disease, consumed their thoughts and broke their hearts every day.

Emma didn't sleep much anymore. She abandoned the pretense of going to bed. She would fall asleep in the living room at some point during the night and sleep until she didn't, which wasn't very long. She would awaken and thoughts of her slowing dying child were immediately at the front of her mind. Sometimes the lack of sleep would catch up with her and she would fall asleep during the day, when there were moments of limited activity.

Christopher was spending more and more time in bed. He was endlessly fatigued by treatments that poisoned his system. The doctors said that the growth of the tumor was being slowed by the treatment, but it had not been stopped; the substance of these reports told Emma and Michael that this was not a battle they would win in the long run. They were trading Christopher's pain and discomfort for an unknown quantity of additional time. The tumor and the treatment were combining to ravage their son, and in return, he might live longer. Were they doing the right thing? One more excruciating question played over and over without an answer.

Emma felt like she was losing both of her men. Her son was waging a battle that was beyond him and Michael had withdrawn into some distant world where there were no answers and where there was no hope. He seldom spoke and moved through life as a somnambulist. Physically present and emotionally on hold, doing his best to feel less and find a way to momentarily stop the pain.

* * *

## July 21
### 11:40 a.m.

Emma glanced at her ringing phone and recognized the number. Dr. Rayburn didn't usually call directly. All appointments were made by staff and the only time she spoke directly to him was at the regular meetings where the latest round of bad news was delivered. She grabbed the phone and swiped to answer. "Hello, Dr. Rayburn?"

"Yes. Hi, Emma."

"Is everything okay?" she asked, concern in her voice.

"It is. We have a major change of plans and I wanted to tell you right away. The new protocol for Christopher will begin tomorrow morning at 8:00 a.m."

"We knew there were new drugs, why is this a change in plans?" Emma asked, confused.

"It's the nature of the treatment, Emma. We are going to start a brand-new regimen with a good success rate."

Emma paused a moment and then asked, "My father brought this to you, didn't he?"

After a hesitation, Dr. Rayburn said, "Yes. The drugs are going to be delivered this afternoon."

"Oh God, thank you," Emma almost prayed into the phone.

"It is exciting news, Emma. See you in the morning."

"We'll be there early and ready," she replied, feeling more encouraged than she had in weeks.

* * *

**July 21**
**3:50 p.m.**
Roland Cook pushed a button and said, "Get Doug Gibson on the phone for me."

"Yes, sir."

Cook made a few notes on his computer and thirty seconds later there was a buzz. "Doug Gibson on line 3, sir."

"Thanks." Cook hit a button and said, "Doug, is there any update on the case?"

"Nothing you don't know about. They set the depositions of Pete McMillan and Sean Garner. I called Pete and Ed Barnes yesterday to tell them that I wanted to get their statements formalized. Pete told me that he would support the company's position on phase three, but Ed Barnes was non-committal."

"What do you mean non-committal?"

"I told him I wanted him to sign a formal statement that makes clear that the company's position on phase three is accurate. He just said he did not want to sign a statement, but he would answer all questions truthfully, so I don't really know what he plans to say."

"Holy shit. That is very disconcerting. We need to know what he plans to say. We'll find out, but we can't let the other side find him, so instruct him to lay low and talk to no one."

Gibson hesitated and then said, "I can't command him not to talk to anyone, but I will encourage that, yes sir."

Cook considered a moment and then said, "I need to make something happen with this case, Doug. The Board would like to see a resolution so we can focus on the distribution of the product."

"Yes, sir. It has just been difficult to make a deal we can live with given the nature of Scott Winslow's demands concerning the phase three testing."

"You're right about that. So, let's change our approach. Let's invite them to the table in an in-person meeting with attorneys and clients. Tell them all limitations are off and that we'll discuss any possible means of settling the case. Then we'll go after them with everything we've got. We'll serve them with a copy of the cross-complaint for fraud, defamation and abuse of process against Cardenas and Palmer and we'll come prepared to discuss what our key witnesses will say about phase 3 at trial. I want to make a big push to motivate resolution before Delexane is released for sale by the FDA."

"Yes, sir, Gibson replied. We can do all of that and project confidence in the result." Gibson was quiet for a moment and added, "I would suggest that we provide a neutral place for the meeting, like a hotel conference room. People can be less defensive when they don't feel they are in the lair of the other team."

"It's in your hands, Doug. Set up the meeting within the next couple of weeks. Give me possible date and time as soon as you can. I'll have my assistants give the scheduling a priority so whenever you and Winslow set it up you and I can be there."

"I'll get back to you as soon as I talk to Winslow," Doug Gibson said.

"Good, thanks," Cook replied and then hung up, leaving Gibson to consider how productive such a meeting was likely to be.

\* \* \*

## July 21
### 6:10 p.m.

"Scott, Doug Gibson on line two."

"Thanks." Scott hit a button and said, "Hello, Doug, what now? You want to tell me that my clients kidnapped the Lindbergh baby or perhaps stole the Mona Lisa?"

"I didn't know the Mona Lisa was missing."

"It isn't, but since when did the real facts stop your client tossing out false accusations."

"Ouch. Another nasty mood?"

"No, sorry. Just on high alert for low flying bullshit."

"You are a piece of work, Winslow."

"Thanks. I'll take that as a compliment."

"I suppose you could if you put on your rose-colored glasses."

Scott was quiet for a moment and then asked, "So, is there an agenda for this call or are we just enjoying exchanging quips?"

"There is an agenda, you just haven't let me get to it yet." He hesitated a moment and then said, "My client thinks it makes sense for the attorneys and principals to sit down and see if we can hash out a deal."

"Right," Scott said, sarcastically. "And this deal will include confidentiality agreements that my clients sign to prevent them from discussing the shortcomings of the drug, but no obligation on your client's part to correct misleading phase three numbers; am I anticipating this meeting correctly?"

"No. We can discuss any possible way of getting the case settled in hopes of getting to some bottom line that works for both sides. Everybody comes to make proposals and both sides listen. Maybe we can't get there, but we shouldn't miss the chance to try."

"If you're telling me that nothing is off the table, we will attend and make one more attempt, but you know what we're after."

"Just don't be closed to other possibilities. Let's all be open to a way to make it work."

"Fine," Scott replied, "where are we going to hold this meeting?"

"Let's pick a date and I'll reserve a conference room at the Bonaventure Hotel downtown. To show you our good faith, my client will pick up the tab for the conference facility."

"That works. My office will get back to you today or tomorrow with available dates a couple of weeks out."

"Sounds good," Gibson replied. "I'll have a few more quips ready by then."

"Good, but let's hope that's not the most productive part of the session."

\* \* \*

**July 22**
**2:10 p.m.**
The Tropics' lunch business was waning as the three women were escorted to their seats on the patio. The margaritas were delivered quickly, and their lunch orders were tendered to a male server who looked some combination of bored and tired.

"Thanks for doing this again," Sandi offered with a soft smile. "Having the chance to be with you helps me cope."

"Are you kidding?" Abby replied with a smile. "Good company and good margaritas. It's really not too hard to take as a late lunch break in the day."

"We should do it every couple of weeks," Jessica said. "Let's consider it a brand-new tradition."

There was a moment of quiet and then Jessica asked, "Did you have your meeting with the detectives?"

Sandi nodded solemnly. "I did."

"And?" Abby interjected.

Sandi shrugged. "Not much news, really. They say that they don't have enough to connect Sean Garner to Art's death to bring him in yet."

"That's it?"

"Pretty much. They are still working at it, but it looks like they are so damned busy that they don't have all the time they need to track all of the evidence. They say that they could bring Garner in for breaking and entering and assault, but they can't prove he killed Art."

Looking for some reason to be upbeat, Jessica said, "At least they are still working on the investigation."

"They are and they say that they will keep me in the loop." She shrugged.

"Are you feeling discouraged?" Abby asked.

"Yeah, a little bit. But I guess they can only do what they can do."

"I think that's the right way to look at it," Jessica added. "Let them keep working it and try not to let it drive you crazy. I hear through Lee and Scott that these detectives are competent at what they do."

"Yeah, you're right. A watched pot never boils and all that kind of philosophical stuff. I'll just let them work it through and tell myself it will all be okay when we get to the end of the investigation."

"I think that's all we can do," Abby replied. "I want you to know, Sandi, Marty talks about Art all the time. He really is an inspirational figure to Marty and Justin."

"Thank you. I want him to be remembered for who he was. It seems that he had a positive effect on many lives."

"He did. He definitely did. To Art," Abby said, raising her glass. "He will always be in our hearts."

The glasses clinked and they took a drink. Sandi smiled, grateful for her friends. Maybe she could find happiness again at some point, and maybe this group would be one small part of that road to happiness. But for now, she had found a purpose and that would help her to survive and she was able to smile. Something that was unfamiliar since Art had died. Sandi was satisfied that this meeting had served her purpose well. If Abby Cardenas or Jessica Morris were asked about her state of mind, they would say that Sandi had accepted the fact that all she could do was wait for the police to complete their investigation.

* * *

**July 26**
**9:10 p.m.**
Sean Garner spent the entire weekend catching up and this had been a hectic Monday. He had thrown himself into all the work he put aside while focusing on ending the Cardenas and Palmer lawsuit. Over the past three days he addressed a multitude of security issues and delegated other issues to members of his staff. All that was going as it should, but Sean found himself getting more and more angry. His efforts to end the litigation had been undervalued and he had been cast aside by Cook. But he knew how close he was to getting these guys to walk away, he could feel it in his bones. One more push and they would make a deal. At the end of the Monday workday, he told his department managers that he would be out of the office for a couple of days. Having cleared his calendar for a couple of days, he was ready to get back to the project that mattered most.

Once at home, he began studying images on Google Earth as a means of accessing some inside information. From his desktop, he watched the street in front of the Palmer house. It was quite a tool, making it possible to case a house, and a whole neighborhood, from miles away. He could see everything as clearly as if he were in the street in front of Palmer's house and walking his neighborhood. And it could all be accomplished without being conspicuous; without watchful neighbors calling the police or coming out to stare at a stranger.

Sean could see what Justin's neighborhood looked like at night — the traffic passing on his residential street, the number of people taking walks in the evening and the nature and extent of lighting in front of the house, and up and down the street. This accumulated data, gathered from the comfort of his living room, would tell him the best time of night to enter the Palmer house.

He decided that Justin Palmer would be the best target because he still bore the physical and emotional scars of the recent attack. He would be vulnerable and could be pushed over the edge. If his trip to see Justin Palmer didn't carry the day, his back-up plan would be to go after Abby Contreras, who was Marty Contreras' greatest point of vulnerability.

As he continued to watch Justin Palmer's house and the surrounding neighborhood, Sean was confident that the back-up plan wouldn't be needed. When people were attacked it introduced a whole new level of vulnerability — a realization that you can never really be safe and that your previous beliefs that you were secure in your environment were simply an illusion.

Sean understood the psychological impact of a life-threatening beating and he planned to take advantage of Justin Palmer's newly discovered reality. One more visit would convince Palmer to make his best deal and walk away from the litigation. It was the perfect time to do it, while the memory of the last attack and its resultant injuries were still haunting him. When it was all done, Roland Cook would learn that Sean had pulled it off on his own. The recognition and the reward would belong to him.

\* \* \*

**July 27**
**5:10 p.m.**
"Scott, Marty Cardenas is on line one."

"Thanks, Nikki. I'll take it."

"Hey, Marty," Scott offered after hitting a button.

"Hi Scott. I have a disturbing update."

"Okay, disturb away."

"Pete McMillan called me, and he seems to be on the verge of a breakdown. He said his deposition is less than three weeks away and he wants us to find a way to let him off the hook."

"Why?" Scott asked.

"Because he has been telling both sides what they want to hear. The defense lawyer, Doug Gibson, talked to him the other day and applied a little pressure to get him to toe the company line. He apparently got scared and said he would support their position in his deposition testimony."

"Great," Scott replied. "So, now that he has given inconsistent commitments, do we know what he's really going to say?"

"He says that he will probably support us if he is pushed, but he doesn't want to do it. He says his wife is seriously ill and he needs to keep his job."

"He said 'probably?' Makes it sound like the truth is whatever is most convenient at the time." After a moment of reflection, Scott asked, "So, what did you tell Pete?"

"I told him I'd talk to you, but I couldn't assure him we wouldn't need to call on him."

"Good," Scott replied. "Let him know that we will need to keep his deposition on calendar and call on him to tell the truth. I mentioned to you that we were setting that settlement conference for a date a few weeks out. As it turns out, the date that works is August 12, which is the day before his deposition. If the case settles, and we have no reason to believe that is likely, then he'll be off the hook. Otherwise, we're going to need Pete to get off the fence and tell the truth. Hopefully, when push comes to shove, he won't perjure himself to keep his job."

"I'll let him know that his deposition has to remain on calendar, and we expect him to tell the truth. I'll tell him that he's not off the hook and that if he lies, he's going to be caught between a rock and a hard place because he told me something different than he said under oath. It may piss him off, but I have to hold his feet to the fire, so he doesn't jump ship."

"I agree, Marty. I don't see any other way. If this case goes to trial, we need to have him locked in just in case he decides it's more expedient to lie when he takes the witness stand."

"You know," Marty replied, sighing. "I had no idea how deep this would go. This battle with Aligor has blown Justin and me out of the job market and made all of our former friends run for cover. Thank goodness Ed Barnes is still on our team." He hesitated and then asked, "He is still on our team, right?"

Scott said, "Yep. He pretty much has to be. We have his signed declaration stating under oath that he knows the phase three realities are what you say they are rather than how Aligor is presenting them. It won't go well for him on the witness stand if he tries to change that testimony."

"He may not like us anymore either when this is all over, but at least we have him committed." Marty shook his head. "After this litigation, we should have a party to see how many of our former friends will show up. We can probably hold it in a phone booth."

\* \* \*

## July 27
### 10:50 p.m.

Sean Garner now knew Justin Palmer's neighborhood better than he knew his own. He spent two days and nights planning and studying the streets that surrounded Justin Palmer's house on Google Earth. He now knew the surrounding streets, the shapes and elevations of all houses on the block and traffic patterns at all hours of the night. Justin Palmer now spent most every night with his girlfriend, sometimes at her condo, but more often at his house. From real estate websites, he determined surrounding houses that were on the market, and of those which ones were unoccupied.

The job should be simple at this point. He didn't have to convince Palmer and Cardenas to give up their claims without compensation. Aligor was prepared to write Palmer and Cardenas sizable checks to settle. As the facilitator of that settlement, his only job was to provide the right incentive. Tomorrow night would be the night. It would even be better if Jessica was present when he arrived, so that she could help convince him that there really was no choice.

Sean enlarged the view of the Swanson Street, which Dawn Avenue, where Justin lived. He would park at 1101 Swanson Street and walk two houses down to 1109, a house that was on the market and from the realtor.com listing, it was clear that it was unoccupied. From there, he would climb the brick wall into the back-yard of 1109 Swanson Street, where he knew that there was no dog. He would cross the backyard and go over the fence into Justin's backyard. He would then enter the Palmer house through the laundry room window. He also made sure that his chosen route was free of closed-circuit cameras. When he left the area, Palmer would want to make a deal to end his litigation and no one would know Sean had been there. It was still twenty-four hours away, but already the adrenaline rush had begun.

He had his tools assembled, including rope, handcuffs and a couple of modified tasers that could be used to impose electrical stimulus in ever-increasing voltage. Sean considered this his final opportunity to get it right and he would do whatever it took to achieve the only possible result.

# Chapter Twenty-One

**July 27**
**11:35 p.m.**

As Sean Garner studied Justin Palmer's neighborhood, a car was parked across the street from his next-door neighbor, in a location that gave the visitor a clear view of Sean's house while keeping the car outside of the glow of any streetlight. The visitor studied the two-story house and its surroundings for a time. Lights were on in the southeast quadrant of the house; the ground floor away from the garage. Most of the other residents on the street had turned in for the night and lights were off, with the exception of security lighting and motion lights that could be triggered by the unwelcome or an adventurous cat. During the half-hour the visitor waited, only one car drove past and it pulled into a garage about ten houses further down the block. No one was on the street. After a time, the visitor then got out of the car and walked slowly towards Sean's garage, and then to the side of the house and inspected the walk-in entry door to the garage. The visitor tried the locked handle of the door and it was locked. Inserting a metallic blade into the handle, the visitor heard a single click as the door lock was defeated and the handle now turned. No alarms sounded. Satisfied, the visitor took a deep breath and then walked back to the waiting car.

* * *

**July 28**
**6:08 p.m.**

Justin Palmer walked into The Briar Patch and looked around. Marty was already positioned at a table in the back of the bar with a beer in front of him and another in front of the empty chair that awaited. Justin smiled and walked over to Marty, shaking his hand and sitting down. Justin glanced around at the dark wood interior of the bar, which looked even darker with the dim lighting throughout.

"Just out of curiosity, how did you pick this place?" Justin asked.

"It was the least conspicuous place I could find. I mean, you can't even see it when you're in it."

They laughed aloud and picked up their beer glasses. "Here's to friendship, survival and vague memories of having a career," Marty offered. They clinked glasses and took a drink. "You're getting around pretty well."

"Yeah," Justin replied. "Physical therapy helps. A minor limp and it doesn't really start hurting until later in the day when I'm wearing down." He was quiet for a moment and then said, "I think getting together like this is some deranged version of good mental therapy. It's comforting to know that someone else is in the same boat."

"Yep, even if it has multiple leaks and is slowly sinking," Marty replied.

"Right," Justin replied. "Here we are with no career, former colleagues and friends who look at us like we're contagious, and the media trying to figure out if we're a fraud of some kind."

"And don't forget the guy who thinks he will end the litigation or end us. Santa, as Jessica calls him."

"I can't forget him. I think about him every day because I think he's going to be coming for us." He paused and then added, "I bought a gun."

"Yeah?"

"He already beat me to just this side of dead once and I think he's coming back."

Marty studied him. "What kind of a gun?"

"A Glock. I'm told it's reliable and it's pretty easy to operate."

"A little scary though."

"Yeah, I never thought I'd have a gun. And I'm not one of those guys who grew up feeling comfortable around them. But then again, I never thought Santa would be trying to kill me either." He shook his head and added, "And Garner has already shown me just how easily he can penetrate my alarm and show up in my house."

"Just make sure you shoot Santa and not Jessica or the mailman."

"Jessica is going to be right next to me and mailman better not show up at midnight."

Marty took a sip of his beer and asked, "So, what do you do? I mean are you sitting up all night aiming a gun at your front door?"

"I installed cameras on each of the corners of the house. Of course, I know that he can probably disable those, too." He shook his head. "And I'm always listening. I stay up late and sleep light. The gun is always within reach."

Marty shook his head. "Sounds like this asshole is getting just what he wants. He has both of us perpetually waiting for the other shoe to drop. I walk around the house with a pipe in my hand when there is any kind of sound or just when I'm nervous. Which is all the time. Abby is trying really hard not to saying anything, but I know she hates it."

Justin's turn to sip his beer. He leaned back in his chair and said, "Part of me wants to go after him and force a showdown to get this over with."

"Perfect. I love a good shootout." He shook his head. "Let's try not to get crazy."

Justin nodded. "I know. I really don't want to shoot anyone. I just want this done. I'm tired of waiting to be attacked."

"I know what you mean. Even while we're sitting here, I keep staring at the door to make sure he doesn't show up."

"Yeah. It's a nightmare that is never over. So, I want to give the whole damned thing a nudge."

"Great idea," Marty replied, shaking his head. "Let's give a crazy person a push towards a showdown."

"All right, I get it. It just makes me feel so helpless."

"You are singing to the choir. Between some asshole trying to do us in, friends that aren't allowed to talk to us, and a great job we no longer have, I'm feeling like the whole world is upside down."

"Yeah," Justin said. "Me too. Any reason of optimism is hard to find."

"I felt a little when you walked in," Marty offered. "It's more than just seeing a good friend, it's an affirmation that we both made it one more day. I'm scared that we are going to set a meeting like this and only one of us will be able to show up."

"What are we going to do about it? How do we break out of this nightmare?" Marty asked, sounding desperate.

"I don't have a clue. You got any ideas?"

Marty shook his head. "Only one. Let's have one more beer while we're both still able."

* * *

**July 28**
**7:45 p.m.**
While he ate a hamburger and waited for Melissa to get home from a late meeting, Lee Henry read the latest stories about the soon to be released Aligor miracle drug and its dispute with the two employees who claimed their stats were fraudulent. Every article had reader comments appended because everyone had an opinion. For some, it was just sour grapes and money that motivated these two former executives. For others, it was big pharma trying to get away with one more rip off and bring in billions of dollars at the expense of the people who struggled to make ends meet.

One of the articles focused on the drugs that Aligor and its two competitors had created and Aligor's lead with the now disputed results of its drug trials. Another article described the roles and work history of Martin Cardenas and Justin Palmer, respecting the creds and portraying them in a favorable light.

The next article that drew Lee's attention focused on the Aligor CEO, Roland Cook. Cook was described as a well-educated and recognized as a man of vision. A leader who made things happen, knew his products inside out, and was also well-connected politically. It was an interesting article about a rich and powerful man. Then suddenly, it was more than that. "Holy shit!" Lee said to the empty room. "Cook has a grandchild with cancer." He reread the passage and he knew exactly who he had to talk to about it. This could be something that made a difference and it was right out there in plain sight. Most people would read right through the passage with a little sympathy and otherwise without a second thought. What he saw was tucked neatly between the lines and it could get him some critical information. He would set up an unexpected meeting and go right at the source.

As the lights of Melissa's car shone on the house, Lee smiled. He quickly checked his GPS tracker and noted that Sean Garner's car was home. For the moment, everyone should be safe. He met Melissa at the door.

"Hi, handsome," she said with a smile.

He took her in his arms and kissed her softly, and then harder. "Welcome home," Lee said, softly.

"You sure know how to make a long meeting a thing of the past."

"How about a glass of wine?" he asked.

"Sounds great," she replied, taking off her jacket. She sat down on the couch and he approached with a glass of wine in each hand. "Thanks." She took a sip and nodded approval. After a moment, she said, "Marty, Justin and Scott are getting quite a bit of media attention these days."

"Yeah," Lee said, "they sure are. What are you hearing?"

"Mixed messages like crazy. From the media blitz out there it's hard to tell if they are victims of corporate abuse or scoundrels trying to blackmail corporate leaders trying to produce a product that the country desperately needs."

"Yep. That's the picture I'm getting as well."

"How about the crazy guy who has been after Marty and Justin, is he still at it?"

"Not tonight. I checked right before you got home and his car is at his house, so unless he's chasing them on foot or with a rental car, they are okay for tonight."

Melissa reflected a moment and then said, "They are probably both pretty nervous at this point."

"They are. I just heard that Justin bought a gun in case Garner shows up in his house again."

She nodded. "I'm not a fan of guns but I don't blame him. In their shoes, I don't know if I'd ever sleep again."

"I don't blame him either and I do think that at some point he's going to come at them again. I just don't know how."

She studied him for a minute. "And you have a way of getting yourself involved when it all hits the fan, so be careful. Please." She leaned in and kissed him.

"I will. I always want to be able to come home to you," Lee said. "Have I told you lately that I've never been happier?"

"Tell me often, because I love it. Just don't make me a widow before we even get married."

Lee reflected on his conversation with Scott about whether that was possible. Instead of commenting about the logistics, he simply said, "I'll be careful."

"I'm sorry," she said, "but I have to spend a couple of hours reviewing for a new project tonight."

"That's okay," Lee replied. "I have some work I want to do as well. As Melissa changed into blue jeans, they had a glass of wine together and then Melissa jumped into her newest project and Lee returned to his computer.

\* \* \*

**July 28**
**10:45 p.m.**
Sean Garner put on his black jacket and gloves. He planned to be an invisible shadow in the night until he was ready to be seen. It would take less than fifteen minutes to get to Justin Palmer's neighborhood with late night light traffic. His tools were in an easy to handle tote in the trunk of the car. Everything was ready and his adrenaline was pumping.

He turned off lights in the house and made his way to the kitchen and then took a step out into the garage. He had taken a couple of steps towards his car when he felt a sharp pain in his neck. Something bit him. He swung his arms around behind him but didn't make contact with anything. He needed to turn on the light to see what had happened and to see if there was a mark on his neck. He grabbed at the light switch and turned it on, then he saw her squatting behind the door to the kitchen. His expression was pure surprise as their eyes met for a moment. "What are..." he started to say and then he silently fell to the floor as the pentobarbital cocktail Sandi had prepared and injected into his neck took hold.

She stared down at the man who murdered the love of her life, wondering if he really thought he would never be held to account. She dragged the dead weight of his body around to the driver's seat of his car. She took the car keys from his pocket and then pulled his lifeless body into the driver's seat, going around to the passenger's side to complete the process of moving him into position. When he was behind the wheel, his face pressed up against it, she returned to her supplies at the back of the garage, placed the hose around the exhaust as tightly as she could, and put the other end of the hose through the driver's window. She started the car and closed the window tightly around the hose, then checked the gas gauge to assure that there was plenty of fuel in the tank. It was three quarters full. She could already smell the exhaust coming in as she climbed out of the car on the passenger's side and closed the door behind her. The injection would put him out for at least an hour, long enough for the carbon monoxide flow to do its job.

Sandi looked at the unconscious Garner seated behind the wheel one last time and then walked over and picked up the full, five-gallon gas can and the supply bag she brought along, which was a lot lighter without the hose she was leaving behind. She glanced one last time at the running car and the unmoving body behind the wheel. Satisfied, she opened the walk-through door from the garage to the side of the house and twisted the lock on the handle so that who-ever found the body would find the door locked from the inside. She stepped outside and closed the door behind her. She stared at the garage door for a time and then turned and disappeared into the night.

# Chapter Twenty-Two

Emma and Michael sat in Dr. Rayburn's office once again, with familiar feelings of anticipation approaching panic. It was as if making them wait was part of the torture; they sat idly with the expectation that bad news that was always just around the corner.

Dr. Rayburn walked into the room and sat down. He was quiet for a moment and then slowly grinned. "It's good news," he offered. "We are seeing the beginnings of tumor shrinkage."

"Oh my God," Emma screamed. "Really?"

"Yes, really. We are only a week into the new therapy, and the drug appears to be working."

"It's the drug my father provided?"

Dr. Rayburn nodded. "It is."

Emma and Michael lit up, grinning widely. "Thank you so much," Emma said. Michael sat speechless for a time and then hugged his wife and they both began to cry, except this time, they were tears of joy.

Dr. Rayburn smiled as he watched their reactions. "It's nice to have good news to share for a change," he said.

"I can't tell you how this feels," Michael said, finding his words.

"So, we keep on with this therapy. I think we finally have the right treatment and if this progress continues, I expect you will begin to notice that Christopher is getting stronger."

"Wow, this is just incredible," Emma said. "I have to call my dad and thank him."

"Yes," Dr. Rayburn replied with a smile. "That sounds like a good idea. See you at our next meeting. If something significant develops before then, I'll call you."

"Thank you, Dr Rayburn," Michael said, feeling a tremendous weight suddenly lifted from his shoulders.

"My pleasure. See you soon," he said, wearing a rare smile.

As they left the office, Emma was already dialing her father.

"Hi, sweetheart," Roland Cook answered.

"Dad, thank you so much. We just left our meeting with Dr. Rayburn and Christopher is doing better. His tumors are beginning to shrink."

"That's wonderful, sweetheart. I'm so glad to hear it."

"He told us it's because of your new drug. Thank you so much."

"I am delighted that my wonderful grandson is doing better. Truly. Do me one favor though, and don't say anything about the drug. We aren't yet authorized to use the drug because the final FDA approval hasn't happened yet, so we need to keep that low profile."

"Got it. No problem, we will keep that in confidence. But I want you to know that whatever happens next, you extended Christopher's life and I will never forget it. I love you, Dad."

"I love you too, sweetheart. Give my best to Michael, too."

"I will. He wants me to tell you thank you from him as well."

"Tell him you're both welcome. And give my grandson a hug for me. Me and your mother will come see him this weekend. If he's up for it, we can take him for ice cream."

"Yeah, he may even feel well enough to enjoy that."

\* \* \*

## July 29
### 11:45 a.m.

Sandi Underwood had arrived back home a little after 1:00 a.m. She spent some time looking at pictures of her and Art, from their early and youthful days together through their wedding and honeymoon in Hawaii. She made her way to more recent pictures and found herself aching to be beside him again as she crawled into bed. She set an alarm for 6:30 a.m. and slept comfortably.

When the alarm went off, she made coffee and then began her day as she normally would. She sent emails to a couple of old friends, making plans for an outing the following week, and then she wrote to Abby Cardenas and Jessica

Morris, suggesting that they select a day for their next trip for margaritas at The Tropics.

By late morning, Sandi was checking the internet for local news. There was no mention of Sean Garner or anyone in the area dying of carbon monoxide poisoning. She began to wonder if maybe he had awakened in time to extricate himself from his assisted suicide. It was possible that he managed to escape the death sentence, but even so, there was nothing that connected her to the scene. Unless he recognized her from the single instant that their eyes met. If that happened, the police just might show up at her door and she would have to feign ignorance of the whole matter. They had no way of placing her at the scene. She had even remembered to turn off her cellphone before leaving home, and left it off all night, so that her whereabouts couldn't be determined.

Sandi decided that she would walk to the park, just like she and Art used to do. She left the apartment and started her walk. It was a cool, sunny day and it felt wonderful to go walking as they had done together so often. As she walked, Sandi looked to the sky and said, "I love you, sweetheart, and I don't know for sure, but I think I got the son of a bitch."

\* \* \*

**July 29**
**5:55 p.m.**
"Mr. Cook, Dan Sturgis is on line 3. He says it's important."

Roland Cook didn't usually take calls from the second in command in a department. He thought about it a moment and said, "I'll take it."

"This is Roland Cook."

"Mr. Cook, Dan Sturgis here."

"Yes, Dan. What can I do for you?"

"Well, sir, we just got word that Sean Garner passed away." No one spoke for a moment and then Sturgis added, "Carbon monoxide poisoning. It was an apparent suicide in his garage."

Cook was momentarily shocked. Would Garner do that? He knew Garner was distressed at the time of the last meeting, but taking his own life? "Dan, please call the PR people. They will need to be ready to respond to inquiries and to put out a statement on behalf of the company."

"Yes, sir. I'll do that right now."

"Thanks, Dan. And you are now the interim chief of the department."

"Yes, sir. I appreciate that." Cook hung up and reflected about the news. He never thought that Garner would do himself in. That aggressive son of a bitch would certainly do others in, but himself? Maybe after the last meeting he considered himself too far out of the running to achieve the future he needed. It also occurred to him that no matter what happened, he no longer had to worry about Garner sharing secrets if he was pressured.

\* \* \*

**July 29**
**10:15 p.m.**
Scott pushed a button on his phone and waited.

"Hi, Scott," Lee's voice answered.

"Did you see the news?"

"I did," Lee said.

"Tell me you didn't have anything to do with it."

"I didn't have anything to do with it." He paused and then added, "But the police have the GPS I put in his wheel-well, so they'll know someone has been watching him."

"Yeah, that's true."

"It's not a problem though, I had good reason to be concerned what he was up to with our clients. The only concern is that I want my GPS back, so I'll make a couple of calls and tell them it's mine. Maybe if I can get it back informally."

\* \* \*

**July 30**
**9:10 a.m.**
Marty Cardenas and Justin Palmer sipped coffee in Scott Winslow's conference room. Donna came in and sat down with them. "We confirmed the news," she said. "Garner really did die and there will be an investigation, but it looks like a suicide."

The two men sat back in stunned disbelief. No shootout, no more attacks, he was gone. Scott walked into the room and sat down.

"I don't believe it," Justin said.

Scott wore a puzzled expression. "It's confirmed. Garner is dead."

"I believe that," Justin replied. "I just can't believe he did it himself. He was one nefarious bastard, but much more likely to kill others than himself. And if he dealt with others like he did us, there's probably a boatload of people who would want to do him in."

"I agree with that," Marty said. "Something had to go pretty wrong for that guy to do himself in."

"Right," Scott replied. "It must have. But you guys didn't do it, right?"

"Nope," Justin said. "Although I would have if he showed up at my house again."

"Well," Scott offered, shaking his head, "do yourself a favor and leave that part out when you get questioned by the police."

"You think we will be questioned?"

"Sure. The news says there's going to be an investigation, so the police are likely to talk to all of those who had a beef with Garner before they are able to conclude that it was a suicide."

"I was home with Abby all night," Marty volunteered.

"And I was with Jessica," Justin said.

"So, you both have alibis. It should be a pretty short conversation." Scott hesitated and then added, "Plus, this guy died in his garage with a hose connecting his exhaust to the interior of the car. It sure looks like a voluntary exit, doesn't it?"

"Yeah, it does," Marty replied.

"Anyway, now that you know he's not coming after you anymore, you should both be able to sleep a little better."

"Amen to that," Marty said. "I know that Abby won't consider this real sad news."

Scott said, "I'm sure it will bring some relief. This was one sick dude. So, go relax. I'll see you guys on Wednesday when we prep for the meeting with Aligor and their lawyer, right?"

"Right, we'll be here," Marty said. Justin nodded agreement.

Marty and Justin left Scott's office and walked out to their cars. "I have to tell you," Marty said, "I am so relieved. I feel like I've taken my first deep breath in weeks."

"Yeah, me too, buddy. There's something refreshing in knowing that the guy who might kill you can't do it."

They shook hands and climbed into their cars. As Justin took off, his phone rang. "Hi, Jess."

"Come home," she said. "I'm already at your place and I miss you."

"On my way," he said. He paused and then said, "I usually don't celebrate anybody's death, but I can't tell you how relieved I feel."

"I get it," Jessica replied. "I never thought I'd say something like this, but I'm so glad Santa is dead."

They chuckled and then Justin said, "I agree but try not to share that with Katy and Joey when we see them next."

\* \* \*

**July 30**
**5:25 p.m.**
Lee entered the medical building and made his way down the hall. He took the elevator to the third floor, where a number of oncologists were stationed. He entered the office of Mitchell Rayburn M.D. and walked to the counter.

"Yes, sir. Can I help you?" the female receptionist asked.

"Yes, my name is Lee Henry. I have a 5:30 meeting with Dr. Rayburn."

"Can I tell him what it's about?" she asked with a friendly smile.

"It's confidential, as I stated on the phone."

"I see. Okay, follow me," the young woman said. She led Lee down a corridor to the same office where Emma and Michael awaited their news updates on Christopher's condition. "He'll be with you shortly," the woman said, and then she turned and left the office.

Twenty minutes later, Mitchell Rayburn walked into the room and said, "What can I do for you, Mr. Henry?" in a voice that said his presence was tolerated rather than welcomed.

"Well, sir, there is a rather delicate matter we need to discuss."

"You are a private investigator you said, is that right?"

"Yes, that's right."

"And who are you here representing?"

"I work for Scott Winslow, the attorney for Martin Cardenas and Justin Palmer in their action against Aligor."

"Well, this should be a short meeting, Mr. Henry, because I don't know either of them, and I have no involvement in the lawsuit."

"All true," Lee replied. "But that's not why I'm here." Rayburn held his gaze and waited for more of an explanation. Lee continued, "I'm here about Christopher Franklin."

"What? Why?" Rayburn asked, looking stunned.

"His grandfather is one Roland Cook." Dr. Rayburn said nothing. "Michael and Emma Franklin are reporting that their son's condition has started to improve."

"And?" Rayburn asked.

"And you've been treating Roland Cook's grandson with a new medication. I need a copy of the child's treatment record."

"That is protected and confidential."

"It is, but one way or another, its content is going to be discovered."

"Meaning what?"

"I will spell it out for you. You have been treating Christopher with a drug that was supplied by Roland Cook and does not yet have FDA approval. The implications of that for your medical license are not good, wouldn't you agree?"

"So, you are blackmailing me?"

"Just looking for a little information that makes a difference to my client."

"I can't share that information," Dr. Rayburn said with determination.

"Well, you can either share it with me or you can share it with a couple of police detectives who will consider it their duty to pass the information on to the California Medical Board."

"So, you are blackmailing me."

Lee shrugged. "I think you did a good thing for this child, so I have no interest in having the licensing authorities examine the matter. In your shoes, if I thought there was a drug out there that would help save a child, I would find a way to get it from anywhere I could find it, regulatory compliance or not. What you did is ballsy and praiseworthy. I simply need a copy of the record and a declaration from you to establish that it is an accurate copy of your medical record. I will not give it to the Medical Board."

Dr. Rayburn narrowed his eyes. "And if I won't do this?" Lee looked at him and said nothing for a time. "Why do you need this?"

"I need a record of what Roland Cook authorized."

"Isn't his action a gesture of bravery as well?"

"To some degree, but it's a little more personal for him. This is his grandchild we're talking about."

"So, you still haven't told me how you intend to use it where he is concerned?" Dr. Rayburn persisted.

"No," Lee replied, "I haven't." Lee leaned forward in his chair. "I can tell you that I don't plan on sharing the medical record or the declaration I want you to sign with the Medical Board. You did a good thing for a very ill child and I respect it and do not want anything negative to happen to you as a consequence."

Rayburn reflected, wearing a troubled look. "I'm supposed to throw Cook under the bus when I think he did a good thing as well?"

"Like I said, my intent is not to go public with this, I just need the information. Alternatively, you could refuse and let the chips fall where they may."

"Let me see the declaration."

Lee handed him a copy of a declaration under oath stating that the attached records were the true and accurate medical records of Christopher Franklin. He shook his head unhappily and quickly signed the document, handing it to Lee. "I'll have the file copied and one of my staff will bring it to you in the waiting room," Dr. Rayburn said, unhappily.

"Thanks for your time Dr. Rayburn."

"I want you to know that I don't like this, or you for doing it," Rayburn said.

"I understand, doctor," Lee said as he stood and made his way out of the office. Ten minutes later, he left the office with the executed declaration and a copy of Christopher Franklin's medical file.

Lee got into his car and put the medical file down on the passenger seat. He reflected on how useful the information might be. Delexane can't legally be used or distributed by Aligor until the FDA gives it final approval, but this is something a guy did to save his grandson's life. Using the drug prematurely may not be legal, but who's going to take issue with crossing a line to protect your grandchild when he is otherwise going to die? Maybe this exercise was just a waste of time. He picked up the file and leafed through it, almost convinced that it wasn't going to be as worthwhile as he had anticipated. When he got to the tenth page of the medical record, he had to do a double take. Could it really be true? Lee checked again, and then again. It was real. He hit a button on his phone and waited.

"Scott Winslow's office," a friendly voice said.

"Hi, Donna. This is Lee. I need to talk to Scott right away."

"Hang on. He's with someone but I'll break him loose for you."

After a moment, Scott said, "Lee, what's happening?"

"I just got hold of the medical file on Cook's grandson."

"You did what?"

"One of the articles covering the dispute between our clients and Aligor had a brief reference to a recent discovery that Cook has a grandson who has cancer.

I started thinking that if his grandson was sick, Cook might be tempted to give him the drug before the FDA approval happened."

"I'm with you," Scott replied.

"So, I found out the identity of the oncologist who had been treating his grandson. His grandson is Christopher Franklin by the way, and I paid the doctor a visit."

"You're making me nervous, Lee."

"I got hold of the boy's medical file."

"His doctor gave you the boy's file?"

"Yes."

"You're not going to tell me how you got him to do that, right?"

"Right. So, I'm reading through the file and, well, you better sit down for this one. You aren't going to believe this."

# Chapter Twenty-Three

**August 2**

**11:30 a.m.**

"Thanks for coming by this morning, Mrs. Underwood," Olivia Blake said as she and Ed Farris walked into the small conference room at the detective bureau.

"Good morning, detectives. I'm not sure why I'm here, but I'm hoping you have found new information about the death of my husband."

"Actually, we want to talk about the death of Sean Garner this morning." Sandi did not react. "You have heard that he's dead?"

"I have heard that, yes. As far as I'm concerned, it couldn't happen to a nicer guy."

"I understand, but what we want to know is if you had anything to do with his death."

"What?" Sandi asked, incredulous. "This was a suicide, right? Who am I, Jack Kevorkian?"

"Yes, it looks like a suicide. We're making sure that was the case."

"And you think that maybe I had something to do with it?"

"We're just checking, ma'am," Farris said. "You did have reason to want him dead."

"No, I had reason to want to see him caught and go to jail. That's what I was hoping that you guys were working on," she replied, sounding indignant.

"And we were working on that, Ms. Underwood. But obviously things have changed."

Sandi nodded. "I wasn't unhappy when I heard he was dead, but last I checked, that's not a crime."

"No, ma'am, it isn't," Farris said. "Anything you want to tell us?"

"Only that I hope you won't give up finding who killed my husband, whether or not that turns out to be someone still alive."

"You think that Sean Garner murdered your husband, don't you?" Olivia asked.

"I think that's a good possibility, but I'm waiting for you guys to tell me if I'm right about that."

Ed Farris smiled and said, "We will let you know if we learn more. Thanks for coming by today."

"You're welcome." Sandi stood and walked from the conference room. She smiled as she exited the building, reflecting on the fact that they never asked her about her background as a nurse. That meant no one found traces of the cocktail she had injected into Garner, and probably, no one looked. They were accepting that this was a suicide and they were just going through the motions to rule out alternatives. It was all good news. She had not felt a moment of guilt since Sean Garner's exit from the planet. It was a matter of accountability that she believed would have happened no other way. She didn't know how Art would feel about what she had done, but she felt pretty damned good.

\* \* \*

**August 4**
**1:30 p.m.**
The three women sat at their patio table enjoying a mid-day margarita and waiting for tacos to arrive.

"Cheers, ladies," Sandi offered with a smile and glasses were clinked.

"Are we celebrating something?" Abby asked.

"It's ghoulish I know, but I guess you could say I wanted to celebrate the fact that karma caught up with Sean Garner."

"Is it karma when someone takes themselves out?"

"Why not?" Sandi asked. "Doesn't matter to me how it happened." She was quiet for a moment and then asked, "Did the detectives interview Marty and Justin?"

"Yeah," Jessica replied. "Justin confirmed that he knew nothing about it and told them he was with me all night. I confirmed that what he said was right and they took off satisfied."

"Same for Marty and me," Abby said. "I had the feeling that they were ruling out people who might have had a reason to go after Garner." She paused and then added, "Pathological and crazy person he was, there might be a lot of people for them to consider."

There were nodding heads and agreement all around. "It may be a terrible thing to say, but I'm relieved," Jessica said. "I mean, Justin was starting to sit up late with a gun in his hands waiting for this guy to invade the house. It was stressful and crazy."

"I'm with you," Abby agreed. "And I know that Marty is glad we don't have to find him waiting for us everywhere we go."

Sandi smiled widely, feeling like her interests weren't the only ones served by what she did.

"What's that major grin about?" Abby asked.

Sandi's smile must have been bigger and more obvious than she intended. She shrugged and said, "I guess I'm just glad to be sharing this day with such good friends."

\* \* \*

## August 5
### 7:55 a.m.

Sandi was getting dressed when she heard the buzzer. Someone was at the front door of the apartment building. Sandi didn't get many visitors, so it had to be a solicitor. They never seemed to read the no soliciting sign the size of a refrigerator that was posted next to the apartment directory. She ran out into the living room and pushed the intercom button. "Who is it?"

"Hi, Sandi. This is Lee Henry. I hope it's not too early to say hello."

She smiled, "It's not too early. Come on up, Lee." She pushed a button and there was an electronic buzz as the front door lock was released.

Sandi met Lee at the front door of the apartment as he got off the elevator. "Come on in," she said. "Want some coffee?"

"Sure. That sounds great."

He stepped inside and they walked to the kitchen. Lee took a seat at the counter while Sandi poured them both coffees. She handed him one of the matching cups and sat down.

Lee said, "Thanks for the hospitality. I've been meaning to stop by and see how you are, so today I decided should be that day."

"Well, thank you, Lee. That's thoughtful of you."

"Are you getting by okay?" he asked.

"I am doing all right. I miss Art every day and that isn't likely to change, but my sons are good men and I get with each of them once a week. They really looked up to their dad, so it has been really hard on them."

"I'm sure of that," Lee replied. "I was very moved by Daniel's words for his dad at the funeral. He did an amazing job of paying tribute to Art."

She smiled. "He did, didn't he?"

"It was so heartfelt. Everyone felt his pain."

"You have good kids," Lee said with a smile.

"I do, for sure. I also made friends with Abby and Jessica and we get together every week or two. At first, I think they were just trying to pull me through, but now I think that they are really enjoying our get-togethers, too."

"Sounds like you are really making your way."

"And you are going to get married in September?"

"I am. I found the woman of my dreams and I'm not letting her get away," he said with a smile. "You'll be there?" he asked.

"Yep. Got the invitation and I'm already thinking about what to wear. Thanks for inviting Daniel and Alex, too."

Lee nodded. "Our pleasure."

Sandi reflected a moment and then said, "Melissa must be a little nervous about the work you do."

"That's true. I'd think she rather I was an engineer or an accountant, but she accepts the things I get into." Lee thought for a moment and then said, "You've heard that Sean Garner is no longer with us?"

"I did and I have to say, it's a relief. I'm sure that Marty and Justin feel the same way. Abby and Jessica have told me that they do."

"No doubt about it, everyone targeted by him feels much better knowing he's not coming back." He reflected and then added, "But you know, I never figured a guy like him to do himself in. He just isn't the type."

"Yeah, go figure," Sandi replied, nodding.

"Knowing that about him, it occurred to me that someone skilled may have had a hand in his demise."

"Really? You think so?" she asked.

Lee smiled. "You were a nurse by profession, weren't you?"

"Yes," Sandi replied, feeling uncomfortable with where this might be headed.

"I've always been fascinated by the inside information doctors and nurses possess."

"What do you mean?" she asked.

"Well, things like what drugs have what effect on the body. What could be used to put someone under for a while. Those kinds of things." He didn't wait for an answer. "I was keeping an eye on Garner, you know. Because of the threat that he posed to Marty and Justin. I found a couple of ways to do that. One was a GPS I placed on his car. The other was a couple of closed-circuit cameras I placed to allow me to keep an eye on his house and the street remotely." Sandi sat in stunned silence, as he said, "Yeah, some nights I actually went out there, but when I wasn't there, I could look at his house and his street from my computer at home."

She was quiet for a time and then asked, "Were you doing that the night he died?" Her stomach feeling like she was hitting the highs and lows of a roller coaster.

"I was, yes. And did I tell you that you can actually look at the surrounding houses and the street?" He smiled and added, "You can even see the license plates on cars parked out front of the house you're looking at." She opened her mouth, but no words came out. He held up a hand so that she didn't feel the need to say anything more. "Anyway, it looks like this was a suicide. If anyone was involved in assisting, I don't think that will ever be known." He smiled. "I was interviewed by the police detectives and told them it sure looked like a suicide. I bet you were interviewed, too."

She nodded. "I was."

"Right. Along with Marty and Abby and Justin and Jessica. I think that they have done it all now and are ready to reaffirm that it was a suicide. So, it looks like Garner chose his own exit." He smiled at her and added, "But if anyone did lend him a hand, the world is better for it."

Lee stood and said, "Thanks for the coffee, Sandi." She still looked a little shell-shocked. He gave her a hug and added, "Art was a very lucky man and I'm glad to count you as a friend. Say hello to Daniel and Alex and I'll see you at the wedding next month."

As he walked to the door, she said, "Give my best to Melissa. And come back again for coffee, Lee. It was really great to see you."

Sandi worked on regaining control of her blood pressure as she watched Lee walk to the elevator. He was a complex fellow. A remarkable guy she didn't know all that well, but with whom she shared a secret that no one else could ever know.

# Chapter Twenty-Four

Scott met Marty and Justin in the Bonaventure Hotel lobby. They both looked a little lost in the strangely shaped hotel. Scott had spent a number of days in meetings here over the years, but the thirty-three-story building was confusing to those who didn't know it, with odd shapes and elevators designated by colors and shapes, like the red circle, yellow diamond and green square. Scott pulled his wheeled brief case towards the hotel registration counter to ask where the meeting was scheduled. Before he got there, he saw the daily directory that had been posted. Among its listings was "Aligor meeting, 232."

The three made their way to the elevator and exited on the second floor, where numerous meeting rooms were housed. They found Conference Room 232, with an open door and containing a conference table large enough to seat twenty comfortably. Parallel to the table was a long credenza that had been set up with coffee, tea, and a variety of donuts and snack foods.

The three made their way into the room and took a seat on one side of the table. Moments later, Doug Gibson appeared at the door with Roland Cook and a big man of about sixty that Scott didn't recognize.

Doug Gibson said, "Good morning, Scott. Mr. Cardenas. Mr. Palmer. You all know Mr. Cook, and this is Mr. Albert Stevens, a member of the Aligor Executive Board." After greetings all around, they grabbed coffee and took a seat on the other side of the table.

Gibson sat between Cook and Stevens and said, "Well, let me start us off. Scott, you know that we think your case has some problems. Our people will testify that your clients are incorrect in what they are urging about the phase three test results and the jury may well conclude that they have manufactured the results that they have been circulating. The evidence will show that this product, Delexane, is revolutionary. It has the potential to help those in the last stages of their lives when nothing else is working. It is important to the company and it is important to the whole of society that Delexane is available for those people who need it most. Many of the people who will turn to Delexane have nowhere else to turn; they have exhausted available potential remedies and they are fighting for one more month, one more week or one more day. Delexane has the ability to extend life and, in some cases, improve the underlying pathology so that life is extended even further. In that sense, it is a miracle drug for our culture. For all of those reasons, we will fight hard against anyone who wants to keep Delexane from bettering and saving lives." Gibson paused, letting his words and his emotion settle on the room. Then he resumed with, "All of that said, we are here today with the intent to see if this case can be resolved in the best interests of all concerned and if you are here to be reasonable, we are prepared to work towards that end. We want to resolve this case, but we also want to get help to the people in need, to provide critical assistance available nowhere else and to extend life. What we cannot do is have third parties dictate the terms of use for this critical drug."

"Third parties?" Marty interjected, shaking his head. "I gave seventy hours a week to the development of Aligor products for over seven years. Now I'm a third party?"

"You are outside the company and you are suing the company, Mr. Cardenas. So, I don't think third party should be an insulting term."

Marty shook his head, feeling the sting but said nothing else.

Scott nodded slowly, and then said, "Seems to me that your words were a little personal for those who have been fired and then falsely accused of fraud by an organization that is actively trying to hide material facts from the public, but let's leave aside whether your comments were offensive for a moment." Scott leaned forward in his chair and said, "What you just described in your introduction is the dream; a dream shared by Mr. Cardenas and Mr. Palmer. Unfortunately, it's not the reality. We accept that you are here in good faith to try to find a way to reach a resolution of this case. That is our purpose as well. That said, a little reality has to settle in if this is going to work. Martin Cardenas and Justin Palmer, along with Art Underwood, were the executives most familiar with the phased test trials for Delexane. They reviewed and measured results at each step along the way. They were extremely excited about the product in phase one and even more so in phase two, where a larger number of subjects had good results. But with phase three, it all came apart. Suddenly, with ten times the number of subjects in the test, the success rate was a fraction of what it had been. Add to that the fact that there were suddenly disconcerting side effects that hadn't been previously noted. How extensive and severe they were remained to be determined.

"Marty and Justin registered complaints with Art and all three registered complaints about the results not being what the company continued to publish. They were told that they needed to wait until the results had been thoroughly reviewed. When that process was complete, nothing changed. Their concerns were raised again." Scott looked at Roland Cook. "At that point Mr. Cook began to perceive anyone who persisted with questions as disloyal and Mr. Cardenas and Mr. Palmer were abruptly fired, the terminations carried out by Sean Garner."

Scott looked at Gibson, Cook and then Stevens. They each studied him. "So, Doug, you describe the dream to benefit society, but when legitimate concerns were repeatedly raised about the effectiveness and reliability of the product, and new side effects were identified, this turned into a personal nightmare for Mr. Cardenas and Mr. Palmer.

"Their only motivation for raising these issues was to make sure that Delexane was safe and effective; which is what everyone supposedly wanted. In response, they are both abruptly fired and isolated. The real phase three results are hidden, a more favorable version created, and Marty and Justin are publicly accused of creating fraudulent data, all so that this inadequate version of the Delexane dream can beat the competition to the market.

"After the unjust terminations, the Aligor Director of Security began a campaign of harassment to force an end to this lawsuit and allow Delexane to hit the market without the deficiencies in the product surfacing. Garner suddenly begins to appear wherever Marty and Justin and their significant others are. He makes threats if the lawsuit isn't resolved, he breaks into Justin's house and then orchestrates a physical attack that Justin barely survives."

Gibson sipped his coffee and then began speaking with a calm, practiced voice. "We think that there is a number of problems with what you just said, Scott. Part of the problem is the distance between your allegations and reality. Let's start with what will determine the outcome of all of this, the evidence.

We will have two key executives involved in the phase three trials testify that your clients' numbers are false, and the real ones are consistent with what we provided to you in discovery. We believe that the jury will understand that we are trying to get a life-saving drug to market and Mr. Cardenas and Mr. Palmer are trying to interfere with that objective for their own personal gain."

"Wait a minute," Justin snapped angrily. "This personal attack on us is bullshit. For the company there is a fortune at stake, but we are trying to do what's best for everyone; for the people who will put their faith in this drug."

"I understand your position, Mr. Palmer, and what I said is not a personal attack," Gibson responded calmly. "I'm telling you what I believe the jury will come to believe after hearing the evidence."

Scott nodded and then suppressed a smile. "The two executives that you are relying on to convince the jury to accept your position are Pete McMillan and Ed Barnes." Gibson remained quiet. "You can own it, Doug, it's not a secret. You identified these executives in discovery."

"That's right. And they are going to make clear that your clients fabricated false test results and the real test results are what we gave to you." Gibson said confidently.

Scott sat back in his chair. He was quiet for a time, studying Gibson and then he asked, "Are they really?"

"Yes, of course," Gibson snapped.

"Well, I think you have a significant misunderstanding about what these gentlemen are going to say when they take the stand."

Gibson narrowed his eyes. "How so?"

Scott considered for a moment and then reached into his brief case and pulled out a file. He pulled out a copy of the declaration signed by Ed Barnes and handed it to Gibson.

Gibson began reading and learning that Barnes would testify that the real version of the phase three trial results was the one Marty and Justin had presented. He then looked up at Scott wearing an angry expression. "How did you get this? Did you approach my client?"

Scott sat back in his chair and said, "No, Doug. And he's not your client. You can check with him. But let's not get caught up in a debate that takes us from the substance of his testimony. I showed you this before trial because we are all here to make efforts to resolve the matter and I am confident Mr. Barnes will tell the truth at trial. I can tell you that Mr. McMillan does not want to have to testify, but if pushed, his testimony will be similar."

"This is bullshit," Gibson yelled angrily. "You have no right to be talking to employees and I'm going to make an ethics complaint to the state bar association."

Scott shrugged. "Mr. Barnes is unrepresented, and I have never spoken to Mr. McMillan. I assume you know that Mr. McMillan has the right to speak to Mr. Cardenas or Mr. Palmer if he chooses. So, before you lose track of where we are you might want to consider that there are no ethical violations here."

"Let's talk," Roland Cook said to Doug Gibson.

Gibson nodded and said, "We reserved the conference room next door as well, so that both sides have a place to speak privately."

"Fine," Scott replied. "See you when you return."

Cook, Stevens and Gibson walked silently into the hallway and disappeared. "What do you guys think?" Scott asked.

"I don't know what they'll do," Marty replied, "but they were pretty shocked to find that Barnes and McMillan aren't in their corner."

"Yep," Scott replied. "Right now, they are discussing the fact that Barnes is locked into his testimony by his under-oath declaration and McMillan's deposition is tomorrow, so he will be on the record if we don't get somewhere today. It gives them some motivation because once McMillan's testimony is committed to a written transcript, the word could leak to the media that he is not supporting what the company is promoting."

When they returned Gibson wore the poised expression of a veteran of countless wars like this one. He grabbed a refill of his coffee while Cook and Stevens took their chairs. When Doug Gibson sat down, he said, "I think you are mistaken about Mr. McMillan. We have different information about what he will say."

Scott shrugged, doing his best water off a duck's back expression. "I guess we find out tomorrow at his deposition when he has to tell us what he knows under oath, right?"

"True," Gibson replied, "unless we successfully resolve the matter today." He paused and then said, "So, let's cut to the chase and get this done. We are prepared to pay one million dollars to each of your clients to resolve the matter today."

"That sounds fair," Scott replied. "What about telling the world the truth?"

"Here we go again," Gibson replied, shaking his head.

"To my knowledge, we never left this issue." Scott looked at Cook and then Stevens, who were both studying him. "Look, we know that Garner was arranging for assault, battery and home invasion to get to my clients."

"Mr. Garner is no longer with us, so he can't testify about what he did or didn't do. But if he was over the top at some point, he was not acting within the scope of instructions from the company."

"But he was keeping the company informed. I can prove that Garner called Mr. Cook around 2:00 a.m. the night Justin Palmer was beaten. At that point he believed that Justin had been killed. And I know that Mr. Cook returned his call around 6:00 a.m."

"You are not seriously suggesting that a phone call that occurred that night was Mr. Cook somehow endorsing beating up Mr. Palmer?"

"No, what I'm suggesting is that Mr. Cook knew what was happening and Garner called to tell him it had all gone terribly wrong."

"I don't intend to listen to this guy suggesting that I ordered anyone beaten up," Cook said indignantly. "That is preposterous."

"Lots for the jury to consider," Scott said.

"Do you want to get this case settled or not, Scott?" Doug Gibson asked, frustration making its way past the perpetually calm voice.

"Yes, but we want something done about the inaccurate data that is constantly being pumped out to the public. This product is not what you thought it was after the first and second phases of the testing."

"What if we agreed to add a fourth round of testing the same size as the third, to check the numbers and further identify and possible additional side effects after the product's release?"

"I think we are on the right track here," Scott said. "But there are a couple of problems. First, the public will have bad information at the time of the product's release and the second is how we know that the results you kick out after round four will be accurate?"

Roland Cook interjected. "We'd be willing to get the new phase completed in five months and allow a third party we have faith in review our results. There is an intermediary to assure the results are published. But we are not going to alter the results of the third phase without the additional testing."

Albert Stevens spoke up for the first time. "We believe in this product and people need it yesterday. We are confident that this is a product that will save lives."

"Are you?" Scott asked and fell silent, leaving the question hanging in the air.

Stevens narrowed his eyes. After a time, he said, "What is that supposed to mean?"

Scott reached into his briefcase and pulled out the medical file Lee had obtained from Dr. Rayburn. He opened the file in front of him and then said, "Mr. Cook has a grandson who has been stricken with cancer and who was nearing the end of life. It put him in a very difficult position," Scott urged looking at Cook, who looked back at him with daggers.

"So, now you're going to tell us that Delexane was used to help a family member before its FDA release," Doug Gibson said.

Albert Stevens said, "You think that you can make something of that? A grandfather coming to the rescue of a terminally ill grandson? You take your best shot."

"You make a good point, Mr. Stevens," Scott replied. "I thought exactly the same thing. If something is technically unlawful but done to save a child's life, who would hold a man accountable?" Stevens nodded agreement. "But then, we discovered something else. Read from pages ten and eleven of this medical record."

Cook was silent and turning white as Stevens studied the medical record. He stared at Cook. "Jesus, Roland, what did you do here?"

Roland Cook didn't speak. Scott said, "He did what any grandfather would do, he used the product that he believed would be most likely to save his grandson. And the product he believed in most was Sutton Pharma's Exerdes, rather than his own Delexane." He let that settle for just a moment and then said, "So, you tell me again that the man at the top of Aligor has total faith in his product."

Doug Gibson, always the lawyer, looked at Scott and asked, "How did you get a confidential medical file without the family's consent?"

"Is that really the conversation we need to have right now?" Scott asked, hoping they didn't need to go down that rabbit hole because he had no good answer. He could hardly say that I think my investigator may have blackmailed the doctor into submission. Besides, he didn't want the distraction from the real point which had hit home.

There was quiet all around. Stevens looked at Cook and said, "Roland, do we have some issues with the product we need to work through?"

"Let's talk privately," Doug Gibson said. The three men stood and walked slowly from the room to go next door.

Marty Cardenas wore a stunned expression. "I can't believe it," he said. "That is amazing, Scott. How did you..." He let his words trail off.

"I don't know," Scott replied. "Lee came up with this."

Marty and Justin nodded acknowledgment as if this somehow that answered the question. "Well, whatever he did to get this information, we owe both of you," Justin offered.

"Amen to that," Marty joined. "I can't think of anything that makes the point that he knew there were deficiencies in Delexane better than him choosing a competitor's product to rescue a family member."

Scott, Justin and Marty refilled their coffee cups and grabbed a breakfast bar. It was 1:40 p.m. and the Aligor team had gone to the adjoining conference room a little before 1:00. At 2:15 p.m., Scott knocked on the door of the conference room that housed the other team. "What is it?" Gibson's voice yelled through the closed door.

"Just wondered if you were making progress."

"We'll come back when we are ready. Be patient." Cook and Gibson both looked frazzled; the look that spoke of obstacles that had not been overcome.

"Okay. We may walk downstairs to the café, but we'll be back in half hour or so."

"That's fine."

Scott, Justin and Marty walked down the hallway to the stairway. "How did Lee get that information about Cook's grandkid?" Marty asked.

"I know better than to ask," Scott replied. Marty looked at him like he might be kidding, but Scott's expression said otherwise.

"Aren't you curious?" Justin asked.

"Yes," Scott replied. "But sometimes it's better not to know. I can say that it was some combination of logic and intuition."

"Hmm. Okay, but how did he get a cancer kid's medical file?"

"Your guess is as good as mine," Scott replied. "I just know it had a pretty major impact in that room. I mean, what's the plausible answer to why a grandfather gives his grandchild another guy's product to save his life when you theoretically have the best one on the market?"

"I can't think of one."

"As you saw from the expression Cook wore when it was revealed, he couldn't either."

\* \* \*

**August 12**
**1:30 p.m.**
Olivia Blake and Ed Farris sat outdoors at one of the umbrella-covered tables of Baccalaureate Burgers, near UCLA, where unhealthy food and higher education came together. A college student dropped off a tray of food and picked up the cardboard number they had been given. "Three Thesis Burgers, three diet cokes and two onion rings," the kid said, not waiting for a response before departing.

Lee walked to the table and sat down. "Greetings detectives," he offered with a smile.

"Here's your burger, diet coke and onion rings," Olivia said, pushing food in Lee's direction.

"Awesome, I'm starved. How much do I owe you guys?"

"This one's on us," Farris replied.

"Okay, I'll get it next time." He took a bite of the burger and nodded. "Excellent." He gave them a grin and said, "I haven't seen you guys in a little while. How's business?"

"We won't run out of work anytime soon," Olivia replied. "But we've been thinking about how you might be able to assist us."

"How?" he asked, intrigued.

"Well, you can move around and do things that we can't, like we found out in connection with our examination of Sean Garner." Farris smiled. "We need evidence before we can get to a suspect and we need probable cause before we can get to evidence."

"Right," Lee nodded. "Pretty much the way it should be, don't you think?"

"Generally, yes. But we keep thinking about how you managed to get cell phone data before we had any basis for a subpoena. We were thinking that maybe you could help us from time to time."

"Here's the problem with that," Lee offered, thoughtfully. "I got you cell phone data when I needed the data for a client whose interests I was representing. If I'm not representing a client and I just out there getting evidence for you guys, I become an instrument of the police. If I'm just working for you, then you still need PC before I can get you what you need."

"So, if there was a client paying you for your time, then it works right?"

"A real client, not just a supplier of money from sources unknown."

"We'll keep working on the idea," Olivia offered. "You are a resource we would like to be able to use to get where we need to go."

"I understand," Lee offered. "As specific tasks come up, we can brain-storm to see if there's any way we can work together. You can't hire me because then I'd be subject to the same rules you are. Freelancing gives me much more room to move."

"We've noticed," Farris said with a grin.

"So, all we need to do is find you a client with interests similar to ours and problem solved."

Lee grinned. "That would work."

They ate in silence for a time and then Olivia said, "We're closing the Garner case as a suicide, but he was certainly asshole enough to have had someone help him exit the planet. You got any thoughts about that?"

"Well, I agree with you about the guy's character. He was a dick. But you didn't find anything that suggested anyone else was involved, did you?"

"No," Olivia replied. "He did himself in using a pretty conventional method of suicide. We checked the scene and didn't find any signs of a break-in or suspicious prints. Doors were locked and he was apparently home alone. By the time the body was found, it was too late for a blood alcohol and there was no reason to do a tox screen on what clearly looks like a suicide." She regarded Lee a moment and then asked, "Do you think someone set it up?"

Lee shook his head. "I doubt it, but who can be sure. I am confident that Garner helped Art Underwood off his fifth-floor balcony, so I don't feel bad about the fact that karma stepped in to make him account."

"Karma, huh?"

"Yep. It's inescapable. The ultimate force to level the playing field."

"So, maybe you can present yourself as working as an agent of karma."

"Nice thought," Lee said. "I think I'll put that on my business card."

"Yeah. That should scare the shit out of people," Farris said. He studied Lee and then said, "You know, I'm not convinced that you would tell us if you had evidence that someone helped Garner make an exit."

Lee looked at Olivia and then Ed. He felt bonded to these guys, like he was with friends. But they were still cops who had a job to do. "It's all speculation. Anyway, you know that Garner was a crazy asshole who didn't make the world any prettier. I'm not sure I'd want to hold someone he fucked over accountable if I could."

"That's the thing Lee, we can't do vigilante justice," Olivia said, shaking her head. "So, if you know something…"

"Wait, it's not like I killed this guy. Like I said, it's all just speculation." Lee paused a moment and then said, "Garner had plenty of reason to do himself in. Maybe he woke up one morning and realized he was a hopeless asshole."

Farris shook his head. "That doesn't seem likely. I've seen a lot of pathological dirtbags and hopeless assholes as you call them, and they seldom have an epiphany and change course towards citizen of the year."

"Meaning what?" Lee asked.

"Meaning he was probably still okay with being a hopeless asshole and not likely to kill himself because of it," Farris replied.

"There's that," Lee replied. He smiled and changed the subject. "You know, I hope we do get to work together again soon. I'm rather attached to you guys."

Olivia and Ed both smiled and it was pretty clear they liked him too.

\* \* \*

**August 12**
**4:40 p.m.**
The Aligor team emerged from the adjacent conference room looking worn down. They sat down quietly as Scott, Marty and Justin awaited some kind of update. Doug Gibson looked at Scott and said, "We have a proposal to make that will require participation by you guys." He drew a breath and then said, "None of this is final because it has to be reviewed and approved by the Aligor Board of Directors. A special meeting has been set on Monday to address the issues if we reach tentative agreement here."

"Please go on," Scott prompted. "We're listening."

"There would be announcement that there will be a phase four of the trials to take place starting immediately and we are going to delay release for one hundred and twenty days while it is completed. It will state that we do not foresee any significant issues, but we want to study it a little further to make sure that we are not surprised by any side effects."

Doug Gibson said, "That's where your role comes into play. Two ways that you are going to participate. First, you add nothing to the press, and you dispute nothing. If asked, you simply state you're glad the company is being cautious."

They absorbed those limitations for a moment and then Scott asked, "What's the second way we are involved?"

"The amount paid to you is reduced by half. You each get half a million dollars. The other half is your participation in the further study you are seeking. If you're all in on this, that shouldn't be a problem, right?"

It made sense to Marty and Justin, but Scott said, "Hold on. These are two separate questions. The damages Marty and Justin suffered as a result of their terminations aren't reduced by the fact that you need to work on the product."

Albert Stevens interjected, "That's the deal. You're contributing to the costs of the phase four testing that you are demanding or there will be no deal."

"We still need the third party appointed as part of this deal to analyze the results and comment if what Aligor says isn't consistent with their view of the results. We also need the ability in the agreement to enforce all of this."

"Understood," Gibson replied.

"Let us talk," Scott said.

"We'll go next door," Gibson said, standing. "We still have files there anyway."

As they walked from the room and closed the door, Scott asked, "What do you think?"

"It works for me," Justin replied. "I'm also okay with them reducing the settlement to help finance the testing. I want to make sure this drug is accurately revealed to the public before they start buying it."

"Absolutely," Marty said. "I'm on board with all of it. Tell them to have the board buy into it and we'll sign the agreement. So long as third party inspector is one of those that we trust, we are good to go."

"Okay," Scott replied. "Let me take one more shot at the money they pay you guys. I know that you'll agree to what's on the table and I'll make sure we don't lose this deal, okay?"

"Sure," Marty said.

Justin shrugged. "Okay, so long as we don't kill this deal."

\* \* \*

**August 12**
**5:25 p.m.**
The Aligor team reentered the conference room and looked at Scott expectantly. "We are on board with most of the terms," Scott said.

"With the exception of what?" Gibson asked impatiently.

"With the exception of the damages from my clients' termination. Let me remind you that their careers were abruptly ended and their ability to work anywhere in the industry was shut down."

The three on the other side of the table looked annoyed, like they were on the verge of shutting down the negotiations. "So, no deal?"

Scott leaned back in his chair and said, "We are okay with the idea of contributing to the testing, but the number should be seven hundred fifty thousand each and we want endorsement from Aligor in the form of letters of recommendation we approve and a general agreement about what prospective employers are to be told about them."

Cook shook his head in the negative. Stevens looked thoughtful for a time and after an extended silence he said, "The letter and the agreement about what we tell prospective employers are fine. We want these gentlemen to find new positions. But the money doesn't work. They said they would be a part of this." Scott waited silently, feeling in the air that his clients wanted him to agree. After a time, Stevens said, "Six hundred fifty thousand each."

Scott nodded and replied, "Six-fifty. That way they are giving you back seven hundred thousand of the two million offered as their contribution to phase four."

Stevens shook his head. He had now taken over the negotiations for Aligor. "No. We'll go to six twenty-five. That's it. You want to be a part of this deal or you don't."

Scott reflected a moment and then looked to his clients. "Done," he said. "We have a deal."

Gibson said, "I'll do a memorandum of the deal points that we can all sign before we leave tonight and then I'll draft a proposed agreement for Scott's review tomorrow."

It was 7:30 p.m. when they walked out of the conference room and went down the elevator to the hotel lobby. "You did a hell of a job, Scott," Marty offered.

Justin nodded agreement. "I feel like a load was lifted today," Justin said. "Thank you." He paused and added, "Thank Lee for us as well. I have no idea how he got the medical file on Cook's grandchild, but it certainly broke things open when you revealed that Cook had used the Sutton Pharma's product to save his grandchild."

"I will tell him, guys. And I'll be in touch after we have the agreement in the right condition for you to sign."

"Great, thank you." Marty gave Scott a quick hug. "Abby will be appreciative as well."

"Yep, Jessica too. She was convinced that I would find a way to get killed or beat up again, so she'll be grateful just to know that the litigation is over and I'm still walking around."

# Chapter Twenty-Five

**August 16**
**8:55 a.m.**
The media was all over it. 'Aligor delays the release of Delexane for one hundred twenty days' Cable news stations posted on breaking news banners that moved along the bottom of the screen. Blogs and Twitter were alight with commentary. Some thought it was a good thing to make sure the product was perfect. Others thought that there must be some problem that had been uncovered. Still others said that it revealed that the fired executives of Aligor had been correct all along.

Their phones rang incessantly, but neither Marty Cardenas nor Justin Palmer would comment other than to say that Aligor was being cautious and that was smart. Their lawyer, Scott Winslow, was equally tight-lipped, but those guys often were.

A cable newscaster revealed that, in related news, Aligor stock had taken a twenty percent hit with the revelation that the release of Delexane would be delayed. Immediately after the announcement, the Aligor public relations team was everywhere, making appearances on many of the cable channels and voicing the importance of making sure that they gave it enough time to make sure the drug was as good as it could be for the many who would be helped by it. Smiling Aligor representatives blanketed cable with statements that in introducing a product like no other to the market, they wanted to make sure that all steps were taken to protect the consumer, so that everyone could have the utmost confidence in this fantastic new drug. They were pretty good at turning this problem into a PR opportunity.

Scott smiled while he listened. It was ballsy under the circumstances, but it was a good campaign. There was a buzz and then the one of the disembodied voices Scott knew well, "Scott, Doug Gibson on line three."

"Got it, thanks Nikki."

Scott hit a button and said, "Hi, Doug. Need more recruits to talk about how philanthropic the company is being?"

Gibson chuckled. "It seems like they have that pretty well covered. I have to say, they are doing a damned good job with the PR."

"I'd have to agree. They've assumed the role of protector of the public. A smart decision and one that we're okay with as long as they really do the job."

"I think your guys will be okay, too."

"With the recommendation letter and the scripted positive words that Aligor agreed to provide to all prospective employers, I think they will too. Justin already has a lead on a good job, so if your people get it right, he should be able to land it."

"Believe me, they will get it right. I've gone over it with them and I know they don't want another lawsuit for costing him a job with what they say about him." He paused a moment and then said, "I am curious about one thing, though. How did you get the information about Cook's grandchild being given the competition's product?"

"That's one of those lucky coincidences that I can't share. It certainly was persuasive though, wasn't it?"

"You could say that, yeah."

"So, unless your guys screw up this agreement and I have to come after them for it, I guess I'll see you on the next case."

"No doubt you will. I enjoyed working with you on this case, Scott, even though you are a pain in the ass."

"Well, that's mutual, Doug. You are a pretty good pain in the ass yourself."

"Thanks."

"But I won't tell anyone that," Scott added.

"Yes, you will. When you talk to your plaintiffs' employment lawyer buddies, you'll tell them whatever you think about me."

"That's true. But you'll do okay in any story I tell."

"That's mutual as well. Take it easy. And, oh yeah, I called to tell you that the settlement checks will be delivered to your office next week."

"Perfect," Scott replied. "And I have one question for you. What did you learn about all the harassment that Sean Garner was engaged in?"

"That's one that I'm going to decline to answer. Take it easy."

Scott smiled as Gibson hung up. The call was a fitting end to the case and both sides were already moving on.

\* \* \*

## August 16
### 11:55 a.m.
Lee Henry waited on hold for about three minutes.

"This is Dr. Mitchell Rayburn," a calm voice finally said.

"Hi, Dr. Rayburn. This is Lee Henry. I'm sure you remember me."

"Yes, I do. I'm seldom blackmailed, so it stands out in my mind. What do you want?" The tone was decidedly unfriendly.

"I just wanted to give you a heads up. I want you to know that I will not be releasing the information you provided. It will not come out in a courthouse or anywhere else."

"I'm glad to hear that, Mr. Henry. I have been very concerned about how such information can be misused."

"I thought that you would be, which is why I wanted to make this call. To put your mind at ease."

"Thank you, sir. Can I ask that you destroy the copy I gave you?"

Lee considered the fact that the settlement had not yet been completed and then replied, "You can, and I will as soon as possible. It shouldn't be long. Until then, it stays confidential."

"Fair enough. In light of this call, I will trust you to do what's right."

Lee paused and then said, "One more thing, doctor. Thanks for being brave enough to do what it takes for children like Christopher. The lives you save will touch many others."

"Thank you for saying that, Mr. Henry."

"Take care, doc."

\* \* \*

**August 21**
**5:00 p.m.**
Emma, Michael and Christopher arrived at the Cook's Westlake mansion and walked in without knocking. Christopher ran ahead and yelled, "Grandpa," as he saw Roland Cook's smiling face in the living room.

"Hi, Tiger. Come give me a hug." Christopher flew into his arms and giggled as grandpa spun him around in the air. He put his grandson down and studied him. The gaunt face had been replaced by cheeks that were rosy and only slightly shallow. His eyes were no longer dark circles but were bright with excitement. His improvement was undeniable. "Oh my God, you look great, kiddo."

"Can I play on the big screen?" Christopher asked.

"Sure."

Christopher ran off into the expansive great room to find his favorite toys. "Hi, Dad," Emma said, hugging her father. She pulled away only slightly and said, "Thank you so much. I know what this cost you."

Michael shook his hand and said, "Thank you. Truly. You can see the difference you've made for him. There is still a long way to go, but for the first time in months we don't feel like we're going to lose our son."

"He does look good," Cook said, smiling.

"Recommending and delivering the other guy's product at this stage in Aligor's roll out of Delexane was one of the gutsiest things that I have ever seen. I will remember it forever."

"Just don't tell anyone that you got an advanced look at Sutton Pharma's product, because it's not yet FDA approved either. And for Pete's sake, don't buy any of their stock. The press would never let me hear the end of it." He grinned. "You guys ready for a glass of wine?"

"I am so ready," Michael said, nodding.

"Me too," Emma added.

"I am so very proud of you, Dad. You rescued my baby and you are my hero."

Randall Cook pushed a tear away and said, "I'm proud of all of you, too. And so sorry for what you've had to go through." He handed them a glass of wine.

At that moment, Helen Cook walked into the room carrying a tray of hors d'oeuvres. "Hi, Emma. Hi, Michael. Why don't you have some goodies while I go squeeze Christopher." She put down the tray and raced off to find her grandson.

"I heard about Sean Garner," Emma said. "I'm really sorry. I only met him once, but that has to be a big loss to you."

Roland Cook nodded. "Yes, I'm not sure what prompted something like that, but it's awfully sad." As he spoke the words, Cook reflected that he wasn't sure how he felt about Garner's suicide. He was a devoted employee, but he was a little too edgy and it was pretty clear that he would do anything to get ahead. He would certainly have thrown Cook under the bus if he were cornered, so it was probably all for the best. After too long a silence, he raised his glass and said, "A toast to Christopher's recovery." The glasses clinked and they sipped their wine. They all anticipated one of the best evenings they had enjoyed in a long, long time.

\* \* \*

**August 21**
**8:30 p.m.**
Within four miles of the Cook residence, The Treasure Chest Restaurant sat at the top of a hill overlooking Westlake Village. The walls were floor to ceiling glass on one side, taking full advantage of the lake and hillside views.

In addition to a panoramic view, the restaurant offered good seafood and steak, and it had a separate dining room perfect for the celebration of the Cardenas and Palmer party. Drinks, dinner and friendship filled the room. Lee and Melissa spoke with Marty and Abby about the end of the case and their upcoming wedding, now less than a month away. Scott and Lisa talked to Justin and Jessica about the daily lives of parents; the joys and frustrations of raising children who were still pretty young, but believed they had all the answers even before their teenage years. Sandi Underwood and her sons, Daniel and Alex, mixed with everyone. Sandi set up the next margarita event at The Tropics with Abby and Jessica, even while they sipped on margaritas this evening. Daniel and Alex were fascinated by the work that Scott and Lee did and spent part of the evening asking about the details of how Scott prosecuted a case and how Lee went about finding evidence.

After they ate, Marty stood at the front of the room and said, "I'd like to say just a few words. I have to start with the obvious. This party could only be made better one way, and that's if our old friend Art was here with us. Bless you, Art. We love you." He took a moment to fight off emotion and then said, "Next, Justin and I want to thank Scott for his work on our behalf; Scott, you were incredible. We also want to thank Lee for his work, which could only be described as divining hidden secrets and then finding a way to get out of the vault that hid them. Amazing."

"Next, to Sandi, Daniel and Alex. We are so glad that the Underwood family is here to help us honor Art, whose work ethic and integrity influenced us every day. We are glad to count you among our good friends." Sandi smiled widely and blew him a kiss. After a moment, he added, "And one more thing, Justin was offered a good job yesterday."

There was a round of applause, and then Justin stood and said, "Which I turned down." There was puzzlement on the expressions around the room until he added, "Because Marty and I are starting our own consulting group for the pharmaceutical industry. Overseeing and analyzing testing and helping them get products right for FDA approval. So, far we have two companies who want our help, and no, Aligor is not one of them. But maybe someday they will be."

The applause broke out one more time and then Scott stood up and looked to Marty and Justin. "Thank you, guys, for inviting Lisa and I to this shindig. Marty and Justin, you guys were exemplary clients and you are good people. You worked hard and wouldn't be intimidated. In the end, you made a difference that will help countless people in desperate need and who have no bargaining position." He was quiet for a moment and then looked to Sandi Underwood. "Sandi, I think that the strength Marty and Justin brought to this was inspired by the man they looked up to most. Art has been a big part of all of this, and he was every bit as courageous as he intended to be."

He turned to Lee. He wore a big smile as he looked at his friend and shook his head, "I don't know how you do it." He paused and added, "and don't tell me," he said, holding up a palm and drawing laughter. "But it's true that you always come up with something that matters, usually, like in this case, something that wasn't even on our radar screen. Nice work."

Lee nodded his appreciation and then stood. He looked first at Sandi, then at her adult children. "Daniel and Alex, I am aware that you know your dad was brave and a man of strong values. In fact, Daniel said it beautifully at the celebration of Art's life. I have seen how Marty and Justin regarded him as well. I only wish that I'd had the chance to know him. But something else you should know is that your mom is of that same strong character. I have had a chance to get to know her and she is courageous and extraordinary. You guys have two wonderful parents to celebrate."

It was clear from the expressions they wore that Daniel and Alex were proud of their mom, but they would never know what he meant about her being courageous. Sandi smiled at Lee but remained silent. What he spoke of in code would always be their secret.

"To Marty and Justin, it was a pleasure to work with you. I believed in your cause and wanted to help find a way to make them account for what they did to you guys and for their misrepresentations about a drug that could save or kill people. It's a pleasure for Melissa and me to count you all among our friends." He lifted his glass, turning his words into a toast and they all drank. "To Scott, thanks for getting me involved in amazing and challenging cases. I'd say the work keeps me off the street but technically it usually does just the opposite. I always love working with you, my friend," he offered, lifting his glass in Scott's direction. "Oh, and thanks for knowing what not to ask."

Everyone laughed at that one, able to relate to that firsthand.

Justin had a twinkle in his eye as he looked at Scott and asked, "How do you know when not to ask Lee where he got something?"

Scott pushed a hand through his hair and said, "Lee has a creative way of getting things done. There are a couple of obvious tipoffs about when not to ask questions. If Lee just came up with something no one else can get to or if he found some evidence that we didn't even know existed, I've learned not to ask how he pulled the rabbit out of the hat." He smiled at Lee and then added, "But I do accept the rabbit with thanks." The room filled with laughter once again.

Jessica and Justin laughed for a time and then Jessica leaned towards Justin and said, "The rabbit out of the hat thing makes me think about something I've been wondering for a little while."

"What's that?" Justin asked.

She had a twinkle in her eye as she asked, "Do you think Lee and Scott know whether someone helped kill Santa?"

"I don't know." He thought for a moment and then added, "But if anyone discovered information about that, it's going to be Lee. And based on what I just heard, if Lee knows something about that, Scott isn't pressing for the details."

"Sounds right," Jessica answered, laughing.

They chuckled, clinked champagne glasses, and watched this group of friends interact. It was an evening to be remembered. Justin looked over at Marty, who smiled and raised his glass. The two new business partners toasted each other, sharing the excitement of a new career and the thoughts of hanging on to this group of friends as a part of their lives.

Dear reader,

We hope you enjoyed reading *A Secret To Die For.* Please take a moment to leave a review, even if it's a short one. Your opinion is important to us.

Discover more books by David P. Warren at https://www.nextchapter.pub/authors/author-david-warren

Want to know when one of our books is free or discounted? Join the newsletter at http://eepurl.com/bqqB3H

Best regards,

David P. Warren and the Next Chapter Team

# About the Author

I am a 39 year attorney with a passion for writing thrillers. My most recent book is 'Imploded Lives,' (2018), focusing on the lives of several people who are about to become hostages in one of the most remarkable bank robberies of our time, and the perpetrators, who will take hostages, and manage to completely disappear, leaving puzzled detectives and FBI agents with no idea how they or the money disappeared. My immediately previous book is the legal thriller 'The Whistleblower Onslaught' (2017), the story of an executive in the energy industry fired for complaints about the company's unsafe conditions in its mines. An explosion in a mine, resulting in one dead and three injured. A lawsuit that gives you a good look at the legal system and a company hiding the truth. Bribery and blackmail to protect corporate secrets and someone who will do anything to stop the lawsuit from reaching trial. I previously wrote 'Altering Destiny' the story of a young woman's flight with found money and something deadly she does not know she had, and 'Sealing Fate', about a newly elected congressman whose affair leads to blackmail and murder. I love characters who are compelling and plots that take you to the unexpected. I am already underway on the next book. Thank you all for your kind words and support. I will do my very best to keep you entertained with interesting characters and plot twists. Thank you to all of my fans and supporters! My website is DavidPWarren.com

# Books by the Author

- Scott Winslow Legal Mysteries

    - The Whistleblower Onslaught
    - Personal Violation
    - A Secret To Die For

- Altering Destiny

- Imploded Lives

- Sealing Fate